TWICE CHOSEN MAN

L LEIGHTON DECORE

 FriesenPress

Suite 300 - 990 Fort St
Victoria, BC, V8V 3K2
Canada

www.friesenpress.com

This is a work of fiction set into an historical setting. The author has placed a fictional character into events involving David Thompson and the war of 1812. The interactions of the fictional character, William Ashford, should therefore be regarded as fiction.

ISBN
978-1-5255-2507-0 (Hardcover)
978-1-5255-2508-7 (Paperback)
978-1-5255-2509-4 (eBook)

1. *Fiction, Historical*

Distributed to the trade by The Ingram Book Company

TWICE CHOSEN MAN

PART ONE
THE COLUMBIA RIVER

London, England
February 4, 1810

Captain William Ashford walked smartly up the hill towards the two large double doors of Whitehall, the headquarters of His Majesty's Office of Colonial Affairs. He wore the green uniform of a Rifleman of the 5th Battalion, 95th Regiment of Foot. His boots, though freshly polished, were not shiny but dull to prevent reflection of sunlight. Only the feet of his boots were visible as the tops were covered by the green trousers of a Rifleman. His short jacket was the same green colour and his short sword hung from a thick black belt leather belt on his left side. He was without his leather cartridge pouch and rifle as he knew that the carrying of firearms into the hall was forbidden. His hat, also green, sat high on his head making him look almost a foot taller than his five-foot ten-inch height. It was secured under his chin with a leather buckled strap.

This was the second time he had entered Whitehall. The first was on the occasion of his attending to obtain his papers confirming him to be a Lieutenant in His Majesty's army. He purchased his commission, a normal practice of the day, as he was looking for adventure.

He pushed open the door and stepped inside. Almost immediately a red-coated corporal approached him and said, "You must be Captain Ashford. We are expecting you, sir. Please follow me." Ashford removed his cap, tucked it under his left arm and followed the corporal up the stairs to what was apparently the outer office of Lord Percival Worthington, Secretary of Colonial Affairs.

"Please sit here, sir." The corporal pointed to one of three chairs in the room and went to another door, knocked quietly, opened it and entered. He held the door open and said, "Captain Ashford has arrived, sir." Ashford did not hear a response as the corporal turned around, closed the door, and left the room.

Ashford sat, alone, stiffly at attention, shifting his short sword to allow more comfort and waited. He had no idea why he was summoned to London from the Peninsular War in Spain, just that he was directed there by his commander Lieutenant General Arthur Wellesley[1].

During the voyage from Spain, he kept asking himself what this was all about. He was simply told by General Wellesley that a man was to be chosen for a special assignment and was to report to this office. Ashford was that chosen man, chosen for the second time, the first to become a member of the 5th Battalion, the 'Chosen Men'.

After half an hour elapsed, Ashford was getting impatient. He wondered how any official of the King could waste so much time without a word. But a good soldier did not to ask questions, he merely followed orders. He was about to rise and pace the floor when the large oak door into the inner office opened.

"The secretary will see you now, Captain Ashford. Please come in." said the short balding man as he held the door for Ashford to enter.

Ashford entered and saw a gentleman clothed in a black jacket and stiff-collared white shirt seated behind an over-sized oak desk. The balding man took a seat to the left of the gentleman. Ashford stood silently at attention and waited.

After what seemed to be forever, the man behind the desk rose, looked at Ashford and spoke.

"My apologies for the long wait, Captain. I had some final material to read before we commence. Please sit down." Ashford placed his cap on a long credenza at the wall on his right and sat stiffly in the large chair directly in front of the desk.

"We shall be as informal as we can as we talk, Captain. You may relax. You are in no sort of trouble. Quite the contrary. That will become apparent as we talk. First, however, there are few questions I must ask. Please answer as fully as you can without fear. Again, that will become apparent as we progress."

---

1 Later to become Sir Arthur Wellington, First Duke of Wellington

"You are William Ashford, Captain in the 95th Regiment of Foot?"

"Yes, sir."

"And as such you are one of the 'Chosen Men'?

"Yes, sir."

"Oh, forgive me. No need to address me as 'sir'. We should be less formal"

"Fine, sir – uh – fine".

"Tell me of your last engagement with the enemy before you were sent here."

Ashford was startled. His last engagement was at the retreat from Corunna, one that made a black mark on the campaign. It was an igno-minious retreat, a solemn one, a stunning defeat about which Ashford and his companions were not proud.

"Sir?" He didn't want to talk of it.

"Something to do with a French general, I believe."

"Oh, that. Yes. It was a very difficult retreat. We had just crossed a bridge and noticed the French were about to follow us. We were desperate and knew we needed more time and we were about to be overrun. I saw the general, think his name was Colbert. And I thought, if I shot him, that might slow them down. So I shot the man in the head. That had an effect."

"Captain, I believe you are being modest. I am told that you shot the man from as far away as 600 yards. Some said it was a lucky shot."

Ashford began to relax. He knew what the Secretary was getting at so he decided to tell the story in more detail.

"Mr. Secretary, yes, it was partly luck and really more like three hundred yards. One of the men near me commented on it being a lucky shot, so I felt I had to prove it was not all luck and shot the General's aide. But I shot him in the torso because he kept lowering his head. You might say there was some luck involved because it was a hot dry day with no wind and I had a slightly downward angle. But the rifle made it possible and the rifle, well, that was the key. I, like all soldiers of the 5th Battalion, carry the series three 1806 Pattern Infantry Rifle. It's the best in the world, even better than the famous Kentucky rifle used by the Americans. We love the weapon. It withstands very rough treatment. It is easy to carry and re-load even while crouched. A magnificent ..." Ashford realized he was rambling. But it felt good and he found he was relaxed and comfortable.

The Secretary made a quick glance to the balding man and to Ashford a slight smile. "Yes, Captain. That is what I wondered about. It is one of the many reasons why we have brought you here."

"Sir – uh – Mr. Secretary?"

Sir Percival looked directly into Ashford's eyes and was startled by the fact that they were green, not the blue mentioned in the dossier. He noticed, also, that Ashford was clean-shaven, did not display a mustache or facial hair of any kind as seemed to be getting more common amongst officers. "I will explain. Your record shows you to be a bright young man, hardworking, admired by your men and your superior officers. You have accomplished a good deal for a person of only twenty-four years in age."

"We have quite a dossier on you. General Wellesley is particularly impressed by your attitude and quick-thinking. It is he who suggested you for this assignment. We are here to invite you to a new and very different endeavor. You may refuse, in which case you will be returned to your former command in Spain."

Ashford straightened in his chair. He was intrigued.

Worthington continued, "The new 'endeavor' will take you far away to the colony of Canada. It will be very different from anything you have done thus far. It will be arduous, long, and completely foreign to you. Above all, it will be challenging, dangerous and a matter of great service to His Majesty. If you accept this assignment, you shall receive the salary of a Major but retain your rank as Captain."

Percival paused to give a moment for Ashford to think and then continued, "You will also receive an additional, though not sumptuous salary, from your new employers." He stressed the word as though to put quotations around it. "You will act, in part, as an information officer, under somewhat of a 'diversionary manner'. It will be a long assignment coupled with hard drudging work of the kind that will be completely new to you and at times under very difficult conditions."

The secretary paused and looked at Ashford. He could see not only surprise, but what he took to mean the expression of a man who was intrigued and eager to hear more.

"Part of your task will be to gather information while working, not as a uniformed officer, but as a civilian, disguised, if you will, so that few people know your real purpose."

Ashford thought for a moment. "Are you saying, Mr. Secretary, that you want me to become a spy?"

"Well, we do not use that term. We prefer to use the expression, 'information officer'."

Ashford looked down. He had to think. This sounded like a great adventure and that is what he sought all his life. But this was a huge change.

"Canada. I know little about Canada. Can you tell me more, sir?"

"It is a very large country. It is at least twice the size of Europe. At least we think so because much of it has yet to be explored and mapped. You will travel the whole length of the country, from the east coast to the west coast. You will have to learn how to paddle a canoe, how to carry heavy loads. You will probably endure the particularly harsh weather of winter which, I am given to believe is itself a challenge. You will live and work with the French-Canadian voyageurs, become 'one of them' so to speak. We are told that you speak French fluently?"

"Yes, well, almost fluently. I never learned to use profane language, sir."

Ashford's mind was racing and the Secretary could see that.

"Perhaps you need a few moments to think, Captain. If you wish, you may step out into the outer office to consider our offer. We are aware that this is a considerable surprise to you. Knock on the door when you are ready."

Ashford nodded his head and rose. The balding man opened the door and let him through.

"Good Lord," Ashford breathed as he seated himself outside the inner office. A few moments later he found himself pacing back and forth, looking at the floor, then at the pictures hanging on the walls, then back at the floor, then at the chair, his boots, his hands. He noted that his hands were trembling slightly so he rose to continue pacing, thinking. His parents were both gone, he had no siblings and that was of some consolation. His friends were the men of the 95th but some had already died. The war in Spain was not going well and was stalled. The wait for action was eating at him and all his comrades and the future appeared to have little for him.

Maybe it is time for a change, he thought. And this looked like a great challenge. But maybe it was too great? What did he know about the Canadas? What did he know except war? That's it. War. Doing what Sir Percival wants was really just another aspect of war.

And war was by no means easy. It was mostly a great deal of waiting followed by hours of sheer terror, brought about by the effect of cannon and musket fire. Then it was like standing in a meat grinder. Fist sized balls, then grapeshot and musket shot would rip into a man's body and it was usually not a clean hit or a hit that instantly killed. It was more like a sadistic maiming.

A bayonet charge was the crowning of the horror. It normally happened at the crucial time when one of the belligerent forces was about to collapse. It happened when the choice was to turn and run or to stand and to fight in a desperate and confusing fight that seemed to have no order or real structure. A bayonet charge was something a soldier would never forget.

Ashford got just a taste of such horror, not a complete taste, but one that seared his mind for life. It occurred just a few months after he was made a 'Chosen Man' at the battle of Rolica in Spain. It was a horrendous battle, one that ended with a bayonet charge. Ashford, as a 'Chosen Man' was lucky not to have participated in the charge but he was unlucky in another way. He was directed to walk the field after the battle, one which saw almost 500 British and more than 700 French killed or wounded.

Ashford was sent, with some of his men, to walk the field and check the bodies of any officers for anything that might provide intelligence on the French forces. It was during that search that he first witnessed the results of a bayonet charge. Scores of men, British and French, were scattered within a relatively small area, all with horrific stab wounds to various parts of their bodies, many of them still alive and moaning with pain and despair as they died.

But the worst part was when Ashford heard a familiar voice somewhere to his left.

"Ash, Ash is that you?"

Ashford turned towards the voice and was shocked to see his friend, James Williams, a Lieutenant with whom he had spent many hours joking, singing, and carousing and a man that Ashford often thought should also have been selected as a 'Chosen Man'.

As he walked slowly to the man half lying and half sitting on the ground just a few yards from a dead French officer that Ashford was about to search Ashford looked to confirm his suspicion.. Yes, it was James and he was in a horribly sorry state. His left hand had been severed, his left eye was gone and his legs were crumpled under him as he sat, hopelessly staring at Ashford. He bent over his friend.

"Ash, I need a favour."

"Anything James," replied Ashford as he knelt beside his friend.

"See that Frenchie, there, the officer?" James pointed with a movement of his head to the officer Ashford was about to search. "He's the bastard that stuck me with his sword. First, he hacked off my hand. Then he got me from behind and I'm sure he cut my spine. Can't feel my legs. Can't make them move. I know I'm going to die here but I need to get even with that bastard."

"He's dead, James."

"I know. I know. But I still need to get even. Look, he has a pistol and it's half-cocked. Get it for me. I just want to put a ball in the bastard's head. Please."

Ashford rose to retrieve the pistol and gently placed it into his friend's remaining hand.

"Just move behind me Ash, so I can get a good shot"

Ashford rose and stepped behind his friend but as he turned to look where he needed to step he heard the shot. James Williams had simply pointed the pistol at his own head and pulled the trigger.

This episode went through Ashford's head, as clear as if it might have happened moments ago. It had burned into his mind and stayed there all his days and, every time he thought of it, he found himself trembling. He knew that it was rare for a 'Chosen Man' to get into a bayonet fight, but it could happen and realized that this new assignment would likely prevent that.

He rose and knocked on the door.

"We are pleased by your decision and, quite frankly, we expected you would agree. Let us get started as there is much to do. We shall begin by describing the background information and, through that, leave you with a good impression of what you will see and what you might expect. We say at the outset that you will be left almost entirely to your own resources save what we shall provide for you."

Ashford shifted his weight as to settle in for a long discussion.

"First the background. Please feel free to interrupt, ask any questions, and provide your thoughts as we talk. All of what we say and do here is of utmost secrecy. Understood?"

"Yes, Mr. Secretary."

"We are almost certain that the Americans will take measures to undermine our efforts in the conflict with Napoleon in Spain and elsewhere. Our informants advise us that an internal and somewhat secret debate is in progress in the United States government to help France by stretching our resources, perhaps even to the extent of invading Canada. Although the Americans will cloak their reasons in some fashion, we are informed that they want to control the whole of North America. We believe we will be well prepared for that but have concerns about the lands in the far west of the Canadas. As you may know, the border between the Americans and Canada has been only partly settled."

Percival stopped as he realized he was not giving Ashford time to absorb all the background. "Please feel free to interrupt, Captain. I'm sure this is a good deal to take in."

"Yes, sir, I will."

"I should explain the border a bit," the Secretary continued. "It is settled that the border is the 49th latitude westward from Lake Superior to the far west, but beyond that point there is some confusion. I will show you on a map in a few moments. The land westward near the ocean is still largely unknown to us except for the work of one man of whom we shall talk later, and that most westerly part of the border will likely be in dispute. Our informants have advised us that a newly-formed American trading company known as The Pacific Fur Company is about to embark upon the work of taking control of the fur trade in that region by the establishing a fort at the mouth of the Columbia River, which flows southward from the Rocky Mountains to the Pacific Ocean. The area is presently known to his Majesty and the Americans as The Oregon Country or The Oregon Territory."

Sir Percival paused to be sure Ashford understood what he was about to say. "We do not believe, at this time, that its founder, Jacob Astor, is part of the plot, but we have strong indications that agents of the United States have been placed into his company. Mr. Astor plans to send a ship from New York to the Columbia River and an overland expedition to secure the fur trade for his company in that region. In doing so, he will compete with and perhaps even squeeze out the designs of a Canadian company. More on that in a moment."

Percival paused, again, in order to say his next words carefully. "I stress, again, that we are certain that Astor's designs are purely commercial and in no way connected to the idea of American control of the west coast of North America. But our sources advise us that his project will open the possibility of the United States to claim the Oregon Country for itself. It is His Majesty's desire to prevent that."

The Secretary continued, "Presently, there are two large fur trading companies in North America. The first and largest is 'The Company of Gentlemen and Adventurers Trading into the Hudson Bay, best known as the 'Hudson's Bay Company'. It has an exclusive charter granted to it by Britain to trade and effectively control all lands that have rivers draining into the Hudson's Bay. The second is the Northwest Company. David Thompson is a part owner of that company."

He paused again and reached into an oak cadenza behind him and unrolled a large map on his desk, making sure it faced towards Ashford.

Poking his finger at part of the map he continued. "This is Hudson's Bay. The present border is not yet settled all the way westward to the Rocky Mountains. There is no settlement, and only a few parts of the lands westward to the Pacific Ocean have been explored. There is a trading post, here, called Spokane House, which was established by Mr. Thompson about three years ago. We will talk more of that later."

Ashford rose to look, again, at the map.

As I said, the other fur company is one established by the Canadians themselves. It is named "North West Company" and to some degree is in competition with the Hudson Company. It is not allowed to partake in trade in those lands granted to the Hudson's Bay Company. However, it is partly owned by a gentleman named David Thompson who was formerly a trader and mapmaker for the Hudson's Bay Company. This man is the key to your work and he is the man I spoke of earlier.

"Key, sir?" asked Ashford.

"Oh, forgive me. We mean Thompson no harm, quite the contrary. I will henceforth refer to all parties without the "Mr." for purposes of brevity, is of extreme importance to, not only his company, but to all of North America. We are in the process of informing the leaders of the Northwest Company of our information and expect them to be fully apprised of the situation within the next week. Our goal is to cooperate with the Northwest Company to assist them in having peaceful trade in Oregon and thereby avoid a takeover of the region by the US."

"Now, this is the important part, our sources show that the agents in Astor's group mean to steal the maps and logs made by Thompson. He is world renowned for his map making and has travelled and mapped much of the west, even parts of what is now the United States. Our sources tell us that those agents intend to destroy or use his maps in order to lay claim to that territory and even more. Equally reliable sources say the Americans plan to claim all of the land northward from here to here." He pointed to the map, poking his finger at the Oregon Territory and sliding it up as far as the Russian territory far to the north. The same sources fear that Thompson's life may be in danger." He paused, certain Ashford would have some questions.

Ashford took the hint. "Some questions, sir. I take it I am to prevent any harm to Thompson and his maps? How am I to travel to the Columbia River? How far is it? How do I get there? How long will it take? What do I do?"

"Good, right to the chase. You will sail aboard a navy frigate to Halifax, here, then by a sloop to Montreal, here. From Montreal you will join a group of voyageurs and travel all the way to this point, a place called Rocky Mountain House. This place is the starting point, mapped by Thompson, to connect with the Columbia River, here. As you can see, the map has almost nothing on it past this point. At any rate, you will accompany Thompson all the way to the mouth of the river. He will map the whole area and that map will be shared between the 'Norwesters'and us in the future. You are to protect Thompson, his maps, and his logs at all cost."

"Cost, sir?"

"You may have to use your rifle."

"I see."

"By the way, Captain, we have arranged for and will have in our possession two new series 1806 Rifles, one for you and one for Thompson, as a gift to him, and plenty of shot and all the trimmings. Also, you will have a full artist's kit to enable you to make sketches of the lands as you progress on your trip with Thompson. Such sketches will be valuable for future navigation and will provide you with a 'story' by which the real purposes of your venture will not be discovered. Those materials will be handed to you as you board the frigate. That will be tomorrow afternoon."

Worthington paused, again, to sip more water. "You should reach Montreal in about sixty days and will be met there by a North West Company employee. You will dress in your battle dress while on board the frigate, sleep and eat with the Royal Marines on board, and assist them should any trouble arise. We have arranged for you to 'become a temporary Marine' and you will act the part."

"And how long will the trip to the Rocky Mountain House take?"

"I'm afraid I cannot give you a firm time. It will take between two to four months. You will travel with a small brigade of what they call 'express canoes'. That is where you will learn the business of a voyageur and of paddling a canoe. I am told you will find it quite fascinating, but hard work. The people of North West Company in Montreal will provide you with all the clothing you will need as the winter and other weather factors require."

Ashford wondered what Sir Percival meant by 'other factors' but decided not to ask, at least not yet.

"You will be in the company of what are known as 'voyageurs", mostly French Canadians. I am told they are somewhat uncouth but very hard working. They are of French or, more likely, French and Indian descent, half breeds, called 'Metis'. These voyageurs are apparently quite the characters and face the weather and hard work extremely well. I am told that once you get to know them they are a very entertaining, loyal, and friendly people. Be careful not to have them know you have been at war with

France as some, not many, still have feelings for France. Undoubtedly you will have a full-blooded Indian with you, most likely Iroquois."

"Iroquois? I've heard of them. I hear they are quite fierce."

"The Iroquois are very war-like and very good allies of His Majesty and the Canadians," replied Percival. "Unlike the Americans, we have attempted to treat the Indian people with honesty and trust. That stems from the importance of the fur trade. Thompson, we are told, has an Indian woman as his wife."

"This sounds more and more interesting both from the challenge and the people with whom I shall live. I hope I will not be overcome by it."

"Captain, the reason you have been once again 'chosen' is that there is no other person as well suited as you for this assignment. The two rifles have been purchased directly from the manufacturer and have no serial numbers, nothing that will give a hint of any military connection. By the way, the manufacturer is a man of German decent, short, has thick brown hair and speaks with a slight German accent. I tell you this as background information you may need."

"Understood."

"Further, to obscure your background, before arrival at Halifax, you will throw your uniform, and all items that have indications of military on them, overboard. You will thereafter dress in civilian clothing. Only Mr. Thompson will know of your true identity and purpose. I have been told that, especially in winter, you should follow the advice of those around you as to how and what to wear as well as when."

Ashford gave a slight nod and stood to study the map. He pointed to various markings on the map and the Secretary immediately gave information of each mark. "Unfortunately, we cannot provide you with a copy of this map. It is still secret."

"That will be all for today. I ask that you come back early tomorrow morning as we must present the rifles, artist's kit, and other items to you and give you a final briefing. Your ship will sail in the afternoon. Good day."

Ashford was then ushered out.

The next morning, he was immediately ushered into the Secretary's interior office and the final briefing began.

"Please open, remove, and examine all items from the duffel bag. As you remove each item you may have a question. I will explain the nature and purpose of each."

Ashford began.

> Item 1- an artist's kit about two feet square and six inches deep. It had two snap clasps that held the kit closed. When he opened the kit, he found it contained three leather-bound books, each of about sixty pages of high quality white paper eight by ten inches in size, perfect paper on which to draw.

> Item 2 – three small three by three-inch tins with screw-on tops labelled 'Lamp Black'. Inside the tins was the powder, made of good quality lampblack which, when mixed with water, would become 'India Ink'.

> Item 3 – a small leather bag containing several pen nibs of varying thicknesses, five of each, all wrapped neatly in a soft cloth.

> Item 4 – four pairs of wool socks tied into a bundle with a leather cord.

> Item 5 – a woolen light grey greatcoat, flannel shirt, woolen vest, two pairs of heavy cotton trousers all neatly bundled together with a similar leather cord.

> Item 6 – a very sharp Navaja knife in carefully wrapped in a soft blue cloth. It was a knife made for killing, very sharp on one complete side and half of the other. It was shaped for slicing and thrusting and had a five and a half-inch blade. It was not a folding knife like the one he kept in his boot that folded into its handle much like a shaving blade, but a straight knife with a beautifully-crafted sheath that could easily fit onto his belt. The sheath had an innovative method of securing the knife. It had a looped strap that clasped together with a brass button that one had to

simply snap into place. It was made for quick retrieval. Ashford tested the blade for its fit to his hand. It was perfect. He would wear it on his left side to avoid conflict with his cartridge pouch and powder horn.

"We are aware, Captain, that you have extensive training in the Andalusian knife-fighting technique and that you carry one in your army-issued boots."

Ashford was shocked as few people knew about his knife. It made him wonder, again how Percival was able to gather information. "You will be fitted with a new pair of boots, similar to the kind you now wear but without any indication of military identification."

"You are quite correct, sir, about the knife, I mean. But I would say that a good Spanish fighter would be a difficult challenge for me. I took the training in Portugal from a Spanish-Portuguese trainer. At first thought it looked like a couple of men playing 'Patty-cake' but once I learned the moves I came to enjoy it. The Portuguese fellow had a modified manner of fighting that did not require wrapping an arm in a coat. I have never had occasion to use it but still practice the moves about once a week. I prefer the rifle. Less personal. I will keep the knife I now have and use this as an extra. My present knife has no indication of anything military."

Item 7 – a leather courier bag.

Percival continued, "I should explain that item. It contains two letters. The one tied with a green ribbon is to be presented to the Captain of the vessel upon your embarkation. He will be expecting you. The one tied with a red ribbon is to be presented to the President of the North West Company upon your arrival at Montreal. His name is William McGillevray. He will also be expecting you. There is one other such letter, not folded as these two, but it is under a false bottom of the artist's kit and can be removed only by carefully cutting along the bottom inside seam of the kit. It is to be given to Mr. Thompson as soon as you arrive. It contains the same information we have already discussed and, if Thompson shows it you, you may read it. All letters bear my seal and are signed by me."

Ashford resumed his inspection of the remaining items in the bag.

Item 8 – a leather bag containing about twenty lead balls for the rifle.

Item 9 – a cotton bag containing the powder horn and about twenty cartridges as well as many already-cut pieces of paper used for making more cartridges. Most interesting was the roll of very fine linen to use as patches to wrap the musket balls when loading the rifle. Linen patches gave more distance and accuracy to the shot and the myth of using silk was just a myth. Silk was too fine and tended to break up when the ball and patch were rammed into the barrel.

As Ashford inspected the rolls of cloth, the Secretary spoke. "We understand the silk gives you better distance and accuracy. I would suggest you prepare to use it only when necessary and use the linen first. That way the spy will not recognize your expertise with the rifle." Ashford nodded his agreement but knew he would toss the silk patches as soon as he could.

Item 10 – a compass.

Item 11 – a leather pouch containing a lead ball mold, ladle and ten one-pound ingots of lead, enough to make about 150 musket balls. There was also a small pot to use for melting the lead.

Item 12 – a spyglass similar to the one used by Admiral Nelson at the battle of Copenhagen in 1801. Ashford admired this item.

Item 13 – a shorter, forest green wool coat, about just knee-high, with toggle straps instead of buttons. It also had loops for the lighter green sash that was pulled through them. Perceval had undoubtedly taken care to use the same green as used by the 'Chosen Men'.

"The rifle you will present to Mr. Thompson is in the captain's quarters on board the ship. It fits easily into the bag. You will carry your own rifle cartridge pouch and other materials with you when you board the ship.

We shall hand that gear to you as you enter the carriage that will take you to the ship. The carriage will collect you at noon tomorrow. As you know, weapons of that kind are not allowed within these walls."

Worthington paused for a sip of water, "A small trunk with an additional 200 rounds of lead ball cartridge paper and patches will have been loaded on the ship by now. We have arranged for it to be kept in the Captain's quarters to avoid pilfering and discovery. You will have a fully equipped cartridge pouch, unmarked by anything military. We are aware that the lead balls for your rifle are different in size from those of an ordinary musket. We have provided the proper balls for you."

Ashford held up one of the lead balls and nodded his approval to Percival.

"Perhaps you should try on the shorter coat. You will note that it is quite loose in fit as you may be in need of more space in cold weather. This coat is called a 'capot'. You will note it is knee length which, we are advised, is the kind preferred by the Canadian voyageurs because it gives more freedom of movement."

Percival waited until Ashford tried on the capot, and then continued. "There are some coins in the pocket and more, together totaling 220 pounds sterling and 200 well used United States dollars, of varying denominations, in the trunk."

Ashford was fingering the coins in the pocket as Percival spoke.

"As for Thompson, he is not expecting you but a letter of explanation will be given to him by Mr. William McGillivray of the North West Company," continued Percival.

Ashford examined the compass. "I am familiar with the compass, sir," Ashford said. It was of good quality.

"One more matter to discuss," continued Percival. "We have placed our own man into Mr. Astor's organization. The method of identifying each other will be by the words written on this note. It is to be done in the most natural of ways. You will notice that there are two parts, one to occur on the first encounter and the next on the following day. If the encounter of the following day does not occur that could mean our opposition is suspicious and may know the words. It will also prevent accidental use of the 'code'. Memorize, practice and then destroy this note. Any questions?"

"Sir, how do we return and to where?"

"We will attempt to have a ship for you at the Columbia River, but that is unlikely. You will therefore have to return, by canoe, to Montreal with Mr. Thompson and others."

'Good Lord!' Ashford thought.

The Secretary then held out his hand and said, "Good luck to you" as they shook hands. "And I would add, as an observation, that you are now the only *twice chosen man* in His Majesty's military service."

"Thank you, Sir Percival. I shall try my best not to disappoint His Majesty."

Ashford loved his calf-length army supplied boots. They were comfortable, had good gripping features and were snug for long-distance running. He couldn't throw them away but knew he had too. So, on the walk back to his Inn he stopped at the cobbler's shop arranged by the secretary and tried on his new boots. They fit perfectly. His plan was to throw away the army issue boots and wear the replacements on board the ship. That would give him opportunity to break in the new boots before having to toss the old ones. The new boots contained a hardly-noticeable slot built inside the boot to hold the Navaja knife. He would stuff the new boots into the duffel bag and toss the old ones somewhere in the Atlantic Ocean.

Upon his return to the inn, Ashford stopped at a barber shop located next door. He knew there would likely be a barber on the ship, but felt he deserved a real barber rather the kind on His Majesty's ships.

When he sat in the barber's chair and looked into the mirror facing him, he got a bit of a surprise. The hair was, indeed, long. It was clean, but somehow, it was not brown. It was getting more on the dark brown side and it didn't seem to want to sit well on his head. It looked, in fact, like it had grown a bit wild. His complexion had also changed. He had lost the ruddy complexion of many Englishmen and his facial features were those of a very healthy person who had spent many days in the sun.

He ran his fingers through his hair again and looked into the mirror at the barber, "Clean up this mess, if you can, please" he quietly said to the barber. "And you might just as well give me a proper shave."

"Right you are sir. Just get off the ship?"

Ashford just nodded and pretended he was too tired to talk.

After the barber, Ashford returned to his room at the inn, ate an early lunch, and returned to his room to read the note from Sir Percival.

Start by first person

> "I would venture to say that you have had some interesting experiences on your voyage?"

Reply by second person

> "Yes, some on the terrifying side."

First person response

> "Well, we must get together over a drink and trade stories."

Next day conversation initiated by same first person

> "I still look forward to exchanging stories."

Response

> "Oh yes. Would this evening be convenient?"

Reply

> 'No. Unfortunately I have a commitment. Would tomorrow morning be convenient?"

> On the third encounter, the next day, the person talking to you will approach and say, "A nice time to trade stories, is it not?'

Reply

> "Certainly, shall we walk?"

"My God! I really am to be a spy!" Ashford said aloud to himself.

Jefferson Town
Jefferson County Kentucky
February 22, 1810

By age thirty, Ronald James Foster was a wealthy man. It took him years of hard work, meetings with the right kind of people, buying slaves, keeping the business healthy, and marrying a beautiful woman. They married with a lavish ceremony to which he invited many prominent people. His property was not the largest in the county, but easily one of the top ten. He had forty slaves, grew vast amounts of tobacco, grew and sold produce and, in his mind as well as those minds of many in Jefferson County, was a man of stature, a man who should run for office, a man who might one day be governor of the State of Kentucky.

This day, February 22, 1810, was a great one because it was the day he was appointed Major of the 17th Kentucky Dragoons, a "Light Infantry of Horse" and part of a network of militias within the state. Militias were the solution to the political situation in the United States of America. Each state had independent control of military state militias which would come to the aide of the United States whenever called upon. They couldn't be forced to do so, but it was expected. They were not, however, expected to see service in a foreign country.

This day, the morning after his induction as Major of the 17th Kentucky, Foster woke a little early and dressed in his new Major's uniform and strode to the table where he knew Morris, his stable slave, would have his mare ready for the morning ride. His uniform was the one to be used for battle. It was, in his mind, one of pure art. The tunic, waste-high for riding, was navy blue trimmed with red lapels, red like the cardinal, the official bird of Kentucky. His breaches, again made for riding, were narrowed at the bottom to accommodate his ring boots and grey like a summer rain cloud. His new sword, not strapped to his belt but to the side of his saddle behind him, was within easy reach. It was a standard cavalry sword, a sabre, meant for stabbing and slashing at close quarters. Its handle was laced with gold-coloured chord. Impressive, indeed. Foster took no training in the use of a sabre. He reckoned there was no need as there wasn't much to swinging a sword at people's heads.

His horse, ah, his horse. She was pure white, like a summer cumulous cloud and appropriately named, "White Cloud". Foster knew she was the finest mare in Jefferson County.

Foster's hat was not quite standard. It was not the usual black or grey horse-hair helmet commonly used by dragoons but the hat of a Colonel or General and topped with a large egret plume poked into a cardinal-red holder. The plume could be easily replaced when it got too dirty. It was his "touch". It set him apart from the others. It made people notice him. It made him feel good. It made him the important man in the field.

But there was one other thing that made Foster proud; the Kentucky Knife. It was really a glorified butcher knife, standard issue for his men. It had an eight-inch blade, which itself would scare the wits out of anyone. It was flat and thick on the top but very sharp on the cutting edge. It was used for everything, for cooking, cutting meat, skinning a deer (not so good for that), and even stirring the pot. But its major use was for a knife-fight. Foster took a few lessons on knife-fighting but was not at all proficient with it, though he thought he was.

As Major he had no use for a rifle. It was too cumbersome, though his men used them. As Major, Foster knew that a fine pistol, tucked into a fine holster at his left hip within easy reach of his right hand provided the superior weapon, and the superior image.

"Good afternoon, gentlemen." Foster said in a polite and respectful tone as he arrived at the meeting with three of his troopers. One of the troopers was his brother, Jacob. "Ah'm pleased you-all could come." He purposely exaggerated his drawl in the presence of his militia men. It was his way of showing them he was one of them. "Please sit. Can I pour you some bourbon?"

The men declined with a collective movement of their heads and sat into the large chairs placed in front of Foster's desk. As they sat, they looked in awe at the huge mahogany desk, the bookcases, the fancy inlaid wood, the green drapes, the fine array of drinking glasses and crystal jugs of spirits, and they were overcome with it all.

"Fine. We'll get down to business. We've got an opportunity for expansion, boys, expansion like you've never dreamed of. As my brother knows, the Pacific Fur Company is planning to send a group of men over land to the Pacific Ocean, 'way out west. They want to set up a tradin' post there at the mouth of the Columbia River. Some people call it the "Oregon Country" but I don't know why. Anyway, in doin' that they're lookin' to set up an American presence in the far west. I have also learned that up in the Canadas, a Montreal company called the North West Company is sendin' a man out there to try and beat the Pacific Fur Company to the place. This man is David Thompson and he's no ordinary man. He's one of them map making guys and has mapped most of the west, even before Lewis and Clark got there. You know who Lewis and Clark are"?

Of course, they didn't know. Of the three, only his brother Jacob could read. The other two could sign their names and that was all. So Foster told them about Lewis and Clark and how, in his view, the expedition was done to lay a claim for all the lands westward to the Pacific Ocean. He added some facts that in 1803 the United Stated purchased lands located in southern USA, from France in what was called "The Louisiana Purchase"

"And all that tells me that it is American's destiny to take it all, and I mean all of the west and even the Canadas to the north. Now, to help make this happen, we have to get rid of all the maps and logs of this man Thompson. And I mean every sign of his ever being there. That means no evidence, none. Do yah follow me?"

Foster knew his men well enough to understand that he was instructing them that they were to murder Thompson, but he was careful to give his command in a way that he could deny ever having done so. His men could not read. But they weren't stupid. "Do you know what I'm sayin'?"

"Yes," said Jacob. The others followed with nods of their heads.

"Fine. You will be given full supplies and new horses and mules, one of each to all of you." Foster was aware that his brother was in dire straits and needed cash and fresh start and had already arranged that with him. They will be yours to keep when you finish the job. You will also be given one thousand dollars each upon completion. You will present yourselves as mountain men out to explore and take furs. You must always act the part. That means you leave your tomahawks at home. Get that?"

More nods.

"Now, I will read you one of these letters. There are three of them, one each. You will sew them into your jackets, like we do before a battle, and put them in this oil-skin packet. The letters are addressed to William Price Hunt who is the leader of the Overlander group. You will meet him and ride with the group. Jacob knows where you will go to find this Thompson guy. But you'll have to get to this fellow Hunt fast. That means leavin' in the next day or so. Understand?"

"Yes."

"Another thing. You will do your deed up north, in the wild lands out west. We don't want this to happen in the United States. All of this is secret. That way no one ends up at the gallows. Get it?"

A collective, "Yes."

"I remind you. No pay until you bring me proof that the job is done. The maps and logs of this man Thompson will be that proof."

"Yes, sir."

"Good, that will be all for now. The horses and supplies will be ready for you at a place only Jacob knows about. You leave the day after tomorrow. From that moment you'll be on your own."

When the men were gone, Foster poured himself another shot of bourbon, sat in his large chair, took a sip and said out loud, "I'm going to make America great and the run for President."

Rainy Lake[2]
May 9, 1810

On this beautiful spring day, David Thompson, with a brigade of thirty large freight canoes, each with twelve men and 3000 pounds of furs and travel supplies, are less than a half day from Rainy Lake near the western tip of Lake Superior. It is the annual spring brigade that brings the winter's store of furs for sorting and transport to Montreal. The French-Canadian Voyageurs are happy with the prospect of their arrival as many of them will remain there a few weeks in preparation for the trip back to the west. They sing. They sing of women and of ale and rum. They are spirited songs, the kind that increases the rhythm of their paddles and presses the canoes to a faster pace.

Thompson is also pleased. It has been a successful season. Only two paddlers have been lost, one to a terrible fall during a high trail portage and another who died slowly and painfully of a strangulated hernia. So few mishaps were unusual and Thompson was thankful for that. At Rainy Lake, Thompson would present his logs and maps to the Northwest Company and rest for a couple of weeks. There was no reason for him to travel all the way to Montreal, and he was anxious to spend time with his wife upon his return to Fort Augustus (near present-day Edmonton) in the prairies.

---

2   Rainy Lake is near the Lake of the Woods area, near the western tip of Lake Superior, present day Ontario and about 2500 miles by canoe from Rocky Mountain House, Alberta.

At Rainy Lake, Kenneth MacBride was waiting for Thompson as he strode toward the post trading house. Thompson could tell by the look on the man's face that something was amiss and immediately worried there would be an argument over the quantity of furs delivered.

"Good afternoon, Mr. Thompson. We must talk."

"Oh, oh."

They sat inside the inner office, the manager behind the desk and Thompson in front to it. MacBride pulled a bottle of very dark rum from his desk drawer and was about to pour some into two glasses, when he stopped himself.

"Oh, forgive me. I forgot that you don't partake." He poured a glass for himself, took a healthy portion and gulped it down.

"Something is wrong, Ken? I've never seen you drink before supper hour."

"Yes, my friend. And it is I that must tell you." He looked down into his half-empty glass as though he was thinking of pouring another portion. "We have received a letter from Montreal. I am instructed to present it to you, talk, and then destroy it." He handed the single page to Thompson.

Montreal, February 17, 1810   for Mr. David Thompson

We have very reliable sources that indicate the Pacific Fur Company is about to embark upon an expedition to set up a post at the mouth of the Columbia River. As you know, that area is the source of very valuable otter fur. You will remember that Mr. John Jacob Astor, its owner, discussed with us the possibility of forming such a company with him for the trade in that region. A ship will sail from New York within the next few weeks to establish the post. There is also strong indication that Astor will send a group over land for the same purpose. The intent is to build the fort on the south side of the river. This will likely have far-reaching effect on our endeavors and upon the future of the whole region. I have therefore instructed Mr. MacBride to make preparations for you to depart with a company of twenty-four men and proceed to that destination and there set up

a post for the Company. McBride is to hand-pick the men who will accompany you – all men with whom you have traveled on other occasions, though you may choose some men from your own voyageurs. All gear and supplies needed to get to Rocky Mountain House will be ready. We wish you the best in this voyage.

William McGillevray

Thompson looked up at him and saw dismay on his friend's face.

How long will it take for us to be ready? I will need two express canoes and eleven men."

"I will pick them for you, my friend. The men in the brigade will be anxious to get home, so we should choose men who are well-rested."

"How long before we have to leave?" asked Thompson.

"Well, we received the letter not one week ago and it will take time to repair canoes and then pack. I have decided that a third canoe will accompany you with additional goods and then return to Fort Augustus for the winter. I would say, oh, ten days. Besides, you need some rest and good food to put on a little weight. You are to sleep in the spare room of my house."

"I thank you for that, my friend." He handed the letter to MacBride and watched as it was gently placed into the almost spent fire of the fireplace.

Halifax
September 10, 1810

aptain William Ashford departed Montreal on September 10th on a long and arduous journey by canoe to Rocky Mountain House. He knew nothing about the canoe, had to buy his own paddle and learn as he travelled. Long before ever attempting the stroke with a canoe paddle, he had begun the preparations for the journey while still at sea. The night before arriving at Halifax, he took off his uniform and all things that might link him to the British army and placed them into a potato sack, added a six pound cannon ball, and threw it overboard. He was already in his green capot and thought to himself, "I am someone else. God help me do a proper job of it."

Ashford quickly learned that his journey would prove to be very hard but intensely interesting work. The experience would prepare him for what was ahead at the far west end of Lake Superior. His travel was by way of the eight-man express canoe. Ashford would, in fact, pass through the post at Rainy Lake and there learn that Thompson had already left for Rocky Mountain House to begin a journey to the mouth of the Columbia river.

Rocky Mountain House
Near the Rocky Mountains
September 12, 1810

Thompson's journey to Rocky Mountain House was faster than usual because they paddled in "express" canoes. The express canoe was twenty-five feet long, carried five to eight men and was packed with only the gear they needed to complete the trip as quickly as possible. Those traveling by express canoes did not have the luxury of stopping to hunt or make pemmican. Time was important. Even on the way back, the express canoes carried no freight as their sole task was to deliver messages as quickly as possible. The men who paddled them were the strongest and best of the voyageurs. They seldom complained. They sang quick-tempo songs to keep their rate of paddle at forty stokes per minute. They joked and laughed most of the time and derided their companions whenever one of them accidently struck the side of the canoe with the shaft of the paddle or when one of them sloppily paced his paddle onto the water and splashed water on the others. They seemed to revel in the hard work.

Thompson paddled much of the way, though he did not have the strength or endurance of the voyageurs. On many occasions, when the water was too shallow or the current too strong, they would physically drag the canoe through the shallows or pole it up the stream, and in the case of hard-current rapids, would line the canoe upstream. Lining a canoe is something only an expert would do. It involved tying a rope to the bow and to the stern of the canoe, and pulling it upstream, or down, all the while steering it in and out of the eddies and around the rocks. A mistake

would result in the canoe tipping and possible loss of all cargo and supplies, or sometimes the loss of a canoe.

Often, they would have to portage the entire rapid. Portaging took
the form of carrying the canoe and all provisions past a dangerous rapid
to get around it. As they were travelling upstream all the way to Rocky
Mountain House in low seasonal water levels, they often needed to drag,
or line, or portage. They were able to stop at posts located along the route
and refresh their provisions, especially the supply of pemmican, which was
their staple food.

They knew when they were close to Rocky Mountain House as they
had travelled this part of the voyage on many occasions. Soon, they spotted
the smoke from the chimneys of its main building. The place was not so
much a "fort" as much a group of structures surrounded by some vertical
pine logs that acted as a rough palisade.

It was near dark.

"Good day Mr. Thompson. You are back early" Georges Lupine said as
Thompson strode towards the main structure.

"True, true, George. I am in a bit of hurry. We shall talk inside." Once
inside and seated, Thompson explained the situation without revealing his
true purpose.

"It is therefore my intention to proceed by way of the pass we traveled
some time ago to Kootenay House, Howes Pass, and then the Columbia
River. It will be necessary to re-provision as soon as we can."

"Certainly, my friend, but there is something you should know."

"Yes?'

"The Piegans. They are quite angry. They are very concerned with the
fact that we have provided the Kootenay with hunting muskets and have
blockaded the route. They threaten some evil upon you should you try to
go through their lands."

"Good Lord!"

They sat in silence for several moments.

Thompson was well aware of the possible evil they had in mind. He
heard of occasions where the Piegans would take their enemies and pull
strips of skin off their backs before killing them and then take their scalps.
He thought those stories untrue but decided he would not test them.

a small river coming from the western mountains and it flows into the Athabasca here, where to it flows mostly northward. There should be a pass up there. That's our route. Problem is, it will take time and we don't know how difficult it will be."

They stood silently and stared at the map.

"We need horses and sled dogs. We need some good ash wood to make sleds and we will need snowshoes. We will need a good quantity of pemmican and trade goods. The trade goods will buy us passage through other native lands and help set up trade for the future. We will need axes; a hand drill to build birch bark canoes on the other side. That also means a large number of men, say twenty-four in total, to get us near the pass, if there is one. We would go over the pass with twelve men. We will also need to re-supply and get messages to and from our route back to Rocky Mountain House."

"Once we get over the pass, we shall not have the luxury of any message system. So we will attempt to reach Spokane House, to the south, here, and you should send any further messages to us there. I will try to send two men back every five or ten days to be sure we are in contact with you and to advise as to any supplies we might need. But once we start the trek over the pass. I'll need all the men I can get, say eight men at least. You will have to send those supplies as fast as possible. When we make our final move over the pass, we'll be on our own. But hopefully, you will be able to follow with more supplies for our return trip."

Thompson paused to think. "We will have to wait until spring before we can make a new canoe. The birch rind and spruce roots we need to build a new canoe will only be ready when it gets warm."

He paced, trying to visualize how they would identify the Columbia River, then spoke, "Once we are on the Columbia, you will likely not hear from us. Spokane House and Rocky Mountain House are our only real contact points. Getting over the pass in the dead of winter will be hard work. I propose to start by proceeding over land to Boggy Hall then to meet the Athabasca River at its juncture with McLeod's river. Hopefully the river will be frozen fast and the horses will be able to walk on the ice, at least part of the time. Tents, we will need tents and furs to sleep, four tents to hold six men each, provisions, winter clothing, good winter moccasins and mittens. How soon can we get that all together?"

Lupine was ahead of Thompson, "Two days, I think. But we need time to make more snow shoes. The native women can do that. I must remember to pack for repairs to the snow shoes. We have almost no ash lumber and will have to use birch and it is less suitable for snow shoes than ash. Let's plan four days to be sure. Will your men continue on the voyage?"

"Yes. They signed up for the whole trip and are good men, picked for the voyage. But perhaps you could select six more men to complement our canoe." Thompson wanted to be sure he could at least get over the pass and extra men would be useful to set up contact with Rocky Mountain House once they found and got over the pass he knew had to be there.

"I have done so already. All but three of the six have travelled with you before, except LaSalle", replied Lupine. "All of them asked if they could go with you."

Office of the Secretary of Colonial Affairs
London, England
Sept 20, 1810

Lord Percival Worthington, Secretary of Colonial Affairs to His Majesty King George III, sat at his desk while he unfolded a sealed letter just delivered to him by a special courier. He noted the handwriting and confirmed to himself that it was genuine, the handwriting of James Wilcox, and a gentleman of wealth, loyal to His Majesty living in New York, USA. He carefully read:

Lord Worthington   **September 10, 1810**

It is of interest that a ship, the Tonquin, owned by John Jacob Astor of the Pacific Fur Company has today departed New York bound for the Columbia River. Of more interest is the fact that she is captained by one Jonathon Thorn a mere Lieutenant of the United States Navy – on leave from the Navy. I find it curious that he is on leave as, to my knowledge such events are unknown in His Majesty's Navy and I question why such would occur. Moreover, the President of United States has forbidden any ship to depart New York, yet the Tonquin has been allowed to do so. The only explanation I can surmise is that the Navy of that country is somehow involved with the venture of Mr. Astor. I have

no further information on this matter but will advise you should I acquire anything more of interest.

JW

Percival frowned, and then breathed just a few words, "Damn! I was right. They're after control of the North West, not just the Canadas. And they are preparing for war."

He looked up and shouted for his aide. "Please inform His Majesty that I have received an important communiqué and that I beg an audience with him as soon as possible." He then rose and looked out his window, deep in thought.

The Overlanders
October 21, 1810

On the 21st of October, 1810, the Overlanders of John Jacob Astor's Pacific Fur Company departed from St. Louis, Missouri on its quest to reach the mouth of the Columbia River. They were to follow the route taken by Lewis and Clark on "The Voyage of Discovery" arranged by President Jefferson.

But their voyage was poorly planned. It was burdened by sixty people, all of whom had no inkling of what lay ahead and all of whom had to be fed. There were horses, wagons, all manner of fancy foods, and even cannon. Of the sixty people, there were thirty "riflemen" intended to control and frighten any Indians they might encounter.

Three of those riflemen were hired just days before departure and were there, on the instructions of Major Ronald Foster, Commander of the 17th Kentucky Dragoons, for the sole purpose of killing David Thompson and stealing his maps and journals. They each carried the famous Kentucky Long Rifle and were militia members of the 17th Kentucky Dragoons. They were dressed like mountain men but, in fact, were just three cutthroats of the worst kind.

Mostly because their numbers were so large, confusion and arguments often occurred, it took until late July 1811 before the "Overlanders" left South Dakota and began the trek over the Rocky Mountains.

It was three weeks later when three Kentucky men left the Overlanders, or what was left of them, somewhere near the confluence of the Snake and Columbia rivers. They were later to show up at Spokane House, a post established by David Thompson two years earlier.

Meeting of the Waters
January 2 - 8, 1811

Thompson's group had no easy trip to the Athabasca River. Temperatures ranged from zero to minus twenty-four degrees Fahrenheit, and the depth of snow from little to three feet. There was much bush and they often had to cut their trail in order to provide sufficient room for the horses, dogs and equipment to pass. When he could, Thompson often went to the high point of land to survey the area and get compass readings on their location and the direction of flow of any river or stream. Often, he could not really see the direction of flow because of the ice and snow. But he was able to make an educated guess at that. He made detailed notes in his log on most days. On November 29th they reached the Athabasca River some miles southwest of where McLeod's river joins the Athabasca. From that point the going was less onerous, but still difficult. For Thompson this was a great relief.

He took the time to record that LaSalle, one of his men, would not join Thompson and the others for supper. That obviously caused some concern because he didn't need a sullen man on this voyage. Thompson made a point of eating with the men. Doing so bought all of them close and protective of each other, a feature much needed when in almost constant danger and hardship.

Several more days of difficult back-breaking drudgery found them at the destination Thompson was looking for, a stream flowing into the Athabasca River from the west. It wasn't much more than a trickle but certainly less than summer flow. This came as no surprise as these mountain rivers were constantly fed with spring water that showed itself from time to time. Thompson could see that the banks of the river, when in full run, were quite wide during spring and summer. There was a very good chance that it led to a pass over the mountains. The water, after all, had to flow both east and west from the top of the pass he hoped would be there.

They had plenty of meat as Baptiste, one of the hunter-voyageurs, shot two very healthy elk each bearing a good deal of fat. But they would need more, just to be sure.

Passage over any pass in winter is worrisome. Thompson did not know how high the pass was or if it was even there, what the snow conditions were, how cold it would be, or how steep the climb. But he concluded it was acceptable, though no place to use horses. All would be on foot; pulling and pushing the sleds to help the dogs along. Careful preparation was needed. Pemmican would be their life source and it was time to make as much as possible and the two elk were a great start.

For the past many days, they were all dressed for winter weather. Each of them wore their cloth leggings under sturdy trousers, flannel shirts with a vest for extra warmth, and a knee-length jacket, known as a "capot" The longer great-coat was too cumbersome and long as they often had to bend and crouch while working on land. Their jackets were held closed by a sturdy sash or cloth belt. Buttons were a nuisance as they kept popping off and getting lost. Instead they had toggles and loops to hold the capot together. They wore mittens made of leather and lined with rabbit fur. Gloves were useless as they made frostbite to the fingers a serious risk. They had two pairs of moccasins, both of them calf-length. Each had a soft thick inside sole. The pair for use while on land was lined with rabbit fur and very warm. They wore calf-length wool stockings while on land and sometimes put on two pairs for extra warmth.

They slept in the tents on top of Buffalo skin for protection from the cold ground and covered themselves with three wool blankets. Most often they wore flannel shirts, clean dry trousers, and one pair of stockings when they slept. If they got too cold, all they had to do was wrap the Buffalo skin around their bodies and they did that often. Work was steady from dawn to dusk. But the men were well fed and happy.

LaSalle, however, was more often sullen. Only occasionally did he eat communally with the group. His mates noticed he swore more often. Not at them, but whenever any small thing happened that displeased him and on most of such occasions his displeasure was caused by his own lack of care. After he pinched his finger or stubbed his toe, or dropped a piece of firewood it would be "Merde!", or "Shit!" in English. And he did so in a way that Thompson would be sure to hear it. Occasionally, one of the men would approach him and say, "Thomas, we are fine, all of us" or offer similar encouragement. But LaSalle's response was usually a sullen pout. Yet, never once, did he say an unkind word to his mates.

The main job was the preparation of pemmican. That would be their staple food for the next several weeks. How many weeks they did not know, and they needed the fat for warmth and the high protein of the meat for energy and quick thinking. As a result, the camp was a beehive of work.

They needed firewood, not to cook the meat, but to dry it. The available wood, however, was not ideal and it was mostly green and set off many sparks as the sap within the wood heated to boiling. It also took a good deal of time for the wood to burn, so the search for dried wood-logs and branches of trees carried down the river and dried-out tree stumps was constant.

They had a good set-up for pemmican. Two racks of green wood were constructed which, for the weather conditions, was ingenious. The racks stood on tripods which supported four main poles, one at corner of a rectangular shape. At each pole a slightly smaller wooden rod was tied to form a four foot by three-foot rectangle. On one of the cross-bars notches were cut into the rods onto opposite sides of the structure. The notches held smaller wooden rods to be placed onto the horizontal rod, about four inches apart. It formed a rack for hanging meat. Those smaller rods held strips of "pounded meat", each about ten to twelve inches long, one inch wide and an eighth of an inch thick. The meat was draped onto the rack and hung down five to six inches down from the top.

While the rack was being constructed, three men were busy cutting and "pounding" the meat. They did it with care. Strips of meat were cut from the elk carcass, as thin as possible, and then the meat was rolled, not really "pounded", on a large flat rock that was close enough to the fire to warm the rock so meat would not freeze to it. They used a dowel-shaped piece of fire-dried wood to roll the meat. As pine or spruce wood imparted a taste of sap to the meat, they used aspen. As the meat was pounded, much of the blood would ooze out so there was as little moisture left in it as possible. The strips were then cut again to conform closely in size to each other. This would ensure that all the meat would dry at the same time.

The "racks", two of them, were placed cross-wind to the fire. Their purpose was not to smoke the meat but to keep it warm, not cooked, until all the moisture was forced out. Every now and then, two men would carefully lift one of the meat-holding rods to the far end of the rack, and then successively reposition the others closer to the fire. This method resulted in a uniform dryness to all pieces of the meat.

The sun was low and there were fewer hours of sunlight in the winter, so it took longer than usual to dry the meat. They took turns, three hours at a time, to keep the fire moderately hot throughout the night. There were some worrisome moments when one of the men saw the glowing eyes of wolves moving silently in the forest, drawn closer to the fire in their desire for fresh meat. But the men were aware that the wolves would not venture too close. They learned to ignore them.

While all that was going on, there was another fire, lower in heat and managed closely to produce heat from the coals rather that a large open flame. A similar rack was set high over the flame to slowly cook and dry the meat. The idea here was not to dry for pemmican but to half-dry the meat so it could be eaten, like beef jerky, as long as it was free of mold. This meat was salted and when ready was stored in much the way pemmican was stored. Pemmican could last for months as long as it is kept dry and out of the light. The half-dried meat would not.

There was another process carried on a third fire, a small one over which they hung their largest cooking pot. Fat from the elk was slowly melted and rendered until they had enough clear fat liquid to add to the dried meat. It was added when all the meat was fully dried. Then it was carefully and evenly mixed with the dried meat. About fifty percent fat to fifty percent meat, by weight, was ideal. It was good for the dogs as they needed fat for energy and warmth.

In the end, the fourth day of work, they had two hundred pounds of pemmican, and eighty pounds of half-dried meat. The pemmican was shaped into blocks about four inches thick, one foot long and eight inches wide and packed individually into square leather bags. The bags were to be packed in separate sleds in case there was a mishap with one of them.

They burned all the marrow bones so as to not encourage wolves to congregate in the area and packed for the trip over the pass. Too many hungry wolves were a great danger to all. Thompson had already walked about a mile up the valley to get a better idea of what the hike up would be like. He noted clear blue water rushing under the ice, not surprising to him, but it gouged its way so far under the ice that it was impossible for him to tell if one could walk on it. They would have to avoid that danger, for to slide into the water or even to get their feet wet would cause great delay and possibly the loss of toes. In places, there was no room to walk along the river and they would have to venture into the woods. That meant they would have to pick their way through a forest laden with fallen trees and snags of all sorts. It was going to be a very difficult climb, certainly not as easy as the Howes Pass.

Sleep was well organized. They now had three canvas tents: two of them large enough to hold six men and the third for Thompson as he needed space for writing his logs and planning each day, as well as a place to keep some supplies safe. At mid-morning of the day before they were to make the ascent, Thompson gathered the men.

"Tomorrow we will climb up the pass. I don't know how far it is, maybe two or three days. But I do know it will be a hard climb. Right now, this river does not look very steep, but I think there will be bad parts. The rocks are what worry me the most because, as you can see, they are rounded by the flow of water and very treacherous for walking. So we will go slow on those rocks and try to avoid them. Two men will lead to make a path in the snow. That is very hard work, so they won't carry freight. We will take turns doing that. The horses and dogs will follow with one man in front and one behind each sled. Each man will carry a light load of goods."

"What about the wolves? They will follow us." asked Gilles.

"Yes, at least for a while. Once we get a few miles up, Baptiste will shoot one of them and that will probably cause then to stop following us. One man in front and one in back will carry a musket. We will do as we always do, hang the meat and pemmican each night.

Thompson paused to allow questions. Then he spoke again. "I think firewood will be a problem. So pick up anything we can burn as we go and lash it to the sleds. It seems to me that, up here, the trees grow very slowly, so the wood we find should burn hot. Keep the pieces small for weight. It looks like the trees will be very small and not high enough to hang our food. So we will camp in places we can hang it, even if we have to a back-track a little to do so."

Despite comforting Gilles, Thompson and the rest of his men were not worried about wolf attack. They tended to avoid contact with humans unless in absolutely dire need and the wolves they saw were healthy and well-furred. If anything, they would only seek ways to steal food. But, one never knows.

"So, let's begin packing for the climb."

A few minutes later Cote gave a shout, pointing towards the big river behind them. "Three men come! On horseback! It's Thomas and Vaudette and another." Two of the riders had another horse, laden with packs following behind them. The third was at the rear of the line.

They all cheered and waved at the approaching men.

Thompson looked carefully at the third man. He was someone new and he had a rifle slung in a leather rifle case at the right side of the saddle. He was a tall man, at least taller than the voyageurs, but dressed like all the others. When he pulled back the hood of his forest green capot, he revealed a bright red toque which he wore snuggly folded over his ears.

They all sat and waited for the group to finish crossing a small shallow in the river, then rushed to greet them. Hugs and friendly punches followed as the men dismounted. Thomas announced there were more supplies and four men immediately moved to collect them. The third man walked directly to Thompson, and said, "Mr. Thompson, my name is Ashford, William Ashford. I came to join you and bring letters from Montreal. Can we talk?"

Thompson's first thought was, "Well, this man is all business." His second was, "Something is afoot." He held out his hand, as did the new man, and they shook.

Come. We can talk in my tent." He said, pointing to the three tents grouped near the large fire. The new man slung his rifle, a short one by Thompson's measure, over his left shoulder and a leather case over the other.

As he entered, Ashford noted there was a small writing table at the center end of the tent, a rolled-up hide next to it and positioned so it could be unrolled into a bed. There was no formal bed but merely a space to sleep on the ground.

"Sir," began Ashford. "I am here for a special purpose which I will explain to you when we are out of earshot of the other men. In the meantime, I will present you with the instructions I have been given. May I?" He motioned with the leather case that he wanted to place it on to small desk.

"Certainly," Thompson's curiosity was almost overwhelming.

Ashford gently placed the leather case on the desk, opened it and carefully reached in to remove and set aside the objects inside. First were the books. Inside one of them was the letter from McGillevray which he presented to Thompson who immediately began to read it. Meanwhile, Ashford continued to empty the case: some cans marked 'lampblack', a small leather bag, a pair of socks for padding. Then he reached down to his left side and drew out a very evil-looking two-edged knife. He took the knife and very gently ran the tip of the blade along the entire edge of the bottom of the case, pealed up the leather, and removed a neatly folded paper which held something inside.

"I am instructed to give you this. I know of its contents but have not read the letter. You will note that it bears the seal of the Secretary of Colonial Affairs of His Majesty King George."

Thompson accepted the package, opened it and began to read. As he did so, his hand shook slightly.

For Mr. David Thompson   London March 4, 1810

We present to you Captain William Ashford of the 95th Regiment of Foot of His Majesty's forces serving in Spain. Captain Ashford is a highly decorated man, a member of 'The Chosen Men' being a special force of Riflemen attached to Lt. General Arthur Wellesley in the war currently at a lull in Spain. He is an excellent

marksman and we are advised one of the best in the regiment. Among his attributes we mention but a few. He speaks fluently in French. His loyalty and perseverance in harsh conditions are greatly admired by his senior officers and his men. He is a gifted artist with the pen whose depictions of scenes and terrain have assisted his superiors in planning for battle. This gift will serve as excellent 'cover' as a means to disguise his purpose with you. Although he has little knowledge of the canoe, we have instructed him to learn and become comfortable in this aspect of his assignment. We are confident he will have done so by the time he reaches you.

The purposes of his assignment are two-fold. First, to ensure your maps, logs, and other information are preserved and kept safe and second to ensure that you are protected. The reasons for this will be explained below.

Our sources believe the Americans are preparing to declare war on Britain. We speculate that they will try to invade Canada in order to aid the French in our struggle with Napoleon. That is one reason we believe they have designs on the west coast.

Credible sources have indicated that Mr. John Jacob Astor is planning to send a ship from New York to the mouth of the Columbia River on the west coast of North America and presently known as 'Oregon Country'. He will also send a party of men over land. Mr. Astor's aim is to establish a fur trading post at that location, a post that will compete with the North West Company. The fact of competition is not the central worry. The same and other sources lead us to believe that the United States of America will place some agents within Mr. Astor's groups to find and destroy any and all maps, logs, or other information you may possess or make of the Columbia River. One less reliable source suggests that your own life may also be in danger.

Captain Ashford is sent for the purpose of protection as it is our belief that the Americans are planning to annex all of the lands of the western coast, up to the lands far north of the Columbia that are under control of the Russians. We have no knowledge that Mr. Astor is aware of the facts stated above. We are quite sure that an agent has been planted in your group, Mr. Thompson. We therefore encourage you to work closely with Captain Ashford and to devise a means of keeping all this information secret and to prevent any harm as above stated. We strongly suggest that no record referring to Captain Ashford should be made on your logs. Captain Ashford is aware of the contents of this letter and may provide you with more information. You may show this letter to him and should then destroy it.

Sir Perceval Worthington
Secretary of the Office of the
Colonial Affairs to His Majesty
King George III

The letter bore the red-wax seal of the Secretary of Colonial Affairs of His Majesty King George III.

Thompson sat and stared at the letter, not knowing what to say or what to believe. After a few moments he grasped what was happening and looked up at Ashford.

"Good Lord! This is incredible."

"Yes, indeed. It means we should be careful and should talk in more detail soon, somewhere we can't be heard."

At that moment there was a loud commotion outside. The men were laughing, some cheering. Thompson and Ashford scrambled out and quickly learned the cause of the noise. Ignace and Battoche were seated on a strange-looking sled and were in the process of hurtling down the hill towards the camp laughing their heads off until they fell over and buried themselves in the snow just uphill of the camp. The other mean cheered and jeered and two more grasped the rope tied to the front of the sled and began to run up the hill.

"That, Mr. Thompson is a new device designed by your man at Rocky Mountain House," said Ashford. "He calls it a 'Toboggan Sled' and suggested you could experiment with it on your, uh, our journey. I've seen something like this before only this one has two small tracks, like the skids of a dog sled. The floor is flat and smooth, like a toboggan to keep it from sinking into snow but the tracks will help it stay in a straight course. It is also a great deal of fun. I might say that I have learned much more that I could imagine on this voyage and some of what I've learned is a bit on the silly side."

Thompson was familiar with toboggans but it never occurred to him that they could use one to haul heavy loads on hills that led in directions one did not want to go. A toboggan tended to slide and skid in the direction of least resistance. If the skids worked, they could carry heavy loads up slanted hills of deep snow. He waited until Ignace and Battoche slid, tipped, and rolled and laughed down the hill.

"Lads, I want you to meet a new comrade! Gather 'round." Somewhat reluctantly, the men did so.

"This is William Ashford. Montreal has thought up a new idea which I think may be a great idea. Mr. Ashford is an artist and he works with the pen. He is said to be very good at making pictures of the hills, rivers, and valleys that God has created. That will help me and others who will later follow us on this great journey. He tells me he is good with a rifle and can help Baptiste on the hunt. Say hello!"

Like school-boys they all hollered a great "Hello" and then came to Ashford to shake his hand and welcome him. Ashford knew immediately that Thompson would be a good man on a potentially dangerous voyage, one adept at maintaining necessary secrets.

Thompson continued as each man welcomed Ashford. "Mr. Ashford will join me in my tent so he can use my table to draw." Then he looked at Ashford with a knowing and mischievous smile.

The men immediately went back to trying out the toboggan sled. Thompson strode slowly past the fire and tucked the two letters into the hot coals at the edge of the fire. Ashford watched as the white smoke of the paper turned into a dark heavy spiral and very slowly rose as the wax seal melted and burned.

"I should get my gear." Ashford said, as he walked toward the pile of bags and other items that were unloaded from the toboggan. "Shall I put them in the tent?"

"Certainly. Put them on the right side. I'll move the desk a little to give you more room." Thompson went to the tent and began to move the desk and chair. Ashford followed carrying his duffel bag and his Buffalo skin, placed them on the floor just as Thompson's bedding, and returned for more. There were only two more items, the small trunk containing more rifle balls with a leather pouch containing a musket mold, ladle and ten one-pound lead ingots and other rifle gear, and, of all things, his paddle. He planted the paddle firmly in the snow as though to say the paddle wanted the snow to melt and the paddling to commence.

"Don't tell me you hauled the paddle all the way here on horseback?"

"I'm afraid I have fallen in love with this paddle. It took a while to get on to it, but it's part of me now," replied Ashford.

"Well, we'll see if it gets in the way. If so, we'll use it for fire wood and make a new one. The lads will have to do that anyway."

"Let's go for a stroll and talk some more." Thompson held open the tent as he spoke and they both stepped outside." Over this way. We'll let the men play for a bit so we can talk." He turned and hollered up the hill. "Be careful lads! We don't want to break the thing!"

At the edge of the Athabasca, Thompson turned to Ashford. "Is all this real?" he asked.

"I'm just a soldier and can't really say for sure. But I think it is. I'm told the Americans are very disturbed about inference with shipping. One of the hints is that there is an embargo in the US that does not allow any ship to depart from New York, yet the plan is in the works to do just that. The ship is privately owned and that will make it look quite innocent."

Thompson seemed perplexed. He took a moment to think and then realized what was bothering him. "Good Lord!" He bent down and, with a stick, wrote the number of days per month, then added them together. "I have wasted, uh, let me think. I left Rocky Mountain House on September 12. That would be 114 days ago. Are we in a race, here?"

"I don't know," replied Ashford. "Depends on how long it takes for a ship to travel around South America and this far north on the other side."

"Well, I have heard from some ship captains that it takes at least ninety days going south, then another ninety days going back north just to reach the Hawaiian Islands. That would be no less than 160 days. We still have time. The problem is that I don't know how fast we can build another canoe. We need warm weather to do that." Thompson's mind was running with figures.

"In speaking with the Captain on the frigate that I sailed on to get to Halifax, I was told that going around the tip of South America can only be done at certain times of the year, summer time. When it's winter in London, it is summer down there. So, a ship would likely make the voyage around the tip in our winter. That would be about now. We still have time," offered Ashford.

That eased Thomson's mind somewhat. He crouched to pick up a handful of snow and licked it. "We are about to go up that hill. I am quite sure it will lead up over a pass to the western side of the Rocky Mountains. The pass is the 'Height of Land'. Some call it the 'Great Divide' because from the top of the pass onwards all the water flows westward to the Pacific Ocean. I have passed through some of the land and have been told the Columbia River passes, going north, that way." He pointed to the north. "Then it bends and flows south and the west to the ocean. My Kootenay friends have told me the 'big bend' happens somewhere near the bottom of this pass. But we shall find out for sure when we get there."

Thompson bent to pick up more snow. "When we get to the other side, we will build at least one birch bark canoe and then paddle to the ocean. At that point our travel will be much easier than what you have endured so far as we will move fast with the current. I am quite sure the horses will not get too far because the snow will get deeper as we climb and the rocks are too dangerous for them. So we'll send the horses back with Thomas and go on without them,"

Ashford waited to allow Thompson to continue, then couldn't hold it any longer, "Is Thomas really an Iroquois Indian? I've hear they are quite ferocious."

"Yes, he is. And yes, they are ferocious warriors. The Americans are deathly afraid of them because they take scalps after almost every battle. But you need not worry about Thomas. He is a loyal and dear friend and I have travelled hundreds, no thousands, of miles with him. He also has good sense of humor which he has picked up from the lads. Thomas is a gifted helmsman who reads the water very well. Ignace and Charles are also Iroquois." Thompson nodded his head toward the two Indians watching the fun with unbelieving eyes. "They are the best of the best paddlers and read the water even better than Thomas. You probably had occasion to pass through some rapids, but nothing like what we will see on the other side. You travelled upstream and in relatively low water. But you should do fine and I will say you will come to love every moment of it, especially right after you go through each rapid."

Ashford nodded, though he couldn't fathom how anyone would like being scared to death. "Oh, almost forgot (a small white lie there), the people in London have given me an Infantry Pattern 1806 Rifle, just like mine. I am to give it to you. It's packed in my great coat at the bottom of the bag. No one has seen it and I doubt that anyone could tell it was in there as it is well padded. They asked me to present it to you as a gift. Since I am here posing as someone I am not, I propose not to let it be known that I am an expert marksman as to expose that would likely let the spy who may be with us know what he should not know. I noticed you did not say anything about that fact when you introduced me to the men and I think that was wise."

"Thank you, Will uh, William. I agree. You will notice that both Baptiste and LaSalle have the American rifled musket. They are good marksmen."

"Just so you know. The series three Infantry rifle is far superior to the Kentucky rifle. I've used both. But we shall not let that be known. In the meantime, I'll make a point of showing I'm not anything more that the average marksman. Should I bring out the rifle for you?"

Thompson paused to think, "Let's wait. Keep it safely concealed as you now do. For now, we concentrate on getting over the pass. One more thing, I do not imbibe in spirits. But I allow my men to do so, very little at a time, so we don't have any brawls. Tonight, we will give all them dram of

49

rum just before sleep and that will please them. I suggest you partake with them as it will help you become one of them more quickly."

"I will, with pleasure. Very few of us army types have objection to a drink or two."

"In future we will have to devise ways to talk in private. We should both keep ourselves alert to whoever the spy may be. I doubt he will make any moves until we are well along in the journey. If he does, it will likely be closer to the end."

With that, they returned to the men, who were tired of the sled and were going about packing for the next day. As he always did, Thompson was about to inform the men as to what lay ahead.

"Ignace and I walked up the hill, about one mile. The rocks are not suitable for the horses so we will have Pareil, Thomas, and Gregoire Cote return to Rocky Mountain House with the horses. We will supply them with twenty pounds of pemmican which will be sufficient for them to get to the cache we made at the entrance to the mountains. They will be able to shoot an elk on the way. Would you wish to return?" he turned to LaSalle when he spoke.

"No, Mr. Thompson. I keep going." LaSalle looked at the ground as he spoke.

For supper they ate fresh meat cooked in a large pot with dried peas. As it was likely to be the last fresh meat they would see for days and they ate it all. A dram of rum and a soothing song led them all to their beds.

As Ashford and Thompson settled into their beds, Thompson turned to him and, in a low vice said, "LaSalle has been complaining for the past several days. He has even started kicking at the dogs. Keep an eye on the man. I will ask Ignace to do so as well."

Over the Pass
January 8 - 11, 1811

It was a bright day though the sun had not yet come over the mountains to the east. Thompson and Ashford had already packed their gear into the toboggan, with the chest and extra rifle securely tucked into the duffel bag. Ashford's rifle and cartridge pouch case were tucked in beside the freight for easy access. Their buffalo skins formed a cover on the sleds and Thompson's notes and maps were placed just under the skins.

Thompson stood beside the toboggan mulling where in the line of travel it should be placed. "William, where would you suggest we place the toboggan, front or back of the line?"

"I was given a demonstration of this toboggan sled at Rocky Mountain House and was advised that it be used at the front of the line. It will pack down the snow and make it easier for the dogs behind it."

A loop was attached to the curved front of the toboggan and finished with another loop made with a Bowline knot which served as a point where two ropes could be attached for the dogs. Each of the sleds and the toboggan would be pulled by two dogs assisted by a man leading the dogs, who also had a rope to the sleds. Behind each would be another man whose duty it was to push the sled, be sure it stayed in line and did not slide off the track. Another man, armed with a musket, was to trail behind all of them. The first two men of the line would tire more quickly than the others. So periodically they would fall to the back where the snow was better packed and all would move forward to fill the vacant space. The party was thus comprised of eleven men, including Thompson.

Pareil, Thomas, and Gregoire Cote were sent back to Rocky Mountain House with letters from Thompson.

They could see water flowing water within the river now and then. In the Rocky Mountains even some of the smaller rivers had water flowing all winter long, the water originating from underground steams. This created a serious hazard because the river ice was less reliable. Water lurked under thin sheets of ice that could easily break. There was danger of being swept under the ice and drowning, perhaps never to be found as the water would trap a man in the ice until spring. Ashford marveled at how the clean, clear water flowed under and over the ice, gouged its way onward with silvery shine and vivid blues. He was astounded how the water, so clear, turned black when it got deep, how it flowed over and under layers of ice, how it seemed to slow down to a crawl and move like black or blue molasses as it passed over the ice. At times, he felt the water was looking up at him, inviting him to come closer, to touch it. Yet it also warned him not to do so.

At the outset of the trek, he was told repeatedly of the great danger of getting his feet or legs wet. To counter that problem, each man carried a spare set of socks and kept and extra pair of moccasins within easy reach. Trousers were kept tucked into their moccasins and that made it almost impossible for snow to get into their feet.

There was no shouting, no song, no ribald jokes as they began the climb, just a few grunts and mild swearing as they made the initial push to get the sleds going into a comfortable rhythm. They soon began to make good time. The slope grew steeper, the snow deeper, and the silence of voices became more pronounced. Finally, Michel Boulard, the one who was always talking and always happy, spoke.

"I tell you. Being near the back of this line with the dogs and Francois farting every minute I think I'm going to die!"

He was met with a roar of laughter.

It was Francois' turn. "Well, maybe you go to the front. Break the trail. We can't hear you up there."

More laughter.

After that, there were many jokes poking fun at the man ahead of each in line and all followed by guffaws from all but one man, Ashford. The pace picked up and the day went well. As they walked the men near the front would periodically pick up a manageable piece of driftwood left high and dry on a rock and above the snow and stuff it into one of the sleds. Sometimes they would break off the track and pull a dead branch off a dried-up tree.

All the men knew they could dry off and have a good hot cup of tea when they made camp at the end of the day. Each man could look forward to a good fire, a good meal and a good sleep when the day's trek was done

Then, a most amazing sight! To their left he saw a steep cliff that was seeping water about three quarters of the way up the rock face. It trickled in places and in others it gushed. But the astounding part was the formations of ice that Ashford could not believe were real. There appeared to be actual tubes of ice with water flowing through them. In other places there were curtains of ice that seemed made to hide actors on a stage. In other places there were long, heavy icicles hanging by some magic from the rock face or from still more ice, and around the sides of the walls there was deep frost stuck to the rock and mimicking a thin layer of wool on the back of a sheep. Ashford had to stop for a minute just to be sure what he saw was real.

"This is a fairy land!" he said.

"Oui, Monsieur Ashford, but a dangerous one," advised Boulard.

The day went well. And, for Ashford, was full of wonder. But the next day they woke to snow—wet, sticky snow.

"Gather 'round lads! We have to move!"

When all were out of their tents and bunched around Thompson, he barked out instructions. "This wet snow means we may have a chinook roaring though here so we have to get over the pass and as far down the other side as we can."

Ashford looked at Thompson, "chinook? Should I get my rifle ready?"

"It's a weather thing, answered Thompson. "Pierre, explain it to him and tell him your story. Pack up fast boys."

Pierre came to help Ashford take down the tent and pack it and to explain the chinook.

"Chinook is weather. Indians call it the 'Snow Eater'. It is very warm weather that come over the mountain and melts the snow. You can tell one is coming from the sky. There is big arch." He drew a big half circle in the sky to the west. "Cold weather and cloud in front, a big clear sky behind. That is very warm weather. I tell you what happen to me one day."

He stood up. "Four men. We bring back carcass of big elk Gilles shoot across the river near Rocky Mountain House on south side of river. It is cold day. We are two mile from river. Fort is on other side. We see the big arch and we know we get chinook so we move fast, in line one behind the other. We wear the snowshoe. Snow is deep. We cannot run. Maybe one mile from river we can feel snow start melt. River is shallow but there is deep part, ice very thick on this side. We can see the post, see smoke from chimney. We start across the river. But suddenly there is big water from melting snow on top of ice. The water come down very fast and I am last man in line. Water is too fast for me to cross so I am trapped on south side of river. The other men, they throw blanket, chunks of wood, pemmican for me. Water only five-six feet across but very fast. I spend two day there. They give me tent. I am safe. Then I get back and they give me big cup of rum."

Thompson was listening. Pierre's story was familiar to him. It was told often and mostly true. And it served to explain the chinook. "We have learned that, on the west side of the mountains the chinook brings snow at first then rain and the rain is often hard. Sometimes there's no rain but clear sky because it has rained on the mountains farther west. But the melt creates big problems. So we have to get over the pass and as far down the other side as we can."

Ashford did not quite believe the story, but he got the message. He had to wait and see.

The men ate pemmican as they packed. They would need the energy from its fat for a hard day ahead. It was easier to eat than the half-dried meat. Dogs received their share as well.

Looking west Ashford could see the broad arch in the sky with clear bright sky behind it. They moved on, as fast as they could. As they rose closer to the top of the pass, Thompson noted that there was almost no new snow. The snow came down only on the leeward side of the pass. That was a good sign. It meant the chinook was not too severe and may not have flooded the valley down the other side. There was a greater flow of water in the river and the air was definitely warmer. The two lead men were quite far ahead and Thompson was about to tell them to slow down when there was a loud shout from one of them.

"Up here! Bring another rifle"! Both men were now waving them up and looking quickly around them. Ashford grabbed his rifle and shot pouch, doffed his snow shoes and ran up with Thompson. When they reached the men, they pointed frantically to the snow at their feet. Tracks! Fresh tracks! Bear tracks! Big, big bear tracks!

"That is a very large bear, probably a grizzly bear. But what the hell is a grizzly doing wandering around in the winter?" They waited until the rest of the men reached them.

Thompson spoke again. "Very unusual to see bear tracks at this time of year. We have to assume it is hungry, or mad. We should keep our eyes open."

Ashford measured one of the tracks with his hand. It was far larger than his hand. "I saw many bears on my voyage up here, but never a grizzly. The men told me about them, how it takes at least five shots to bring one down. They said these bears avoid people. Is that true?"

Boulard provided the answer, "Yes, Will. But you surprise him, he attack. If you see one, even a black bear, never look him in the eye. He take dat as threat."

"How do we know it's a male?"

"Two reason for dat. Momma bear is with cubs, very warm somewhere, sleeping. These tracks very big. The bear walk that way". He pointed towards the right side of the valley." Maybe he will smell our food. Maybe he is very hungry. We keep watch and go fast."

"Mr. Ashford, please take the front of our line. LaSalle, you take the back as you know more about these creatures than William. It's not likely it is ahead of us, but it could swing back behind us. Let's get moving. We might post a guard tonight. See how far we get."

Ashford still had trouble understanding the chinook. It seemed unbelievable. Yet, it all happened so fast that he had to believe it. This land is full of wonders, and strange ice formations and snow melting like it was on fire. Now big bears. What else would he see? As he walked at the front of the line he kept looking behind, looking to the right and to the left, hoping he would not see a huge grizzly.

After about four hours walking, any thought of the bear was gone. They made good time but were nearly worn out.

Thompson noticed that the pace had slowed and there was an odd stumble with the snowshoes, a few grunts of "Merde" and no joking. It was time to look for a place to camp. It took another hour before they found a suitable spot, and the light was failing. It took longer than usual to set up the camp. But it was well planned and quite suitable. A good feed of half dried meat and a dram of rum and they were all asleep. No need for a guard as they found one tree large enough to hang the meat and felt they had travelled far enough not to be bothered by a bear.

The next morning was a fine, clear and warmer than previous but just below freezing. The snow was hard, so no need for snowshoes. Thompson ordered Thomas and Vaudette to take the lead and to space themselves further ahead than usual. He wanted to know when they reached the top. The toboggan and sleds had to be man-handled to keep them from sliding on the hard snow as there was a slant to the left, towards the river's edge and they had a tendency to slide in that direction. That ate up a good deal of energy and pemmican as they worked, so they traded positions more often. The dogs were doing fine, although they often had trouble sliding on the harder snow.

Thompson noticed that LaSalle was kicking at the dogs again so he moved the man to the back of the line.

After two hours of hard slogging, there was a shout from the lead men. Ashford looked up and saw them waving and jumping up and down. He knew what that meant. They were at the top!

Once all the men and dogs were assembled at the top, Thompson looked down.

He could see for miles. The valley was different, the mountains more rounded than jagged and, as far as he could see, there were layers upon layers of mountain ranges each range progressively a lighter blue-grey in colour as though painted from the imagination of a drunken artist. Most important of all, however, was the sighting of two small half open-lakes about five miles below them. It was obvious that the waters were flowing west into those lakes. Yes! They were over the pass!

"Lads! If we can make it down to those two lakes today, we have a good camp and a great fire. Francois, did you bring your packet of spices for split pea soup?"

"Oui, Monsieur Thompson. And I think it is good day for good soup!"

Ashford was sure he heard a great cheer from the men, but they just stood there in awe of the sight. He knew that, in their hearts as well as his, there was a loud cheer.

"Francois' soup will be great. But best of all is that all of you can wash your clothes and stinky bodies in that lake," said Boulard, always the friendly joker.

A great roar of laughter and joy rose to the tops of the mountains, and then they all started down the hill. It took only three hours to get to the lakes.

They decided they would bathe and wash clothes in two shifts. One shift would gather firewood while the other bathed. Francois took the second shift and, while the others washed, he began the preparation of his famous split pea soup. He used dried green peas rather than the usual French Canadian yellow peas. Ashford watched as he prepared the soup and Francoise gave him a running description as he worked.

"The split peas should be soaked for a few hours so they cook faster. But I have a secret way. I crush the dried peas."

He scooped several cups of spilt peas into a fine buckskin bag, took out a rolling log similar to the ones they used to pound the meat, only not stained by animal blood, and crushed the peas into tiny pieces. Then he placed them into a large pot of water and hung it over the fire.

"When the pot boils I raise the pot up to get less heat. After that we let it cook very slow. But I have a secret. I show you when the soup boils."

When it just started to boil, Francois lifted the pot higher so it would simmer rather than boil. Then he reached into another bag of fine buckskin and brought out several smaller ones and from each small bag took out a pinch or two of their contents. "Dried spices and things, a little garlic, some bay leaf, some rosemary (he pronounced it "Rose Marie") and, very important, a handful of dried potatoes. The potatoes make soup thicker." He threw in dried potatoes followed by a handful of pemmican for flavor. "I make these dried things myself, all summer long, and I keep them for winter."

The men of the first shift were returning, laughing and joking. Thompson was amongst them. They hung their wet clothing on crude racks near the fire, cross-wind of it to avoid smoke, donned dry clothing and gathered around the fire for warmth. After a few moments they went out for more firewood. Francois gave instructions to keep the fire low and he and Ashford joined the second group.

The soup was great. They ate it with slices of half-dried meat, talked and joked and wondered aloud about what the coming days would bring and were content. It was dark and Francois had already placed another pot onto the hook over the fire and now he rose to look into the pot, turned to Thompson, and gave him a small nod.

Thompson rose. "Well lads, it's time for green tea."

"Green tea! Green tea!" It was a joyous chant as the men rose. All, except Ashford, had smiles on their faces.

Green tea? thought Ashford. Sounds interesting, exotic, maybe.

They formed a semicircle around Thompson, who was holding a pot of something and a tin cup. Each man brought his own cup, the one they used for eating the pea soup, and waited. They looked at Ashford as if to say, "Well, come on. Join the line!" Ashford did so. Francois held a small pot he had placed over the fire came to stand beside Thompson who was holding an empty tin cup and a small barrel of rum.

As Thompson was a non-believer in the medicinal values of sprits, he began the ritual. Francois poured a measure of the tea into a tin cup and Thompson quickly downed it then chased it with pea soup. "Ah, green tea, nothing like it."

Thompson then approached each man, one at a time. Francois then ladled a measure of the tea – about two ounces – into each man's tin cup and waited until each of them in turn drank the tea and chased it with rum. Each of them, after finishing the rum said, "Ah, green tea, nothing like it." Then they passed the tea cup to the next man.

Finally, it was Ashford's turn. Francois ladled the tea into the tin cup and Thompson poured the rum into Ashford's own cup. Ashford then made a mistake. He tasted the tea instead of shooting it as the others did. It was bitter, very bitter. Well, not just bitter, but… he could not place a name on the taste.

"Drink it fast," someone said. So Ashford shot the rest down and chased it with the rum. But the rum didn't help. His taste buds were already frozen with the bitter taste. But he knew he had to say the words, even if he had to choke while doing so, "Ah, green tea, nothing like it."

All the men burst into laughter.

"You have just had your first taste of winter green tea." said Thompson. "It's made from spruce needles and brewed like tea. It's not so bitter when we use tender spring boughs and it's really no joke. Our Indian friends, including Thomas, Ignace and Charles taught us about this many years ago. It prevents scurvy and in the winter months we have to take it, otherwise our teeth will fall out and we eventually die. We drink it every few weeks.

Ashford understood. But, of equal importance, he realized that he had just joined the group. He was one of them, a comrade. He felt that even more so when each of the men, except LaSalle, gave him a hefty bear-hug and spoke words of brotherhood. LaSalle simply placed his hand on Will's shoulder, turned and walked away.

That gesture dampened what was otherwise a great evening and made Ashford wonder even more about what was in LaSalle's mind.

Thompson and the others thought the same.

Thompson wanted Ashford to try to find out what was on LaSalle's mind and had already told Ashford to be wary of him. So he ordered Ashford and LaSalle to lead and watch for game. They were to shoot anything they thought appropriate and it was not long before the spotted a somewhat emaciated deer. It walked slowly in front of them, not really aware of the presence of men. It was about 150 yards away.

"Show me how you shoot that fancy rifle," LaSalle said as he pointed toward the deer with his head.

"It's a little beyond my limit, If he was about fifty yards closer, maybe I could do it, but ..."

"Oh, give it a try." They were both whispering.

Ashford raised his rifle, took aim, and purposely missed the deer.

"Shit." The deer scrambled into the bush.

LaSalle simply let out a grunt.

When they went back to the middle of the line, LaSalle made sure everyone knew Ashford missed a deer. It was as much to demean Ashford as it was to show that LaSalle was the hunter, but Ashford was expecting that. It was the price he had to pay for what he was really doing.

That night, as he and Thompson settled into their beds, Ashford used a soft voice to tell what really happened. "I have to tell you that I purposely missed that shot. I feel LaSalle was trying to find out how well I shoot for some other purpose and I feel he will try a more serious test later. I am now convinced that he is our spy."

"Yes. I was convinced when he refused to properly acknowledge you at the green tea ceremony. The man is jealous of you and he hates you. Be careful. I will no longer allow him to hunt with you, and the lads will think it is because you're a lousy shot."

"One more thing," said Ashford. "I noticed that the two Indians didn't drink the rum in the green tea thing and, come to think of it, they never have taken any. They don't like it?"

"No. I will not give spirits to our Indian friends. They cannot handle it and often get into fights. They could even end up killing someone. Our company often uses rum to trade. But I refuse to do it and they are fine with that. It's unfair and not good for them. The Company has learned to not provide rum as a trade item. Ignace and Charles learned that a long time ago, and avoid it as best they can. Besides, they grew up with spring tea or winter tea, and I think they prefer the taste of it compared to rum."

Ashford thought for a few moments then asked, "How, may I ask, did you tell the Company you would not use spirits for trade? It seems to me the company would profit from it."

Thomson smiled as he explained. "Well, I put the kegs of rum on a particularly unruly horse, one who never liked a heavy load, then pulled him through the forest. The horse would use the trees to rub off and break the barrels. After about the third time, the company quit supplying me with spirits for the Indians. Eventually, they stopped using rum altogether."

Both men laughed.

Desertion, Deception and Ambush
January 13 – 26, 1811

The next morning was a fine one. Thompson, as he did each day, wrote his morning entry in his log, a simple note on the temperature. It was fourteen degrees Fahrenheit and would get warmer during the day. LaSalle was sent out to hunt but returned less than an hour later, grumbling and asking for meat. Francois was stunned! It was not yet time for eating meat and told LaSalle he had to wait.

LaSalle's response was, "What in shit do you take me for! A god damned horse? No one can go so long without meat!" Thompson could see that Francois was visibly shaken. The meat supply was getting short and LaSalle knew it, and to Thompson this felt like the last straw. It was time to part to take some sort of action, but what? For now, Thompson would have to think about how and when to do it. The man still had some value as a hunter and he could not spare him, yet.

As it turned out, the idea of waiting to get rid of LaSalle was a good one because the next day the man was able to bag two young male elk. They ate fresh meat and made more half-dried meat. That took a whole day. Still, Thompson worried. Sooner or later LaSalle would pull the whole venture into failure and the men were getting despondent. He could see that the men were uneasy about being near LaSalle. The days ahead would be extremely difficult.

Thompson knew he had to make a difficult decision, not just about LaSalle, but about which direction to travel, southward or northward. He still had difficulty believing that the Columbia River, at this place, would flow north and make a hard turn to the south as his Indian friends told him. It didn't seem right, because Thompson had seen the Columbia travelling southward along this valley.

Thompson decided he would wait on any action concerning LaSalle. He was still of use and what lay ahead regarding the river could mean he would need LaSalle for a day of so longer.

The next day LaSalle began to beat the dogs senseless. This time he kicked and punched the dogs and went after one of them with a wooden club. The poor dogs howled in pain and tried in vain to escape the blows until Boulard intervened.

"LaSalle, my friend, please! The dogs are our companions. They do you no harm. Please! Leave them in peace!" As Boulard spoke, three of the other men stepped next to Boulard as if to tell LaSalle he would be beaten himself.

It was time. The man was a danger to the whole venture. Thompson walked between the men and Boulard, with Ashford close behind, and spoke.

"My friend, you are unhappy. I ask you to calm yourself. These dogs are very important to us. Perhaps you should return to Rocky Mountain House?" It was more a suggestion than a question.

LaSalle replied with grunts and incoherent mumbles and strode into the forest. Thompson knew the man would likely desert and was worried. But, for now, this was all he could do. To expel LaSalle might lead to violence and violence, right now, was no option.

Thompson walked past Ashford and spoke quietly, so no one but Ashford could hear, "Keep watch on that man. We have to keep the peace." Ashford gave an almost imperceptible nod.

Their course took them into a valley with a gradual incline on the north side where the south-facing slope was almost bare of snow, with few tall pine trees. The south side was steeper and snow-covered and had more, but smaller trees. It ended with a small rise at the south end, then another steep course. To the west, the direction of travel, it sloped gently downward and ended with a short easy climb upward to the top of a small ridge that seemed to show the valley's end. Because the North Slope faced the hotter south sun, it was less treed and those were taller trees of pine rather than spreading spruce.

Ashford commented on how pretty the valley was as they passed through it. "Were it not for the weather, I could see myself living, in summer, in this valley."

When Thompson saw the steep hill just over the ridge on the bottom end of the valley, he called a halt.

"We will camp here, on this ridge. There's good firewood and not a likely place for an avalanche. We are tired and I don't want any mistakes. Mr. Ashford, since you are in love with this valley, I invite you to make a drawing of it. Please mark the compass heading as to the direction of your view."

Ashford cleared a spot looking back in the direction they had travelled and took out his drawing kit, mixed a small portion of the lampblack and began. He drew each of the large trees on the north side with great care and a little less care for the opposite sloop. His ink was beginning to freeze. But he managed to draw an accurate picture of the valley.

"Here it is, Mr. Thompson. I had to stop because the ink was freezing."

"Very well done, though, next time you will have to devise a means of keeping the ink warm." Sometimes I place my ink well on warm flat rock. I carry one in my case."

"You never stop learning," Ashford thought to himself, then added, "and there is still a lot more to learn!"

One day's slog later, on January 26, LaSalle, LeTendre, and D'Eau deserted. That did not become apparent until about two hours after they disappeared, and when Thompson realized that he went immediately to his tent and looked for his log book and his book of map sketches. They, too, were gone.

"Francois! Find Mr. Ashford and tell him to come here as soon as he can!"

"Oui, Mr. Thompson."

Minutes later Will reported back, asking what the urgency was.

"LaSalle, LeTendre, and D'Eau have deserted. My logs land maps are gone and I am sure LaSalle has them. I don't think the other two know that. They are just lazy men with small hearts and small minds. You have to go after LaSalle. Be sure you have enough supply to spend the night because they have a two-hour head start. All I need is the return of the logs and maps, so try to avoid violence."

Ashford immediately began to pack a backpack. He purposely chose a small one that would allow him to run with ease. The pack was quite similar to the ones he wore with the 95th. As much of the surrounding area was clear of snow, and since he had to do a great deal of running, he decided to wear his boots and pack the rabbit-fur moccasins. The folding knife went into the boot pocket. He packed an extra set of trousers and a flannel shirt to wear should he sweat too much and need to spend the night in the cold. Two blankets, two pounds of pemmican, extra socks also went in. He made sure his compass was securely attached by a lanyard to the leather loop at the front of his capot, tried on a pair of leather gloves he might need, then cut off the trigger finger of the right glove and stuffed them both into the proper pockets of the capot. He would wear mittens until he knew he would have to shoot. He slung a bag of water over his shoulder so it sat comfortably at his left hip, then tied it to his hip so it wouldn't bounce as he ran. Almost as an afterthought, he stuffed the spyglass into the cartridge pouch. He then tied his snow shoes to the outside of the pack.

"It should take less than a day, maybe two days. I will hope to arrive back here late tonight. Don't want to sleep in the cold unless I have too. Can you have one of the men keep a large fire? If it's dark when I arrive I'll fire a shot as soon as I see signs of the fire. Oh – this toque is too bright. Can I borrow yours? The green colour will be better." They traded toques and Ashford turned and left.

Thompson didn't have time to say "Good Luck" as Ashford was already trotting up the hill.

Ashford ran at a trot holding the rifle in one hand and shifting it to the other every now and then. He knew LaSalle would have to take the same trail back to Rocky Mountain House and, since there were three of them, all tired and angry, they would be slow. He reckoned he would need three hours, so he ran a modified "Rifleman" style, ten minutes at a trot, then four minutes at a walk. He didn't need a watch to time himself.

As he ran-walked, his mind went through a number of possible scenarios of what would happen when he caught up with the three men. It was likely that shots would be fired. But the others had no musket, no rifles. It would be LaSalle who would do the shooting. He would have to let LaSalle shoot first and LaSalle, being the coward he was, would likely shoot from 150 yards or more because he thought Ashford could not shoot with accuracy at that distance. Ashford had no choice. He would, if need be, give LaSalle that first shot.

On second thought, he decided that was not a good idea. This was not a sport.

As he ran and walked he thought about what could happen. LaSalle's actions had shown that he was dangerous, a bully and a coward. Only a bully would treat Francois the way he had and only a coward would beat the dogs as he did. Did he know that Thompson would send Ashford after him? What would he do? Ambush! LaSalle would set up an ambush! But where? How?

Ashford stopped and cut off a piece of pemmican and started chewing it, not much chewing because it seemed to melt in his mouth. He was getting to like the stuff!

Back into the trot. He continued on, trotting, then walking, then trotting. More thoughts came to his mind. How would LaSalle set up an ambush? If he thought Ashford could not shoot more than 100 yards he would set up a range of more than that, maybe 150 yards. Few people are good at 200 yards. He would want the advantage of height, so he would likely find a spot for that. It was now almost noon. The sun would be from the south, a bit low. He would take that advantage!

Ashford slowed to a walk.

The valley! thought Ashford. The valley I drew! LaSalle was away "hunting" when Ashford drew it. He knew LaSalle would set up just a little above the floor of the valley and for a shot where they had walked. To get a good shot at LaSalle, Ashford would have to do it from across the valley and the sun might not be good. He would have to get up behind him and pick a spot above where he would most likely wait. The valley was about half an hour away. LaSalle would likely set up so he could see anyone coming. That means he would be on the south side near the west end of the valley, on the right.

Ashford stopped. The south side of the valley had a gradual slope that joined with the steeper slope further on. There were lots of trees along that slope and the trees thinned out about half way along the valley to the east. He was sure LaSalle wasn't that good a shot, so he would probably wait until Ashford entered the valley. That meant a slog through the snow to get behind and above him. He was probably up there now, Ashford thought. What should he do? Maybe he should wait until LaSalle's hands became numb in the cold. Ashford knew LaSalle did not have gloves, only mittens, he always shot with his trigger hand bare.

Ashford convinced himself that LaSalle was not there yet. LaSalle would have to double back, and he couldn't go straight up because his tracks would give him away, He would double back through the trees at the far, east end of the valley then back-track to set up about half way up the valley. A slog up through the trees would be the best thing to do. Ashford could wait until LaSalle arrived, and hoping he was not there already. He would have to take that part slow and quiet.

Ashford slowed to a walk. He needed to find the route he would take but couldn't waste time.

Then Ashford noticed what looked to be similar to a path, likely a game trail. The slope ended almost like someone built a path up around the right side of the valley. It turned to the left and then faded out in the trees. He could get up through there. But damn, he might need to wear the snow shoes.

He thought for a moment about putting on his moccasins. They might fit better in the show shoes, but then decided he would not. There was no time. He had to move fast but silently and set up his own ambush.

Ashford cut off more pemmican as he knew he would use considerable energy tracking though the snow, then he hung his pack into onto a branch of a pine tree, just high enough to be sure wolves could not reach it, then began up the slope. He stopped and loaded his rifle. He then placed a leather bag over the end of the barrel to keep snow out and a wool sock over the firing pan for the same purpose. His boots fit reasonably well into the snow shoes and there were few snags to impede his walk. In half an hour he got the first glimpse of the valley below him. He crouched and surveyed the valley and the low ridge above. That would be where LaSalle would come. A person down in the valley would not see his tracks in the snow as the ridge dipped just enough to obscure them. He scanned the line of the dip and could see no tracks.

"Good. He's not here yet," he said to himself.

Ashford looked for a better place for his own position, but soon realized there was none. He had to stay at this spot. But there was high ground above him and if LaSalle climbed up there it would mean his own certain death. He pulled the spyglass from the inside pocket of his capot and carefully pulled it open. His purpose was to see if there might be tracks at the far end of the valley, tracks to show LaSalle was climbing higher. A careful scan showed no tracks and told him it would be too long a shot from up there. But Ashford decided to scan it again to be sure. He braced his arm against the tree and looked again.

"There he is, the bastard."

Ashford could see LaSalle making his way along the line, keeping down low, his Kentucky rifle at the ready. The man had a backpack, a small one, slung over his blue capot. His hood was up and he didn't seem worried about anyone being above him. He was in a hurry, seemed to be more concerned about getting to some specific point, so Ashford panned ahead of his direction of walk. About 500 yards ahead of LaSalle he saw a rock protruding from the snow, dark on this, the sunny side as well as on the left, towards the downslope end of the valley.

It looked like a good spot to set up an ambush. It had good cover for hiding. It was about 150 yards from where Ashford stood. Easy shot. He decided to wait for LaSalle to set up, but not too long. Ashford knew that LaSalle's heart would be pounding from the effort of the climb and that his aim would be unsteady.

Ashford settled in position to shoot in the direction of the rock and waited while LaSalle made his way there. Then he noted the small backpack LaSalle had strapped to his back likely held Thompson's map and log book.

He wondered where the other two men were. They could not be within easy rifle range and probably didn't even have muskets. Only LaSalle would have one. He would worry about them later. LaSalle was the threat now.

It took LaSalle almost ten minutes to get to the rock. The snow was obviously deeper there and that made it a tougher job for him. When he reached the rock, he took off the pack and set it down out of sight from anyone in the valley and crouched behind the rock. The hood of his capot was down and he wore no hat under it. From where Ashford was he could see that LaSalle had chosen good spot. His shot would be about 150 yards down to where they walked the day before and 150 yards from where Ashford was waiting.

Ashford took a deep, silent breath and focused his aim directly at LaSalle's back. That way, he would take only a small movement to take final aim before the shot. By that time, LaSalle was well-settled, calming his heartbeat and waiting with his rifle at the ready.

"Up here, LaSalle!"

LaSalle rose, much faster than Ashford thought he would, and swung his rifle towards the sound of the voice, but before he could find the source, Ashford fired.

The ball went right through LaSalle's capot, vest and shirt and mangled his lungs. LaSalle's rifle fired in the imagined direction of Ashford's voice as LaSalle fell to his knees, now seeing Ashford rise to stand beside the tree. His face contorted with real terror and he began to cough blood into the snow. Then he fell completely, face-forward.

Ashford quickly re-loaded his rifle and waited. He knew the coward was dead but did not know where the others were. He waited, ten, maybe fifteen minutes, and then rose to approach the body.

Yes. It was Thompson's bag. But where was the rest of his stuff? Why would he take this with him when he was trying to ambush Ashford? He must have wanted to make sure it was safe. His other gear must be with the other two.

Ashford made a quick search of LaSalle's body. In the pockets of the man's capot he found two bracelets, each with a name engraved into the brass plate attached to them. The names plates on the bracelets were LeTendre and D'Eau. Such plates were common amongst some of the Voyageurs who wanted to be sure their bodies were identified if they were mangled in rapids or by falling from a height. He also found two leather purses, each with the initials of the two men and each containing several coins of varying denominations—their gambling money.

Ashford sat for a moment and concluded that the son-of-a bitch murdered the other two. But he had to find out for sure. He picked up LaSalle's long rifle and his cartridge pouch and powder horn and slung them over his shoulder.

As he didn't know how much farther he would have to hike, Ashford went back down to his backpack, put on his moccasins and started back up the hill and into the valley where to snow on the south-facing hill was almost all melted away. Half an hour later, he came upon the bodies of LeTendre and D'Eau. One of them had been shot in the head and the other in the back. That second body was up higher, in the snow and just at top edge of the valley. It appeared to Ashford that this man was trying to run. A few yards uphill he found the men's large packs and, farther to the south side, the tracks LaSalle made as he went up the hill for his ambush. As Ashford had neither use for nor the ability to carry the packs, he left them there. He also had to leave the bodies as he found then as he had no means of burying them. It would be dark in about two hours so he had to move fast.

Before leaving, he stopped to search LaSalle's pack. The man stole some pemmican and it might be of use to us, thought Ashford.

After about two hours spent sliding downhill, walking and running when the ground was level, stopping now and then and proceeding much more slowly in the dark, he saw the glow of the camp fire reflecting off the snow at the sides of the valley. He pointed LaSalle's rifle skyward, fired off a shot and hoped he would have a nice cup of pea soup when he reached camp.

Three men, including Thompson, were waiting for him when he arrived. There was a small pot of soup staying warm near the fire. The others men came from their tents to join them. As he drank his soup, with the permission of Thompson he told everyone about what happened and produced the items he found. "It is my suggestion that whatever is in the purses be shared amongst the lads, or given to their families," he said to Thompson.

"The two had no family. The lads will share it," said Thompson. "Leave it to me."

The *Tonquin*
January 26, 1811

John Jacob Astor's ship "*Tonquin*" sailed from New York to Hawaii, arriving there on 10 January 1811. It then departed for the Columbia River on 20 January. On board was Gabriele Franchere, a seasoned French-Canadian voyageur, now clerk for the Pacific Fur Company, and as such, in charge of Stores and Trade at the ship's destination. He was then twenty-seven years old and very familiar with the life of a voyageur and with the fur trade.

They were at sail with favorable winds on the 29th of January. That night, a clear sky with bright stars and little swell. Franchere, for some reason suddenly awoke, which was unusual as he never had trouble sleeping on board the *Tonquin*. He decided he would go on deck, get some air, and then settle back to his hammock. As he walked past the storeroom door, he reached for the paddle lock on the door to be sure it was locked. But at that moment he heard voices coming from inside the room.

"So he said to me, 'Will you do it?' And I thought about it for a few seconds and said, 'Yes. But I will not kill Mr. Thompson. He's a good man. I know him. But I will steal his logs and maps if I have the chance. I will do that for 200 dollars.'"

"Really?" said the other voice.

Franchere froze. He knew the voices. The first man he heard was Simon Cambray, one of thirteen Canadian voyageurs on board. The second was Albert Belton, also a voyageur.

"Oui, but I was not to be paid until I brought them the logs, so I tell him it would be very hard to keep those things hidden and I would need

300 dollars. He said, yes. Then he said to me I hope you succeed, but if not, there would be Riflemen waiting for Mr. Thompson on his way back. I hope I will succeed. Thompson is a good man."

It was obvious by the way Cambray slurred his voice that they had broken into the stores and stolen some rum. Good. They were unlikely to realize someone heard them. Franchere silently went back to his hammock where he lay, unable to sleep, until dawn.

Boat Encampment
January 29 – February 4, 1811

The trip down was quite pleasant compared to the slog up the pass. The snow was deep, often very wet and soft, but they managed. By late afternoon they spotted what Thompson knew had to be the Columbia River. He was now certain of it because it matched with what the Indians told him two years earlier. The Columbia headed north, and then at the confluences of two rivers, it turned south and flowed to the Great Sea. He could see the water, obscured in places by ice and snow, flowing to his right, to the north. The trees around him were massive and unlike any Ashford had ever seen. There were pine, spruce, and cedar trees, all of massive size and girth. But there were very few birch and they needed birch for canoe-making. Thompson would have to scout the area but, for the moment, it was time to make camp.

Though supplies were low, Thompson gave double rations of pemmican, hot tea, and a dram of rum to all the men. All slept well knowing they were much nearer to the end. Nearer, yes, but still very, very far from the end.

The next two days were spent looking for, finding, and testing the rind of birch trees for the canoe. Ashford accompanied him, carrying his loaded rifle in case of wolves or cougars. As Thompson tested, he explained 'the rind' to Ashford, "See, you can peel this off. It comes off in a nice shape and we try to make as long a piece of it as possible. This is not the bark of the tree. The real bark is just under it. When we peel off the rind, the tree will easily recover by producing more. It's a form of protection the tree gives itself against weather. That's why I don't feel guilty about doing this to birch trees."

"You learn something every day," Ashford said to himself.

"Look at this," Thompson said while pointing to the strip of bark that he peeled from the birch. "To be useful for a canoe, the rind has to be at least one quarter inch thick. I now believe that all the birch trees on this side of the great divide have thin rind. Useless, except for starting a fire. Also, these horizontal cracks are too numerous and there is potential for leakage from them. I think it's because of the mild weather on this side. There is little need for them to protect themselves from the deep cold of the east side of the mountains. Also, the only time we can harvest the rind is in warm weather, spring and summer, so we wouldn't have birch until mid-spring. Around here, spring comes early, about mid-February to early March. This stuff is of no use to us. I will look more, but I fear we shall make our canoe some other way."

"We will make another kind of boat?" asked Ashford.

"Yes. We can make one of cedar. But we need warmer weather for that as well. The thing to do now is to make a more permanent camp, a log house for us, and then a cedar plank canoe. We have a lot of work ahead. I'll need you and Baptiste to hunt, get as many provisions as you can. Never hunt alone. The bears might be thinking of waking and the wolves and cougars are hungry. In the meantime, I have to design a cedar canoe and the lads will start cutting down pines for a shelter."

When Thompson informed the men of their predicament, there was a long, collective groan.

During their lives as voyageurs, all the men had been stranded somewhere and they knew the best thing to do was to keep busy. So they got to their tasks right after a breakfast of pemmican and tea. Baptiste and Ashford set off for game and in no time ran across a small herd of red deer, shot two, and then proceeded to gut them, a task Ashford had to learn from Baptiste as they went. By the time they had hauled the carcasses to camp, Thompson and the men had chosen a site. It was in a small clearing within easy reach of the river and well treed with a few pines and many cedars.

It was only then that Ashford noted that the pines tended to grow in small groups where there was good sunlight while the spruce and cedar grew in dense stands creating shade on the ground but reaching ample sunlight higher up. Two men had already cut down several pines and were busy chopping off the branches to make simple logs. They decided not to de-bark the logs though they had the tool to do so. Right now, they needed the shelter. Everyone knew they would be here for some time. They also decided that, after constructing the frame for a roof, they would construct a roof with cedar boughs. A sturdier roof would come later.

The construction site was bustling with activity. The men were not happy, but busy and not complaining, and in two days they had the temporary cabin, a permanent fire site with log benches and a crude table topped with split pine boards. In the process they noted that the pine, though green, split easily.

After six more days, their work became more efficient and the supply of meat more abundant, most of it in the process of being dried for pemmican. The men were happy. Fresh meat each day undoubtedly helped in that regard. Helping their moods was the fact that each day was warmer than the last and the accumulated snow in the forest was beginning to melt faster. Their hearts were more at ease and the men were again making stupid jokes, laughing, and singing.

They were a family, again.

Each day, Thompson and the two Iroquois would go into the forest and test the pines to determine if sap was starting to flow. There was no sign of that.

But Thompson did find a stand of white, or yellow, cedar, the best wood with which to construct the frame of a canoe, better than the more common red cedar because it was stronger and lighter and, when split green, was best for the frame because it was more pliable and easily molded.

There was, however, one moment of despair for Ashford. His paddle was packed at the bottom of the toboggan sled, carefully placed under a cover of his grey greatcoat and when he remembered it was there, he peeled up the coat and received a terrible shock. The shaft was broken in two places! He picked each piece up and cradled all of them in his arms, walked a few steps towards Thompson and sat down in despair.

"My paddle! My paddle! It's broken!"

Cote and Boulard gathered near him, looked and Boulard said in, mock sadness, "Oh, how terrible, then began to laugh. We told you, we should have used it for firewood!"

Ashford was not amused.

"But do not worry, Mr. Ashford. We will help you make a new one, even better than this. A paddle you make yourself is the best. You will see."

"Yes, Will," said Thompson, "We all need to make paddles and it's true. The one you make yourself is the best. You might want to keep that one as a template for the next one. We always make extra ones as well."

"Oui," said Cote, as he offered Ashford a hand-up and then gave him bear hug.

Around the fire that night they discussed what they had to do next. Thompson began the discussion. "We'll build a cedar canoe. I found a stand of good white cedar for the frame and we'll start as soon as it gets warm enough. In the meantime, Ignace will continue to test the pines for sap. We need a lot and we'll all have to get involved in collecting it. While we wait for the sap, I suggest we cut down some of the red cedars and start building a proper house."

"Why do we need a proper house?" asked Francois.

"Well, I am sure we are near the spot where the Columbia runs south. The river's direction of flow tells me that. The river flows north. It should bend around and flow south somewhere downstream. But I don't know how far it is before we turn south. I still don't know which way to go from here. Besides, I think it will take some time before we have enough pitch and even more time to make the frame for our canoe. We also have to make the bench and locate good pine roots to sew the wood. The ground is still frozen and without the roots, no canoe."

"Ignace, what do you think?"

"Yes. Spruce tree here, not enough. We must to use the pine. I think also we should make a long, uh, bathtub to help make wood soft and a shape to bend wood around for inside of the canoe, like we do at home. We can make shape with a big log of cedar. I show you as we build." Ignace had built many birch canoes and although the others built some as well, he was by far the best suited to take charge of the task.

"And we have to keep busy or we'll lose our minds," added Thompson. "Agreed?"

The men agreed.

"Fine. Tomorrow one group will cut down pines while Ignace will find a red cedar we can hollow out to make a trough for hot water and make a shape for the canoe frame. How long should the log be, Ignace?"

Ignace rose and paced out about twelve feet.

"Sharpen your tools in the morning lads. Now let's have a dram. I hope we don't run out."

After the rum they all went to bed in their new, but rough and half roofless cabin.

The *Tonquin*
March 22 – 25, 1811

For some weeks Captain Jonathan Thorn of the *Tonquin* had been showing signs of instability. He grumbled to himself constantly. He leered at the crew and the Canadian voyageurs as though he knew they were plotting against him. Worst of all, when he was alone, he talked to someone who was not there; someone who was taunting him, yet also guiding him, someone he was compelled to listen to and someone who frightened him.

The voice began with someone waking him at night, just a voice, at first and then a bright, harsh white light, a light that illuminated his entire cabin and pulsated with the rhythm of a panicked heartbeat. Then it grew. It stayed with him most of the time. It grew inside him like a malignant worm and became so much a part of him that he ceased to notice that it was something that did not belong.

The crew took note of his change. At first, they thought it was just a general grumpiness, but as the days passed they became concerned. They whispered to each other about his demeanor and Thorn's mumbling and began to discretely avoid him.

They worried.

On March 22, while fighting a very mean storm blowing in from the northwest, the *Tonquin* reached the mouth of the Columbia River. Several years before this day, in 1791, Captain Vancouver of the Royal Navy had reached the same spot. Vancouver noted the shoals and currents from the sea and concluded the site was not suitable for his ship. He did not enter the mouth of the river. But for Thorn, the voice kept pushing, demanding

Thorn show the world how great he was. The voice also told him it was his duty to do so.

Thorn kept his ship safely out to sea for one day, then slowly bought her closer to the mouth of the great river. With his spyglass he was able to see a dangerous sand bar that posed a serious problem for his ship. Moreover, the storm, although abated, still presented dangerous waves that confused the river current and the Captain. He considered backing away but the voice came to him, strong and demanding, "Get up that river, you damned fool! Find the way!" it said.

And Thorn responded, "Five men! You, you, and you! Thorn hollered as he pointed to three men, "And you two! Get into that jolly boat and find me a channel. Do it now!"

Every man on board was astounded. No man should go out in that water, in those waves and into the river current in this weather. "Captain, no. It's too rough. Please!" shouted the first mate.

"Shut your mouth, you're a damned old woman afraid of the water!" Thorn shouted. "Get moving you men!"

Some of the men heard the first mate's words as he boarded the small boat, "This is it for me boys. Don't expect to live through this."

It was a difficult struggle for the five men to launch and then board the jolly boat. The waves from the sea, in their battle with the river current, were not just huge but were terribly confusing. There was no rhythm to them, no way to predict or see any pattern that would allow them to get even close to shore, much less take soundings of the water's depth. The waves hurled them erratically, at times even lifting the boat out of the water. It tossed them about like a wooden toy and then flipped the boat end over end. All of the men, along with the boat, disappeared, and though the crew on board the Tonquin looked feverishly to find and rescue them, it was no use. All were lost, never to be found.

All on board were horrified.

Thorn watched, not in horror, but in disgust for the men he had just sent to their doom. "Yes, yes! I know! I'll try again, tomorrow!" Thorn said loudly to someone his crew could not see and ordered the ship to stand off until the morning.

Thorn awoke the next morning with venom in his mouth. "Damned cowards." He stomped to the deck and began barking orders. "You!" Thorn shouted, pointing at the second mate. "You think you know more that I! You get the other jolly boat and find me that channel!"

The second mate knew it would be considered mutiny if he did not do as ordered. There was only one thing he could do. "Sir, yes sir. But I will not choose the men to go with me, sir. I ask you to do so, sir."

The second attempt also ended in failure and nearly cost the lives of all five men. They had to struggle with all the energy they had to make their way back to the ship. That brought Thorn to a vicious rage. He turned to the third mate and selected four more men to accompany the first mate on another try. Two of those men were Canadian voyageurs named Belton and Cambray, the two men Franchere overheard talking in the store room days ago. The other two were Hawaiians who joined the crew during *Tonquin's* brief provisioning stop. Thorn's order was to wave a flag when they found the channel and, in that, they succeeded.

But, without first making any effort to have the longboat return, with the men on board, Thorn proceeded into the channel. As the longboat crew attempted to return, the ebbing tide sucked their jolly boat away from the ship with unbelievable speed and they were unable to board the ship, instead, they were dragged out by the tide. Thorn guided the ship past the small boat without effort to aid them. As he passed the foundering men, several members of the crew hollered for the captain to stop and get them on board. But he kept on, ignoring the men and leaving the longboat to its fate. All on the ship witnessed the boat get carried outward then flip over in the huge waves. All saw the third mate and one of the Hawaiians get swept away and drown. They all saw the remaining men struggle to right the boat and climb into it and looked on in horror as the Captain continued to sail up-river.

One of the three men in the boat succumbed from hypothermia during the following night and the other two were able to swim ashore the next morning.

Eight men died and Thorn appeared unaffected.

Boat Encampment
February 5 – April 4, 1811

The sap in the spruce and pine trees began to run freely in early April. Though it was possible to harvest frozen sap, most of which flowed from injuries on the trees, the voyageurs preferred to take fresh spring sap as it had few bugs or other impurities stuck into it. But now fresh, clean sap was flowing and that meant it was time to gather sap and make pitch. That, in turn, meant Ashford had to learn how to collect sap and prepare the pitch needed to seal the boat.

It was a sticky, menial job, a never-ending, sometimes frustrating task that caused him to become the brunt of several French-Canadian jokes. As instructed by Pierre, he first cut a large right-angle triangle into the bark of several trees. The cut was made in the tree so the triangle stood tall and the sap flowed downward to the base of the cut. In a few days, it would gather enough sap to allow Ashford to scrape it off with a stick. The trick was to get it off the stick and into the pot. Pierre purposely didn't tell Ashford that he should wet his fingers before pushing the sap off the stick and on Ashford's first few tries Pierre and the others made a point of watching as their friend pushed the sap with one finger, then with another finger, then another; each time getting more goo stuck to his fingers, only to collect more spruce and pine needles, leaves and bugs while he tried to rub it off. They watched, holding back their laughter, until finally all of them burst into gales of laughter when he tried to lick it off only to find that it didn't taste so good.

That was when Ashford realized they were watching him, waiting for just such a moment. "What? How do you get this off?" That was when

Ashford looked at them and realized he was set up and burst into laughter himself.

"Monsieur Ashford, be careful now when go for a shit. You don't want the leaves or your fingers to stick to your ass." It was Boulard, the joker, who brought more hoots of laughter from the men.

Pierre then demonstrated the best way to do it. He took the stick from Ashford and first dipped his fingers into a cup of water before pushing off the sap. "Get fresh water often," he said, then patted Ashford on the back and walked away. The others all came and gave him a similar pat on the back, smiled and went back to their jobs.

I was a healthy joke. It made Ashford feel even more a part of the group. It made him appreciate how laughter and fun had to be part of their work and how it made them a great team. As he rose from the first successful push of the sap, he turned and saw Thompson, who had obviously watched the whole scene, and noted the suppressed smile on the man's face.

Ashford knew now that he was really part of the team which gave him the right to play his own jokes. In the meantime, he would gather sap every day, warm it in the pot and then add charcoal. Soft wood, like that of a pine tree was more suitable for the charcoal. It was easier to crush into powder. The crushing was done with two flat rocks. Then the powder mixed into a paste with the warm sap resulting in glue that was waterproof and could be applied to any leaks just by warming it again. In fact, voyageurs always had a pot of pitch handy to repair their canoes when needed. Though Ashford, in making the powder, expected some other kind of joke about a pitch pot, it never came. Everyone was just too busy.

The ground was still frozen, so it was not quite the time to gather pine roots. They had to use pine because the ground was too rocky and the spruce roots got too tangled in trying to weave around them. Pine grew in drier soil with fewer rocks and the roots grew straighter. Besides, that chore would be done only when they were ready to sew the frames and boards to the new boat.

None of the men had built a canoe with lumber rather than birch 'bark' so the job was half-planned and half-experimental. Thompson and Ignace were kept busy trying to devise the construction so Ashford assisted in the downing of a large red cedar, taking his turn at chopping at the tree, then stripping the bark with the draw knife. The job was to make the large 'bath tub' in which they would boil water to soften white cedar boards, each about one and a half inches square. Those would form the ribs of the canoe.

But first, they had to make the bath tub and, on the advice of Ignace, they would make the shapes for those ribs at one end of the log tub. Getting the water to boil in a wooden container without setting it afire would be an easy, but time-consuming task, as explained to Ashford. Red hot rocks would be thrown into the water causing if to boil and give off steam. That was an old trick used by the natives of North America to boil food, often in large hollowed out trees just like the one they were building.

Splitting the large twelve-foot long tree trunk was a job to be done by the experts. Ignace and Charles took turns doing it. First, they began by splitting off, wood, an inch at a time, to make a flat base on the trunk so it would rest securely on level ground. Splitting the tree had to be done slowly, along the seam of the rings in the tree. The technique fascinated Ashford.

First, Ignace would select the point at which to start the split by placing an iron wedge at the desired point. Then Charles would lightly tap the wedge until it began to split. Then the draw-blade would be inserted and tapped carefully until the whole length was reached. It usually split with a loud noise before they reached the end of the log. In most cases a good long board would spring off the trunk. In some cases, the split would happen prematurely so they would have to split the remaining part off to maintain the line for the next split. The shorter pieces were set aside for future use and very little went to waste. It took all day just to get the tree ready for gouging out.

During the process, Ignace explained that it was easier to split a tree and bend the boards while the tree was still green. Dry wood tended to break in the wrong places and wet, new wood was easier to bend for the formation of the frame. He explained that they would do the same process for the boards to be used for the skin of the canoe. Those boards would not need to be steamed as they would be easy bent to the gradual shape of the frame. But the boards had to be green and had to be attached while they were still pliable.

Whenever anyone went near the river, they would bring back any large stones they could find, preferably not one of the wet ones, but those from the outer edges of the water. Cold wet rocks tended to explode when they hit hot water or when the water within the rocks turned to steam, so the rocks were placed in a dry place, exposed to the wind. That reduced the chance of explosions. Exploding rocks tend to injure people, even take out an eye.

As the process continued, Thompson approached Ashford. "Will, I think it's a good time to let the lads know I have that rifle and for you to teach me the proper way to use it. My birthday is April 30. Most of the lads know that. But we can use it as an early excuse to bring out the rifle. I think I should get comfortable with it, just in case we meet some unfriendly Indians and, though I always try to stay friendly with them, we may have a problem. The Americans have passed through some of the territory ahead of us and, in my view, tend to shoot too soon. They are deathly frightened of Indians and we have to bear the burden of any rash things they may have done. I propose you take me on the hunt tomorrow and we shall practice."

"I agree. You wait here. I'll go in and get it, make a speech, and set it up. Act surprised."

Ashford went into the tent, pulled out the rifle, cartridge pouch and horn, and then checked the rifle to be sure it was not damaged.

"Lads, gather 'round. I have an announcement," said Ashford. The men immediately noticed that Ashford had two of the same kind of rifles in his hands and gathered around in curious surprise.

"I am told that Mr. Thompson's birthday is coming – uh – on the thirtieth of April?" He turned to look at Thomson who nodded and tried to look like he didn't know what was happening.

"Well, I'm tired of lugging this thing around and think he should do it himself from here onwards! Sir, I present you with a birthday present, a few days early. Here is my gift to you. Happy Birthday!" He handed the rifle to Thompson.

It took a moment for the men to overcome their surprise before a unified cheer of Happy Birthday rose in the forest. All, in turn, came and shook Thompson's hand, some showing guilt that they had no gift to offer, but all cheerful and pleased with what Ashford had done.

Thompson then stepped forward. He paused a moment as if he did not know what to say, and looked down at the rifle in his hands. He weighed it, looked at Ashford and the men and spoke, "Thank you. I think this is one of the few birthday gifts I have ever received. I even forgot my birthday was coming. Thank you, Mr. Ashford. Thank you. Now you have to teach me how to use it."

"Oh, I assure you Mr. Thompson, I will teach you, not as a birthday gift, but for my own protection."

The men roared with laughter. It was clear they not only respected Thompson but loved him.

"Mr. Ashford, I propose I go on a hunt with you tomorrow. I am eager to learn. But I can tell you I am a reasonably good shot. I hope I can do this instrument justice."

The next morning Ashford and Thompson went for the hunt. It was a good time to talk and plan for what might come ahead. As they walked Ashford explained the differences between this rifled musket and an ordinary one as well as the famous Kentucky rifle.

"You will have noticed this rifle is shorter than the normal musket. It's really the King's answer to the Kentucky rifle but what makes it unique is the short barrel. The short barrel allows it to be carried more easily and loaded in a crouched position, making it and easier to avoid detection by the enemy. It is as accurate at long range as the American one. I believe even at longer ranges. It is used mainly by the "Chosen Men" who are soldiers of the 95th Regiment of Foot."

"Our job is to act as skirmishers, to harass the enemy and most important, to kill the officers of the enemy. In some ways this rifle is more difficult to load than an ordinary musket because of the rifling inside the barrel and the fact that it has to be loaded with wadding around the ball to get maximum velocity from the explosion of the powder. Push the ramrod down easy, then harder as you get the ball down farther. Don't just tap it. You need two hands, one down low to be sure you don't bend the rod at the end of the loading process."

Ashford kept talking as he loaded the rifle, "The greatest feature is the adjustable sight. It can be adjusted to two hundred yards and, in the hands of an expert, accurate to 270 yards or more. I can re-load this rifle at the rate of three shots per minute, but most of the 'Chosen Men' will take a little longer than that."

"The Chosen Men?" asked Thompson.

"They are a breed unique in warfare. The men are 'chosen', not volunteers, though most soldiers now aspire to become one. They are chosen when their officers recognize them as exceptional marksmen and soldiers. They are chosen for their stamina, for their calmness in battle, for their ingenuity and ability to act as a team. They all read, know how to use the compass, and can survive in the wild on nature's bounties.

"Once we are selected to become 'Chosen Men', we undergo more training, not just with the rifle, but with new ways of fighting. With this rifle we can run, not just march, long distances. We can slow down our heartbeat before a shot. We almost never miss. We are proud of being the best warriors in the world. Uh, sorry. I got carried away."

"No, no. Don't be. I can see why they sent you here. I think the threat is even more serious than I thought."

"I don't know, but His Majesty is concerned about war in Canada. I might say, Mr. Thompson, this adventure with you and all the others I have met is incredible. This country has filled me with wonder. These men with us are unbelievable. I am honored to be part of it and to know you. Now, let's learn about this rifle."

Ashford took Thompson through all the moves several times, naming each step and then calling out the steps as he watched Thompson go through them. He started with just the ramrod, and then added the powder, then the ball. He demonstrated it with a chant of each step and, then when loaded, instructed Thompson to fire at a target set up fifty yards away. His pupil took well to the instruction and turned out to be a good shot, even at one hundred yards. They fired no less that twenty shots when Ashford stopped. "I recommend you clean the rifle often, even when not used for a few days. You will also learn to prepare your own cartridges. Tomorrow we'll do a real hunt."

When they returned to camp they saw that Ignace and Charles had already scorched the log and begun digging out the burnt wood. The 'bath tub' would be ready for use tomorrow. Splitting of more cedar for the frame would start at the same time and, while that was going on, the men would chop down more white cedar and make ready to split planks.

Putting the canoe together was the next problem, as they were not yet sure of how to do it.

The next morning Thompson gave instructions to build a 'table' upon which the canoe would be built. He also instructed Ignace to design and prepare to construct the 'form' for the frame. That, he knew, would take time as they might have to wait a day or two to have suitable pine roots and they weren't sure exactly how to do it. In the meantime, they were to make racks for the production of pemmican and half-dried meat just as they did previously. This time, it was easier and faster because it was warmer outside.

Thompson and Ashford went on the hunt. It was another pleasant, warm day. Most of the snow was gone and only patches were left in places where the trees provided good shade. The two men walked silently, took care not to step on anything that would present a noise, and constantly looking in all directions for game. It took only two hours for them to spot a beautiful buck about one hundred yards away near the edge of the forest.

"Your shot," whispered Ashford.

Thompson carefully aimed and hit the deer. He could see the look of surprise from the deer. Then he saw the deer seemed to realize something was wrong and took about three steps, not at the run, but more in confusion, and then it fell, twitched a few times, and died.

"I'll make a 'Chosen Man' out you one day, my friend. Great shot."

They approached the deer, confirmed it was dead, and immediately prepared to gut and quarter. Gutting took only a few minutes as Thompson was practiced in the art. When they were about to begin quartering it, Thompson froze.

"Quiet", he whispered. "Hear that? Don't move." He slowly turned to look down wind. "Bear. A grizzly. Trouble. He's about two hundred yards, there." He pointed with a small movement of his head.

Ashford slowly looked in that direction and was astounded. It was very large brown bear, mangy-looking but fearfully huge. Its face seemed flatter and more rounded than the many black bears he'd seen and there was a hump above his shoulders which made him look even more danger- ous. Ashford's heart thumped a few loud thumps and then settled down. Slowly, very slowly they half rose and grasped their rifles.

Thompson slowly put his hand on Ashford's shoulder and whispered, "Keep low. Don't make eye contact, just know where he is. Back away slowly. Don't run, don't turn your back. He wants the deer. If we have to shoot, I'll shoot first to scare him away. If he keeps coming, be prepared to shoot. Don't shoot for the head unless you think you can get him in the eye. Aim for the shoulder to cripple or slow him down while we re-load. The deer is his. That's all he wants but he'll kill us to get it."

The huge bear snorted and sniffed as it honed in on the smell of the deer, seemingly oblivious of the two men. Then it stopped. It rose on its hind legs, looking around at first, then in the direction of the men. He had picked up their scent but was unfamiliar with it. It sniffed and snorted, still looking for the source of the strange scent. Then it saw the men, but because of near-sighted vision, could not tell what they were. It only knew they were close, too close, to its next meal. It let out a loud 'huff' and started a trot in their direction. The trot increased to a run and was taking it directly towards Thompson and Ashford. It was now about 150 yards away.

"When I say so, rise up. Make yourself look tall and be ready to shoot. I'll fire first, over his head, and then we wait for his reaction. I will re-load. Don't shoot until I tell you. All he wants is to protect his food," whis- pered Thompson.

"Now." Thompson did not shout. He talked in a soft voice to be sure not to startle the bear.

He rose. Thompson took aim to a spot well above the bear and Ashford drew a bead on the bear itself. Thompson fired. The bear skidded to a full stop. It was confused. It looked to his right and saw the deer carcass. It looked at the strange creatures ahead of him and then again at the deer. Then it snorted and walked directly to his meal.

Thompson stopped his re-load and the two of them backed away while the bear sniffed at the deer, glanced up to look in their direction and then dug its teeth into the carcass. The men continued to back away until they were sure the bear was happy with his feast. Once satisfied they turned to walk away, confident the bear was no longer concerned with them.

"That was close, too close," said Thompson as they walked. "Best not to shoot when you don't know you can kill. We don't have any use for bear meat, not with all the deer and other food around here. I think it best we return to camp and avoid this area for the next few days. That creature will stay close and protect his meal until he eats all of it. When we see vultures circling the sky we'll know he is about done."

"I will admit that thing had me worried. My God! What a massive beast!"

"I think this was probably its first good meal since he woke from winter hibernation. He was quite skinny and he would fight hard to protect his food. We are two lucky people. I broke a rule today, always keep watch downwind. It's the great sense of smell that all bears have that gives them the edge. We'll tell the men to keep out of this area."

As they walked, Thompson kept looking back and then downwind. Then it occurred to him that he should talk more about looking 'in the eye'.

"By the way, we will undoubtedly make contact with some Indian people. You may notice that sometimes they will not look at you directly in the eyes when they talk. That's because they live in nature. They observe wild animals and respect them. For the animals, say, bears, wolves, all the predators, looking directly into their eyes is taken as a threat. It is a challenge to fight. Our Indian friends look upon strangers in the same way, so they avoid eye contact, even when they speak. It's not that they are lying or that they don't respect you. It's because they don't want to provoke a fight. It's a sign of respect, that they come in peace. It's only after they know you that they make eye contact. I just thought you should know that because it may help avoid trouble and will certainly allow us to make friends easier."

"Right. I noticed that on our trip along the Saskatchewan River. Glad you explained that. It now makes sense."

"Of course, the same applies to all predatory animals. They avoid making eye contact with another of their species," added Thompson. They walked on.

"You come back early. No luck?" asked Boulard when the two walked into camp.

"Gather 'round, lads. We have something to tell you," said Thompson. He told them about the grizzly and advised them not to go near the area of the kill for the next few days.

Over the next few days, Thompson and Ashford continued to hunt and more. Thompson decided he would teach the 'Chosen Man' about using the sextant in a mountainous terrain. He was aware that Ashford took lessons in the art aboard the frigate from London to Halifax, but wanted to show how to find the horizon in a sea of rock and hills.

Work progressed. Meat was being dried. The cutting and bending of the frame parts and the ribbing for the canoe showed promise and one of the men found the ground and pine roots suitable for harvest. However, they would first have be sure they had a very good supply of cedar planking and Ignace had already begun the task. Two medium sized and straight red cedars were cut and the process of spitting them into planks of about one-half-inch thick would soon begin.

The next day, Ignace did his first test of the hot water-steam bending. He had to make a 'form' under which to place the framing boards for the ribs of the canoe. He had done that may times and learned that the best way was to make the central two ribs first, then place the next rib under that one then the next and so on. The process would be repeated with the second central rib. Once the ribs were set, the planking would follow. As they had no metal and could not make a steaming oven, he would have to use the 'bath tub' and place a canvas cover over it to make each rib. Steam would be produced by tossing red-hot rocks into the water. One tent had to be sacrificed for the job, but that was no worry as there were now only eight men and they had a spare tent. Besides, the canvas would still be useful for something later. It might even still end up being useful as a smaller tent.

The progress in making the ribs began. It took two days to perfect it but Ignace was happy with the result. In the end, all went well and it took a week to make the ribs to form a good canoe frame. The process of unloading the cooked stones from the 'bath tub' then adding water, then heating up it up again with dry, red-hot rocks was very time consuming. All the while, two men were busy scraping off the bark of pine roots in a specially-designed form and splitting the root in half with their finger nails. The thinned-down roots were then placed into the tub and softened to become almost rope-like. All went well and they began splitting cedar planks.

But there was a problem. Should they fit and attempt to glue the boards on to the ribs for a smooth surface, or construct a clinker-built canoe? Clinker-built boats were made since the Viking age. It consisted of placing each plank partly over the previous one, sewing each where the boards over-lapped, and using the pitch to glue each board into place. That would make the canoe water tight. After a day's debate, the clinker method was chosen. It would make a stronger canoe.

They were now ready to place the planks.

The process was very slow. Without nails, they had to sew the planks onto the ribs of the canoe using more split pine roots as a thick thread. Since they had a hand drill, they were able to drill holes into each plank at the point it touched the canoe ribs, and then sew the plank to the frame at that point. Each drilled hole was glued and water-proofed with pitch and later covered by the over-lap of the planks. Pitch mixed with dried moss was then pushed up into the overlap along the length of the plank. This sealed the canoe and made it water tight. Thompson decided to sew on each alternate rib, and then sew the next plank on the in-between points of the ribs. The result was a strong canoe that presented less likelihood of causing the rib to break. They made a point of making the bottom as a hybrid of the clinker and the flush-fit method. Their end result was a canoe ended with a slightly rounded bottom rather than a pronounced 'V' shaped bottom. In rapids, a keel was unwanted as it made quick turns very difficult.

It took a week, largely because they wanted green, freshly-split planks that would bend to comply with the form of the ribs. On April 1st, they were done. All of them stood back and looked at it. With all the waiting for good weather, searching for suitable rind, designing a form and a frame, gathering pitch, and splitting planks, Thompson was delayed in his quest for the mouth of the Columbia River by sixty-eight days.

The canoe was a thing of beauty. It had a high prow and a high stern, the better to shed water in the rapids, and carried a shape very similar to a birch bark canoe. It was twenty-four feet long with eight benches; one very near the stern, then six more in the centre that could hold one man on one side of the canoe with the next man on the other side. This allowed for freight to be stored as a counter-balance on and under the unoccupied side of the bench. The steersman and bowman would occupy the each of the two benches on the ends.

Those benches were narrower and made for only one occupant. There was extra space between the stern bench and the group of four in the centre to allow for storage of gear and supplies and more foot-room for the helmsman as he would often stand while paddling in the rapids. The forward bench was set back from the bow to make room for the bowman to stand with his long paddle. There was also extra space between his bench and the most forward of the four-bench group which had small platforms on which they stood in heavy water.

Ashford noted that and asked, "I have been told not to stand in a canoe because it will tip, but saw the men in front and back standing and I see a place for them to do so in this canoe. Is that safe?"

"Yes. Is safe" answered Ignace. "You see, she is a long canoe and more than four feet wide. She rides the water well. But man in back has to see, read the water. Front is high, so he stands and paddles with the long paddle. Sometimes man in the front will stand to make the quick turn. He uses the long paddle too."

The next job would be a test for leaks by placing it in the water, loading it to weigh it down to the normal paddling draft and waiting to see if there were any leaks. When they lifted it to place it in the water, they found it was even lighter than a bark canoe. She was a work of art! By morning they would know if there were any leaks.

Thompson stood back in admiration, "I believe this calls for a good measure of rum and a good sleep. Here's to our new canoe. May she float like a white cloud on a clear day."

The next morning Ignace awoke before the others and walked apprehensively to the canoe. Moments later, there was a loud shriek, followed by dancing as singing. "No leak! No leak!" he hollered. Everyone rushed out of the tent and joined him.

About one hundred pounds of pemmican had been made and about thirty pounds of half-dried meat, and was made and a stock-taking showed they had enough peas to make two meals of pea soup. Francois also had enough of his spice for the soup. They were ready to move!

It was time for one of Thompson's speeches.

"Lads, I believe we are, indeed, on the Columbia River. The problem is that I don't know what the river is like downstream. I am almost certain it bends southward and flows to the Pacific Ocean but we know nothing about how many portages we will make or what the rapids are like. I do know from what the natives have told me, that there is a very serious set of impassable rapids somewhere along our route that way." He pointed to his right, to the north and the west. "We need to re-supply and I have decided we will paddle and line this beautiful canoe upstream to Kootenay House. I'm not sure how far it is, but think it is less than ten days. From there we go over land to find a way to join this river again because it turns southward in between this range of mountains and the next one. The portage from Kootenay House to this river is only one short mountain range to the west. I hope you are not disappointed by my decision, but this is the safe way to go."

None were disappointed. All knew that David Thompson was the best frontier explorer in the world and he would do all he could to keep them safe.

"Let's get packed up! We will leave just after daybreak tomorrow. We'll have half-dried meat for breakfast and pemmican on the river. We will have about fifteen hours of sunlight and long days of paddling!"

All the men, including Ashford, gave a loud cheer.

More Death in the North Pacific
June 3-5, 1811

Captain Thorn kept the *Tonquin* anchored fifteen miles up the Columbia River for sixty-five days in order that a fort could be at least half constructed. The assistance and tools of the ship's carpenter were needed for that task. John Jacob Astor had directed that a large plaque was to be mounted on the gate. It was to read "Fort Astoria" and Gabrielle Franchere volunteered to make the plaque.

During most of those days Thorn secluded himself in his cabin. Members of the crew could hear him pacing, talking to someone they knew was not there, and knocking his sword against the furniture. He hardly ate. He demanded that the cook leave his meals at the door and retrieved them after he knew the cook was gone. Eventually, he looked into the mirror and was surprised by what he saw. His normally well-trimmed beard was long and straggly, his eyes bloodshot, his face wrinkled from lack of proper diet and his hair far too long. He realized at that moment that he had to shape up, so he shaved, cut his hair and ordered a boat to take him ashore. He was not interested in visiting the fort. He just disappeared into the forest. He did that once per day for three days, then shouted for the second mate, who was now the *first* mate and ordered him to prepare to sail. "We shall sail north and trade with the Indians," he said. It was June 1ˢᵗ, 1811.

Had he bothered to seek advice from Franchere, he would have learned how to approach and deal with the Indians he would likely meet. There were ceremonies, ways of approaching them, methods of gaining their trust and becoming friends. But he didn't bother because he had two reasons to sail farther north and only one of them was to get rich on otter skins. The first and most important reason was to establish a 'presence' and thereby a means for the United States to claim the lands. Instead of including a professional fur trader, he took only his 'interpreter'. That was Lamaze, a half Chinook Indian who also used the name, George Ramsay, a man with some knowledge of the language of the Salish Indians.

For the next two days Captain Thorn carefully, and with very little confidence, sailed north staying at about ten miles off the coast at all times. He took sextant readings each noon and made no attempt to go ashore. Then, in the early afternoon on June 3rd, after he calculated his position to be almost directly on latitude 49, ordered the new first mate to sail into a cove and drop anchor. In a matter of minutes after the anchor was set a group of Indians appeared on the shore waving at the ship.

"Mr. Ramsay, on deck, if you please," he hollered.

"I want to talk with those savages," said Thorn. Wave them to come aboard. You speak their language, don't you?"

"Yes, sir but ..."

"No buts. Get them to come out here."

"Sir, I propose we approach them, unarmed, and talk fist. It is best to make friends first. I have never done this before and it seems to me it is best we start as friends," pleaded Ramsay.

"Fine, fine. Just get the process going." Thorn was impatient.

It took some minutes for Ramsay to launch one of the voyageur canoes. When he was well under way, Thorn went to his cabin and wrote an entry in the ship's log:

June 3, 1811

Have taken readings and confirm we have reached the 49th latitude off the coast of North America. Have begun the process of trading with the natives. When we complete our trade, I shall erect a cairn on shore stating our arrival and claiming the land south of this point to be the property of the United States of America.

Meanwhile, on land, Ramsay tried his best to set up a 'mood' or a 'method' by which he could begin to trade with the Indians. Through the process, he came to realize that these people must have had prior contact with white people as he noticed the odd piece of iron, such as an iron head on a war-club, a tin can, a few arrows with iron tips, and, most intriguing, an iron cooking pot. He surmised that these articles must have come from Russian traders, as he was aware that the Russians, for some time, were trading along the west coast and even claimed what would one day be known as Alaska as their territory. He also noted that iron seemed to be limited, which indicated to him that the Russians were careful in how much they gave the Indians. Good. The rarer a commodity, the better leverage he would have in trade negotiations.

Thorn was anchored in what is now known as Clayquot Sound off the coast of Vancouver Island. A boundary agreement had not yet been made between the US and the British this far west of the headwaters of the Missouri River. The area from there westward was known only as 'Oregon Country'. It consisted of the lands west of the Rocky Mountains to the Pacific Ocean, then northward to the Russian territory now known as Alaska. Disputes as to whose land it was would be were to continue until 1846.

Thorn did not know that he was on an island, not the mainland of North America as, in his caution to stay away from dangerous shoals and rocks; he kept the *Tonquin* so far off shore that he could not tell the difference.

Trade with the natives of Clayquot Sound went well, at least on the first day. Thorn was adamant that the Indians would come on board to trade as, being fearful of 'savages' he wanted a measure of control over them. He felt it important to show the natives what a great vessel he had and how powerful he was.

Proceedings began when four large canoes shaped not so much as a bark canoe, but much larger, with very forward-reaching high prows and sterns approached the ship. Each canoe carried ten men, though there was clearly room for twice that number on each vessel. At the bow of the lead canoe stood a tall, magnificent-looking man dressed in a fine robe of otter furs and holding a staff crowned by eagle feathers. He was obviously their chief as the others were not nearly as well-dressed.

Verbal communication was a difficult matter because the language of the Nootka was not well known, even to Ramsay, who could communicate in the Salish language. After some confusion and touching of the ship, the chief and four men were allowed to board while the natives on the other boats waited. Sign language, more like friendly gestures than a 'language' was used. Soon there was a rhythm to it and it appeared Ramsay and the chief were able to communicate.

The Nootka presented a few pelts of reasonably good quality beaver, fox, even a rather impressive black bear. In turn, Ramsay showed the Indians the usual trade items; similar to those he saw while on shore. But the Indians produced no otter and otter was the one reason for Thorn's trading expedition. Thorn would have made himself a fine fortune in otter fur. And, having seen the appearance and density of otter fur elsewhere before and noticing the quality of fur with which the chief was adorned, he was determined to get some. He handed an otter pelt to Ramsay and instructed him to ask for such fur. Ramsay did his best to do so and, after a few more gestures the Chief and others departed to return the next day, according to Ramsay.

Thorn went to his cabin to grumble.

Next morning the canoes approached, with fourteen men on board each vessel, and the same 'ceremony' of having the chief come aboard took place. Only on this occasion fourteen of the men in the chief's canoe were allowed to board the ship as well. Each of the men carried a bundle of furs as they boarded the ship. Again, there was more ceremony, this time shorter than the day before, and the chief sat to begin the barter. Furs were exchanged for iron arrow-heads, needles and other goods and the process was proceeding very nicely.

But Thorn was impatient. The voice in his head told him to 'hurry up'. He once again asked Ramsay to show the otter fur and ask for some. The chief understood and produced an otter pelt. It was an old one, somewhat worn, and not of good quality.

Thorn snatched the pelt from the chief looked him in the eye and shouted. "Damn you! What do you thing I am, a fool? You bloody god-damned savage!" and threw the pelt at the chief hitting the man squarely in the face.

No word was spoken. The chief slowly rose and looked at Ramsay as if to say, "I'm sorry," and made some friendly-looking gestures to Ramsay before departing.

"The chief is saddened. But he will return tomorrow with more furs, Ramsay told Thorn.

The next day's approach and ceremony was the same. The chief, with two canoes of fourteen men each approached the ship. The Chief held up what appeared to be a fine otter pelt and motioned his desire to come aboard. When the chief and all his twenty-eight men were on board, each of them produced a war club, the chief a knife, and they began clubbing and hacking at the crew. Thorn was the first to go down, his head crushed by an iron-headed club. Thorn had not taken the precaution of distributing muskets or any other kind of self-protection to this crew and men fell from the blows of war clubs and stabs of knives.

Ramsay saved himself by jumping overboard. All but five of the men were killed. It was only when one of them was able to get hold of a musket and fire a shot that the Indians fled.

The five remaining men, for a time, let go some shots of lead in the direction of the Indians, and then quickly threw the bodies of their fellow seamen overboard. That night they crouched, shaking with fear, debating what to do and knowing they could not sail home by themselves. One man, James Lewis, urged them to stay on board and try to sail away, but the others refused. Fear of navigating the sea muddled their courage. They knew they would wallow in the ever-lasting ocean until they starved or would send the ship crashing into the shore where they would all drown. Lewis tried to tell them how difficult it would be to travel overland in territory they did not know but was known to the Indians, but the men would not listen.

The four men decided to make for shore and escape overland but, when they made their attempt the next morning, all of them were killed within minutes of reaching the shore. Lewis had no choice. He was wounded and unlikely to survive. He could see the natives gathering to make another assault of the ship. He knew he had to keep the arms and powder safely out of their hands so he decided to set fire to the ship's powder magazine.

As he lit the powder line and watched it crawl into the room, he said a quick prayer and waited.

The *Tonquin* blew apart with a huge fire ball.

Thorn's log went down with the ship.

Years later, Ramsay would appear at the site of fort at Astoria. His story, though embellished somewhat, told of the events of how the ship exploded, how he was rescued from the water by some Indian women, and how he remained a slave for two years. Few believed him.[3]

---

3   The wreck of the *Tonquin* was found in Clayquot Sound, BC, in 2003.

Another Difficult Trek
April 5 – June 19, 1811

There was little snow on the ground at the Boat Encampment because it faced southwest and had received less snow that usual the past winter. But there was a great deal of snow on their southern trek. Thompson and his men paddled whenever they could, which was not very often. It was mostly poling the canoe though shallow water, lining it, walking it in even shallower water, and even hauling it over ice and snow. At one point they stopped at a long narrow lake and waited three days for the ice to thaw enough for the canoe, only to find that Mother Nature was not ready to provide that luxury. So they built a sled, mounted the canoe on it and dragged it eleven miles south to find open water on the Columbia.

They then paddled, poled, dragged, and pushed the canoe upstream to a point Thompson was familiar with and which he had earlier named 'McGillevray's Portage'. It was May 8th, 1811.

They spent another thirty-two days, with good deep water to paddle, all of it upstream and facing many small rapids which cost them a great deal of energy and the disintegration of the canoe. They walked the last two miles to Saleesh House, where they rested and built another canoe. From there, they paddled to Spokane House, a trading post founded by Thompson two years earlier.

It was at Spokane House that Thompson and Ashford heard some interesting news.

"David, how good to see you again," said Jacques Finlay as he approached with his hand outstretched. Jacques was a French Canadian with a name that didn't sound French but was proud of being one of the great voyageurs. He was of average height for a voyageur, about five feet six inches, and walked with a slight limp; like his friend, he had fallen from a height while on portage and, like Thompson, did not have his leg properly set. His easy smile presented his character as it really was, a gentle, wise man respected and trusted by all who met him. His command of both the French and English languages was almost impeccable. He and Thompson spent many years paddling and exploring together making their relationship respectful and friendly.

"And good to see you, Jacques".

"Come, sup with me and we will talk. I have some interesting news. Oh, forgive me. I'm being rude." He turned to Ashford and pushed out his hand.

"Ashford, William Ashford. My pleasure sir,"

"Can Mr. Ashford join us for supper?" asked Thompson. "I'm teaching him and he is with us as an artist to make sketches of what we see for our records."

"Of course, of course. Let's say, in one hour? I bet you've had no fresh pork for some time and that's part of my news. We plan to raise pork here and now have our second litter. Don't ask me how we got it here."

"How is the trade going? Busy?" asked Thompson when they sat down to a meal.

"Quite well. The natives provide good beaver pelts, though I have warned them not to trap all the beaver because they will have no more pelts to trade in the future. We have seen very few white men the past year, a few Americans, but otherwise just the voyageur brigades and express canoes."

"Americans?" Thompson's curiosity peaked like the explosion of a volcano, thought he tried to conceal it.

"Oh, we get some Americans here, yes. Some of them I'm not sure about. They don't look too experienced though they act the part."

"Oh? Tell me," said Thompson.

"Well, four days ago, three Americans came; didn't act much like trappers, but, dressed like they were. They all had those Kentucky Long Rifles, carried the same knives on their belts, big knives like butcher knives with wooden handles, like they were triplets. And they asked questions, strange questions."

"Ah Jacques, you must be dreaming," said Thompson.

"No. No. They even asked about you. They told me they have heard about you and were hoping to meet you."

Thompson and Ashford exchanged glances.

The conversation turned to why Thompson was at Spokane House and Thompson explained without mention of the problem concerning the Oregon territory. Thompson did tell his friend that he planned to ride horses to Kettle Falls rather than paddle because his earlier exploration of the Pend Oreille River, northward from Spokane House showed him it had too many portages. "But don't confirm that with anyone for now. I don't want word to get out that we are bound for the Pacific Ocean."

"I will be quiet," said Jacques, then looked at Thompson with an 'I-suspect-you're-worried-about-something' look. Thompson returned the look with a 'I-can't-tell-you' smile that cut off that part of their conversation. Jacques didn't press the matter.

Thompson provided Jacques with a list of his needs: pemmican, half-dried meat, dried peas, extra tobacco, trade goods and, most important to his men, a small keg of rum. They ran out several days ago. They would leave the next morning.

That night Thompson sat alone in Jacques' house and composed a letter. In it, he was careful not to reveal Ashford's real name, but knew he had to make sure all concerned knew who he was talking about. As he wrote, it occurred to him that he might suggest to the British that they do something about the fact that the ship sent by Astor might beat Thompson to the Columbia. He reasoned that, since he was cooperating with His Majesty, the British just might do the same in return. It was worth a try. He decided to ask a favour in return. He would suggest something that might still allow the North West Company to control the Columbia River trade.

June 18, 1811

For Mr. McGillevray and others in London

It is my pleasure to advise you that I am presently at Spokane House. As you will have learned from previous letters sent to you from Rocky Mountain House,

we suffered serious delay by reason of the blockade by the Piegans of our passage by way of the Saskatchewan River. We were thereby forced to proceed by way of the Athabasca River and find passage through the mountains near that river. Further delay resulted in our being unable to build a bark canoe and to wait through winter to construct a cedar canoe.

We are about to embark from this point to the Columbia River which is about three days ride from here and will hopefully arrive at our destination by mid-July. I also add that there have been some Americans in this area and they have in inquired about me. Mr. Ash is on high alert.

I add that I have received information that the Americans have sent a ship to that place. Mr. Astor is an honourable man, but, if he were told that His Majesty will send his own ship to the Columbia, Mr. Astor might be convinced to sell his established place for a fraction of its worth. I say this in the event that I do not reach the Columbia in time.

I ask you to pass this letter on to the people in London by hastened means and to hereby advise them that their concerns were indeed, correct. Also advise them the services of Mr. Ash have proven very valuable the past months and I believe shall be in the future.

It is important that you present this letter by the earliest means. Discretion is important.

David Thompson

Moments before departure, Thompson presented the letter to his friend. "Jacques, I give you this letter for swift delivery to the head office in Montreal. It is of a sensitive nature and has been sealed in its own package. Do not open it. I am not at liberty to tell you more at this time."

Jacques took the letter and smiled at his friend, "I had the feeling something was in the wind. I don't want to know. We have a brigade leaving in two days and I will see to it. Bon Chance, my friend."

Three days by horseback later, Thompson and the group arrived at Kettle Falls where they had to build another canoe for the final push downstream on the Columbia River. By this time, they had so much experience in the art that it went much more quickly than any of the previous builds.

Paddle to the Mouth of the Columbia River
Avoiding War and Death by Indians
July 3 – 15, 1811

All the men looked forward to this leg of the trip. They knew it would be mostly paddling and they would see great new sights. Paddling was their great joy. They were about to make history. People would talk about them; women would swoon over them. Their names would be known throughout the Canadas.

Kettle Falls was a magnificent place; a great place to start an historic journey. The Salish called the place '*Shonitwa*', meaning '*the roaring waters*'. And it was just that. There were wild rapids, steep and impassable falls with many channels through which the river boiled and foamed with unrelenting fierceness. The most interesting aspect of the falls was the fact that many Indian people gathered there from June to October of each year to harvest salmon, a spectacle no European had seen before. Thompson was again amazed at the custom of indigenous people to name places in terms of nature. It reminded him of the Saskatchewan River, its name given by the Cree Indians meaning, '*swift-flowing*' and demonstrated their reverence of nature. He found that reverence existed in all the tribes he met, even the most war-like of them.

What Ashford found intriguing was the way the natives fished. It was not by rod and hook but by spear and woven baskets on long poles. Men with spears stood precipitously on rocky points in the middle of the rapids and jabbed at the fish when they saw one near. The spears consisted of long poles onto which they attached three flexible prongs that would spread apart when they entered a fish and, in that way, held the creature until it was launched backward onto the shore. The baskets worked much the same way except they simply held the basket in the water and the fish swam right into it. When they felt the fish, they would pull the basket out and fling it on shore. The women would immediately club the fish and start cleaning them. It was an efficient production line.

Thompson and the group built their new canoe at the foot of the falls, purchased smoked and dried salmon with trade goods, and joyously began the trip. Ashford was about to feel the beauty of the paddle as he never thought he would. It was his new paddle and, as he was told, it was even better that the one that broke. He soon came to agree that the paddle you make yourself is definitely the best.

He would come to wonder even more at the skills of the voyageurs and to share their joy and harmony with the world. It would become not just work but a worship of nature that Ashford would never lose. But, as he would also learn, this voyage was also filled with great danger.

There were now ten men in the group, including two Simpoil Indians that Thompson found at the falls. The Simpoils traded with the people at Spokane House, spoke some English, had their own paddles, and were anxious to get back to their village about seventy miles downstream. During conversations with them Thompson learned there was a serious rapid not far downstream. Contrary to the usual flow of a river, the outside of a curve being where the more dangerous water and rocks lay, this one had the rocks on the inside curve. That meant the group should scout the rapid first and pick the line. The Simpoils also informed Thompson that the rapids on the Columbia, north of these falls, were impassable and the portage long and difficult.

It was a hot July day, the group changed to summer clothing and paddling gear, a change that came as a small shock to Ashford. All the men wore loin cloths with cotton leggings and a light linen shirt. Thompson noticed the shock on Ashford's face and offered the explanation.

"We paddle naked most of the time". The expression 'naked' was not the same as 'nude' but of almost nude. "Reason for that is that we get wet, then we get hot, then we get wet, then hot. The leggings are to avoid sunburn. Somethings the lads take off the leggings and the linen shirt. We wear the shirt for the sun and mosquitoes but often take off the shirt when we are not bothered by mosquitoes. We wear hats as a protection from the sun as well."

The men all put on their jockey caps which are similar to modern baseball caps and Thompson tossed one to Ashford. It was, by coincidence, forest green in colour.

It was the two Iroquois, Ignace and Charles, that shocked Ashford most. In their paddling garb, leggings and loincloths with leather vests, they looked like sketches of the North American natives he was shown some years ago. Mean! Dangerous! Frightening! And Ashford was soon to look just like them.

"Voyageurs have a song they sometimes sing when approaching a difficult rapid. It tells them to doff their coats and get naked because, if we tip and have to swim, the water-soaked clothing will take you down and we drown," added Thompson.

Within minutes they were in their rhythm. Even Ashford was paddling in time with the others and all were stroking their paddles with efficient ease. After a few miles one of the Simpoils waved ahead and said, "The big water! We stop, look!"

It took an hour to scout the rapid and, as the guide pointed out, there were dangerous rocks on the inside of the curve. But the water, though heavy with large waves, showed the centre and right of the curve would be the safer route. The rapid was short; about half a mile long, but the portage would be three times longer. All voyageurs preferred to risk their lives in a rapid rather than do a slippery portage. Carrying heavy gear up and over a pass, along narrow paths next to a steep and deadly cliff, sweating, suffering and dying from a hernia were things they would rather avoid.

They would run it.

Ignace seated at the stern of the canoe and acting as the 'steersman', as Thompson described him, rose to a standing position as they cautiously approached the boiling water. The bowman and the steersman both used longer paddles. The shafts were longer as were the blades. That allowed them to stand, especially when running rapids, to see where to 'pick the line' in order to safely navigate the rough water.

Their 'hybrid canoe' was twenty-six feet long and fifty-four inches wide. That made it more stable than a smaller regular North Canoe. The bowman and the steersman often had to stand in order to see over the higher prow. As they stood, they would brace their lower legs against the gunwales for stability and power and guide the canoe though the rapid. The other men, seated on four benches in the centre, provided power and speed and, at times, helped reduce speed. Often, they would lean the canoe into a turn to avoid the "upstream lean" which would flip the canoe. The lean was particularly important when moving into or out of an eddy. The stronger the eddy, the more it became a whirlpool and whirlpools were a great danger. Ashford learned about the "upstream lean" on his trip up the Saskatchewan River but was by no means expert at avoiding it as timing was important.

This rapid was a mean one. Its waves were high; sometimes well over their heads as they half-sat and half-kneeled with their legs tucked under the seat making them more a part of the canoe. That added stability. The current was very swift. There were numerous strong eddies, too strong in which to seek refuge and sometimes so strong that they became whirl-pools. But Ignace was able to pick the safer route through the confusing the water. Towards the end of the rapid, however, he had to steer through a V-shaped chute to avoid very high waves and rocks on both sides. The problem was a huge wave at the bottom of the chute and, as the canoe went over it, then suddenly downward, he was vaulted out of the canoe and into the water.

"Ignace is gone!" hollered Cote,

"We turn and find him!" shouted Charles, at the bow. He was now in command.

The bowman commonly initiates the fast turns in the bow. A good team like Ignace and Charles could do all that without a word or a shout. It was automatic because each knew what he had to do and when. But without the help of the steersman, it was more difficult and Charles had to shout orders.

He jabbed his long paddle into an eddy behind a large rock and the canoe swerved around 180 degrees to face upstream and stayed there. In that eddy he was able to spot Ignace, floating towards them but to the right of the eddy. "We go right!" With that order all the men provided power to punch the boat out of the eddy, lean downstream, and come about just as Ignace passed them. Once out of the eddy, they easily maneuvered to Ignace, who was by then downstream of the canoe. Ignace knew exactly what to do. He did not claw at the gunnel or try to climb into the canoe. Instead he did as they often practiced; he worked his way to the rear and grasped the foot-long rope loop at the stern and stayed to the rear. In about one minute they ferried to shallow water and Ignace stood up. He was still clutching his paddle.

"Merde!" he said in French, "I broke my paddle." The blade was snapped in half.

"Paddle? Your paddle? You're alive!" Boulard, always the joker, said with a tone of admonition.

During those minutes and the rescue of Ignace, Ashford was terrified. He was accustomed to danger, had even 'stood the line' with regular British troops as the enemy advanced on them. He fired, re-loaded, and fired again and again while the enemy advanced. He faced death from musket balls but never experienced this. The waves seemed to come at them from all angles. The water boiled. The canoe seemed to get thrown wherever the waves wanted to send it and it rolled from one side to the other, almost tipping into the torrent.

When it was over he experienced the results of adrenalin and an urgent thirst for water. He scooped water with his hand and tried to shovel it into his mouth and with that was able to calm himself. Then he suddenly realized he must be mad because he loved it! He loved every moment of it! Fantastic!

Ignace was still staring down at his broken paddle when Cote and Gregoire jumped from the canoe and then ran at each other to crash together chest-to-chest.

"My God! That is some rapid!"

"Check the cargo." said Thompson. There was a look of great relief on his face as he spoke.

Some water entered the canoe, so they unloaded, checked to be sure the pemmican was dry, untied a spare long paddle and turned the canoe upside down to empty it. They would make another paddle from a plank of white cedar the cut just for that purpose and they had another, shorter paddle, for the next such occurrence. Broken paddles were not uncommon and they always had spares or the means to fashion a new one.

They took their time in returning to the river in order to allow Ignace more time to recover because all of them knew that to having to swim in a cold rapid cost a great deal of energy. Scouting the river provided that time. From the hillside they could see the river for miles. It was without rapid, even looked calm, though with a swift current to the next range of mountains far in the southwest and they knew that for the next hours, possibly the whole day, they would enjoy a swift, safe river.

The crew celebrated their deliverance from the rapid with a measure of rum before supper, all the time making jokes about how Ignace thought he could fly, or how they couldn't believe he could swim, or that he didn't know what he was doing. Ignace took it all as a compliment and joked with them. They slept well.

The next morning was a glorious one. When Ashford emerged from his tent, he saw Ignace and Charles standing in the canoe at the stern and the bow, holding their paddles and swinging them in all kinds of directions. They were practicing; trying to get more accustomed to the placing of their feet and knees while standing in a rocking canoe. Their experiments led them to place small fitted pieces of wood, glued in with pitch, on the gunnels. The ridges of wood would provide a means to better brace themselves in the rapids.

After a breakfast of pemmican, the men once again checked the pemmican supply, confirmed it was dry, and continued the voyage.

This time it was quite different. The swift water took them very quickly downriver. No rapids! It was when the water slowed that Ashford came to learn more about these men: the singing.

Voyageurs sang whenever they felt like it, most often when the water was smooth and a little slow. They did so to uplift their spirits and to set the rhythm of the strokes and their favorite song. The one they usually started with was the old French-Canadian song, a song about plucking a bird: Alouette.

Ashford had trouble understanding why anyone would want to pluck a lark. It is, after all, a small and pretty bird with a pretty song and not like a dirty cannibalistic chicken. But he decided not to ask.

The great thing about this song is that they could speed it up and thereby speed up the paddle rate and the O-o-o-oh part could be hammed-up to a jolly sound. The sound of songs rang through most of the day until they reached the site of the Simpoil Indian village.

In one day they paddled seventy miles!

Thompson was here to set up a fur trade, to make friends, and not to take land from the Indians. To show he was a friend, he had a process that almost always worked. When he saw an Indian on shore, or when he expected to see some, he would walk onto the land where all the crew would sit in a circle and smoke. That was a sign they came in peace and wanted to talk. Usually one or two natives would cautiously approach and Thompson would present them with a gift of tobacco and request the chief come to talk. The first-contact natives would always take the tobacco back and the chief, with others, outnumbering Thompson's group, would cautiously approach. There would be speeches made by the chief and they would sit down to talk.

Tobacco was presented in the form of a rope of braided tobacco and more would be given to the chief after the first talk. The tobacco was stored in a waterproof keg as a rope of several feet in length. They would cut from it for purposes of trade while the voyageurs would look after their own stash of tobacco. After the initial talk, when the Indians knew he came in peace, Thompson had to endure a welcoming ceremony. Some were short, others long. Most involved a dance by the men and women and his men were often asked to take part. Then they would talk and visit, sometimes for two days but more often just a few hours. The talk was all about wanting to trade, make friends, and find out what the natives needed.

There was another equally important reason for the smoking and talking ceremony. Thompson knew it was an insult to enter and leave the territory of a chief without permission. Violence could result. He also wanted to be sure that, on his return trip, the Indians would know who he was and that he was a friend. In most cases the friendship established by these ceremonies would last forever. More important, other traders who used the same contact methods would be treated as friends and friends were greeted with pleasure and not so much ceremony. Those who did not use such a process were considered ignorant and unwanted.

Shooting first was the worst possible thing to do. It would end in bloodshed and all villages would thereafter treat the perpetrators as their enemy. The natives could recognize an enemy in minutes and they somehow knew when a man talked with a 'forked' tongue.

On this first meeting with the Simpoil Indians, all went well. The chief asked for axes, knives, iron spear-heads and arrow-heads and flints. He also asked for a musket.

Thompson explained that they had come a very long way and could not spare a musket. But he also assured them that they would soon be given a musket in return for firs. He also explained that he would give all other tribes the same kind of musket as he wanted them used for hunting and not for war.

The Simpoil agreed to hunt and find furs. Thompson explained to them that he was here to find his way to the sea on this river, and if the river was good, a ship, a very large canoe, would come and they would all prosper. This village, and others, came to like Thompson quickly. They often helped his men on long portages, lent them, and even gave them, horses. They even gave Thompson and his men smoked salmon though their own stores were short.

Every departure from such meetings ended with a speech and a prayer to the Creator. They would ask for safe passage and a safe return with trade goods. They would give long friendly good-bye waves as Thompson's canoe paddled around the first curve of the river. Thompson and his men would return the waves. There was hope for everyone. There was no war.

The two Simpoils stayed with their village and the men pressed onward. They now had no guide.

The next days were long and joyful. On this leg of the journey Ashford was exposed to his favorite song. It was one they sang for hours and ended only when voices began to fail. In French it was called, "*En roulant ma boule*" (We make it up as we go along). A 'leader' would initiate the song on some theme, usually women, but often about nature or about what happened that day or yesterday, or about someone in the crew. On the latter theme Thompson would always caution the men not to go too far as he didn't need the men starting a brawl. They sang the song sometimes in French and sometimes in English. As for the French, Ashford was often at a loss of what was said because he had never learned the profane words in French.

Today's first song went like this;

Leader:
Sing, sing, sing
We sing this song all day long
We make it up as we go along
The Group
We make it up as we go along
We make it up as we go along so the words are never wrong.
Leader (begins the theme)
By Charles – Ignace is crazy and thinks he can fly
Next time he tries it we'll just pass him by
Chorus – Sing, sing, sing we make it up as we go along
Reply (by Ignace) Charles is good at making fast turns
But sometimes I think he wants to paddle the stern
New singer (Cote)
Boulard is a man of many stories and jokes
Most often his words just make us choke
Reply (Boulard)
Cote is quiet man does not talk so much
Most time he paddle and not say much
New singer (Bordeaux)
Francois he cook and make pea soup just fine
But he never bother to serve us wine
Reply (Francois)
Michel Boudreaux his name sound like wine
But his taste so bad he should not whine
New singer (Pierre Pareil)
Ashford is English and speaks French quite well
But we should work hard and teach him to swear
Reply (Ashford)

Pierre swears a lot but only in French
If I knew what he says it would corrupt my mind
Thompson (to change the theme)
We are all good friends and great comrades
Let's change our song to stay good friends.

The men passed many hours singing this song. Boulard's verses were the best and always very funny; often so much so he would throw off the cadence of the paddlers as the laughter would be loud and infectious. His humor was good for the team. Some of his gems included;

"Ahead and to the left are two large mountains
To me they look like great tetons" (breasts in French)

"Ashford he has sticky fingers covered with pitch
I wonder how he takes a shit."

Boulard's jokes, though sometimes crude, were fun and really a value when the repeated dipping of paddles became a bore, bringing the men together as a team.

Thompson and the men continued the voyage, stopping to meet and talk with natives, smoking pipes with them, and giving gifts of clay pipes and tobacco to the chiefs while explaining why they were there. At the confluence of the Columbia and Snake Rivers he did something he had never done before. He erected a pole with a note attached stating:

Know hereby that this country is claimed
by Great Britain as part of its territories,
and that the NW Company of merchants
from Canada hereby intends to erect a
factory at this place for the commerce
of the country around.

Later, he and Ashford took a walk around their campsite, out of earshot of the men, and Thompson explained why he put up the notice.

"I am aware that Messrs. Lewis and Clark have come this way on what their president calls a 'Voyage of Discovery'. But it is more than that. One must remember that the United States recently purchased land from the French, which they called 'The Louisiana Purchase'. The Americans want all the land, all of North America, to be theirs. The 'Voyage of Discovery', I believe, was another land grab. I have come to believe that they will claim the Oregon Country and even more. If a war starts between the Americans and Britain in the Canadas, that will be proof of their intentions and this may have an effect on all that. Stealing my maps and logs will wipe out any evidence of a claim for Britain and leave the doors open to the Americans. And yes, I now think they will go so far as to kill me. Now, I do not say that their President is involved with what they plan in my regard, but someone high up in the United States must be. There are many people who think that way, many over-zealous persons. For the present, this is all I can do. I point out that Lewis and Clark built their fort on the south side of the Columbia River and my action today may have some small effect on claiming the land north of this great river."

He paused, then continued, "Well, that was quite a speech"

Thompson had more to say, "When I put this all together, keeping in mind that the Americans wish to take control of all North America, it makes me think of what may be in store for us, all of us, on this voyage. As for me, once I return to Montreal, there will be no need to kill me. But while we are here, in this wilderness, all of us are in great danger."

Thompson paused again, "As for you, my friend, I believe Sir Percival has already thought that out. He is aware of England's lack of resources to fight another war so far from home and is trying to prepare for what he thinks will happen. The Americans will invade the Canadas and you have been selected to do what can be done to stop it. There is more in store for you when we complete this voyage."

Ashford was not surprised by Thompson's words as the same thoughts had been swirling in his head for some time. "Quite frankly, I agree. It's the reason I have been sent here. As for whether more is in store for me here in the Canadas, I can truthfully say that I am prepared to stay, not only because it is my duty but also because I have fallen in love with this land and its people. Now, don't get me wrong, but Sir Percival, I know, has very professionally slipped me into all this, even manipulated me, and that does not bother me. I even look forward to what he will have me do in the future."

Thompson and Ashford walked back to camp in silence.

The date on the post was July 9, 1811. Thompson and the men were just six days from the mouth of the Columbia River. In the remaining days, they would travell from Kettle Falls to their destination, a distance of 280 miles, in less than two weeks. Three of those days were spent making friends with the natives.

It was a far cry from the hard labor on the trip to Spokane House. As they paddled, they encountered some vicious rapids requiring portages then noticed the river began to slow.

Five days later, as they rounded a curve of a noticeably slower river, Thompson spotted the smoke of what he knew must be the fort built by the Astorians. He was too late. He therefore decided he would show he was not completely defeated and stopped to dress in his finest clothing and erect a small flag pole, at the stern of the canoe.

It bore the Union Jack.

Thompson, Ashford and the others had travelled, on foot and by canoe, close to 4000 miles from Rainy Lake to this place, much of it in extremely cold weather and frequently passing through lands and rivers not yet explored by Europeans.

The Astorians greeted Thompson with grace. They welcomed them, fed all of them, and gave them supplies, even though their supplies were merger because the *Tonquin* had gone missing. They put the men and Thompson up in a small cabin meant for storage of material still on board the ship and treated them with hospitality. It was on the second day that Gabrielle Franchere approached Ashford.

"Mr. Ashford. Walk with me. I want to show you around. See what we have done with so few resources."

"Glad to, Mr. Franchere."

As they walked, Franchere made a demonstration of pointing at things that were not that noteworthy and Ashford began to wonder what this was all about. Then Franchere stopped and looked at his companion.

"I would venture to say that you have had some rather interesting experiences?"

Ashford suffered a momentary shock and was sure it was noticed. It took a moment to recover. But he knew that Franchere had just given him the code established by Percival "Yes, some on the terrifying side," he said.

Franchere responded correctly, 'Well, we must get together over a drink and trade stories"

"Oh, yes, would this evening be convenient"

"No. Unfortunately I have a commitment. Perhaps tomorrow morning?"

At about 9 am the next morning Franchere walked calmly to Ashford and said, "A nice time to trade stories, is it not?"

"Certainly, shall we walk?"

As they walked, Franchere began by making s small speech. "I signed up for this job because I missed the adventure of my younger years. I spent several years in the fur trade, working with the Hudson Bay Company, and came to enjoy it. Then I joined the Pacific Fur Company on the urging of John Jacob Astor. I still live in and regard Montreal as my home and am proud to say I am Canadian, not just French-Canadian, but Canadian. You must not therefore judge me as some kind of traitor to Canada. I am not. I believe one should lead his life with honor and honesty. I still regard myself as part of the Canadas and have respect for my home country. That is why I will tell you what I know." His command of English was perfect, though he spoke with a hint of French-Canadian accent.

"I understand completely. I am British, but I can tell you I have fallen in love with Canada and the people."

Franchere then began to tell his story. He started by revealing what he knew and thought of the Captain of the *Tonquin* and the events on approach to the Columbia River. He provided his opinion that Thorn was interested in something other than just setting up a fur trading post and how he came to that opinion. He explained that Thorn took the ship north to trade with the Indians but knew nothing of the fur trade and less than that of native people. It didn't make sense. He couldn't understand how a Lieutenant in the US Navy could go on leave to captain a privately-owned vessel.

Then he told him of what he heard that night as the ship sailed from Hawaii to the west coast. "I was shocked at what I heard. I refused to believe it. When I heard what those two men said, I wanted to return home. Of course, it was too late."

He ended his story with another speech, "I did not have the pleasure of meeting Mr. Thompson until he arrived here. But I know much about him and regard him with the greatest admiration. He would not hurt anyone. He loves the woods and his fellow voyageurs. He is a man who should be respected, not threatened." They continued the walk for a few minutes, talked in an animated manner, with Franchere pointing here and there in case they were observed and parted when they returned to the fort.

"Thank you for your candor and your views, Mr. Franchere. What we have said these past two days will remain secret, except for Mr. Thompson, and no word will ever be spoken to anyone in the future, even by him. We have suspected this but as yet we don't know who gave the order for the possible killing of my good friend. Until we know that and until we solve the problem, I shall keep a close watch."

"Agreed," replied Franchere. "I can say that Mr. Astor would never even think of such a crime and when asked to do this work for Sir Percival I was not advised of any plot to commit murder. I assure you of that. I was interested only in my Canada."

Ashford did not hurry to tell Thompson about the conversation. It was best to do so at some time and place where it was completely safe. Early in the return trip, would be the best time.

Return to Spokane House
July 22 – August 12, 1811

The day before their departure, Ashford browsed in the Astoria's trade house. He was doing so just out of curiosity until he saw tomahawks offered for trade, something he had not seen in the North West Company stores. Tomahawks were weapons of war and that was not the Canadian way. Without consulting Thompson, he purchased two of them, one for Ignace and one for Charles. He would keep them hidden until he talked to Thompson and placed them in the bottom of his duffel bag, hidden in the forest green capot which was of no use for in the hot July weather. Ashford had worries of great violence in the near future. He also purchased a sack of dried green peas, tea, sixty pounds of pemmican and a small cask of rum then proudly showed them to Thompson a few minutes later. Those purchases were gladly welcomed, though he was asked how he paid for them.

"American dollars, of course," was his answer.

Thompson just smiled.

When they were well away from the fort, Ashford stopped paddling and spoke. "Mr. Thompson, I have something important to say. We should talk privately and then share it with the men."

After half a day's paddle, Thompson directed the men to beach the canoe. He and Ashford then went on a short walk and Ashford told him about his conversation with Franchere. He also revealed the fact that he purchased two tomahawks. They might be useful in the days ahead. They quickly decided that they would tell the group the whole story and, in the evening, give the two Iroquois their gifts. Any man who did not wish to continue would be allowed to return to Astoria, though Thompson was sure none would go back.

Paddling upstream is always just grunt work. Most of the summer melt was gone and the river was only rarely swift. There were many times they had to ferry across the river to find gentler water and few times they had to drag the boat through the shallows. But they made good time, better than expected. That day they traveled about twenty miles. Camp was made on a grassy plain above the water. That evening, Thompson made an announcement, "Gather 'round lads. We have something important to discuss." He and Ashford then began to tell them what they learned. They made no mention of Franchere, and no questions of how they got the information were asked.

"It's time to tell you what's going on." Thompson's demeanor was serious. "I have been advised by high authority in the government of Great Britain that the Americans are probably gearing for war. It is believed they are preparing to attack Canada. They will claim it is for the indignities His Majesty has done to American sailors, but we think it is a nothing more than a land grab. I will give you some background."

He paused to sip some water from his metal cup. "In 1803 the United States purchased a vast tract of land called the Louisiana Territory from France. That almost doubled the size of the USA. Since then there have been many indications that they, the Americans, want the whole of the North American continent and that they should start with Canada and the Oregon Country. That's where we are now – the Oregon Country. Right now, Great Britain in involved with a very difficult and costly war against Napoleon, the emperor of France, and that leaves the King less able to stop an invasion of Canada. Our people in London have strong indications of a coming invasion of Canada. They also believe the Americans want to claim all the land west to the Pacific Ocean."

Ashford stood as Thompson sat down. "Those people in London have spies everywhere. The information we have is that some people have been sent to steal Mr. Thompson's maps and logs so no record of his travel to the west coast will be found. LaSalle, when he deserted this venture, took those maps and logs with him and I was sent to get them back. That's why I am here – to protect those records and to protect Mr. Thompson."

"What? Protect Mr. Thompson?" asked Boulard.

"Yes, because British intelligence believes some people were sent to overland to get the records and to kill Mr. Thompson if they have too. I was also sent here to protect our man." He pointed at Thompson. "We now have good reason to believe an attempt will be made on him. When we were at Spokane House, Mr. Finlay told us about three suspicious men who were there just a few days before we got there. They were dressed like trappers but did not behave like trappers. They asked many questions about Mr. Thompson and then disappeared. We have since learned more. We believe there will be an attempt to murder him. From the description of the men we believe they come from Kentucky, a part of Untied States. They carried Kentucky long rifles, just like LaSalle's, that one." Ashford pointed to LaSalle's rifled musket."

There was a long, stunned silence.

Francois stood and walked around, trying to understand what he just heard. The others just sat in silence.

After about two minutes, Ignace stood. "I know of these Kentucky men. They call themselves 'Riflemen' because of those guns. They carry tomahawks and big knives and they call those their 'scalping knives'. I know them. They have killed many of my people. We must prepare for them and be ready to kill. I will kill."

"Well, we should devise a plan." Thompson's words broke the long silence caused by Ignace's words. "In the meantime, there are two things we should do. Number one, Ignace, you know how to use that thing," he said, pointing to LaSalle's rifle. You are now in charge of it. Charles, I assume you know how to use a musket, so Mr. Ashford will show you how to use mine. We will keep then loaded at all times. Number two, Ashford has a gift for both of you. He purchased them at Astoria because he thought it might be useful. Will ..."

Ashford began, "Before we discuss the gift, I have to tell you about who I really am. I am a rifleman of the 95th Regiment of Foot of the British army. We are called 'The Chosen Men'. We are trained on the use of this rifle and have very different ways of fighting. I suspect our ways are more like our Iroquois friends. I will tell you more about that as we travel. But now, to the gift." He bent and reached into his duffel.

"Charles, Ignace, I present you with these two gifts, the kind of gifts one hopes never to use. Please step closer,"

They did. And Ashford handed each of them one of the tomahawks he purchased.

After a few moments Ashford reached into the bag and pulled out the Spanish knife and strapped it on to his belt.

"We may be at war, gentlemen. Tomorrow we will spend an hour or so re-training with the rifle. Ignace, Charles, I assume you know how to use those things?" He pointed to the tomahawks.

Charles stepped closer, "Yes, every Iroquois young man is taught how to use it. I not use one for some time so we will play with them."

"Good. We need a measure of rum, then to bed. We will talk more about this as we travel. For now, we have nothing to worry about". Thompson knew the men were in somewhat of a shock.

After the rum, everyone crawled into their bedding. Some remained restless.

The next morning went well with Charles practicing with the new rifle. It was obvious he had good knowledge of the musket and it made Ashford wonder why Charles had never told anyone. But that, Ashford knew, might be the tendency of Indian people not to boast to white men.

The day's paddling also went well as the river seemed to become slower. That allowed them to talk of plans.

They reasoned that those three Kentucky men were hanging around Spokane House, so there should not be much to fear until Thompson's group were close to the post. Thompson's group would be travelling there by going upstream on the Snake River and, as the Kentucky men had no canoes and the mountains were very rugged, it was unlikely any move would be made until after they reached Spokane House. It was reasoned that the Kentucky men would not take any action near Spokane House, but somewhere away from it, somewhere in the wilds where no one would see or hear anything.

Just the same, they would keep muskets loaded at all times.

"One more thing to remember," began Thompson. "We will stop and meet our native friends on our way back. I think it would be wise that Ignace and Charles not wear their tomahawks when we meet. They may take it as a threat."

"Yes, yes," both of them agreed.

At the confluence of the Snake and Columbia Rivers, near the place where Thompson erected the pole claiming this land for Great Britain, he ordered a stop. He then directed Cote to cut down a small fir tree, strip it of branches and make a pole. After digging a hole in an open area as deep as they could get with the axe, they placed the pole into it, so it stood straight and reinforced it with rocks planted firmly around it. Atop the pole was the Union Jack.

The flagged pole was on the north side of the Columbia River.

On August 12, 1811, they arrived at Spokane House and were warmly and eagerly greeted by Jacques Finlay.

"Oh, oh so good to see you my friend. I have news, important news and a packet to give you. Monsieur Ashford please come, also. Pierre! Come! We need you to tell us!"

A man who was standing nearby accompanied them as they walked.

They sat in Jacque's office and he began with no further pleasantries. It was obvious he was concerned about something.

"Those three men, the ones who claim to be trappers, came back. They asked about you again. Pierre was suspicious of them so he started snooping around. He went at night and watched them, listened to them at their camp. They didn't know he was hiding in the bush. Pierre, tell them."

"I sneak up on them. It is dark. They sit by fire and talk. I listen. They talk of many things but then I hear them say 'Thompson', my ears perk up. They say like this: 'We can't do it here. Someone will be bound to find out and we'll face the gallows. We do it north of here as soon as we know what route they take.' Those are exact words I hear, so I tell Mr. Finlay."

Finlay thanked Jacque and dismissed him. Ashford and Thompson were not surprised and that shook Finlay.

"Monsieur Thompson, they mean to kill you!"

"It's fine, my friend. We were sure these men were up to something like that. Mr. Ashford has suspected it since the last time we talked. We will be fine. Tell me what else you know."

"The men stayed nearby for another day, then they came and asked me again where they might meet up with you. I know you will go back to Kettle Falls and I think they know that too. So, I told them you usually go by canoe and on foot up the Pend Oreille River. But I know you have a shorter way across the ridge, the way you came today."

"Thank you, Jacque. You did well. I think we will go back that way, as usual, but we would like to drag our canoe up there. We've spent too much time building canoes. The route is not so bad now. I noticed that you have cut a good road. If we have good horses and a travois to carry the canoe, we'll make good time. Can you lend us the horses and a couple of men to help? They can bring the horses back. Besides, the Pend Oreille route is really tough, even on horses, and we might be able to get ahead of them. When did they leave?"

"Four days ago, David. That's quite a lead."

"We have to try. Anything else?"

"No, Oh! I almost forget. A packet for Mr. Ashford arrived here about ten days ago. It has a seal on it, so must be important. I will get it for you."

London, March 15, 1811   **for Mr. Ashford**

Our sources have confirmed that three men are on route with the intent to intercept Mr. Thompson. We do not know their names but have learned they were sent by a Major R. Foster of the 17th Kentucky Dragoons. These 'soldiers' are militia, not regulars. They are famous for rather harsh treatment of native people. We are certain they mean great harm to Mr. Thompson and advise that you take careful precautions. We fear war is imminent. Further instructions will be given to you at Rocky Mountain House or Henry House as we are making preparation for further endeavors by you. Good luck.

                        Sir Percival Worthington
                        Secretary of Colonial Affairs
                        To His Majesty King George III

The letter, as usual, bore the heavy wax seal of the Secretary of Colonial Affairs. Ashford showed it to Thompson then turned to Pierre, "I cannot show you this or tell you what it means, Pierre. May I burn it in your fire?"

"Of course, of course. As you can see, there is still some flame. And I don't *want* to know anything. I may live longer that way"

Ashford then placed the letter into the fire and watched as it burned; first with a white smoke, then with a spiral of heavy black smoke that slowly crawled up the chimney.

Murphy Creek
49th Latitude
Near the present Canada/US Boarder
September 4, 1811

The ride to Kettle Falls was uneventful except for having to man-haul the canoe around trees because the travois needed more room. They did it in three days and began the paddle upstream as soon as they got there. During the paddle, they quietly discussed what they might do to protect themselves. It was also when they were told about how the 95th Rifles worked, using ambush if needed, and about what they were likely to face. It seemed the men were no longer as shocked at the revelation that people were out to kill Thompson. It became obvious that all of them, including Thompson, that all were looking to Ashford as to how to deal with the situation.

Thompson, as usual, made several compass readings on route and made detailed position notes by sextant at noon each day. As they paddled they talked, planned what to do, and did little singing. Evening was devoted more to speculating about what was ahead, discussing how they would protect themselves.

"Tell me what you know about these Kentucky fellows. It will be useful?" asked Ashford.

Charles was the first to answer. "They are stupid men. They think their way is the only way to live. They hate my people but they fear my people like no others. Even Charles can read better than those men. But they are very good forest people. They shoot like they were born to shoot."

Thompson added his thoughts. "Yes. We should not underestimate them. They are extremely good hunters and very resourceful. As far as I know, they know little about the canoe. Pierre said they travelled here with three mules and lots of supplies. That means they will not use the canoe and will stay on land."

"So, if they have to cross a river, they have to find a shallow spot, and on this river, that may be hard to do," And those rifles they carry tell they will try and ambush, just like LaSalle, shoot from afar."

"Yes. They will shoot from high place. We stay away from high place," added Charles.

"What about those big knives?" asked Ashford.

"Big knife. Use for everything. Take scalps. They are good warriors but do not follow orders." Charles undoubtedly had come across these people before. Charles was anxious and spoke quickly.

"Do they fight with the knife?" asked Ashford.

"Yes. Charles will practice with you. I see them do it. Mostly they stab and try to slash at body. They use tomahawk too. But no one talk about them having tomahawk. Maybe they hide them."

"Thank you, Charles. In the morning we will practice. I'm afraid I know little about how to defend a tomahawk."

"We will play so you learn."

"About crossing the river ..." wondered, Thompson. "Why would they? Where? How would we know?"

"Well, just as well we watch for that. It might be easy to find tracks that cross the river. With three horses and three mules, they won't be able to easily hide a crossing. Seems to me Ignace and Charles would be best at finding that, so we should be watching for it wherever there is a place they could cross. We have to know where they might strike."

"They might just shoot us from the shore as we paddle," offered Cote.

Ashford thought for a few moments then realized he had the answer to that idea. "No, don't think so. The information we have leads me to believe they have to bring the maps and logs back to their boss as proof of success. They do this for money and will get paid only when they prove they did it. Shooting us from shore would likely result in the loss of the logs and maps."

At noon on the third day of September, Thompson announced, "We have crossed the 49th latitude. That means we are close to the point where the Pend Oreille River should join the Columbia. It will flow in from the east, on our right. I think the Kentucky men will be travelling that route, on horseback. So we are now in great danger."

Ashford then provided his plan. "We will look for an open place to camp every night. Open spaces will allow us to see if anyone approaches. We will stay far away from places where high ground allows them to pick us off from above. At the same time, we have to find a way to 'invite them in' so they can get close enough to shoot. In other words, *we* set the trap; not them. They won't expect that. Also, I don't think they will attack at night, but you never know. In daylight they can see better and will be cocky because they don't realize we know about them. That's our advantage."

"One other thing, if you see them, do not holler, make like you didn't see them, just quietly tell me. We have to make them think we don't know about them. Each night we will set up our camp with that in mind. I think they will attack us today or tomorrow and they will be waiting for us. We have to think of what they expect or want us to do and do the opposite. Never do what the enemy expects you to do. Make them do what *you* want them to."

He stopped for a further thought. "Mr. Thompson, you have that pistol. Keep it on you at all times, especially at night."

As they paddled, they were constantly alert to finding places where horses and mules could ford the river but found only two places and they were out in the open with flat plains on both sides. No tracks. Then, at about three o'clock in the afternoon they came upon the confluence of the Columbia and Pend Oreille Rivers, just as Thompson described. Now they were really alert.

A little further they came upon another place where horses could ford the river. They swung the canoe to the west side of the river for a better look. As they straightened their angle near the shore Charles quietly spoke.

"A man sits on top of hill, right side." informed Charles.

"Nobody looks up there!" ordered Ashford. Keep looking to our left. Charles, it's probably one of them scouting our arrival. Ignace, you look for tracks. Charles, what's ahead? Look as far upstream as you can. We may stop ahead."

"No tracks," Ignace reported.

"A creek coming in from the left. Good place for camp. Maybe one mile," Ashford said. "Charles, is there a place to camp on the right side, below that steep hill?"

"Yes, just below where the man was. He is gone now."

"Good. They expected us to camp there because they're on that side of the river. That was their first mistake. Maybe wishful thinking on their part. They thought we would camp on the right, just under the hill where you saw the man. We make camp on the left, by the creek. I see there are trees along the creek bed. But we need an excuse to stop. It's too early to make camp. Any ideas?

Cote, the quiet man, immediately spoke. "We pretend canoe leaks. We stop and look. Set up to look like we try to repair canoe and have to camp."

"Good thinking. Bail water on the left side so they can't see we are acting. Show you're all worried. They're probably still watching us. When we land, jump out and unload everything, then turn the canoe over up towards the shore so they can't see there's no water. Francois, Boulard, you have some water ready to spill on the shore side of the canoe when we empty it; lots of water. I want the ground wet as we tip the canoe so they can see it. Hide your bailing pans when you go on shore. Everyone else help unload and tip the canoe. Make a big deal of it."

The men did a great job, like watching a stage performance. There was loud talking and swearing, even a few kicks at the canoe. The best part was when Boulard stood and pissed on the bow.

"Merde!" said Charles. I have to sit there!" All of the men stifled a laugh.

"Now, Ignace, you inspect the outside and then inside the canoe and point out the place it's leaking. Then we'll haul the canoe up the bank like we need to do repairs. A little more acting, boys, but not as showy. Nobody looks up at that hill. Remember, it's too far for them to shoot from the top of that hill. They have to come to us."

The boat was hauled up and the gear followed. Ignace and Charles began preparations for repair and the others began setting up camp. Ashford pointed out the positioning of each tent and the fire by placing rocks at the spots he wanted the door of each of them. When all was done he directed Cote and Boulard to act out the repair. Then he took time to survey the land near their position. To the south, downstream, there was long open plain, more or less flat and with grass about 18 inches high and few trees. Those trees were small Ponderosa Pine, trying desperately to get enough moisture to grow; they provided almost no protection or place to hide.

"Ignace, Charles, take your rifles and make like you're hunting. Charles, you go up the hill and along that ridge, just half way up and far enough to see what's there and where a likely route is for them to come on the attack or where we can hide and wait."

"Ignace, you walk upstream on the river bank and see if there's a place they can ford the river up there. Go wherever you can see at least three miles upstream. If there is a ford, look for places we can hide for the fight. Make like you're looking for game and, if you see something you can kill and carry, do it and bring it back."

Ashford turned to Charles, "Same for you, Charles. We want to take a deer because if we take a deer that will convince them we plan to stay awhile. If you see them trying to cross, find a place to give me hand signals. If you spot them fording the river stand where I can see you, hands like this."

Ashford put his rifle down and placed his hands on his hip. "I will take my cap off and wipe my face with it to show I understand. Return if you spot them, but take your time. If you have to take cover, do so." Ashford took off his hat and wiped his face with it.

"Charles, I think they will have to cross downstream. So stay out of sight of that place we thought was a good spot. Let me know if they cross with horses and and mules by crouching down like a horse. No acting, no snorting, please."

That little joke calmed everyone.

"When you both return, I'll tell you my plan. We will have our own little surprise for these thugs."

"Thugs?" asked Charles.

"It means bad men, robbers, men who hurt people. Off you go. Remember we don't know they're here."

With that Ashford strode into the trees behind their tents as though he was going to relive himself. His purpose was to scout places from which to shoot because he reasoned the Kentucky men would approach through the trees. It was too open in any other way and their shots would have to be much too far. He went further into the creek and found it flowed with little water but was wet and muddy where the water flowed.

The creek valley was moderately deep, about twenty feet below the level of the plain and it contained some large cottonwood trees, some small spruce and a fair amount of underbrush. There was an animal track along the south side of the creek on the bank next to where the tents were being erected. He slowly walked the track upstream, being careful not to leave any sign that he passed, until he saw a sharp turn in the trail, to the left and up a hill of about ten feet. It formed a small slide, about eight feet long and thirty yards from where he stood. He mentally marked a place to hide yet still see their approach along the slide.

The killers would have to come down that track and watch where they walk. They won't want to slide down the path and make any noise. We'll set up to take them as they reach the bottom. No. It would be best let them pass a few yards. We have to know where all three of them are before we take the first shots, he thought.

Ashford backtracked looking for spots to hide and wait. As he did so he repeatedly looked back to see if he could still see the slide. It disappeared but then became visible again about fifty yards from where he stood and about twenty yards ahead of where he judged the tents to be. Mentally, he made a note that he would park himself there. His second place, after firing a shot, would be just five yards away to his right.

He reviewed his thoughts, and said to himself, Good. Now he had to set up the positions for Charles and Ignace." By retracing his steps back up stream, he found two ideal places, along with secondary places for them to hide. All had good views of all their shooting positions and the sliding path. Ignace, Charles, and he could see each other, but the Kentucky men could not at the angle of their approach. A good set that- up.

Ashford walked out of the bush to the camp site. "Mr. Thompson, what time is it?"

"Five o'clock."

"When is sunset?"

"About eight-thirty or eight-forty-five." Thompson was impressed. "Now I know why they call you 'The Chosen Men'.

"Thank you. But we shall see. There is still more to do. I think we'll send Charles up the hill again tonight to check that route."

An hour later, Ignace returned. "No shallow water, some steep banks. There is an island, close to this side, two mile, but water very swift and river bank is very high. Horses cannot go up. Mule will not swim across river there. They come from there." He pointed downstream with his head and glanced up in Charles' direction. "Charles makes signal."

Ashford looked up and saw Charles standing with his rifle down and his hands on his hips. Ashford took off his cap and wiped his face. Charles then crouched on all fours. Then he stood and waved, indicating the Kentucky men were almost across. Then he pointed to his own eyes, to the direction of the approach and then covered his eyes. Ashford took that as meaning the Kentucky men could not see Charles or Ashford. He waved his arm at Charles motioning that he should return, fast.

Charles was down in minutes.

"Gather 'round. We have more to do."

They all formed a circle around Ashford.

"The thugs are on their way, coming by the downstream route. They come on horseback with their mules. I am sure they will come from behind the hill where Charles was and make their way into the bush at the top end of the creek, about there," he motioned with his head to the trees to his left. "We'll wait for them down in the creek bed. Charles, were the mules packed?"

"Yes, full packs on mules."

"Good. That means they have no idea of what we are doing. It also means they are tired of waiting and want to get this over with. They will be careless. And that's good for us. So here's what we do. They know there are eight of us, so I want them to think we're all bunched up around the camp. They will stop and watch us from the hill up there. We won't see them and we won't look up for them. Understand?"

A mixture of 'yesses' and 'Ouis'.

"One danger about my plan. These men might decide to come in from that direction." He pointed with a head nod to the south and the long open plain of grass, "If they do, someone in the tent will have to slide into the bush and tell us. We will know what to do. One man will stay with Mr. Thompson. Cote, can you do that? There should be no danger and Mr. Thompson has his pistol."

'Oui."

"David, it is unlikely, but you may have to use it."

"I damned well will!"

Ashford continued his instructions. "We have to smuggle Charles, Ignace, and me into the trees behind the tents. We have to cut a hole in the back of the tent so we can crawl through it. I know that's not such a great idea but our lives may depend on it. Cote, you and Boulard will have to figure that out. Maybe you could design it so we can use the spare tent and patch with that. Also, when we go out, we leave our shirts inside, have another one underneath. We go in the tent and you come out wearing our shirts also, all of you will change into same colour trousers as I have and my cap. Charles, Ignace, you must wear trousers while outside, now, to show you are here but when you come through the tent wear your war clothes. That will scare the hell out of the bastards if they see you. Wear something green or brown, no bright colours. We will hide in the bush. As for the rest of you, as soon as you hear shots, all of you go and hide in the bush, *close to the shore*. We will do most of the shooting away from you but those men will not. So, find low spots to hide. Nobody comes out of the bush until one of us says so. Understand?"

A collective nod.

"Good. Now the three of us Ignace, Charles, and I will go into the bush and set up our shooting positions. My suggestion is to shoot and then immediately move to another shooting place about five yards away. Smoke tells the other side where you are.

"We'll go in so we know where you are. After your first shot, move and make a war cry. That will scare the hell out of them. No war cry means you have stayed where you are. Reload after you move. First shot, first kill. *First shot, first kill.* Got it?"

"Yes"

"And know where each of us is, watch our backs."

"Yes."

"Good, now let's get ready. By the way, all of you deserve a prize for good acting. We'll drink to it later. Oh," Ashford looked at Ignace, "No scalps, please."

Ignace replied with a mock indignation, "Ignace and Charles live too long with white man, do not take scalps."

Ashford placed the men and made sure they knew their secondary positions, and then spoke in an almost-whisper, "Wait here. No movement. Wait until they are fully between you and then let them have it. Let the first man go by. I'll get him. Charles, when both of you have the second and third man in sight, you shoot the one in front and Ignace shoots the one behind. I will take the leading man right after you shoot. If the leading man is far ahead and the others have not come down that slide, you wait. But if they have come down, be ready to shoot early in case the lead man is too close to the camp because I'll have to shoot."

When he was in position, he disappeared under some low-lying bushes, settled in, and hoped he didn't forget anything and that the three men would walk into the trap. If the Kentucky men came over the level plain in front of the tents, they would have to move fast and it would be a difficult fight. He felt sure, though, that they had to come in by way of the creek. "Well, we'll find out soon enough," he said very softly to himself.

It was a long wait, more than two hours. During that time the men at the tents made things look normal, talked to each other, and moved about as though they had no care in the world.

Then, there was a sound, the sound of a foot sliding on the path. Ignace, Charles, and Ashford froze.

A minute later Ignace and Charles simultaneously spotted one man slowly and carefully making his way through the trees and toward the back of the tents. But there was no second man.

They waited and waited more, then mentally heaved a sigh of relief as the other two came down the "slide". They were about fifteen yards behind the first man.

At the same moment, Ashford saw the lead man and slowly raised his own rifle to keep a bead on him, waiting for two shots from the Iroquois.

He had to move slowly to get his rifle around a small tree or a branch as the man moved. That was hair-raising because he could not touch a leaf, show movement, or make his rifle stand out in any way. It seemed like a very long wait for the shots he hoped would come, and all the while, his kept his sights on the lead man. Then came two almost simultaneous shots followed by two blood-curdling war cries and Ashford squeezed the trigger of his own rifle.

The battle, if one could call it that, took less than thirty seconds.

But Ashford quietly told the men to wait. Always wait. Always make sure. Ignace and Charles did the same but the men at camp noisily thrashed their way into the bush.

"Done, lads." shouted Ashford. "We got 'em. All clear!"

A very loud cheer came from various points in the trees.

"Check the bodies, boys. Search them. Search their pockets, their boots, everything. We have to know as much about them as we can!" He turned his target onto his back, unbuckled the man's belt and immediately noticed the large knife attached to it. Out of curiosity, he pulled the weapon from its sheath and examined it. It had a long blade, about eight inches, sharpened only on one edge and with a black wooden handle that was smaller than the blade. Then he flipped open the buckskin jacket. It was quite soft, probably comfortable, but likely provided resistance to a blade.

Ashford patted down the body, looking for things that should not be there. Nothing. He then pushed his hand into the two outside pockets of the jacket and found only a clay pipe and some tobacco. Next, he looked at the jacket. He felt the whole of the jacket by pressing it between his hands and, as he was working on the left side, felt a crinkly sensation.

There was something sewn into it. The jacket had no lining but there was a patch sewn in, obviously a hidden pocket.

Ashford used his knife to cut out the hidden pocket and pulled out a small oil-skin packet, carefully and precisely folded to protect something inside. He cut that open. Inside was a folded paper with handwriting on it.

"Well, I'll be damned!"

Mr. William Price Hunt   January 17, 1809
Pacific Fur Company

    Sir,

I present to you one Jason Williams, a member of the 17th Kentucky Dragoons, which I am proud to command. We have been informed of your coming expedition to the west coast of North America and commend you on your endeavor. I offer this man as a member of your group. He is an experienced horseman and an excellent marksman and I ask that you give him good consideration to accompany your group on this great venture. I advise that I shall pay Mr. Williams from my own resources as a token of my admiration for your expedition. I have provided a similar letter to two other men for the same purposes. I ask that you return this letter to Mr. Williams as he may have need of it should he encounter difficulties and is thereby in need of supplies and I shall reimburse others who may in such circumstance provide him with assistance.

    We wish you the best
    Ronald Roy Foster
    Major, 17th Kentucky Dragoons

Ashford finished his search, placed the packet and letter in his pocket, wrapped as it was before he opened it, picked up the Kentucky Long Rifle, its cartridge pouch, and the man's belt with the knife attached and hurried back to camp. When he arrived, he learned that Ignace and Charles bought back the rifles and pouches of the other two men but not the belt and knife. They did not discover the hidden pocket so, before showing anyone what he had found, he went into the bush and retrieved the same items from those two dead men.

"Gather 'round men. I have something to show you,"

Charles immediately noted that Ashford had the knives and belts and did not move. He had a look of horror on his face.

"Charles? What's wrong?" asked Ashford.

"Kentucky man's knife is bad medicine. It is meant only for killing. We do not want it."

"Oh, I'm sorry. Please forgive me." Ashford immediately went to the river, walked downstream about ten yards and threw all three belts and knives into the river.

When he returned, Charles simply said, "Mr. Ashford, you are good man" and joined the group. Ignace joined with him.

"Thank you, both of you. I didn't mean to insult you. Now, we have made an interesting discovery. He then showed the packets and the letters, read one of them and explained it all to everyone. But then, something struck him. He pulled out the other two letters and scanned them. They were identical except for the names of each man. One was Gordon Wyles and the other one, Jacob Foster.

For a moment, Ashford was surprised, but then he understood.

Thompson too, was surprised but not for the same reasons as he did not yet grasp the significance of the names. He turned to Ashford and said, "I repeat what I said earlier. Now I know why they call you 'The Chosen Men'."

Ashford gave a small smile and added more of his thoughts, "There's one more thing. We have to move the bodies, keep them far apart so the bears and other creatures will all have a chance to dispose of them. Charles, Ignace we have to find their horses and mules and set them free. I'd bet they're tied or hobbled somewhere. Also, we might find more information in those packs. Mr. Thompson, how long will it take before the local natives find these men?

"We haven't seen any for days. I don't know. I don't think they set up their villages in this open country. Too open a space. The bears, wolves, and coyotes will probably be on them mid-day tomorrow. The horses will be good gifts when the natives find them. So will some of the stuff they have. But we must be sure no weapons of any kind are left. We don't want to start any wars."

"Let's go."

With that Ignace, Charles, and Ashford began a steady run, south, in the direction of the river crossing. The mules and horses were hobbled, ropes tied onto their front feet so they could walk and fed on the grass but could not walk too far, and the mule packs were hastily thrown on the ground. A search found few useful things, more musket balls, a small cask of powder, a good deal of beef jerky, some blankets. But there was one thing, an utterly useless thing, which caught Ashford, a flag. It was about three feet long and two wide, white with dark blue lettering and the image of a bird, a cardinal, in the top right third of the map. The bird, of course, was red. The words on the flag read:

17TH KENTUCKY

Ashford showed the flag to his companions and was surprised by the reaction on Charles' face. It turned ashen, full of dread. He was about to ask what Charles was thinking when Ignace spoke, "We must return to camp. The night is coming."

It was dark when Ignace and Ashford returned to the camp and the group had not yet begun their evening meal. Ignace and Charles were talking together near the river's edge and the other men were all seated on logs dragged into the site, waiting. Ignace approached the group. Both had smiles on their faces though Charles seemed a little in other thoughts.

When the two of them took places by the fire, Thompson rose for another speech,

'Lads, we have had a difficult and, I may say, an exciting day. It was made difficult by three persons intended great harm on all of us and made exciting by our good friend William Ashford. We owe him much and we give him our thanks. Charles has advised me that he and Ignace have been talking of giving Mr. Ashford another name, not a nickname but one that tells us what we they think of him. Ignace, Charles, please tell us what you think."

Ignace began, "We have to say something before we do anything. When we looked at the Kentucky men's horses and packs, Mr. Thompson found a flag. It was the flag of the Red Bird. We must tell you about it."

Ignace looked down, not quite knowing how to begin. "Charles and I have been given our names by the people of the Seneca and we must first tell you of our names."

Charles rose to speak, "My brother is called 'Stands-in-Rapids'. He was given that name because he is the best at seeing the waters in a canoe. He stands tall in the back. He knows how and where to go, to be safe. He has taken many of our people through very big rapids and has not let the river take any of us. All people of the Iroquois Nations know he is the best." Charles sat down.

Ignace stood to talk. "Charles has been given the name, 'Red Bird'. The white man calls it the cardinal. He was given his name because, as a boy, he learned to speak the language of the Red Bird. He protects the Red Bird and the Red Bird protects him. It tells him where to make a safe camp, where to find food, where there is great danger. Today, we saw that the men who came to kill Mr. Thompson have a flag with the Red Bird on it. It made my brother very sad. He fears the Red Bird will no more talk with him. He feels he must do something to be sure he can speak with it when we return to where the Red Bird lives. He feels we must kill the man who sent these Kentucky men to kill Mr. Thompson. He must do that to show the Red Bird he is still a friend." Ignace sat.

The men sat in silence, not knowing what to say. They, too, were dismayed, saddened by what Ignace said. After a few moments, Boulard, the one who always had a joke to tell, rose and sat beside Charles, put his arm around Charles and spoke. "Red Bird, you are our brother. You will always be our brother and we will help you find this man. We will help you to be sure the Red Bird and you will talk to each other." Charles looked at Boulard and smiled.

After a few moments, both Ignace and Charles rose and faced Ashford, "Mr. William Ashford of the 'Chosen Men' we have decided you should be given a proper name, one of our people's names. We have decided to give you a Seneca name. It is one that tells all who you are. Your name should be, *'tha-yo-nih'*. It means *'wolf'*. We tell you why we give you this name." Charles turned to Ignace.

"Wolf is great and sacred animal to our people. He is loyal to his family like Ashford is to this family of ours." Ignace swept his hand in the direction of all the men as he used the word "family".

"Wolf is very smart. He thinks better than human, like Ashford." added Charles.

Ignace spoke, "Wolf plays with family and makes all feel safe, like Ashford does with jokes."

"Wolf is very patient, he waits, he listens, he plans what he will do, like Ashford does," Charles said.

Ignace added, "Wolf is great hunter. Ashford is great hunter. He showed us this today and when he hunts for food. Wolf is sacred Seneca animal. He is respected. Man who has his name is also respected. Ashford, *tha-yo-nih* , we honor you. You are our brother." Both bowed respectfully to *tha-yo-nih.*

Ashford didn't know what to say. He had come to love these men, all these men, and he knew it was a great honor to be given a name, especially one so important to the Seneca people. He had to respond.

"My brothers, you have taught me much and I hope I will honour you with my actions and my words. It is because of you, of what you have shown me that I have come to love this land. You have shown me the wonders of nature. You have shown me the respect you have for all things around me. You have changed my life and I hope you will continue to do so. You will be my friends, my brothers, forever. And Charles, Red Bird, I will help you find this evil man and together we will kill him."

He was unable to say more as there were tears in his eyes. When he recovered, it occurred to Ashford that Thompson must also have an Indian name. He had to ask.

"Mr. Thompson, do you have an Indian name?"

"Oh, yes, it is a Cree name, '*Koo-Koo-Sint*'. It means 'Star Gazer'. My Cree friends took notice that I spend much of my time looking at the stars and the sun. They noticed that I seemed to know where we were all the time and knew it was because I looked at the stars and the sun. In fact, I believe I lost the sight in my left eye from looking at the sun through my sextant. I have to live with that, now. But I too am honoured by having been given the name."

That night Ashford lay awake in his blankets. He felt different. He was confused. He felt warmth in his heart but could not figure out why. Yes, it had to do with his two Iroquois brothers, but there was something more. His mind took him over the words he spoke to Ignace and Charles. Those words were all true and he felt at them from the bottom of his heart. But there was more to it than that.

He stared up at the ceiling of the tent and watched as shadows formed by the firelight danced on the tent roof. The shadows looked people dancing around a bright light. No, it wasn't that. It was a family of people and they were holding hands and walking in a circle around their new house. And there were other people with them, people who appeared to be the ones who helped them build the house. Some of those other people wore brightly-coloured sashes around their waists, and were singing in French. Others wore leggings made of buckskin. All were happy and smiling and he knew they were looking to a wonderful future.

At first, Ashford did not realize that he had been dreaming. But as he lay, truly awake in his blankets, he came to realize what the just saw. He was now truly and forever part of a large and wonderful family.

This was the first time he felt like this and he could not quite understand it.

Return to Rocky Mountain House
September 21, 1811

he journey up the Columbia was without significant difficulty. It was mostly plain hard work with Thompson mapping the whole route; setting up the latitudes, longitudes and all information needed for future ventures on the Columbia. As the trip progressed, the changes in the forest were astounding. Sparse growth of Ponderosa Pines grew taller and more numerous, then gave way to large stands of Doulas Fir, some of them over 150 feet high and equally large stands of glorious red cedars. Each stand of forest had its own 'flavor' as they could smell the fresh growth of new needles. At times the forest was so thick it became impassable on foot or on horseback. At other times, the high canopies of trees made the forest floor look like a giant green cave. And all the way, small or larger streams fed more and more water into the Columbia. At night, it was almost impossible to see any stars as the canopy was just too thick. At times the relative sparseness of trees and open sky made them feel like they were in a large and endless world.

As the men rounded the bend at the north end of the river, they knew they were close to 'The Boat Encampment' and, when they arrived, were greeted by a small surprise. The place was thriving. Two additional buildings were erected and the first rough cabin was converted into a firewood storage area. There was permanence to it and it was obvious the boat encampment was now a well-built trading post.

But what was even more exciting was the news that canoes were left waiting at 'Meeting of the Waters' which was now a permanent launch place for treks to the boat encampment and at a point about half way down the valley. The result was that Thompson could now take a canoe from 'Meeting of the Waters' to McLeod's river and then, by a now well-set overland 'road', to Rocky Mountain House. Thompson was also advised that the total time to pack over the 'Athabasca Pass' in spring, summer and fall, was only two days from Meeting of the Waters.

The team reached Rocky Mountain House on September 21st, 1811. There, Ashford received the message he was expecting from Lord Worthington. It was addressed to *Major* William Ashford:

Major William Ashford   **March 18, 1811**

Congratulations on your elevation to the rank of Major and upon your successes in your present assignment. We request that upon your arrival at your new assignment, at York[4] in Upper Canada, you prepare a detailed report on what transpired and have same sent to us as soon as possible.

We advise that war is now imminent between His Majesty and the United States of America. As a great many of our resources are engaged with Napoleon, we presently have few of assets to assist our forces in the Canadas. We have thus decided that you shall be placed in charge of forming a group of men modeled after the 5th Battalion of the 95th Regiment of Foot in that location. To that end we have sent to you the uniforms and equipment required, including the Model 1806 Rifles for up to twenty-four men, 'Chosen Men'. All necessary ammunition, uniforms, and supplies to do so will accompany the shipment. By the time you receive this message, the said materials will have been delivered to Major General Isaac General Brock, who is also on route to York. We understand that you may need some additional supplies that would be useful for the winters of the Canadas and have arranged for funds to be presented to you for that purpose. The weather and other

---

4   Present-day Toronto, Ontario

conditions in that area will, we believe, present some different approaches and we are of the view that you have the best experience for such a command.

We do suggest, however, that you present yourself to Major General Brock in the attire fitting a member of the 95th. He shall be expecting you and will assist in 'choosing' the men from his troops. You will present this dispatch to the General upon first meeting him. Your new uniform will be waiting in storage at Fort York. Good luck.

> Sir Percival Worthington
> Secretary of International Affairs to
> His Majesty King George III

The dispatch was, as usual, sealed with Sir Percival's large red wax seal. Ashford wondered what would happen if he were to put it on the fire, then smiled and tucked it into his art kit.

The Rocky Mountains were surprisingly warm during the autumn months and the colours, mostly greens and golds of birch, poplar and larch, with some reds, were beautiful. The air seemed almost still, but hinted at the coming of winter. Trees near the top of the pass were almost non-existent. Signs of avalanches at the pass were numerous. The river, now named by the voyageurs as the Whirlpool River, was fast-flowing and a pleasure to paddle in a small canoe as it was mostly rapids of varying intensity. The trees on the east side of the pass were disappointing compared to the huge and majestic trees west of the pass.

One feature struck Ashford the most. On early mornings, when the sun shone onto the mountains, they glowed. Sometimes that light would show pink on the mountain-tops, then pure white as the sun rose higher. Sometimes the shale and granite rock would turn golden and, as the sun moved across the skies, the nooks, crannies and cracks stood out like they were painted onto the rock. Alhough Ashford was more than thirty miles away, he felt he could just reach out and touch them with his fingertips. But on other days, when the clouds were low or the light was grey, the mountains showed their other side, the dark, dangerous and foreboding side.

The prairies east of the Rockies at that time of year had more birch and poplar than the west side and were bare of leaves. Once into the prairies, there were often places with no trees, even along the river banks. The rivers, though flowing without hindrance, flowed evenly and with reasonable speed. As a result, the paddle by express canoe to York was much faster than Ashford's trip upstream almost a year earlier.

They arrived at York on January 14, 1812.

PART TWO
THE NEW WAR

ASHFORD – WAR of 1812

Training for the New War
Fort York, Upper Canada
January 16, 1812

Thompson was to leave York the day after their arrival. He decided to live with his family in Montreal as his work was done and it was time to take a less demanding role in the North West Company.

Ignace and Charles decided they would stay in the area to be close to their Seneca friends and families and the French-Canadian voyageurs were to return to Montreal with Thompson. All were weary. All felt they needed at least a rest or perhaps even a more normal life. Ashford, as was his duty, followed orders and went directly to the barracks at York to clean up and prepare for a meeting with Major General Brock.

The first thing he noted while dressing was that the new uniform fit perfectly. He had not lost weight but merely put on a good deal more upper body muscle. The second thing he noted, while pulling on his boots, was that the right boot had that knife pocket built into it. "Good Lord! The people at Worthington's office are great on detail!"

He was able to secure an appointment with the General at 11:00 am the next day. So, at eight the next morning, dressed in the green uniform of a Major of the 5th Battalion of the 95th Regiment of Foot, he walked to the beach where the voyageurs were preparing to depart. They were just about to step into the canoe when they saw Ashford approach. At first, they thought it was a mirage or some kind of trick, but then realized it was, indeed, Ashford, the soldier, not the voyageur, who approached. Each walked to Ashford and, in turn, gave him a huge bear-hug, expressing sadness upon their separation.

"We will miss you. We will miss talking and singing with you. We thank you for being one of us," said Gregoire.

"You are one of us. We wish you could stay," added Francoise.

"And I will miss joking about you, my great friend," croaked Boulard.

"Bon chance, my dear friend" Cote could hardly form the words.

"I know you have saved my life and I wish I could tell the world of what you have done. May providence shine on you." Thompson was also in tears.

With that, the team stepped into the canoe, which was facing stern into the water, and shoved off. They all paddled backwards, looking at Ashford, tears rolling down their cheeks.

Ashford stood at attention and snapped a proper soldier's salute, holding it as the canoe pulled away. There were tears in his eyes. Then a cheer came from his brothers;

> Bon Chance, tha-yo-nih!
> Bon Chance, Ignace!
> Bon Chance, Charles!

That was when Ashford realized that his Iroquois brothers were standing behind him, both with tears flowing down their cheeks.

He turned to them and gave them the same bear hug as with the voyageurs.

Ignace spoke first, "Tha-yo-nih, we have heard stories of the Americans killing our people, our friends. We must go to war. We wish to go to war with you."

Charles added, "I have been told my great uncle was killed and scalped by the Americans, the Kentucky men. I must go to war. Can we become part of your fighting men?"

"My brothers, if I have anything to do with it, yes! I will ask my new General if I can have you with me and I say it will be a great honor. In fact, I am to see him in an hour. Where can I find you?"

"We will wait, up there, this afternoon," answered Charles as he pointed to a small bench in the grass above the beach.

At eleven, with his cap tucked under his arm, Ashford was ushered into the office of Major General Isaac Brock and stood at attention facing a man seated behind a modest desk in an equally modest office. General Brock stood and looked at him.

"Sir, Major William Ashford ready for duty. I am to give you this dispatch."

"Relax, Major. I am not a stickler for pomp. Please pull up a chair and we shall talk. You can leave your cap there." General Brock pointed to a small table at Ashford's right. Ashford placed his cap on the table and sat.

"I have read your dossier and must say I am impressed. I am pleased that you have been assigned to my command and can say, from my own experiences and from what I have read about you, that you will be of great value to our cause. I say this because I have had the dubious distinction of being shot by French sharp-shooter, and by that, learned of the value of fighting men like the 'Chosen Men'. We will talk of that in a few moments. But first, I ask you tell me of your experiences while on the voyage to the Columbia River. It will allow me a better understanding of how to set up our new Brigade and how that experience might be of help to us."

"Sir, it's hard to describe it in a short dissertation, but I shall try."

At that Ashford spoke for about ten minutes, describing the work, the men, the natives, the paddling and building of canoes and the attempted attack; the way they learned of the men who perpetrated it, and how valuable the two Iroquois were to the whole adventure. At that point he interrupted himself and made an additional comment.

"Sir, in regards to the two Iroquois, I have a great admiration for them. They were not just good at the canoe but are excellent fighters and I must say that both of them approached me this morning asking if they can go to war with me. Their families and friends have been killed by the Americans recently. In addition, they can help a great deal training the new brigade for warfare in the forest. They are familiar with the Kentucky Long Rifle and I suspect would prefer to use that instead of the 1806 model. I would ask your permission to include them as part of the 'Chosen Men' of Canada. I do not propose to dress them in uniforms and would prefer they wear their own war clothing. The sight of them will terrify any American. Also, my plan is to modify the new brigade, make it a little different from the force as it is in Europe and more suitable to this country."

"Major, you will be in charge of the training and all of the matters dealing with the new brigade. You will, of course, be under my command and will be directed in all actions by me. But the manner of training and such is your job, just so long as the men are disciplined and ready. By the way, we have time and it is my wish that your groups be kept somewhat secret. There are many US spies lurking around us so I have arranged that your training will take place some distance from this fort, in the forest. We are in progress of setting up the camp now."

"Thank you, sir."

"And, Major, I agree on the two Iroquois men. This will be a different kind of war than the kind we fight in Europe and we will all learn from each other. I will make it a point to attend and watch the training, learn from you and your Indian friends, and learn a new way of fighting a war. I would add that yesterday I had the great privilege of meeting with Tecumseh, the great chief and leader of all the tribes in this land. He and his warriors will assist us. Between you and your two warriors, we will learn a new way of fighting a new kind of war."

"Thank you, sir. I may forget to explain this to you so I will mention it now. In the case of riflemen, we are much more informal. The officers eat with the men, treat them as brothers. I'll explain more on that in the coming weeks. Also, we do not salute our superior officers while near any battle. To do so marks an officer for death. Our training is unorthodox and necessarily so. Also, sir, at an early opportunity I would invite you to come and see how we use the 1806 Model rifle. That will provide a better understanding of how and why we do things that may be strange to you. It may also help in deciding how to best use the brigade."

To better illustrate his new methods, Ashford then recounted, in detail, the events at Murphy's creek. General Brock was astounded, not just about how Ashford set up the situation, but also that the actual shooting took less than thirty seconds. That made General Brock even more interested in the 'new' method of warfare.

Ashford added more comment about the Iroquois, "I've had the honour to fight with these two men and learned a great deal. They work with silence, with stealth, with patience. I hope to instill the same methods into the new brigade. It would be their great honour to meet you."

"You may tell them that it will by *my* honour. Perhaps we could meet, say about three today?"

Ashford then thought of an idea that would benefit all of them. "I will say that it took me some days to learn about the patience, how to use the woods as an aide, even to learn how to live and work with the voyageurs. As for the two Iroquois, I have an idea. Mr. Thompson made it a constant to always sit and smoke and wait for the natives to approach. In that way he showed he came in peace. He would start by presenting them with tobacco and pipe for the chief and things would develop from there. It might be a good idea to meet my two brothers in some kind of way that involves tobacco. Just a gift of it to them would do."

"Thank you, Major. I will prepare for that. One more thing, time is becoming important. I have selected twenty-four men and they are standing ready."

"Sir, that brings another thought. Lord Worthington has provided me with some extra funds. It being winter and the fact that we have to use discretion makes me think I should buy twenty-four capots, green of course, for the men. Also, some fur-lined moccasins. We will use the moccasins often as we will train in the bush as much as we can partly because the moccasin is much quieter. I will present the proper uniforms after we have done some training. I also propose to have the Iroquois men teach me and the men about the bush. As we often use a form of "sign language", we will train the men to do so as well. You will, at times, think the things we do are strange. So, do not hesitate to ask me why we do whatever concerns you. As things progress you and I will come to know how and when to use the men."

They talked more, especially about the Columbia voyage, and Ashford left with the feeling that this man would understand the new brigade and how to best use it. He looked forward to the next day and the beginning of the work.

After a short discussion, Ashford went directly to the North West Company post, about half a mile away and ordered his supplies. It would take time for the North West Company to get twenty-four new green capots and the moccasins. As another thought, Ashford ordered three dozen forest green toques. That would take more time. Upon checking with the stores at Fort York, he found the crates of series 1806 rifles, their cartridge pouches, powder horns, and even extra ram-rods. That was another wise detail as troops learning to use the rifle often bent the rods. There were also all materials needed to make cartridges and to manufacture more musket balls.

He then made arrangements through General Brock to have the new men march to their outpost fort with the rifles and ammunition tailing along in wagons. The march would be one small test of the new men to see if they could do the march in full gear and with their Brown Bess muskets and do so within a reasonable time. General Brock would follow some days later and at his convenience.

Ashford wondered if he should bring Ignace and Charles in now, or wait until they were at the new post. Maybe he should ask General Brock about that. He felt it best to keep the General informed.

A quick consultation with General Brock was scheduled for later that afternoon at the time Ashford was to meet with his Indian brothers. It was decided that General Brock would meet his two Iroquois not at the General's office but near the beach outside the fort. General Brock thought it best to meet them in a less-military environment, a place more in keeping with that of the Iroquois.

He is a wise man. Not at all pretentious, thought Ashford.

Ignace and Charles were unlikely to forget the meeting. General Brock arrived, dressed as a General of His Majesty's army, sword and all, and alone. There was no entourage, no guard. He approached the two fearsome-looking natives, who were dressed for war, gave them a slight bow of respect and the handed each of them a packet containing a clay pipe and a leather pouch of tobacco.

"I am honoured to meet you," he said as he gave them a respectful bow. "Major Ashford has spoken very highly of you. He has told me that you have honoured him by giving him a Seneca name and that you are both his brothers."

Charles, though nervous, was the first to respond. "*Tha-yo-nih* is our brother. He has protected us, worked with us and played with us. We are proud to have him our brother."

More pleasantries followed and then General Brock ended the conversation with his thoughts. "It is my pleasure to welcome you as our great allies. I hope you will accompany Major Ashford in the march to the post we have established for the 'Chosen Men'. I have given instructions that you be treated with the respect of all the men. We know that you will teach us much and we are eager to learn. Thank you."

Ignace and Charles were very impressed and, when General Brock was out of earshot, they turned to Ashford, with wonder in their eyes, and said, in unison, "This is a great man."

"I believe so," said Ashford. "He is one who learns. A good man never stops learning. He knows he will learn from what you will do with us."

Early the next morning, the twenty-four men were mustered in the parade grounds of the fort and were lined up in proper order waiting for their new commander and for two Indian men who were to join the force. When they saw Ashford, flanked by two Iroquois braves dressed in their battle attire, almost naked in the snow, but carrying their green capots, the men could not believe what they saw. The tomahawks worn by both made them look even more like the myths the men had heard. The men were absolutely silent, their jaws half-open as Ashford approached.

"Gentlemen, I am Major William Ashford, your new commanding officer in what will be an experience like you have never known. These two men with me are my brothers, Ignace and Charles. They will teach us, and that includes me, many tricks, many ways to wage war Rifleman and Iroquois style. They will also learn from us. Together we will find new ways of fighting, ways to survive in the forest, ways to scare the devil out of our enemies. We will live together, eat together, and learn together."

The men were still aghast, mouths still open.

"Today we will march to our new post, all of us together. Three wagons will follow behind and I am willing to wager the wagons will not be able to keep up with us because we start now. We start now with a different method of waging war. As the days procced, you will find my methods sometimes confusing. But you will understand why as we learn, together, because I too have much to learn. For now, we will leave this great fort in proper formation. When we arrive, we shall settle in and the next morning we shall begin."

"Sergeant, form up the men."

The march began and it was impressive. With typical British precision, discipline and pomp, they marched out of the fort in perfect order and accompanied by a drummer. The three wagons followed behind them.

Their new fort was really not a fort. It was more like a post or a very small version of the one at York. It held a barracks large enough for twenty-four men with a separate room for the sergeant, a potbellied stove for heat, bunk beds in one tier with foot lockers at each bed and few windows. There was a separate but smaller building for its superior officer, with a very small office large enough for a desk and three chairs. There was a parade ground just large enough for Ashford's men. The stockade around it was comprised of pine logs fairly well lined up to provide some cover but with only one platform on each wall that could hold five men. There was a cookhouse, fairly large and workable and it came with its own cook staff and food supplies. There was a very large stack of firewood covered by a large sail-cloth that would likely collapse from too much snow and that needed extra shoring. It was clearly a temporary 'fort' but was suitable enough.

But there was no room for the two Iroquois. Ashford did not want them to be segregated from the troops but worried other men might be uneasy with them at close quarters, at least until the men came to know the two warriors better. So he ordered an annex to be made against his building, with a proper entrance from his own building (not a separate entrance) as he reasoned there would be a good deal of planning done by the three of them. As there were still carpenters on site, work began immediately. In the meantime, Ignace and Charles would sleep on the floor in Ashford's quarters.

As for the wagon supplies, there was a problem. There was no place to store them, so the cookhouse had to be the place. Munitions had to be kept away from any source of fire. With the assistance of the cookhouse crew, they were able to construct a temporary room set apart from any source of fire. Construction of a munitions shack near, but separate from Ashford's cabin began.

Within three days all that would be completed and, in the meantime, training would begin, including an introduction to the series 1806 rifle. For now, the troops would have to continue wearing their regular army uniforms as they all had proper great coats for cold weather and warm boots.

The next morning all the men assembled in the cookhouse for some 'orientation'. As they entered the room, each of the men saluted their commanding officer with a sharp British salute; palm outward, arm level, crisp and clean. All of them sat at the long tables and waited. Then the Iroquois entered and there was a hush, even though Ignace and Charles were dressed in their green capots and not in Iroquois battle mode. They walked in, silently, and stood at the front of the hall near Ashford.

"Men, some rules, and there will be more of them as we go along. But today there are some things you must know and get accustomed to for the moment. First, you will not salute me except while in the fort at York and other places where the show of the salute is important. Why? Because the salute to an officer is like raising a flag showing the enemy who to kill. I want to stay alive. Second, we stay informal because all our lives depend on helping each other, working with each other and, above all, *thinking* like each other. Third, you will learn how to properly use this," he said and held up the rifle.

The men were not surprised. They heard rumors.

"For now, I will tell you more about my brothers." Ashford waved his hand towards the Iroquois. These men are expert canoeists. I had the honor of travelling with them all the way to the Pacific Ocean and back. We faced great hardship together, came close to starving, and were attacked, not by Indians but by Kentucky riflemen. More on that later."

"I will call each of you by name and, since one of my weaknesses is remembering names, it will take time for me to remember all of your names. I will not be insulted if you correct me in that regard. You will call me Mr. Ashford or, if you feel comfortable you may call me 'Sir', especially where brevity and quiet is involved. Now to the rifle."

Three muskets were leaning against the wall behind him. He picked up the Brown Bess first. This, as you know, is the musket you presently use.

It has only a rudimentary sight and is by no means accurate. It is meant for 'standing the line' and delivering a volley of lead. It is almost useless beyond seventy yards but it is deadly in close quarters."

He paused and picked up the Kentucky rifle. This is the Kentucky long rifle. Yes, a musket. But what makes it different is what we call 'rifling'. There are groves in a spiral along the inside of the barrel. Those grooves make the musket ball spin and the spin makes it go farther and straighter. It is accurate up to 270 yards."

The men responded with a 'wooo!'

"The Kentucky is very long." Ashford held it next to the Brown Bess and the 1806 so they could readily see the difference. It appeared to be at least one foot longer the Brown Bess.

"The long barrel, in my opinion, makes this Kentucky more difficult to load. One has to be standing to do it, though some of the Kentucky people can, I am told, do it in a crouching position. Its major weakness is the sighting mechanism. It cannot be easily adjusted and that means only a man who has shot it a thousand times can be accurate at 270 yards. Until now, it has been the best hunting musket in the world and deserves that respect. You will notice that Ignace and Charles use this rifle. They prefer it because they have used it. By the way, the two rifles they now have were taken from three Kentucky men who attempted to ambush us on our trip to the Pacific."

Another, 'wooo!'

"Now to the 1806 Rifle. It works the same way as the Kentucky. But it has a very accurate sighting system and its shorter length makes it easier to load. I will brag a bit. I shot a General on horseback from 300 yards with this rifle."

Another 'wooo' followed with muttering between the men.

"The drawback of these rifled muskets is that it takes longer to load them. I assume, because you have been 'chosen', you could load your muskets and fire off four shots in one minute, including the one you already had loaded. An expert on this rifle can fire only two or sometimes three shots. But you will see why we use this one as we go along."

"By the way, if you have a question, please stand and let me know. We learn from each other. Say your name for me as well.

"Any questions?"

Silence.

"Today, as you leave this assembly, you will hand in your old muskets and all shot and even your powder horns and trade them all for the new ones. You will not try to load and fire the rifles until you receive proper training, but I encourage you to carry them, get used to the weight and the feel of them. Do not adjust the sights until we instruct you how to use them. Questions?"

One man stood. "Wilks sir, Brian Wilks. When do we get to train on the new ones?"

"Thank you, Wilks," Ashford was pleased that the men were anxious to get started. "For now, I encourage you all to carry the rifle and get used to its weight and how it feels when you are about to fire it. We'll start indoors, here, and then go outside. I don't want to blow any holes in the roof."

His comment was met with laughter. The men were getting to know Ashford and to relax.

"Your new uniforms are here, but we'll practice a bit in the ones you now wear one for a few days, at least until we get comfortable with this thing." He held up the rifle.

"Now about my brothers. Charles, please tell the lads my name in the Seneca language and about the Seneca and the Iroquois nations. Ignace, you can help him."

Charles, who was seated cross-legged on the floor, rose. "First I tell you about how Ashford has become our brother." He looked to Ashford as if to ask permission and was rewarded by a slight nod. As for the men, they appeared to be shocked that the Indian could speak English so well.

"We have given our brother the name 'Tha-yo-nih'. It means 'wolf' in our language. We call him wolf because the wolf looks after his family, protects them, teaches them. The wolf is very smart. He is a very good hunter and he is patient. He plans well. Tha-yo-nih is like the wolf and he does all those things, like the wolf does. He is our family and we made him our brother."

Ashford could see the men warming to Charles.

Then Ignace spoke. "I tell you about our people. We are Seneca. There are six nations of the Iroquois. Seneca and Mohawk are warriors. Seneca protect the west gate of our lands and the Mohawk protect the east gate. We have suffered much at the hand of the Americans. We have learned that many days ago, Americans came to a village where some of family was visiting with our Delaware friends. They burn the village and kill the uncle of Charles. We are at war. We ask to join Mr. Ashford in war. Mr. Ashford has asked the great General to let us join. We are here. We are here to help our people and help Mr. Ashford. We are honored to fight with tha-yo-nih."

There was a long silence in the room. Then one man stood up and, with some trepidation, walked to Charles and Ignace and shook their hands. The others followed. The reaction to this gesture was great as you could see the smiles on the Iroquois' faces a mile away.

"That's it for now," Ashford said. "I ask that all of you pitch in to making sure there is enough firewood for warmth and for the kitchen. We will meet again at noon lunch. I have a surprise for you then."

At lunchtime the men arrived, all carrying their new rifles. They were quite animated, anxious to be there. They were not accustomed to a lunch break or to be given lunch as they usually fended for themselves and often didn't have lunch. But they were indeed met with a surprise.

"Sit, men, and we will have the first and only 'formal' lunch you'll ever have in this company. You will learn to eat lunches on the fly, in strange and uncomfortable places."

Most were already seated and most of them noticed a 'something' on the table. It was flakey-brown and about one by two inches in width, length and about an inch thick. "Gentlemen, what you see before you is called, 'pemmican'. It is the super energy food of the natives and the voyageurs. You will be eating a lot of this, so get used to it. I recommend you eat it in small chunks." Ashford broke off apiece and began to chew, not chew so much let it melt in his mouth. The men did the same. Some of the scowled at first, then seemed to like it. Others liked it immediately.

"Brannon, sir," said a young red-haired Private as he rose. "This is not so bad. What is it?"

"Pemmican is made of dried meat, not cooked or smoked, but *dried* meat mixed about fifty-fifty of dried meat and animal fat. The animal fat comes usually from the deer or animal you kill and is 'rendered' so it can be poured into the dried meat. The meat gives you strength and muscle and the fat gives you energy. You will need a lot of both, especially in the winter, and we eat it almost every day. On the trip to the Pacific we would have starved without it. There will be times when we will all work to make it. It lasts almost forever, as long as it stays dry and out of sunlight. We will carry it with us when we venture out on long assignments. We will always have some with us for the energy it gives us."

"Now, as you munch on it, I will ask that each of you stand, starting there and going up each row, and tell me and the others about yourself. I will start. I'm William Ashford, born in Newport, England. My parents both died so I spent several years at an early age in France and learned to speak French quite well. I learned more French from the voyageurs, and while on the Pacific trip came to respect those men a great deal. I served in the peninsular wars of Spain as a 'Chosen Man', a Lieutenant, and became a Captain after one year. I was sent here by His Majesty's armed services and on the Pacific trip before that. I have tried to learn the Seneca language but Ignace and Charles say I have no hope in Hades on that."

Big guffaws.

"By the way, Ignace and Charles speak French and, like me, have not learned how to use profanity."

Each man then stood and told everyone something about their background. Ashford asked each of them some questions, to which all responded. The questions were designed to be sure the men were well-selected, questions such as how well they could read, could they use a compass, had they been in any battles. He came to the conclusion that the men were almost evenly divided into persons of Scottish, Irish, and English background. A good mix. He learned from their demeanor that they were all excited and eager to be one of the 'Chosen Men'. The lone sergeant seemed the best of all.

"In a few days, for our morning run, we'll so something very different. Snowshoes!" He waited for reaction but got none because, he suspected, the men didn't believe him or simply did not know what he was talking about. "Snowshoes are exactly that. We strap then onto our boots and are able to walk in deep snow without disappearing. But there's a knack to using them and I suspect you will be using them a good deal in the years to come. Trust me. It'll be a riot of fun. We will walk and run, if you can call it running because it is not like walking or running with boots. We will start in them without the rifles, then more and more after that." Ashford had a huge smile on his face as he told them and almost reveled in the fact that they seemed to know nothing about it.

"Any questions?" there were none.

"Thank you all. Now, I'll take some time to tell you a little more about the 'Chosen Men', what we do, how and why. We do not 'stand the line' unless there is a real need to do so. We are 'skirmishers'. We are not 'pickets'. We go to harass the enemy and to confuse them. We make it easier for the main battle group to fight because we set the enemy in chaos and cause them to fear what is ahead. More importantly, we shoot and kill. We kill from a far distance and in almost every case the enemy is dumbfounded when we do it. We shoot those men who will present the greatest threats to our main battle forces, the officers, those ones carrying long rifles, the leaders. We have also learned to shoot the drummers while the columns advance. I am aware that most of them are young boys, but we noticed that when the drummer goes down, the men in column lose their step. They don't walk in proper unison and sooner or later they tend to trip all over each other.

Ashford paused, "In many cases it takes time for the enemy to figure out where the shots come from. That's because we are hidden, not standing in the line with bright red coats. Please, don't get me wrong. The red coats are needed. They separate us from the enemy and keep our own forces from shooting each other. And I know the sight of all the Redcoats marching and standing the line with pure un-waving discipline scares the devil out of the enemy."

"We work in pairs. We know at all times where our partners are and where all our men are. As partners, each man protects the other. We protect the main force from snipers. We often take part in the planning of a battle. We may go out on our own missions as assigned by the commanding officer. We assist in retreat or fallback of our forces. We shoot from behind logs and trees and bush and anything that gives us cover. Above all, we move. We move fast. All of that will be better understood as training progresses."

The men appeared to be getting fidgety, so Ashford stopped and drank some water.

"You will find that we often work in silence. No shouting, sometimes talking or whispering. Ignace and Charles have begun to train me in the use of what we call 'sign language', talking and directing each other with our hands and head movements. Complete silence. We will learn that together under their instruction. I can tell you that, when attacked by three Kentucky Riflemen, we used sign language that allowed us to dispose of them in quick order. We planned. We stuck to the plan. We also had an alternate plan to fall back on."

Ashford paused and then continued, "For today, we will go on an hour-long run. We will carry the new rifle and learn the way we get to where we need to be fast, so gear up, greatcoats and full dress. Leave your Bessies behind and form up in a column of twos in five minutes. I am told each of you has a pocket watch but we'll work on how to use them later because much of our work will depend on timing. Five minutes."

The men scrambled and were formed in exactly five minutes.

"Gentlemen, it will be easier to do this running while wearing capots. They are coats that are just longer than knee length. That allows us to run more freely. I've ordered the capots, which should arrive soon. We will do this run each morning before breakfast because we will need to do it often in the future. We do this by running for ten minutes then walking for four minutes. It's my modification of the 'Chosen Men' run. Charles, Ignace and I will lead. We will all do this together, every morning; until we are so good at it we can do it in our sleep. Let's go!"

The men were in remarkably good shape and took to the timing so well that Ashford was surprised. When they returned, he directed the men to assemble in the cookhouse for instruction on the rifle which caused a buzz of excitement as the men almost knocked each other over to get into the building.

"Here it is, gentlemen. Loading and firing is similar to the Bess, but more difficult. But first I want to show you the unique sights on this rifle." He walked to the centre of the room and motioned the men to gather around, even stand on the benches for a better view. He then showed how the sight could be elevated to a 200-yard shot. "To do so requires an adjustment of the sight with small screwdriver and that takes time. The screw driver is in this little compartment of the rifle stock."

Ashford then recommended not taking a shot longer than 150 yards, for now, unless there was loads of time to make adjustments. The ideal distance was 150 yards and at that one could easily shoot a man in the head. "We keep the sight at 150 and make adjustments visually to shoot farther or shorter distances. You will also note the very small notches on part of the sight. It tells you the distances in another way, fifty yards at a time."

"But today, we will leave the sights at 100 yards, then go out and practice. There's one thing you should all know. With the Bess, you're not looking for great accuracy, but with this rifle you are. I'm sure that some of you realize that the chances of your flinching with the musket are very great. So we have to practice not to flinch. The best way to learn that is to sight your target using something steady like a log or a tree trunk, anything that will hold the rifle absolutely steady. Over time you will learn to do it in all different stances without having to steady it on something. So let's set the sights at 100 yards. One at a time, please, so I can help."

They did so and all eventually passed the 'test'.

"Now to loading this rifle." Here's how it's done.

Ashford then went through each step, pointing out the similarities and differences between the rifle and the Brown Bess to the men as he demonstrated each move.

"One: Load and prime the pan – same as you do with the musket, then half cock it. Remember to shake the pan, like this," he tapped the pan with his powder horn after he poured just less than a tablespoon of powder into it, just like you do with the musket."

One of the men rose, "Perkins, sir. Why shake the pan? With the Bessie we just raise and fire it."

"Good question. Most of the time we are running with the loaded rifle so we shake the pan to be sure it stays in place. We want to make sure the rifle will fire whenever we need it and it gets bounced around a lot. We run with the pan covered and the rifle in half-cock" All the men nodded.

"Two: Place the rifle between your knees, just like you do with the musket and pull a cartridge from your pouch. It holds up to sixty cartridges. Bite off the top end and keep the ball in your mouth while you load the powder. You load the powder just like you do with the Bessie." He poured the powder from the paper pouch into the barrel.

"Three: Here's the big difference. You pull patch from the pouch, by the way, there's a small patch-holder here, in the stock. I prefer to have patches handy in the cartridge pouch as it's easier to get to because to use that one in the stock you have to lift the rifle. However, it will be useful to you when you are crouched behind cover, so remember it's there. Result, I carry only fifty cartridges and have a compartment in the pouch just for the patches. Your pouches have that little compartment in it, so you have only fifty cartridges and a few more balls in case you swallow one and end up crapping lead for the next week."

That caused a good deal of laughter.

"The patches are linen, not silk, partly because linen holds the spit-wet ball in place and partly because it doesn't come apart when you push down with the ram-rod. They are not greased because the grease will eventually foul your barrel. Here's the tricky part. You have to hold the patch over the muzzle, like this, and then tuck the ball into it, like this. Sometimes, in cold weather, it's hard to centre the patch, but you'll get onto it."

"Four: This is where the biggest difference is. You have to ram the ball and patch into the barrel, all the way down. It's not just a jiggle and a small push like with the musket because the groves inside the barrel and the patch make it harder to ram the ball down. You must – I repeat - you must use *both hands* to ram the ball down. If you don't, you'll end up bending the rod and when that happens, you're in deep trouble." He demonstrated that move. "As you can see, I have to use more pressure that you would with the musket, especially when the rod is down deeper in the barrel."

"Now you're ready to aim and fire. Here's the other big difference, though. You really aim, not just point. You take your time to aim. As you use the rifle more, you will find you will aim and fire very fast, but that takes a lot of practice. You'll get onto it fast enough." He demonstrated the aim.

"Five: You will likely see your kill if the smoke is not too bad, but sometimes you will not. But you will just know dammed well you made the kill. That's how well you will know your rifle. In the bush, you will shoot and move to a second position because the smoke will give you away. We'll practice that later."

"Now, let's have each of you go through it, one at a time, and we'll learn together. Sergeant, you will go first."

All the men went through the routine with Ashford verbally repeating each step as they went and, when all were loaded, they donned their greatcoats and went out for target practice.

At supper, Ashford simply announced that each morning would be the same: an hour-long run, followed by breakfast and discussion, then target practice. His goal was to get the men to automatically do all the steps without thinking.

At all meals, he encouraged the men to ask questions, present their ideas, joke around and become familiar with each other, as comrades who would help and protect each other. In the evenings, he had them set up an assembly-line where they would put together new cartridges and pack them into their pouches. During the process he stressed that the measure of gunpowder in each cartridge had to be the same because a variance in powder would result in differences in length and accuracy of a shot. The men learned quickly

The process went on for two weeks and in that time the capots, moccasins, and toques arrived.

"Gather 'round, men. I have another treat." Ashford said as he entered their quarters after target practice. As he spoke, two of the men followed him carrying large bundles of 'something". I have some new and different kind of clothing for you."

He drew his Havaja knife and cut the twine holding the bundle together. The knife prompted a murmur among the men.

"Yes, I know you've been wondering about this. It's something I picked up in Spain. It's a fighting knife and I'm glad I haven't had to use it. A knife fight is something to avoid. Anyway, let's look at the new clothing."

He held up a capot. "This is called a capot. It's used by the voyageurs as it is warm and short. It's perfect for us in winter and it allows you to run, crouch, push, roll and work easily in the forest. I wore one like this through two winters and can say it's the best for winter warfare. The colour makes it harder for the enemy to see us, just like your new uniforms. I'll show them to you in a few minutes, but, for now I want each of you to come and try them on. One size fits all and you will notice they feel a bit loose. That's because there will be times when you wear layers of clothing underneath. We'll use them mostly in cold weather and almost always in the bush. Tomorrow is day one."

The men came forward in turn and each pulled on his capot.

"This is a 'toque', another French-Canadian thing. It will keep you warm in winter, like this," He pulled one onto his head and folded it to cover his ears. "It will also make it more difficult for our enemy to spot you and we'll use it in most night operations. We will even wear it in the summer because it will allow us to blend into the forest." He tossed the toques onto the table and each man took one to try on.

"And these are moccasins." He held one up. "There are varying sizes, a few extra for that reason. They are fur-lined. These shoes are used by our Indian friends and keep you warmer than any boot the army might give you. It will take an hour or so for you to get used to them because they are soft compared to the typical army boots, but you'll come to love them more than the boots. Charles, Ignace, and I wear leggings under our trousers, the capot moccasins, and the toques, and we stay warm all day. Tomorrow we will start wearing these and train with them in the cold. I will appreciate your comments on them when we finish our first run."

"One last thing. We have your new uniforms, the uniforms of the 'Chosen Men'. Brannon, Clark, if you would go out to the wagon and bring in the army boxes. You will notice that each uniform comes with a short sword. It's the answer to the short barrel of our rifles and designed to replace the bayonet, which scares the devil out of me because I never want to be in a bayonet fight. I found the swords more useful to open a can than anything, but you never know when we might have to use them. We might do some practicing with the sword as a bayonet because I've been too long as Chosen Man. We are seldom called to use the bayonet, so I will need some practice. You men will probably delight in teaching me."

"Right you are, sir," replied the Sergeant. With that all the men grunted out a sound that Ashford took as approval.

There was one more thing Ashford had to show, or demonstrate, to the men; the *Iroquois war cry*. With a nod, he instructed Ignace and Charles to come to the front of the room. Both of them covered their faces with their toques as though they were wiping sweat off their skin. When they reached the front, they kept their backs to the men.

"One more item, gentlemen. Show them, my brothers ..."

Charles and Ignace turned to face the men and let loose. "Eeeyah! Eeeyah! Whoop, Whoop. Whoop!" They were wearing their red and black war paint. Their eyes shone with the look of a wolf attacking its prey as they made like they were about to attack the men. They held their toma-hawks in the ready to strike and the moved menacingly towards the men.

The men were stunned. They recoiled in fear. Some tried to duck under the table.

"That, gentlemen, is the Iroquois battle cry! Ashford waited for some of the men to get back in their chairs and continued, "It varies, not always the same, but it scares the devil out of the Americans. We will all learn it, practice it, and then use it for that purpose and for signaling in battle."

The men looked at each other, partly in disbelief and partly in the hope they would have joy in learning it. Ashford could tell that some of them could hardly wait.

There's some little boy in everyone, he thought to himself.

"There is one thing you should remember. That war cry is to be used sparingly. You will not use it anywhere except this room, or where you are instructed to use it. You will not use it in some pub when you want to show what 'Chosen Men' can do. It is from battle only and anyone who uses it in some pub or public place will be immediately sent back to stand the line. Understood?"

A collective "Yes, sir!"

"I will leave you now to try on the uniforms, moccasins and all, and have you gathered in the cookhouse in one hour. Sergeant, please arrive about fifteen minutes before that to assist me on another matter."

It was time to pair up the men and Ashford would take advice from his Sergeant, who knew the men well, in forming the pairs. Wilson was expecting the job as it had been mentioned to him a few times during the past week or so. As a result, he had it all figured out. He observed the strengths and weaknesses of each man and would pair them so that they would complement each other. He suggested the idea to Ashford who not only agreed but was impressed by the Sergeant. Wilson also suggested that paired men would also be bunked next to each other as it would build a closer trust. It would help each pair to think the same, to anticipate what his partner would do. Above all, it would lead to each man protecting his partner.

The next morning all men were partnered and thereafter, walked, ran and marched next to each other.

Training went on for another month. Ashford, Ignace, and Charles were constantly with the men. In the evenings, when they were not building cartridges, they learned sign language, rehearsed it and practiced it until they could almost speak a detailed language with their hands and head movements.

"Men," began Ashford, "I believe you are ready – except for two things. You will all learn how to paddle a canoe. But we will wait for spring before we start with that. Secondly, and even though we have to learn about the canoe, it is my pleasure to advise you that, upon completion of a ceremony which will be held in few minutes, you will all be "Chosen Men".

There was a stunned silence, perhaps because to be rewarded with a ceremony was a surprise.

And the ceremony was The Green Tea Ceremony.

When it came for the men to all drink the 'tea' in unison, there was sputtering, coughing, gaging and a whole lot of sputtering followed by just as many 'blawhaaas' as they drank the rum. It ended with large guffaws and smiles and looks to Ashford as if to say, "That was a good one!"

"Congratulations, lads! You are now all 'Chosen Men' and I commend you." announced Ashford. The men replied with a loud *"Hip, Hip, Hurrah! Hip, Hip Hurrah! Hip, Hip, Hurrah!"*

Ashford felt obliged to tell them why they had to drink green tea. "The green tea is made with spruce needles. In winter it is much more bitter that the tea made of fresh spring bows, but there is a purpose for it. During winter, when we have few fresh vegetables, we stand a good chance of getting scurvy. It's a condition that makes your teeth fall out and, if it goes on too long, you will wind up starving to death. Our native friends have taught us to make spruce tea and it is even more effective that having to chew on a lime as the navy does.

"In two days General Brock will pay us a visit. I plan to show him what you men are all about. I plan to surprise him with your shooting and your discipline, show him how you work together, how you move, how the best shooters in the world can wreak havoc on the enemy. So, tomorrow, we will set up our surprise, rehearse it, and the next day we will put on a really great show."

The Big Show
February 24, 1812

A shford stationed Charles about a mile up the road approaching their 'fort' with instructions to silently run back and advise of the approach of General Brock. His reason was the need for surprise. His men were all properly dressed in their army-issued green uniforms of the 95th. Their short swords were in the proper position, their cartridge pouches filled and ready, and their caps strapped on. They were milling around the gate as Ashford had ordered. At 2:00 pm, Charles came running to the gate, which opened as he approached, and went directly to Ashford's cabin.

"They come now. Four men, on horseback."

"Thank you, Charles, you may now hide the men as we practiced."

With that, Charles took the men, in good order, outside the 'fort' and into the trees just across the road and a distance far enough that no one could see them. Ignace took his position near the gate, inside the fort. They waited.

About ten minutes later the four horsemen arrived and the gate opened magically as they approached. Standing alone in the centre of the parade ground Ashford greeted the General with a crisp salute, and then walked towards him.

"Sir, Major William Ashford at your service."

All five men returned the salute, dismounted and, with General Brock in the lead, walked towards Ashford.

"Major, a pleasure to meet you again." General Brock said as shook Ashford's hand and continued, "I have received your dispatches and am also pleased to learn you have finished the training. May I introduce to you some of my officers whom I thought would benefit from knowing all about your work here: General Hale Sheaffe, General John Vincent and Lt. Colonel John MacDonnell."

Ashford shook hands with each of them in turn, and then directed the men towards the doorway of the cookhouse. "Gentlemen, I have arranged a demonstration of the firepower of a team of 'Chosen Men'. Please stand here. It may be a bit safer."

He nodded to Ignace who pulled open the gate, gave blood-curdling war cry and stood back as the whole team ran, in double file into the yard, then spread out in twos and took positions behind small haystacks, a wagon and other objects scattered throughout the parade ground.

"Please note the twenty-four paper bags located around the enclosure. Each of the lads made one from sheets of paper. They are filled with ashes so you will be able to see how my lads do. I have instructed each of them to pick out an assigned target, kill it and then reload their rifles. To allow you to be able to see each shot, I have instructed them to, on my command, shoot their targets, not in unison as would be done while standing the line, but counter-clockwise in a successive manner. When done, they are to reload." He waited a few moments.

"Have at it lads!"

In about ten seconds all of the paper bags burst open, one after the other, their load of ash exploding as the shots hit, and the ash dust filling much of the compound. All hit their mark and all were reloaded within thirty seconds. It was a demonstration of the clockwork precision of the 'Chosen Men'

"If I may suggest, shall we go inside and I'll tell you of the training and the reasons for it; how we would operate and other matters. In the meantime, my lads will go to their quarters and dress in their winter and forest uniforms. That may surprise you, but I will explain." Ashford waved the men toward their quarters. Ashford held open the door as they entered. He did most of the talking, about their job as skirmishers, how the men were teamed in pairs and covered each other. Some questions were asked, which he answered.

He took more time in answering a question as to whether the men should 'stand the line' with the regular troops. "The rifles take more time to load than the Brown Bess, so that makes them less effective in the line. However, these men were already trained to stand the line and will likely do quite well. The accurate range of these rifles in as much as 270 yards. By that I mean we could kill or severely wound a man with a shot to the torso at that range. We would prefer to start the shoot at 200 yards. At 150 yards, we are absolutely deadly in our shots. Although we can, as you have noticed, accurately do a head shot; we will concentrate on the torso. If we miss and get a leg or an arm, we will have still taken one man out of action. More than that, it will take at least two men to help the wounded man and that means two men less enemy troops in the battle. As for officers, we shoot to kill because without leadership an attacking force is lost."

Ashford's superior officers were somewhat surprised with the coldness in which Ashford spoke, but they understood and became convinced that his insights were correct and the use of the 'Chosen Men' would be of great benefit.

"I would add, gentlemen, that we shall be facing a good number of Kentucky Riflemen or other militia groups who use the rifled musket. We shall target those men first and that will reduce long-range casualties on our part. With the permission of our superior officers, we will also set ourselves out, hide if you like, in appropriate places on the periphery of a battlefield to take out the riflemen at the very start of the action. To do so, we may even go out the day before battle to surprise the enemy. We will use ambush. We move fast, and shall demonstrate that when we return to Fort York with you. You may be surprised by our winter outfits. By now, the men have dressed and should be awaiting us in the compound. I should point out that I learned how valuable these outfits are while working, mostly in the snow, with the voyageurs on the trip to the Pacific Ocean. They give us warmth and, above all, the freedom to move fast."

"How will the men survive in the cold all day?" asked General Sheaffe.

"They already have, General. We have taken the men out on two occasions, in the clothing you will see and stayed as if in ambush the whole day. One of the things we did was eat pemmican those whole two days. That's another thing I learned from our French Voyageurs. During the winter, at minus twenty-four degrees, we made pemmican and would have starved without it. We have already begun make it with the men, to teach them so we are always ready. I have even trained the men on the use of snowshoes and can say they can use them almost as well as any voyageur."

He then led the officers out and waited for their reaction as they saw the men.

It's hard to convince a General who is accustomed to complete order, discipline, and precise movement of troops to understand this new concept and Ashford knew that. He also felt that the generals were not yet convinced, but he was confident he would convince them on the return trip to Fort York.

"Gentlemen, it may be a little late for you to return this day. We have little to offer in terms of comfort, but I have arranged to have you stay in my quarters overnight. There is room, but you will have to sup with the men in the cookhouse. I do ask one thing, though. I have instructed my men to never salute an officer in or near a battlefield. In fact, we seldom do so as it marks an officer as a target. When you sup with us, you may be surprised by how informal it is. I always eat with the men and with my two Iroquois brothers. At any rate, you will find it interesting and will undoubtedly wonder at what appears to be a lack of discipline. I assure you it is not a lack, but a necessity, because we depend upon each for our lives. We work as a close, small team."

By then, the Colonels and Generals we so taken by what they saw, they had little concern about decorum. They actually looked forward to it.

The supper went very well. At the suggestion of General Brock, the four senior officers dispersed themselves amongst the men, making it a relaxed visit. During that time, they learned more about the team and of Major William Ashford. Stories were told, not just about their training but also about what they knew about Ashford. It was obvious they would protect him and die for him.

The return trip to York was another masterpiece. With the Generals' approval, Ashford and his men led the way. He moved his men with a brisk and disciplined step. About eight miles from the fort, with the prior approval of General Brock, Ashford had the men do his modified run-walk. They disappeared from sight in moments. But later they appeared, just one mile out of Fort York, standing at attention along the sides of the road. Some of the men were carefully holding something that seemed to be steaming. They were holding mess tins of hot pea soup. Others held fresh-baked buns; others bottles of wine, and others, white napkins. One man held a pork roast and a rifleman's short sword as a carving knife. Beside the road was a table set for five with chairs neatly tucked under them. The table was set with knives, forks, spoons and pewter wine glasses.

Ashford made a quick, but not showy salute and said, "Gentlemen, my men thought you may be a little cold and hungry from your ride. We have therefore arranged something to chase the chill." As he did so, he handed a bottle of cognac to General Brock.

A Meeting of Colonels and Generals
Fort York
February 26, 1812

The day after the return to Fort York,[5] Ashford received a request to meet with General Brock at 6:00 pm on the February 26th. He was expecting it later rather than sooner as the generals had to digest what they had seen over the past days.

When he got to General Brock's command building, Ashford was led to a room he knew was not General Brock's office. It was instead a dining room containing a fairly large table, large enough to seat twelve people but set for only five. The Lt. Colonel and three Generals were milling near a table topped with bottles of spirits and glasses and were in the act of choosing what they wanted to drink. All turned to look at Ashford as he entered and smiled.

"Good afternoon, Major." said General Brock. Glad to have you join us. After the informality of your command, we have decided to reciprocate with our own form of informality. "What can we get you?"

"Some rum would work, sir."

As he handed Ashford a rather fancy glass containing about two ounces of rum, General Brock motioned for Ashford to sit in one of the chairs. "We have much to talk about. Let me begin by saying we were very impressed by our meetings with you over the past days and I must say the welcome to Fort York was a masterpiece of logistics and of, uh, shall we say, 'style? How in the world did you pull that off?"

---

5   York was the town located where Fort York was also located.

Ashford was now relaxed as he knew he was not in any kind of trouble. "Sir, I planned to simply wait for you near the gates but we got there early enough to visit a pub in town and convinced the owners to provide us with the food and drinks. We were lucky because they had already baked the bread, just out of the ovens, and the pork, same thing. So we decided to add that 'touch'. What we wanted to demonstrate was that we could run faster, in good form, than the average horse walks, and we could do it for a long distance. It worked out even better that I thought and I have to compliment my lads on that."

"Well, we compliment you on all of it and we learned a great deal", said General Sheaffe. "We are impressed and want to discuss more on how to use your force."

An enlisted man, dressed in a black waistcoat and white shirt entered and stood at ease near the door.

"Leave us a few minutes, Private. I'll call you when we are ready." That was an indication that General Brock wanted to stay informal and that there was much to discuss.

"Let's start with what, how, and why you did what you did with those three Kentucky riflemen. You've already told me the bare bones of it and I think a more detailed account will help us in what you say will be the use of ambush."

Ashford told them how Charles spotted the man on the hill, how they decided what to do, to fake a leak in the canoe to draw them in; how he wanted to lure them in and not so what they expected but to do what *he* wanted them to do. He explained how Charles and Ignace did the scouting that helped set up the fight and how it happened. He even told them of the hilarious part of the deception – Boulard pissing on the bow of the canoe. That brought out a hearty laugh from all of the officers. In the end he simply said. "They expected to make an easy job of us, but they were all dead before they knew what happened."

As they ate, Ashford was asked and answered many questions about the Pacific trip and what he learned from it. He also answered many questions on how they operated including one asked by Lt. Col MacDonnell. "Have the 'Chosen Men' ever experienced being mistaken by our own forces and fired upon?"

"Yes. We usually do not suffer casualties, at least not many, because we are so spread out. But it requires the other troops and their command to know where we are and to avoid, especially, grape shot in our area. When it happens, we run like the devil or dig ourselves into the ground. We prefer, with the permission of the commanding officer, to deploy without a column, without any show of force. In doing so, we accomplish two things. First, we are not shot at by our own forces. Second, the enemy does not know who or where we are."

"Would wearing a red toque help to identify your men?" asked Colonel MacDonnell.

"Frankly, I think you have a good idea, at least for winter. But the more important thing is for the regulars to know what we look like ahead of time and where we are likely to be. In summer, the red will give our position away to the Kentucky men and they are, as you know, expert hunters and marksmen. Perhaps it will be a good idea to do some maneuvers with the regulars. That way we can work out some solutions. In Spain we did not have the deep forest of this land and our forces could easily see our movements. The surprise to our enemy was the range of our rifles. Neither the French nor the Spanish used them. But here, it will not be like that because of the Kentucky men. And I daresay all the US militia use the rifle. We do have to think that out."

More questions were asked and answered and more stories told as they ate. Then, at about 8:00 pm General Brock stopped the discussion by handing out cigars. "I have small announcement to make, well, three or four."

Though the room was silent, the officers all looked at Ashford with a smile.

General Brock noticed all eyes were on Ashford and paused a second before he continued, "Number one, I shall be taking your sergeant. We have decided to make more units like yours and we believe he can do the job. Do you agree?"

"I do. He is one of the most capable and I think he should even be given a promotion. But, before he goes I would wish him to help me select a replacement from amongst the men. And I will expect him to continue the 'Green tea' ceremony.

"Green Tea?" asked General Vincent.

"Oh, I'm sorry I didn't mention that earlier." Ashford then told him of the ceremony made with Thompson and the one at the little fort. He explained it had become part of his solidifying a family of fighters. They all laughed.

"Second, you will be assigned to my command and you will command them under my command. We will have to arrange that as soon as possible and to show the regulars what it's all about."

"Thank you, sir, I am honored."

"Third, it is a lieutenant who usually commands a platoon of twenty-four men, not a Major. And since Sergeant Wilson will command and train more of them I will promote him to that rank."

"I agree, sir."

"Last, you, as a Major, will command a full company of at least seventy men which will contain your chosen men and you will accompany them in all their tasks. You will, of course direct the regulars under your command and, in the process, educate them as to the methods of the 'Chosen Men' enough that they know what it's all about."

The General took a sip of Port.

"Your command will always be close at hand to me. Later the new rifles will be assigned to these gentlemen." He waved his hand to sweep in all the other officers. "You may be asked to assist in that regard. Also, for the new riflemen, I propose to have them dress in green capots, exactly like the ones you have. I have ordered an additional two sets of twenty-four. I do so because the formal uniforms may take too much time to acquire. I have also ordered the same number of 1806 rifles and believe they are on route to us now. They should arrive in less than ten days. In the meantime, I plan to have your group move around throughout Upper Canada, from fort to fort in order that each command becomes accustomed to your capots. That will help prevent unwanted fire on the riflemen. I have done this with our own resources and wish to keep this quiet for the present."

General Brock rose, as did all the others, and concluded by saying, "Major, take three days off. You need it. We will meet from time to time. For the moment you will be billeted where you now are, but we will arrange for a place with your new command in the next days."

The next few months were somewhat boring but busy for Ashford. He felt he didn't belong in so large an organization as he was accustomed to the smaller groups that filled his life in war the past several years. But, he was a soldier and a soldier obeys orders. He had to admit, though, that working with the larger group was valuable because he was able to set up a system that might protect his companions from the horror of being fired upon by his own army.

In the process he had two occasions to meet and discuss his work with General Prevost, Governor General of Upper and Lower Canada; this caused Ashford considerable worry for he concluded Prevost was incompetent as a soldier, too cautious, too protective of his own status as Governor General, and completely without imagination.

He also felt General Brock thought the same and he hoped to hell he would not fall under the man's direct command. General Brock and his officers were quite opposite Prevost and not stuck with useless insistence to stupid dress codes as was the Governor General. An example of that was the governor's insistence that the troops wear the neck stock: a stiff black collar that forced the chin up and left little room for movement downward. It was the most useless piece of any soldier's uniform.

Ashford did, however, take the time to prepare a detailed report, sealed in its own package, for Sir Percival Worthington. Care was taken not to mention Gabriel Franchere, the French-Canadian working for Jacob Astor, though he knew Percival had contact with the man. Little detail about the killing of the Kentucky men was given, but one of the letters, the one containing the name 'Jacob Foster' was included in the package. Ashford knew Percival would realize its significance.

Ashford informed General Brock of the contents, asked him to read it, then had it sealed by the General and placed for immediate delivery to London.

It was late May, 1812 before Ashford was able to arrange for canoe training. To that end, he acquired three North canoes and with the great assistance of his Seneca brothers, began training. For the men, it was a good deal of silly fun. They started with a fear of tipping over and drowning, but overcame that when they learned how stable the big canoe was compared to the smaller two-person boat. It was the paddle that bought out most of the laughter, cusses, and friendly scraps when one man would accidentally-on-purpose splash another. That usually broke out a water fight that would last until Ignace would shout out some insult telling them to behave like adults.

They progressed well, but the banging of paddles on the gunnels proved to be a problem. Each time it happened Ignace or Charles would shout out, "Quiet, you old women! Too much noise!" There were, of course, other less polite words. But the banging continued because the men were not holding their paddle out and more vertical to the water. That caused them to strike the gunnels with the shaft of the paddle.

Finally, Ignace realized he needed to demonstrate how bad it was. He arranged for all the men, including Ashford, to stay on shore while he and Charles went paddled out, almost a mile, and banged their paddles on the gunnels just as the men were doing. Ashford stayed on shore and explained, "The canoe is like a huge drum. Every time you even touch the gunnel with your paddle, the noise carries over the water for a long, loud way. It's even worse in cold weather. Do that too often and we may all pay for in it blood. To avoid this, you need to lean out a bit and place the paddle into the water like this." He demonstrated the movement.

The banging and noise ceased and soon the men were competent paddlers, at least in calm waters.

News from the Secretary of Colonial Affairs
June 12, 1812

Ashford was settled into his new quarters at Fort York. During his meetings with General Brock, which sometimes included the other three officers, Ashford spoke frankly about the use of the 'Chosen Men'. He was pleased at the news that his group would be expanded to seventy men, though somewhat dismayed that they would be spread around between generals. He felt that seventy men could be of great help in the conventional 'standing the line' and needed some way to prevent that, or at least to find a way to have all the men under his direct command. He also felt that having Ignace and Charles at close contact with the men would be the best way to make the whole group more cohesive. The two Iroquois were the added ingredient that made the 'Chosen Men' of the Canadas more unique and more suitable to the kind of war that would be fought in Upper and Lower Canada.

For now, though, he had to give way to General Brock's approach that he would prefer keeping the first 'graduates' as the core of his men and to have Ignace and Charles play a large role in leading them. The two were trusted men, took orders very well and were respected by the twenty-four graduates. They would all follow the Iroquois anywhere and the men knew his brothers were exceptional scouts and understood the concept of 'standing the line' almost as well as the men who experienced it.

"Sir, I would like to keep them as leaders, sergeants, if you will, so they can lead, guide and encourage the men. I propose, once we have trained the additional complement to seventy, to have them train in a maneuver that would involve standing the line. I would then have the graduates divided into three groups of twenty-four. Two groups would be led by Ignace and Charles. I'll explain why in a moment, and the other by me. The Iroquois would take positions nearer the oncoming force, hidden and placed there by me and Ignace and Charles. Their principle job would be to ensure no enemy sharpshooters enter our field of battle or the periphery of it. These men are experts at hiding and silently disposing of the enemy, but even better at discovering any infiltration of sharpshooters on the periphery of battle. Once they are satisfied that the sharpshooters are dealt with, they can commence shooting at any advancing enemy troops."

Ashford didn't want to plead, but he felt he had to stress the matter, "The third group would be led by me. All groups would be interchangeable as we all act and do the same. Each group would be independent, yet part of the whole force at any given battle. I ask that we use them in that manner."

'Major, I agree completely. That's what your group is all about. In fact, I have arranged for the two Iroquois to be paid a salary equal to that of a Sergeant, starting today."

"Thank you, sir. I will inform them. I have some other thoughts on how to deploy my men, in the line, if need be," Ashford replied.

"I might also say that taking steps for the possibility that the 'Chosen Men' may have to stand the line is a good idea. The process will also train the regulars and the artillery on how to be aware of their movements."

"Thank you, sir."

"Please, go ahead. One of the things any commander must do is never stop learning." General Brock was just that kind of man. He knew it was dangerous to assume he knew everything he needed to know.

"Sir, do you have some paper and a pen, or better still a pencil, I can use for diagrams?"

General Brock rose, pulled several pieces of paper from the shelf behind him, picked a pencil from the brass cup on his desk and placed it before Ashford.

"As I have said before, my riflemen are not really meant to stand the line, but there are times when that may be necessary. In fact, there are times when it will be a good maneuver at the start of a battle. Here's what may be a good move."

Ashford used the pencil and paper to draw his thoughts explaining the use of greater long-distance accuracy of the riflemen. The idea was simple, but, he thought, ingenious. A group of forty-eight plus their commanders would be sent out to wherever commanded of them; even hours before a battle, even the night before, and would be placed to act as skirmishers in the usual manner of the 'Chosen Men'. The remaining twenty-four would stand their own line at the very beginning of the advance of enemy troops. Perhaps the occasion may need more men to stand the line at this moment in time ..." He paused for General Brock's reaction.

"It seems to me that may even depend upon the width of the attacking column or whether to 'Chosen Men' should be used at an earlier stage. But I follow you, please continue," offered General Brock.

"They would form up in the line, as normal line troops do, in two ranks to form a small 'line'. At 200 yards they would fire their first volley, not as accurate as 150 but enough to strike the many of the first lines or two of the enemy column. That will come as complete surprise."

Ashford drew in the place where the 'Chosen Men' line would be. "Then, a second volley at about 150 yards. That depends upon how fast the enemy approaches but I think they will slow a good deal after the first volley. At that range, barring any serious problem with smoke, they can let loose the third volley. At that range I would say each man would kill or severely wound his target. Perhaps we could practice that maneuver, in all kinds of wind situations, so it should be brought to play very quickly. Then, when the volleys of Brown Bessies are of greater value, the sharpshooters would be moved off the field to take skirmishing positions as directed by the commander."

"I must say, Major, this is quite possibly brilliant. We will begin practicing as soon as possible. I would add that having you in this command is likely to be of great benefit." General Brock paused.

"Now Major, another matter. I have here a letter from someone who is very important, Lord Worthington, no less and you are directed to read, and then destroy it. I have already read it and no one else has or will." He handed the letter to Ashford:

For Major General Brock,   London, April 10. 1812

Major Ashford

We have received your report on events of his voyage with Mr. Thompson and we thank you for same. It was enlightening to say the least, as it confirmed information received from other sources. We have learned the name and some facts about the identity of the person who directed the attempts to block Mr. Thompson's efforts. He is identified by us as one Major Ronald Foster, commander of the 17th Kentucky Dragoons. We note that his brother, Jacob Foster, was one of the three men assigned to deal with Mr. Thompson. The Major, we are told, is a vain man with a mid-level education and one who struts around like a peacock. His habit is to wear a black cocked hat with a large white feather plume. You might want to note this because our sources indicate he and his dragoons will join Major General Harrison in an attempt to 'solve the native problem' in the northwest of America. His dragoons number about sixty men, all reasonably well-equipped.

War is imminent. We have no present information on how or where it will begin, but suspect Upper Canada to be the first phase of the North America portion. We shall communicate any further information directly to General Brock with the suggestion that he share same with Major Ashford.

We would add that we are most pleased that both of you have been able to join forces in this problem and wish each of you the best of success. Destroy this document.

> Sir Percival Worthington
> Secretary of Colonial Affairs
> To His Majesty King George III

General Brock smiled as he watched Ashford read the letter and quietly said, "A very interesting life you have, Major. I envy you. We shall work together on this matter as well as on your intriguing thoughts on the use of the 'Chosen Men'."

Ashford turned to look at the fireplace. It had a small flame burning quietly and steadily at the center." May I, general?"

"By all means, Major."

Ashford rose and placed the paper into the flame and watched as a black spiral of smoke rose from the flame and crawled up the chimney.

The "Hawk Congress"
Washington
July 1812

The United States of America had good reason to declare war on Great Britain. She was embroiled in a costly war with France; costly in both money and loss of men. In order to control the shipment of arms, materials, even food-stuffs to France, Britain used its powerful navy to control the seas and in the process, went too far, even arrogantly too far. It began to intercept American ships, raid them, and take away anything that might assist the French in making war. Part of that arrogance was the kidnapping of American sailors, mainly sailors who had deserted from the British Navy, and 'pressing' them into the Royal Navy. The Americans took the position that the British sailors, the deserters, who were pressed back into the navy, were American citizens.

Although some of those men were wrongly pressed, most were real deserters who, upon payment of a fee, were given instant citizenship in the United States. At that time, it took five years residency into the USA to become a citizen but, for a few dollars, these men were instantly declared American citizens. The Americans continued to protest and Britain continued the practice, even after a threat of war from by the US.

On March 4, 1811, what became known as 'The Hawk Congress' met in Washington and indicated they would support a war against Britain, and on June 18, 1812 the United States declared war.

It was debated, yes. But it was done in secret and there were *other* motives in the minds of many of the newly-elected Members of Congress to declare war. Various speeches made in favour of war demonstrated their position, speeches made in large part from the elected congressmen of Virginia and Kentucky with words such as:

> "We can take *the whole of North America* because God has given us the power."

> "Taking Canada would be a *mere march.*"

> "The conquest of Canada is part of America's *destiny*."

One of the most vociferous on the matter of war with England was Henry Clay, Speaker of the House of Representatives of the United States Congress. In a lengthy letter titled, "Letter in Support of the War," he argued there was no danger in going to war with Britain because she was embroiled in a costly war with France. He knew that Upper and Lower Canada had no armed force large enough to challenge the United States.

During the same debate, another Congressman, John Calhoun of South Carolina, stated that, within four weeks of the start of a march into Upper Canada, the United States would have all of it and most of Lower Canada. The young Congressmen, all eager to make their mark in life and all convinced that the people of Upper Canada would cheer them as America took over Canada, pressed for the vote.

The *Louisiana Purchase* led the Americans to think in terms of further expansion. France was at war with Britain. Canada was left for the picking and when the US began its invasion, all were convinced that the people of Upper and Lower Canada would welcome them as providing freedom from British oppression.

The US had a meagre standing army of about 7000 'regulars' and several state and local militias. The army was ill-equipped, under-trained and inexperienced. It had only few old officers who had not gone to war and none who had ever 'stood the line' in battle. The militias were even worse off. They had those greatly-feared sharpshooters but there were far too few of them. Most were just farmers or businessmen. Some militias didn't even have enough muskets to do an adequate job at any kind of battle. Without real experience, they were nothing but a crowd of men without direction. Discipline was almost non-existent. In addition, the mandates of most militias did not allow them to cross borders into another country. The result was that many refused to do so. Their job, as they saw it, was to protect, not to invade.

The British, though greatly outnumbered, were well trained and disciplined. They feared but did not shirk the walls of musket fire and the horrors of hearing and seeing the balls fly at them or of the cruelty and butchery of a bayonet attack.

They were battle-hardened, so much so that many of those who stood the line claimed they could see the musket balls coming at them. Some even claimed they saw the very ball that hit their body. Though, in Spain, Ashford was lucky not to have been hit while standing the line, he saw those musket balls coming towards him and it was terrifying.

The Battle of Fort Detroit
August 13, 1812

Fort Detroit was heavily fortified. There were strategically located hills and mounds around the fort which exposed any approaching army to withering cannon, canister, grape-shot and rifle fire.

On the 11th of July, 1812, United States General Hull led 2,500 troops across the Detroit River in an attempt to invade Canada. It went well at first as he was able to set up a temporary command post in a farm house just across the river in Upper Canada. He believed that it was a matter of marching into Canada and it would be over and done. So, instead of pressing the attack he stopped and issued a written proclamation to be distributed to the people of Upper Canada. It read, in part, as follows:

> "The standard of the Union (USA) now waves over the territory of Canada. To the peaceful and unoffending inhabitants it brings neither danger nor difficulty. I come to find friends, not to break them: I come to protect, not to injure you. I have a force that will break down all opposition, and that force is but the vanguard of one much greater ... should you take part in the approaching contest, you will be considered and treated as enemies and the horrors and calamities of war will haunt you...."

But the Canadians, with the assistance of their Indian allies, were not about to surrender and while Hull waited, the supply lines to his troops were cut off, swarms of Indians gathered to oppose him and he had no way to proceed further.

Hull's great fear of Indians was deeply imbedded in his mind. He had heard stories of them taking scalps, of the fierceness of the Indians, of how they fought at night and made sure every one of their enemy knew they had come. He knew that, if he provoked these people, the result would be horrific. He could wait no longer as he knew he would soon be cut off, without supplies and about to face the most fearsome warriors on earth. He retreated to Fort Detroit and waited.

His invasion lasted one month.

Two days after Hull's retreat back to Fort Detroit, General Isaac Brock, the new Lieutenant Governor of Upper Canada, arrived at Amherstburg, just across the river from Fort Detroit, to meet with his officers and with the Indian warrior/leader Tecumseh. Major William Ashford, invited by General Vincent, was one of the officers present. Ashford would never forget meeting the great Tecumseh and he was impressed, as were the other officers, by Tecumseh's command of the English language, the metaphors with which he spoke, and his wisdom.

"My warriors are ready. More come each day, like the spring swarms of wrens; they come to defend this land. The Americans continue to take our lands and kill our people. They are hungry for land and it is time to stop them and to make them victims of crows as they lay in the field of battle."

There was much discussion, and as it continued, Ashford's admiration of these two great men grew. At the meeting's end, General Brock announced his plans, "I have dispatches and documents taken from a ship we captured. They indicate that this General Hull is deathly afraid of your people and I mean to remind them of why. We will attack that fort across the river in three days. Major Ashford, kindly prepare your 'Chosen Men' to assist in providing covering and suppressing fire to keep the American cannons from firing upon us. We will plan that early tomorrow morning."

For the next two days General Brock, who was outnumbered two to one in troops, paraded local militia dressed in old British uniforms in view of General Hull to create the image of a very large force. He also bombarded Fort Detroit from across the river as though preparing for an attack. But his best move was a note he sent to General Hull:

> "It is far from my inclination to join in a war of extermination, but you must be aware that the numerous body of

Indians who have attached themselves to my troops will be beyond my control the moment the contest begins."

By this time, General Hull had witnessed the gathering of those most-feared of fighters, the Iroquois. He and his men saw them parading without fear, holding what looked to be scalps and apparently boasting to each other about how they took them. He heard the warriors shouting war whoops and saw their faces painted with black and red war paint.

There was no battle. General Hull was certain that he, his men, and all the civilians would be killed and scalped and left to rot in the sun. His fear was so great that he was unable to move from his quarters, much less attempt a defense. He stayed in his quarters, hidden from view, almost catatonic, unable to make any kind of decision. After two days of indecision, and having read the note from General Brock several times, Hull surrendered. More than 2100 of his troops were taken prisoner. All the stores, cannons, muskets, shot, powder, and food supplies of Fort Detroit were also taken by the British/Canadian/Indian force.

The first attempted invasion of Canada was a huge American debacle and not even a shot was fired by the people being invaded.

The Battle of Queenston Heights
Near Niagara Falls, Upper Canada
October 13, 1812

On the 8th of October, 1812, Ashford's group, now forty-eight men plus Ashford and the two Iroquois, were sent to Queenston Heights to familiarize the regular troops with his men. It was important that the regulars knew how they moved, where and how they were dressed. Their green uniforms, made to be less visible and their green capots, made for the same reason, were likely to be taken as American militia or troops. Being fired upon by his own army's cannon was what Ashford dreaded most, so he maintained the usual pattern. His men would rise at about 6:00 am, form up and go for their one hour run-walk, then return to the fort. On every such maneuver they would scout the land, become familiar with each nook and cranny, learning where to hide, if needed, and provide that knowledge to the artillerymen and other fighting men of the British Redcoats. In no time the place was accustomed to the men's routine preparations.

The morning of October 13th started as normal. His men were about to depart, the gates already open. Suddenly a heavy cannonade erupted from the United States side of the Niagara River. Ashford immediately knew an attack was imminent; he stopped the run and shouted up to the look-out.

"What's happening?"

"They're coming, sir! Crossing the river in large boats! Looks like they mean to land a little downstream, just below the hill, there!" The look-out pointed to the bottom of the hill almost directly in front of him.

Ashford had taken his men into that area almost every time they ran and knew it well. "Please advise Captain Cameron to commence and continue return bombardment. Tell him that I shall be down the hill, just over the rim, with my riflemen. Your grapeshot should go over our heads. We will slow the landing as much as we can. Go!"

"Men, find your spots and prepare to repel!" He knew the American crossing had to be done with bateaux, flat-bottomed boats that could uncomfortably hold up to thirty men, as it was the only way to transport so many men across the river. "Take positions and shoot at the man in back of the boat, the one with the long ore. He's the steersman. Take out the men in front next. Shoot any man who tries to replace them! Keep firing and keep you heads down. Grapeshot from our side will be flying above our heads!"

In minutes, they were ready.

There were many boats, so many that Ashford didn't try to count. Each was crammed with men, some of them standing, others sitting on the gunnels. Ashford was familiar with the bateau; they were flat-bottomed boats, with no keel, that needed constant adjustment by the steersman in order to keep the boat in the proper direction. Otherwise it would simply drift with the current. The 'head man' in front was the one to initiate the landing. If any of those men, especially the steersman, were out action, the boat would drift with the current and the wind and become a perfect target for deadly grapeshot that mowed down men like an invisible scythe.

Ashford's riflemen did as told. They were calm and deliberate in picking off the steersmen and the bowmen. The cannons from the fort opened up on the drifting boats with horrifying effect. Ashford and his men could see ten, twelve men get torn apart by the lead marbles as they hit. They could see men screaming, grasping at the gunnels to get back on board and being shoved back into the water by panicked men on board. He saw men drowning in terror. One or two boats made it to shore and its men were blown away by grapeshot. Entire boats were torn apart and sunk. And all the while, his men rained down precise shots at all those in the boats. Many of the bateaux began to drift without control as their steersmen were killed. Some drifted so far downstream as to make the troops they carried of little worth in the battle.

But there were just too many boats. Many made it to shore, discharged their men and turned back to get more troops. At that point it became a matter of the 'Chosen Men' trying to pick off as many men as they could, one at a time.

Far to his right, Ashford could see that some landed American troops were met by others who had apparently landed sometime in the night gathering for an assault up a farmer's path. They had to be stopped, or at least slowed down. He shouted to his men to follow him in a desperate attempt to head off the Americans. He could see them forming up into a long, snake-like column and marching in good order up the path. By then, Ashford's men were getting close to running out of cartridges and he knew they were greatly out-numbered. They had no option but to fire off two rounds to cut down as many man as possible then turn to withdraw to the fort. Each man made his shot deadly and the column began to slow down. The 'Chosen Men' now had to retreat and, as they did so, were greeted by several red-coats approaching in good order, led by Major General Isaac Brock.

General Brock knew that all he could do was slow the American advance and hope help came fast. He was out-numbered. It was a bold move on General Brock's part, one that had to be done, the only way to slow the attack.

General Brock's counter attack was both brilliant and bloody. In quick order, his men formed 'the line' and opened fire upon the approaching troops. He could see the impact of the first volley on the Americans. They faltered, then re-formed, then came on again and again. General Brock was about to be overwhelmed, but he kept up the fire on the enemy as long as he could.

Ashford learned later that General Brock heard the cannon fire and rode, alone, with Lt. Colonel John Macdonell close behind, in an effort to join the fight. He also learned that both had been killed but were able to stall the attack and make the Americans re-form.

Queenston Heights was in grave danger of being overrun.

When General Brock and Macdonell were carried from the field, all thought the battle was lost. And it would have been had it not been for General Roger Hale Sheaffe. He was more cautious than General Brock, but a great tactician. He brought many troops with 120 Iroquois warriors and attacked the right flank of the US troops in a last-ditch attempt to save Queenston Heights.

It was the presence of the Iroquois that saved the day for, when the Americans heard the whoops of the Indians, they broke and ran in complete panic. They ran back down the path in an effort to get to the boats and back to safety. But the boats they wanted to use as their escape were almost all gone and there was nothing they could do but surrender.

The battle was clearly won by the British. Five hundred Americans were killed or wounded and 900 taken prisoner; only fourteen British were killed with seventy-seven wounded. No scalps were taken.

This second attempt to invade Canada was a failure, but a close one. And Ashford's men, who were dressed in capots and thought to be mere militia, were part of a heroic stand that would make their reputation one of envy of many commanders. It would put the 'Chosen Men' into very great demand.

Ashford was proud of his men. The battle proved the value of his command and the concept behind it underpinned their tactics. But he acted without orders in a move that could end the career of any officer and he worried about that for the next few days.

A few days after the solemn burial of two great heroes, Ashford was summoned to a meeting with General Sheaffe, who welcomed Ashford with genuine respect, "Thank you for coming, Major. Please, sit."

Ashford did as asked and waited while the General offered him a cigar and lit his own. "I've asked you here for two reasons. First, I commend you on the action taken by you and your men in our recent battle. You reacted swiftly and properly, even though it might have been prudent to get orders first, and your actions were of immeasurable help in allowing our cannonade to decimate the American attack. It was, I add, a move of great brilliance. I am pleased to say this but also concerned. That is my second reason for having you here today.

"Oh, oh," thought Ashford.

"I'm not concerned about propriety of your quick action. Quite the contrary what I'm concerned about is our friend, the Governor General. He now wants your men for himself. As you have gathered, General

Prevost is a very cautious man but a very ambitious one. He revels in his desire to be famous and I fear he wants you under his direct command to heighten his own reputation. By the way, this conversation never took place, understood?"

"Yes sir. But I must say that I agree with you on your observations and will say no more."

"Good. I am about to lose a very valued officer and there's not much I can do about it except to keep trying to get you back in our house as soon as possible." Sheaffe paused and puffed on his cigar. "I have been directed to have you and your men transferred to Fort Wellington. It is near the town of Prescott, about sixty miles downstream of Kingston on the St Lawrence River. At least we are fortunate that he has not directed you farther downstream and into Lower Canada. I think because it would be too obvious if he did so. I am saddened to say you will depart, with your men, the day after tomorrow. You will go by way of bateaux and join with Colonel Pearson, at Prescott. He is more like us, not so cautious and certainly not a man who seeks glory for the sake of being famous. So you'll be in good company in that regard. I must therefore direct you to ready your men."

Ashford could do nothing but voice his assurances to General Sheaffe. "Sir, I will do my duty but at the same time look forward to re-joining you at some future date. How soon are we to leave?"

"Give it another week. We must all recover from our recent ordeal and there appears to be no great worry. Just the same, I have a great respect for Colonel Pearson, so we should get you there in reasonable time."

Sheaffe rose and reached to shake Ashford's hand. It was then that Ashford realized that the cigar in his right hand had not been lit, so he hurriedly stuffed it into his mouth and shook the General's hand, and turned to the door.

The moment he closed the door behind him Ashford softly said, *"Merde."*

Battle of Mississinewa
Southwest of Detroit, in Indiana
December 17, 1812

In mid-October, 1812, Major Roy Foster received a request from General William Henry Harrison, commander of the US Army of the Northwest, to present his Kentucky Dragoons at Franklintown (now Columbus, Ohio) for deployment on an expedition to rid the nation of the troubles caused by the Indians of the Indiana territory. Harrison was openly anti-Indian. He was convinced that the concentration of the mostly Miami Indians of the Mississinewa region were a threat to him and to the United States. Some say he was even looking to profit from such a venture by speculating in land taken from the Indians. Some say he just hated them. In any event the expedition was designed to destroy the concentration of Indians in the Mississinewa area.

Foster jumped at the chance because it fit perfectly with his own view of the Indians. He had all the men assembled and ready to go within one week. He knew that glory would present itself and that his name would become known to all of Kentucky, perhaps to all of the people of the United States of America. He and his 17th Kentucky Dragoons arrived at Franklintown on December 6th 1812.

Harrison calculated that a winter operation was the best as it would destroy the villages and food supplies of the Indians and that would result in a difficult survival mode, one where all they could do would be to survive the winter, much less help the British in the war. Harrison did not differentiate between the Iroquois nations and other Indians. He hated them all. Many of the targets were Delaware or others who had nothing to do with the British. But that did not matter to Harrison.

While at Franklintown, all militia were required to hand in their long rifles in exchange for a shorter-barreled rifle more suited for Dragoons on horseback, a pistol and a sword. Most of Foster's men just hung the sword onto the saddle as they had never used one, but the pistol, they thought, was a nice thing to have. By this time, Foster had his own beautiful sword, decorated with gold braid and gold handle, laced onto the left side of his saddle within easy reach.

Shortly after dawn on December 17th, the force crossed the Mississinewa River and the battle began with the 17th Kentucky, mounted, behind the Pittsburgh Blues, who were on foot and proceeding with good form towards the village. But as they approached the village, they noted that it was almost completely deserted. The Indians had fled. Foster, upon seeing a chance to show the value of his Dragoons, made a loud yell and motioned his men to charge. The Dragoons of the 17th galloped into the village at full haste and in the process, they trampled several members of the Pennsylvania Blues militia. One of them was killed.

The fleeing Indians responded with an attack of their own. It was an attack not so much to win the emerging battle as to give time for the retreating women and children to escape and to take as many winter provisions with them as possible. That was made evident by the fact that the Indians seemed to be concentrating their musket shots at the American horses more that at the men themselves in order to prevent the Americans from pursing the Indians.

All that was left for Campbell's group was to burn down the village and destroy the food caches.. They even killed all the Indian livestock, though they could have used the meat for harsh winter survival for themselves.

Foster's group, not even aware that they had killed one of their own allies, continued the rush to catch up with the departing villagers. It was during this charge that Foster got the chance to show his "bravery".

An Indian man showed himself, shouting at the troops across a small river. He was shouting in his own language and the troops, not knowing what he as saying, fired at him. The poor man was hit several times but refused to stop shouting. Instead, though badly wounded, he wrapped a blanket around himself, fell to his knees and looked at the Americans in bewilderment and despair. Foster, on horseback, saw this and simply dismounted, walked up to the Indian, who was now saying, in English, "Please, spare me. I am Delaware, I am Delaware. Not Iroquois!" Foster shot him in the heart and the young man fell, face-down in the grass.

Foster bent down, placed his knee on the man's back, grabbed his hair, lifted his head, and scalped him. He then rose to his feet and held the scalp high as he turned a full circle so all the troops could see. His eyes glistened with pride and glory.

In the nearby forest, three young Indian boys, about thirteen or fourteen years of age, lay concealed in the underbrush, trembling in fear, and watching as Foster took the scalp of that Indian man. They remained motionless and quiet, no whimpers, no talking, and waited. They waited in silence for dark, until they knew it was safe to move, and then rose to race for the protection of their own people. Their story would spread like wildfire throughout the Indian Nations northward, to the six Nations of the Iroquois and beyond.

Foster volunteered his men for only three months. There would be spring work to do and whatever meager living the men could scare up would have to be set in motion by early March. Although he did not realize it, his leadership and his men were not well regarded by other militia and regulars.

The loss of one of the Pittsburg Blues through the negligence of Foster was taken very hard by the "Blues" and by all other militia and regular troops. Some officers wanted Foster 'dealt with', but the higher command decided to do nothing as they *might* need the 17th Kentucky in the near future. So Foster was allowed, actually encouraged, to return to his home town of Jeffersontown and wait until needed.

Foster had no idea that most of the officers completely despised him. He returned thinking he was a national hero and unaware that most of the superior officers thought of him as nothing but a toy soldier, a 'dandy'.

He felt more of a hero because of the reception he got when he and the men returned. Under his instructions, one man rode ahead, fast, to arrive at Jeffersontown and inform the populace that their heroes would arrive within the next two hours. The same man then rode back to join the force and, as Foster hoped, the whole town and surrounding citizens lined up the main street to welcome their heroes. It was a smashing parade! Sixty brave soldiers rode in a column of fours, with Foster at the front. In their minds, and in the minds of the people of Jeffersontown, they were great heroes. Mothers and fathers cried. Young women swooned. Storekeepers and others offered gifts of beer, food, flowers, alongside gifts of home baking and many hugs and kisses. Foster was, at that moment, the happiest and proudest man in America.

And he made sure the whole county knew it. One week after his return he organized a very grand party at his estate. There he recounted many great adventures during his time at war, all fictional and straight out of his imagination, and he would become an even greater hero. Local and state politicians were invited and came to the gala and Foster made every effort to impress them with abilities in battle. He repeatedly told the politicians that his force would be ready, willing, and able when called for duty. For the next several weeks, people waved at him, thanked him, gave him free drinks or home-made pies and pointed him out to their children as he passed. Yes, he was a great hero. And he would, in the future, do more to save America!

But, as the months went by, the glow of glory seemed to fade.

By early May of 1814, Foster was yearning for more. He began to write letters to various congressmen and others stating he and his men were ready to resume the great battle and inviting them to include the 17th Kentucky Dragoons anywhere needed and as soon as possible. There were few replies but that presented no worry, for Major Ronald Roy Foster knew in his heart that he would be called back soon. America needed him.

It would be a long wait.

Battle of Ogdensburg, New York
November 22, 1812 - February 22, 1813

A shford and his men arrived at Fort Wellington, near Prescott, Upper Canada, on November 22, 1812. He found the quarters suitable as they were newly-constructed, and judged Colonel Pearson to be a competent commander. It took no time for Ashford and his men to fall into a routine that included the morning run-walk.

Many of the Fort Wellington's force were militia, not comprised of regulars. But they seemed to be reasonably well-trained. Colonel Pearson, commander of the fort, began by explaining the situation, pointing to the fort across the river, "As you know, that fort across the river is occupied by American forces. Some of which are riflemen. I suppose that is why Governor General Prevost has arranged for you to occupy our location. By the way, I have read some accounts of the action taken by your command. I am impressed and eager to learn more about your men. For the moment, we will look at our situation here and then plan how best to use your men."

Prescott and Fort Wellington were directly across the river from the American garrison of Ogdensburg, commanded by Major Benjamin Forsyth, a man who, for the past months, was getting under Pearson's skin. Forsyth kept making incursions across the river, stealing supplies and generally harassing the local population. There were, as yet, no serious injuries. But matters were escalating. Forsythe's troops were taking to looting.

But there was a larger problem. Prescott/Ogdensburg was a strategic point. To the southeast of Ogdensburg was Sackett's Harbour, an important ship-building place where various warships were under construction.

If the Americans kept control of this point of the river, they would have a stranglehold on the supply lines to the Great Lakes.

No matter how many times Pearson suggested to Prevost that Ogdensburg should be taken, Prevost refused. His stance was always defensive and he did not seem to realize that sometimes a bit of offence is the best way to set up a good defense.

Pearson, nonetheless, started taking 'measures' to prevent the Americans from taking Prescott and thereby controlling the St Lawrence River. He began doing 'maneuvers' on the river ice which he planned to continue through the winter. You never know, he thought.

Each time Pearson commanded those maneuvers, he did something new, something small and not easily noticed. One day, he would come closer to the US side of the river. On another day, he would drag an eight-pound canon onto the ice and even get it stuck in the snow so the Americans would stand on their ramparts and laugh at him.

Pearson kept requesting authority to make the attack. The river was frozen fast. It was a perfect time to go. Prevost kept refusing to give him authority. He even went further than just a refusal. On February 21, 1813, Prevost arrived at Fort Wellington on his way to Kingston and took Pearson with him to Kingston. He then left written orders that Major MacDonnell, who was second in command, was not to attempt an attack unless the Americans had substantially reduced the size of their force and there was an excellent chance of victory.

Prevost went so far as to leave written orders to Macdonell,

> "... I remind you that no action will be taken to dislodge the Americans from Detroit. You will make demonstrations and take such action only if there is very strong evidence that the Americans have greatly reduced their numbers and I see no reason for them do so or for our forces to change the status quo."

The US forces consisted of 500 regular troops, about sixty of them riflemen, which were a formidable barrier, especially in the eyes of the US commander, because the British troops had no riflemen and he was unaware of the 'Chosen Men'.

On the 22nd of February, with Prevost and Pearson well gone, MacDonnell began the usual demonstration; only this time some of the men, Ashford's men, were wearing snowshoes. That was noticed by the look-out who immediately pointed out the fact to his Major in command.

"What of it?" replied the American commander? "They're just practicing and don't know what the hell they're doing. Just keep watch on them."

It was then pointed out that the men with snowshoes were headed for the gun battery located on the east side of town. Forsyth suddenly realized it was an attack and, half in panic, ordered his men to make ready to repel.

MacDonnell's attack was divided into two columns; one on the left, to attack the battery of cannons directly, and another on the right, to attack the old French fort just west of the town. That force was to cut off any attempt to retreat. Such retreat would occur on the British right and would likely take a course away from the river and the fort toward Sacket's Harbor.

The right column had no snowshoes and were seriously bogged down by heavy snow drifts on the American side, but Ashford's column, on the left, was able to get quite close to the fort before the Americans woke up and began a heavy cannonade of grape-shot in their direction. The first salvo went mostly over the heads of Ashford's men. By the time the Americans re-loaded their guns, the second salvo did little damage as the steep downward pitch of the guns was not suitable for grapeshot. Meanwhile, the right column became bogged down in snow over their knees with its cannons solidly stuck in the deep snow. Then it came under fire from the old French fort, barley used, to the southwest of town. The column had to make a temporary withdrawal.

On snowshoes Ashford's men were able to almost surround the left battery. After several of the US artillerymen there were shot, the others broke and ran. Ashford's group raced through the town, silencing musket shots coming from the second story windows where some American troops were hidden and in only one hour were able to secure a surrender of the whole area. It was a small battle but an important one.

It brought complete control of the St Lawrence River to the British. US forces never did re-occupy the fort. The Americans left most officers and seventy men behind in the fort, all of whom were taken prisoner. Most of the US force retreated to Sackets Harbor. The British force burned some ships under construction and took most of the useful stores, cannons, and powder back to the Canadian side of the river.

Ashford's personal action on this battle consisted of killing three artillerymen located at the gun battery. He could tell from the reaction that the Americans were completely surprised to have riflemen shoot at them.

The most amazing part of the whole operation was the fact that when Governor General Prevost heard of the successful attack, he amended his order, which previously forbade such an attack, to say he authorized it, taking credit for the victory.

Ashford was not surprised by Prevost's claim of victory, but he was saddened and could hardly wait to get back under the direct command of General Sheaffe. He didn't have to wait long. Two days later Prevost directed Ashford to return with his men to General Sheaffe's command, probably because Prevost didn't want anyone to know he amended his previous order. Ashford could do no more than stay quiet. But he secretly despised the man.

Ashford's next few months were without incident. They were even boring. He missed some important battles that were too far away, the burning of York being one of them, and he was deeply saddened by the death of the great Tecumseh at the Battle of Thames. He also missed the Battle of Chrysler's Farm, a very decisive battle won by the British and Canadians.

All he could do was to wait, wait for action and keep drilling his men.

There was, however, one very promising development. Ashford, General Sheaffe, and the Colonels practiced a maneuver Ashford suggested if the need came for the 'Chosen Men' to stand the line. No musket balls, just blanks with the normal amount of powder, were fired as it was an attempt to determine how to best use his men; how to time their actions, as the enemy line approached theirs; how and when to re-load; when to break the line and have the Redcoats take over; and how smoke would affect the maneuver.

They practiced having infantry advance the British line and timed them in comparison to the time it took for the' Chosen Men' to re-load, without a ball in the musket, and prepare for another volley. It worked out that the twenty-eight seconds it took for each re-load allowed an opposing force to advance a maximum of fifty paces. That left time for three volleys before the troops with Brown Bess muskets to ready for their volleys. To be safe, they decided Ashford's men would fire only two volleys. That would give them more time to leave the field and establish themselves in the periphery for more sharpshooting and more time for the Redcoats to take over. It also gave time for the smoke to help disguise their movement as a panicked retreat while the Redcoats formed their line.

Smoke was always something to keep in mind. If the wind was calm, it was difficult for Ashford's men to properly target the individual enemy troops. Real sharpshooting required good visibility. So the maneuver could be used only then wind conditions were such that, while re-loading, the smoke would move enough to allow a good view of the enemy. A gentle cross wind was ideal.

They also practiced the maneuver of sending his men to new locations and continue the act of picking off the enemy. That was done so the rest of the force knew where the 'Chosen Men' were at all times. Cannon fire from their own army was the main horror to Ashford and his men, especially if it involved grapeshot because grapeshot came at them in huge terrible blasts, at a much longer range than the effective range of the Brown Bess muskets.

HMS Racoon at Astoria
November 30, 1813

While the British warships, *HMS Phoebe* and *HMS Cherub*, were searching for the *USS Essex*, *HMS Racoon*, a British eighteen-gun schooner, preceded to the mouth of the Columbia River. Her orders were to take the fort at Astoria or destroy it. The fort was more than 6000 miles from Valparaiso, Chile and she arrived at Astoria on November 30, 1813. Captain Black, of the *Racoon*, was able to anchor within the bay and then take a longboat up the river to the fort. His hope was to convince the inhabitants to surrender the fort and take it as a prize. But, when he got there, he was confronted by two surprises. First, a Union Jack was fluttering on the fort's flagpole. Second, the 'fort' was really nothing but a poorly-constructed palisade of hastily-cut logs and a house. He commented on it by saying he could level it with a four-pound gun in two hours. With one of his eighteen-pound cannons on the *Racoon*, it would have taken half an hour to make matchsticks out every log and board. He learned that in late October some Northwest fur traders came to Astoria and informed those at the fort that British ships were on their way to blast the fort to kingdom-come.

That meant Thompson's suggestion, made in his letter of June 18, 1811, had its effect. There was a good chance the Columbia would be controlled by the North West Company, even if Thompson arrived there late. The North West Company, taking advantage of the situation, purchased the fort and all contents from the Astorians at one-third its value.

Unfortunately, that left Captain Black of the *Racoon* with no prize to take and even if he did, it wasn't worth much.

Black decided there should be a ceremony to formally proclaim this place the property of His Majesty, King George III. So, accompanied with the beating of a drum, he broke a bottle of Madeira on the flag pole, pulled down the old flag, and replaced it with a new, fresh and shining Union Jack.

Then he left.

The Battle of Valparaiso, Chile[6]
February 9 - March 28, 1814

B y 1800 a system of rules and conventions had developed regarding the taking of vessels as prizes of war. Any nation at war with another nation could take the enemy's ship, whether military or merchantman, by capturing it and claiming it as a 'Prize'. The prize would be shared, half to the Admiralty and half to the crew of the ship taking the prize. Most often captured military vessels were just re-fitted, re-named, and placed into the service of the nation that captured it. Merchant ships were generally auctioned off with the nation whose vessel it was given the opportunity to bid in its sale.

There were some established rules regarding the taking of prizes into the ports of nations who declared themselves neutral when war broke out between other nations. Those rules included the following:

1. No warship could bring more than three prizes (ships) into a neutral nation's port at any one time.
2. The neutral port was not to be used as a place to convert non-military prizes into military vessels.
3. Neutral ports were not to be used as a haven or a place from which to engage in military action with a belligerent nation.
4. If two belligerent nations should enter the port of a neutral nation, both would be treated with respect and be allowed to replenish food

---

6 A detailed blow by blow account of this battle can be found in the Master's Thesis of Kenneth M Hillyard titled "Diplomacy, Neutrality and the Naval Engagement of Valparaiso, Chile, 28 March, 1814.

supplies in that port. It was to be done in twenty-four hours unless there were extenuating circumstances that required more time.

5. If two belligerents were in the port, the one entering the port first would be allowed the first to leave and the other vessel would wait twenty-four hours before leaving the port.

In June 20, 1812, just days after the United States declared war on Britain, the *USS Essex* was sent into the Atlantic to harass British shipping and to take British merchant ships as prizes. The *Essex* was rated at thirty-six guns, but mounted forty-six. The *Essex* was captained by Captain David Porter, who did well with the instructions given to him. In just two months, he took ten British merchant ships as prizes. That, of course, infuriated the British. Plans were made to deal with him. The British Navy was ordered to find and take or destroy *USS Essex*.

In the meantime, the US navy decided to have the *Essex* re-fitted with carronades, a short-barreled cannon used mainly to shoot grapeshot and with a much shorter range than her eighteen-pound long guns. Porter knew that would place his ship at the mercy of British ships equipped with longer range 'long guns'. He complained, to no avail.

In January, 1813, The *Essex* was ordered to the Pacific Ocean and there harass British merchantmen as much as possible. Porter did a good job of it and eventually took a whaler, the *Atlantic*, flying the flag of England. He took that vessel to the port of Tumbes, Peru, a neutral nation, and had the whaler converted to a twenty-gun sloop which he named *Essex Junior*. This amounted to a breach of convention as no effort was made to allow the British, or any other nation, to bid on the ship.

The British had been following the *Essex* for months and soon learned that Porter was in the Pacific Ocean, had claimed the *Atlantic* as a prize, and had her re-fitted in a neutral port. Two Royal Navy ships were assigned to take or destroy the *USS Essex*. Those two British ships were the *HMS Phoebe*, a thirty-six-gun frigate, and the *HMS Cherub*, an eighteen-gun sloop. A third ship, another eighteen-gun sloop the, *HMS Racoon*, was to meet the other two at Rio. Her job was to proceed further up the Pacific to Astoria, on the mouth of the Columbia River. She was to take or destroy the small fort set up there by John Jacob Astor. Her orders also included instruction to destroy anything American.

War was about to come to the very place that Thompson and Ashford had been almost two years earlier.

United States Captain David Porter was a capable seaman, brimming with confidence. So far, he challenged only unarmed merchantmen. Now, he felt he had to make his mark by engaging and destroying a British *warship*. He had to prove he was the best. He wanted to do something "splendid", something that would solidify his status as a great Captain. And what better a way to do it than to take on the two British warships he knew were sent to capture him.

Porter was not without his own connections. US spies and diplomats were located throughout the southern hemisphere where the influence of the United States was growing. As a result, Captain Porter was able to obtain information, influence weak governments and obtain valuable assistance from them. The government of Chile was one such government. Porter received permission to sell his prizes in the port of Valparaiso, Chile. He was able to persuade the government to ignore rules regarding prizes of naval warfare.

Porter knew the British were coming and knew that the best place for the battle would be near Valparaiso, Chile. There were two reasons for his belief. Firstly, American diplomats had the government of Chile wrapped around their little fingers. Chile had just gone through a revolution. She was a country in despair and disarray. She was a country that could easily be manipulated. She was, temporarily, under the great influence of the United States and Porter had that nation under his thumb. The second reason was that Valparaiso was the a place where Porter could abuse convention and use the port as a base from which to conduct war.

Porter continued taking British whalers as prizes in the Pacific. He took twelve in total, including the whaler, *Atlantic,* the only one of the twelve ships that was and sold under the convention, the one where the United States was the only prospective purchaser, the one that was converted to an eighteen-gun warship and renamed *USS Essex Junior*.

The British frigate *HMS Phoebe*, captained by James Hillyar, was ranked at thirty-nine guns, but fitted with forty-six, most of them eighteen-pounder long guns, a feature that would prove important in the days to come. Hillyar was not aware that Porter had taken and re-fitted the *Atlantic*.

Porter arrived at Valparaiso, with *Essex* and *Essex Junior*, on February 2, 1814. He anchored *Essex* and instructed *Junior* to cruise outside the port to intercept any British merchantmen and to watch for any British ships of war. He also anchored three prizes, all of them British whalers, within the port of Valparaiso. One of those prizes was named *Hector*.

Royal Navy Captain Hillyar, with *Phoebe* and *Cherub*, arrived at Valparaiso on February 8th 1814. He too had his secondary ship, *Cherub*, stay outside the port to patrol international waters. In a gentlemanly show of mutual respect, the two captains agreed to meet aboard the *Essex*. That is when Hillyar noted that Porter's vessel was equipped mostly with carronade, guns vastly shorter in range that those of *Phoebe* and *Cherub*.

At this time in history, the waters within cannon shot of a sovereign nation were that nation's waters, beyond that were international waters. If Chile was neutral, then the waters within cannon shot of her shores were neutral. It was contrary to convention for two belligerent nations to wage war within the distance of cannon shot of a neutral nation.

Following the convention, Hillyar did not dally in Valparaiso because he knew Porter had the right to leave first and, if he did, Hillyar's ships could not pursue the American for twenty-four hours. Porter would likely escape. Hillyar re-provisioned and departed the port to set up a blockade the American ships.

On 25 February, Porter made his first move. He towed the *Hector* into the middle of the harbor and set fire to her. At the very least, Porter should have put up the ship for sale. It was, after all, still not his property. Hillyar had no knowledge of this until he received a letter, signed by six merchants of Valparaiso advising Hillyar of what happened. They had met with the Governor to complain and demand that Porter be forced to depart Valparaiso. The Governor waffled for a day or two but eventually ordered Captain Porter's ships to leave. He advised Hillyar that he asked Porter to depart and that Porter no longer had the protection of a neutral port.

Porter stayed.

Some days later, with his ships still in port, Porter attempted to make a *night attack* on *HMS Phoebe*. He manned his long-boats for the purpose of boarding *Phoebe*. But, when his armed boats pulled close to the *Phoebe*, Porter could hear the men aboard talking and realized Phoebe's crew was actually ready for them. The attempt to attack the ship was given up and all the men returned to Porter's ship. This was another act which broke neutrality rules as Porter used neutral waters from which to conduct war. Porter did not make an entry in the ship's log about this attempted night attack. But a midshipman on board *Essex*, David Farragut, later wrote about it. Farragut would later become the first Admiral of the United States Navy.

Porter had other tricks up his sleeve. He even tried to entice *Phoebe* away by setting up a phony attempt to escape the blockade by night. He sent *Essex Junior* out in the dead of night, with a light showing to entice Hillyar to follow. That would allow Porter to sneak away without a battle. The ploy didn't work. Porter had to come out and fight.

He knew Hillyar would attempt to rake *Essex*. Raking an enemy ship is the most devastating and horrific attack one can make. Using this method of attack, Hillyar intended to have *Phoebe* pass by *Essex*, perpendicular to *Essex's* stern. *Cherub* would do the same at *Essex's* bow. Raking would send cannon balls down almost the entire length of an enemy ship. They would slam into wood, chains, and stacks of cannon balls. The large, heavy cannon balls would cut sailors in half, blow away their arms and legs, and splatter shrapnel and body parts throughout the ship.

But, in a brilliant show of seamanship, Porter was able to set his vessel into the proper wind that would not allow either of the two British vessels to bring cannons to bear on his stern or bow. *Phoebe* was able to fire only three shots and *Cherub* could not get even one shot at the enemy. All the while, Porter fired at both British ships with the only long guns he had. The night before Porter had moved his long guns to the bow and stern of his ship just for that purpose.

Hillyar's vessel took moderate damage to her rigging, as did *Cherub*. But the battle was far from over. Hillyar knew that there were no long guns available to Porter that could be used in a conventional side-by-side attack. He also knew that his own long guns had much greater range than the carronades fitted to *Essex*. The battle would be an uneven, relentless, and bloody pounding at *Essex* until she surrendered.

It took two and a half hours before *Essex* struck her colours and it was over. But the cost was grave. *Essex* suffered fifty-eight killed, sixty-nine wounded, thirty-nine of them severely. The ship's compliment was 250 souls. *Phoebe* suffered four dead, seven wounded. *Cherub* suffered one dead, three wounded.

Essex Junior returned from her attempt to lure the British away several hours later. She surrendered and was disarmed by Hillyar.

Hillyar then allowed *Essex Junior* to return to US soil, with all sailors but *Essex*, a military ship, was taken as a prize and sailed to England. She was repaired, re-named and served as a British troop ship for the next twenty years.

The Call to Arms
Jeffersontown, Kentucky
May 22, 1814

Major Ronald Roy Foster, commander of the 17th Kentucky Dragoons, was near despondency. He had heard nothing from the politicians and friends for too long. He was beginning to slide into depression. His life, he thought, was in ruin, even though his crops were excellent and his finances very good. He began drinking too much and knew his career as a military commander was fading fast. Little wonder that his heart thumped wildly as he opened an official-looking document from the war department.

It was what he hoped for all these past months.

He was requested to prepare his sixty Dragoons for insertion into the war. The document was short and to the point. There no mention of the greatness of his force or his leadership, no mention of what, exactly, he was to do, only a request that he make his men ready and report to Washington for instructions. Of course, he was to bring as many of his men as he could muster.

"Washington, boys! Washington!" he said to the men who gathered at his estate four days later. "We've been asked to go to Washington!"

The men, fifty-four of them, let out a great cheer. Each individually shook Foster's hand and hurried home to make preparations.

What Foster didn't know was that considerable pressure was being placed on the war department to include his men, though many top officers did not want him or his men anywhere near a major battle. Kentucky was providing by far the most men for the war effort, more than any other state so, for political reasons, Foster's men were included. Nor did Foster know that he and his men would be placed in a safe situation where there would be no military action and little harm could come from such an undisciplined mob as the 17th Kentucky.

On June 1st, 1814, Foster and fifty-four men rode out of Jeffersontown in a column of fours with fife and drums announcing their greatness to the crowd of more than two hundred people cheering, as their husbands and brothers passed.

"What a great day. What glory is ahead. To Washington," thought Foster as he led the column past the town hall.

Napoleon Abdicates
11 April, 1814

After attempting to invade Russia and taking a beating from both the Russian forces and the Russian weather in 1812, the French were restless. Napoleon Bonaparte, Emperor of France, soon to be Emperor of all Europe, had become too autocratic and unstable. He was forced, by the French people, to abdicate his throne on April 11, 1814. He was done, at least for now.

Britain had many troops located throughout Europe but, rather than sending them home, King George sent many of them directly to the Canadas. He now had the means to properly fight the American attempts at invasion. Shiploads of troops were sent Nova Scotia. It would take some time before most of them reached the Canadas but they would be welcomed as they supplied more resources to fight off the Americans.

Battle of Lundy's Lane
Niagara Falls, Upper Canada
July 25, 1814

Lt. Colonel Vincent of His Majesty's army at the Niagara region, whom Ashford knew and respected, received his promotion to Major General and was transferred to Kingston. Before leaving however, he informed his replacement, Major General Riall, of Ashford's ideas on the use of the 'Chosen Men' in standing the line. Riall, in turn met with Ashford to learn more. The two of them got along very well as Riall understood the idea and the kind of work and value they had as skirmishers in battle. He also understood why the 'Chosen Men' seldom stood the line.

On July 23, 1814, Ashford and Riall rode the portage road from the north near Lundy's Lane. The lane joins the road from the west and is boarded by forest on the east and west sides of the road. To the south is a large open area stretching southward to the Chippewa River. Near this spot the Niagara River forms the border between the US and Upper Canada and, about one mile north of the falls in Upper Canada, there is a road running north along the river. It is the portage road used by fur traders to by-pass the horrendous falls and the rapids below them.

"The reason I have invited you on this scouting trip is to learn how to use your men in what I believe will be a very difficult battle. Two days ago, at Chippewa just south of us, my scouts encountered what we believed was just another bunch of militia. We were wrong. I mean, really wrong. They were regulars; well-trained regulars all dressed in fine grey uniforms and they appear to have been trained in the French style, forming in columns, marching and then forming a line for close battle. I know you have fought the French in Europe and need to know how to best use your men," Riall said as they rode, slowly down the road past Lundy's Lane.

Ashford responded, "Sir, the essence of my team is to keep harassing the enemy. That makes it hard for them to keep the column in form. We shoot from a distance, from the sides, even from the rear. I have noticed that when we do it well, the enemy seems to pack together in a tighter column. The shots coming from their flanks bring down several men and they have to close the ranks. Not only that, they naturally huddle together. That brings instability to the column. And when they lose more men, they are near panic. Half the time, they can't tell where the shots are coming from and that creates more fear. I believe it greatly slows the speed and cohesion of the columns, partly because they have to keep stepping over their fallen comrades as they advance."

They rode on a few yards with Riall looking and considering Ashford's words.

"This whole area is ideal for a frontal attack by the Americans," said Riall as he pointed to the open field and swung his arm as though painting the whole area to the south. "It's an ideal place for an attack in force. Further south, beyond the Chippewa River there is more open field, perfect again for an attack. We know the Americans are planning something and I'd bet it'll be here because they must follow the portage road, more likely near it rather than on it, to get here. There will be too many men to move along that narrow trail with ditches on both sides. Further south the ditches are too deep. The field south of here is much like this and the ground well-suited for troops, horses and gun carriages. So, how would we best use your men if such an attack takes place?"

Ashford was concerned about another matter, the road they just rode. "Sir, this road could be used as a route to bring their guns to bear on us. It's a potential problem."

Riall was ahead of Ashford, and said, "I have already ordered that very large trees, as many as possible, be cut to lie across the road. You can hear them starting the cutting up there. I have ordered them to be cut with as many branches covering the road as possible. It will take days to clear the road, so I'm not too concerned about guns being brought up this far." Riall gave a wise smile as he spoke.

They stopped and dismounted about 200 yards south of Lundy's Lane. It was a great place to view a soon-to-be battle field. Both officers surveyed the site for about two minutes before Ashford spoke. As he did so he pulled out a small bundle of paper, knelt down and prepared to sketch the area. He explained as he sketched.

"The best place to put cannons is up there on the hill, just this side of the road, Lundy's Lane. It's only about twenty-five feet higher than the bottom but ideal for grapeshot because it is only a slight rise and very close to a level field. It's a long march for any column. Once the enemy gets close, before the grape, I would use exploding shells and plain cannon shot, perhaps even canister. The canister will bounce off the field on that slightly downward angle and cut apart the enemy at their knees. They will see the balls coming at them and that will be very demoralizing. But they will still advance. Walking up this slight hill will be hard, especially when they have to step over their dead and wounded.

"So, where is the best place for my men? I have seventy, plus my Iroquois brothers. Where would I use them?" He paused and drew in the forest to the east of portage road. Then he drew in the larger forest at the west side of the field including the peninsula of trees that stretched about 200 yards eastward into the field. He concluded that the encroachment of the forest would naturally force the enemy to stay to its right and avoid the forest altogether.

"Right here, where the forest encroaches onto the field from the west, there is a narrow point. The normal attack by French columns is usually forty men wide by eighteen men deep, or eighty men wide by nine deep. I would think the Americans, since they are trained by the French, will advance in the same way. Here they would go for only forty men wide because of the forest encroaching onto the field of battle. They will not march the attack into the forest as they will be unable to hold the line together. How many troops do we face?"

Riall thought a few moments, and then replied, "We believe they have trained a total of about 3000 regulars. But we don't know all of them are here. I anticipate I shall be asked to take a perfunctory attack father south, near the town of Chippewa. If so, I hope to reduce their numbers. But we must assume a full 3000 in the attack here."

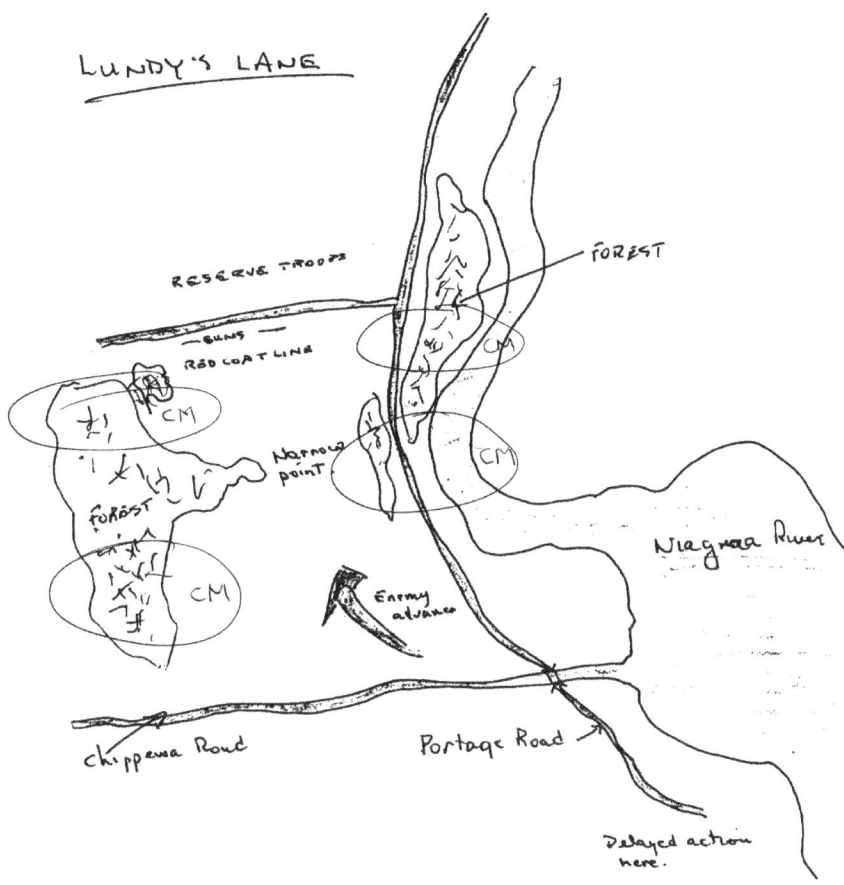

"Fine, we can use the forest. I would *not* put my own men in the forest, here, where it encroaches eastward on the field. They'll get torn apart by our own grapeshot. I would put about twenty-four of my men here, in the trees just east and west of the road. The trees you cut down will be a good place to shoot from if the enemy decides to have some men come up the road. But I don't think they will because they will be anxious to get formed up for battle on the field."

"Later, I would move more men there. He drew a circle around the letters 'CM' in the forest. I would scout out these areas as soon as possible, and then plant the men there at night, long before we think the battle will start. That way, we can devise places to give maximum protection against the grapeshot. Also, my thought is that we will set my men in such a manner that they can move up to the hill as the enemy moves. That will create the impression that there are more of us than there really are. Same on the far west side of the field. I'd put twenty-four men there" He drew a circled 'CM' in that area.

Ashford paused to review his sketch, "Right here, at this narrow point where the trees encroach from the west, is the best place to fire the grape-shot. The Americans will all be packed in there. I looks like about 600 yards from where to guns would be. I'll instruct my men to avoid those trees as the Americans approach. That way we won't be cut apart by our guns."

"That would use up the first forty-eight of my men. I have another twenty-six, including me, to use. I would place them in front of the guns, after the grape shots are done, of course, and have them stand the line, then open fire at 200 and 150 yards. That will bring down at least forty men, most of them at 150 yards. At that range my lads almost never miss."

Ashford continued, "Then, after we fire the second round, we would have them run like the devil, like they were retreating, and have the regular red coats stand the line where my men were. The Redcoats should be placed somewhere so they can re-form a line fast and it would come as a shock to the enemy when they appear near the top of the hill looking down at them, especially if we are lucky to get a minute or so of smoke to obscure their movement. Don't get me wrong. I don't mean to look cowardly, but our regulars are the best in the world at standing the line. My boys can't beat them at that because we can't load our rifles as fast as they can."

"What happens to you and your twenty-four men after they stand the line?" asked Riall.

"I propose they go half to each side of the field, then join our other men and continue harassment from the sides. Also, that could concentrate most of them close to the guns on the hill in case of a breakthrough. We can't let the Americans get to the guns. My men can assist in preserving the guns if the Americans get too close to them."

At this point, Ashford paused. He paused because he realized he had just told his superior officer that he and his own men would likely get involved in a bayonet charge. The thought tore through his mind like a thunderbolt. He could feel his hand beginning to tremble, so he hid it by tucking it behind him and waited for the General to speak.

"Major, I am indeed impressed. I now give you orders to send your men into the areas on both sides of the field as you have documented and plan for a coming attack. If I may, I will take your drawing with me to share it with General Drummond. You are also to prepare the others for their role. I believe we have little time, thirty-six hours at most.

"Thank you, sir. We'll get right at it."

That afternoon Ashford gathered his men and laid out the plan. He was careful to point out the need to stay with the enemy, keep up the shots, and then be sure to be well-placed near the top of the hill.

"Lads, gather your gear. Make ready two cartridge pouches and bring two, I said two, rifles. We may be in the field under fire for more than one day and there will not be enough time to clean the rifles if they foul. If you end up having to use the second rifle, hide the fouled one and remember where it is so we can recover it later."

"Be sure you bring your short swords as you may need them to dig a hole to hide in overnight and you may need it for silent killing, even for a possible bayonet attack. Make sure they are good and sharp. Bring two gourds of water and one-pound pemmican each. You will likely stay the night holed up along the firing positions. This looks like it will be a long and hard battle."

He could feel his hand begin to tremble and his backbone shoot a shock to his brain. He began to worry if he would make it through the next day. He suddenly felt great fear that he would let his men down. Above all, he worried he would freeze in uncertainty at a crucial time.

But he knew he had to hide those fears. He had to do what had to be done and do it without thinking. God, he hoped he would!

"Ignace, Charles, you will lead two groups of twenty-four here and here." Ashford pointed to a large sketch of the area similar to the one he provided to General Riall. "Your job will be to prevent any sharpshooters from getting into these areas and then work your way up the hill while shooting at the enemy troops. Be prepared to use the tomahawks, short swords and knives for silent killing. We've practiced that. I suggest that four men be located at the southern ends of each area for the sole purpose of guarding against any sharpshooters. Remember, know where your partner is, and protect him while he re-loads."

"The second job is to harass the enemy. It is likely they will come up in columns French style, and then form into line. You'll know when your area is clear of skirmishers and at that time you will commence shooting at the enemy columns."

Ashford went on to explain how he wanted to force the enemy to bunch together and how grapeshot would be used, how they have to use positions that offered protection from grape and cannon shot. He turned, again to the men.

"You all know how to do the Iroquois battle cry. We'll use that near the top of the hill, in the bush, if we are needed to protect the guns. Hold the yell until directed to use it. I'll be there to help on that. When Charles and Ignace, or I, make the battle cry, you will add yours and you will attack the enemy as fast as possible. Fix bayonets before you make the assault. I suggest you identify two spots to dig in. The first will be farther down the hill, to the south and the second will be up closer to the top of the hill. In other words, you will move up as the enemy moves up."

"Use signing instead of talking and follow instructions given by Charles and Ignace. They've done this sort to fighting before. You will all go tonight, when it's very dark, and set up your positions. You'll stay where you move up with the column until the war cry tells you to join the fight to protect the guns. Be ready to move fast. Spare your water if you can because it will be a long day. Understood?"

The men offered a collective "Yes."

"I will be up at the top of the hill, near the guns. Lieutenant Wilson and I will stand the line with twenty-four men and fire two rounds into the enemy, and then run here and here." He pointed to the trees on each side of the field. "We'll make it look like we are running away, but we will really be positioning ourselves to harass the enemy and then, if needed, to rescue the guns. It will be some time after that that you may hear the battle cry. By that time, you will be up the hill, close to where my twenty-four will stand the line. When that happens, you are to come to rescue the guns, not before, even if things look bad. Also, when you do, fix bayonets. Protect your partner at all times. Understood?"

Ashford and the men were familiar with standard bayonet practice where the men in line would act as partners. One, usually on the left, would often lunge with knee bent low to either stab or deflect a bayonet thrust against his partner while the other would stab high or deflect the thrust from above. The whole idea was to set up your enemy while he thinks he can stab your partner but gets the surprise of a stab from another man. The problem is that in a real melee of bayonets, it's hard to hold positions in 'a line' if the line had already collapsed. When that happens there is a tendency for each man to act on his own. Knowing this would likely be a bayonet charge in an imperfect or non-existing line, Ashford was instructing the men to act in pairs to always protect their partners.

And as he did so, he felt the confidence begin to drain out of him.

Ashford had to stress the bayonet problem. "If the line collapses, standard partner moves with the bayonet will be hard to maintain, so you'll have to take that as it comes. Just stay close to your partner and use whatever means you can to protect each other. Stab at any part of the body you can. Wound, draw blood, stab anything, but try to keep the partnership solid. Understood?"

"Yes, sir."

That eased the fear in his mind. But he still worried if he could give the order to do the charge. He had to find a way to be sure he would. His answer to that problem was Charles. He would have Charles close by, for confidence and help.

"Charles, when we find ourselves up near to top of the hill, close to the Redcoats, I want you close to me. Find me as soon as you can once we get to that point."

Ashford looked at his men again, "And remember, first shot, first kill. Take your time when aiming. Understood?"

"Yes."

"Good, make ready to go down there at about eight o'clock tonight."

Ashford could tell the men were more excited than worried. He also knew they were ready and anxious to show their worth. At 8:00 pm Ignace and Charles gathered their forty-eight men, divided into two groups of twenty-four, and silently walked , two by two and five yards apart, into the forests on both sides of the field.

On the British right flank, Ignace waited until all were assembled in the forest, then gave a hand motion, 'follow me'. He knew the men could see his hand signals in the moonlight and that they expected to see them. He waited until the hand motion was passed down the line and he was satisfied that each man had received the instruction. Then they all proceeded slowly, without talk, with their powder horns covered by socks to prevent any unwanted noise. As they did so, Ignace pointed to various places suitable for a man to position himself and each man, in turn pointed to other places for the men as they proceeded. They were careful to look back at each selected site so they could recognize it from the other direction.

At one point, Ignace made another hand signal. He turned and held up two fingers, then pointed in the direction of the sites he identified, motioning with his hands that those sites were to be the ones they would move to while the columns were advancing along the field. He then pointed his right hand further in the southerly direction and motioned with his hands 'first sites for shooting'.

When Ignace reached what he thought to be the best place to begin the action, he stopped and signaled that point to be the farthest they would go. It was, in fact, only about one hundred yards north of the place Ashford said the enemy advance would start. Then, he pointed to five men and motioned for them to follow him farther down the southward direction. The 'Chosen Men' were to be the first defense against any enemy riflemen sent as skirmishers to shoot from the forest. They practiced this technique many times and even practiced how to take two enemy men in the same manner that Ashford used at Murphy Creek on the Columbia River. If two enemy were approaching, Ignace would give two quiet 'chirps' letting his partner behind him know that two of the enemy were approaching. He would wait until the second of them was in killing range of his partner, and then move to attack the second man. At the same time, his partner would attack the first man.

The 'chirp' was a very soft 'tick' made by placing the tongue on the top of the mouth and then pulling it back to make the sound. If one pulled back too hard, it would be too loud; but softly done, it sounded like a beetle chirping with its wings. They had to be careful not to pass the 'chirp' along the line as it would sound like all the beetles were lined up, an unnatural situation.

Charles was doing the same on his side of the field. But his area was somewhat different. There was a small path, probably the first portage path used by voyageurs to get past the falls. It was a curvy path and a natural way for skirmishers to make their way northward towards the hill. Charles made sure that his men were placed so each man could see someone approaching at a curve. Charles knew that there would be a tendency for enemy skirmishers to bunch up along such a path, so he decided he would place two more men at the southernmost section. They would have to be close together in order to make a silent kill of more than three men. He then signaled for the men to take their places, with both rifles close by, and settle down for a silent night.

It stayed silent until about 2:00 am. Charles heard a voice, followed by another, about twenty yards to the south. The voices were soft spoken and he could not tell what was said. Very gently, he set down his long Kentucky rifle, drew out his tomahawk and waited until a few moments when he saw a man bending low beneath a tree branch as he crept towards Charles. The man wore a grey jacket. Charles judged that the man would pass close to him, about two yards, to follow the less obstructed course, but he could not see the other man, so he waited. The second man appeared in the darkness as his grey jacket reflected more of the low light than Charles' forest green capot.

He waited, but gave a soft double 'chirp' as his notice to his own man, a few yards in the direction of travel of the lead soldier. Ashford told Charles that the French did not use skirmishers, so it was reasonable to assume there were none. But he had to make sure. He noted that neither of the enemy carried a long rifle but an ordinary musket instead.

They were scouts, not skirmishers.

He watched both men, concentrating on the second one but glancing over to where Reilly, his partner, was. He could see Reilly, but only because he knew the man's position. Then, swiftly and silently, he rose, took one step, and buried his tomahawk into the back of the man's skull, just above the neck. He knew from experience that a strike at the lower part of the skull would kill instantly. He caught the scout before the man made any sound by dropping his musket and gently placed his victim on the ground. As he did so, he heard the sound of Reilly's short sword cut through the lead man's throat, followed by a soft shuffle as Reilly gently placed the man on the ground.

Both men waited. There might be other scouts, though they doubted that. They waited about five minutes then dragged the two corpses into the cover of trees and low shrubs where they would not be found and waited again.

Nothing.

On Ignace's side, similar events took place, with similar conclusions.

Both Ignace and Charles waited for another hour to be sure no other scouts came, then quietly retraced their steps to visit each of their men and tell them to take one-hour naps, one man in each team of two, while the other kept watch. They were all to be awake and ready at sunrise.

Ashford talked with his other twenty-four men who were to stand the line. He and Lieutenant Wilson would stay with them. No need for two rifles. Ashford only wished he could rehearse all the movements first, but time and the possibility that the enemy was watching prevented that.

In the meantime, General Riall told Major General Drummond of his instructions on the use of the 'Chosen Men'. Drummond agreed with the plan and pointed out that, when the time came, he would make as many straight-forward frontal attacks as he could. Ashford's men were to wait until, in Ashford's opinion, there was a need to send his men to keep the guns out of enemy control. But Drummond anticipated the enemy would break and run as they usually did.

Gun positions were set up and waiting. They were ready for battle and close to the chosen firing line. In the meantime, Drummond learned that the enemy was advancing near Chippewa, about three miles to the south. He would attempt to stop them or at least slow their advance there. Riall was sent to make contact and do as much damage as he could at Chippewa.

Although Riall knew the enemy had 'regulars' as part of their force, he had no real idea how many or how well they were trained, so naturally thought it was not a great problem. He was aware that Colonel Winfield Scott had been training his troops with the help of French officers but did not know that Winfield Scott trained 5000 men and that 3000 of them were massed to join this battle.

Although Riall valiantly fought at Chippewa, he was forced to withdraw and in the process, he was badly wounded and was carried off the field. The shout; "Make way for the General!" was heard as the stretcher-bearers carried him out of harm's way and directly into the American forces who readily made way and even showed where to go. Riall was taken prisoner.

Drummond was now without his capable second-in-command and the enemy was advancing, fast, towards the hill and the field mapped out by Ashford and Riall. Riall's force was able to withdraw to the hill position and prepare for the main battle. The guns were readied and in position and all waited. Ashford's and Lieutenant Wilson were ready to move and stand the line for the first two volleys as planned. It was 4:30 pm and the greatest part of the battle was about to start.

The Americans advanced up the hill in good order. They were regulars and very disciplined. The first twenty-four of Ashford's, in the side trees, opened fire, taking their time for each shot and with equal discipline taking turns shooting in pairs, one to shoot and then the other while his partner re-loaded. The result was a pause between each shot, not volleys, but with a pattern as though to say, "Wait, there's more to come." That in itself was disconcerting to the Americans because they did not anticipate there would be sharpshooters in the battle. The apparent mechanical timing with which Ashford's men fired was also a shock.

The US troops soon began to feel like fish in a barrel. The shots were incredibly accurate and their comrades were dropping like flies. That made them huddle, even crowd together. And that, in turn, made the canister and then grapeshot that rained down on them more effective.

When the guns opened first on the US columns, the smoke was horrendous. There was a cross-wind, and each volley of the guns filled the air with dense smoke that lingered several seconds, and then floated away. Each gun fired off about nine volleys and with each, after the smoke cleared somewhat, you could see the enemy faces cringe as the rain of lead marbles ripped through the ranks. On the command by Drummond the second twenty-four, plus Ashford and Wilson, assembled in their 'line'. When the smoke cleared, the enemy looked up the hill to see two ranks of British soldiers, dressed in different uniforms, looking down at them. The green uniforms were unfamiliar and naturally the Americans thought it was mere Canadian militia at the top of the hill. No Problem. They would over-run them with ease.

Then, while the columns were two hundred yards away, the Americans got their first surprise. Twelve men went down, dead, and another seven were badly wounded. But they kept on. The second volley accounted for at least twenty dead. It shook them. But still they came on.

Again, using the smoke as cover, the red-coated men formed their line and volley after volley slammed into the US force. At seventy yards only about fifty percent would hit a target. The kill/wound rate was, at first, very light. But it got worse for the enemy the closer they got to the red-coats. Firing was intense. The British were trained to re-load within twenty to twenty-two seconds, faster than any force on earth, and they kept up the fire even when smoke completely obliterated any sign of the enemy. At the centre and far right of 'the line', an officer was positioned to point the line of fire. He did so with a long spear painted white so it could be seen by the troops. There was a tendency for the men in the line to shoot too high when smoke obscured vision and this helped prevent that. All they had to do was glance at the spear and they would know that, when they fired, they would be pointing in the correct angle. Meanwhile, sergeants pushed and prodded men to close the ranks when one of them went down.

Though casualties were mounting, the Americans still came on.

Each volley was a horror. The sound of 200 muskets firing at once was terrifying. It meant a wall of lead was about to smack into the receiving troops. It meant that legs, arms, heads, thumbs, fingers, ribs, eyes and any part of their bodies would be mangled. But still, the Americans came on, stopped and fired, re-loaded and came on. These were very brave men!

By 6:30 pm, the two forces were just five yards from each other. Both formed in 'the line' and firing at each other as fast as they could. Both sides were close to breaking and near exhaustion, but the shooting continued.

Then something rarely seen happed. The British forces began an orderly withdrawal backwards, past the artillery.

The guns were now exposed. The Americans rushed in, with bayonets, and killed many of the British artillery men. The battle was now at the edge of a defeat for the British.

Ashford knew his own men would soon have to join a bayonet fight. The thought shook him.

Drummond then counter-attacked. He had to because he could not allow the Americans to get the guns and train them on his own troops. He made three such attacks in a one-hour time period, all without success, but at least the cannons were not yet completely under the control of the Americas and were not brought to bear on the British forces.

Ashford could not intervene as his men would get shot by the British as they made each counter-attack. The fighting went on until well into darkness. Bodies of dead and wounded were so numerous that they hampered both side's ability to mount a decent attack.

Then, Ashford saw that the Redcoats were again close to breaking. He looked around to find Charles and saw that his brother was close at hand. He stood to make to Iroquois' battle cry but found he had no voice to do so.

As if he could read Ashford's mind, Charles placed his hand on Ashford's shoulder and spoke, "Can Charles make the cry now?"

Ashford nodded and Charles rose to do so.

The cry was repeated again and again and he knew, even in the darkness what effect it had on the Americans. There was a sudden lull, more than a pause, but definitely a slow-down of firing. Then the firing picked up again, only this time from the left and right flanks of the American forces and, immediately after that more battle cries and a rush of men with bayonets hit the American troops from both sides. Ashford and Charles were in the middle of the melee in no time. Ashford with his short sword fixed for bayonet and Charles with his tomahawk in his right hand. Having Charles by his side was what he needed. He would make it. He would not let his men down.

Men fought men at very close range. When threatened by a US bayonet, the partner would stab the threatening troop wherever he could, in the torso, the arm or leg. And Ashford fought for his life. This was not the long-range shooting of a 'Chosen Man'. It was a madhouse of thrusting, stabbing, pushing kicking, yelling, tripping, doing anything possible to stay alive. At one point, while Charles fended off a high thrust at Ashford with a block that shoved the enemy musket upwards and away from Ashford, he thrust at the man's chest and almost missed. Instead his short sword was swept upwards to the man's neck. At that moment, the harsh glow of a flare caught the American's face as the blade entered his neck. Ashford was looking into the eyes of the man and could plainly see the man did not show fear, or shock, but sudden sadness in knowing that he was about to die. Then Ashford felt hot wet blood as it sprayed onto his face when he withdrew the bayonet.

Ashford thought it strange that he so clearly saw the man knew he was about to die and even more strange that there was no fear. For a second, he wondered if he was just imagining it all.

From that moment things seemed to move in slow motion. Ashford could see each step, each thrust, and each flinch, each drop of sweat that ran down over his eyes. He knew exactly what he was doing. He knew he was killing on a very personal level, on the level of near butchery. And he knew he had to keep doing it or die.

That look of sadness in the eyes of the man he skewered would haunt him for many months. Somehow this close quarter and personal way of killing was different, especially since he bore no hatred of the man he was fighting. It felt too close, too unnecessary, and too barbaric.

Charles was fighting the bayonet charge in his own way, without a bayonet, but with a tomahawk. His Kentucky rifle was in his left hand and he used it as a club, or a blunt spear, or an instrument to deflect bayonet thrusts at him. The long rifle proved useful in giving him for time to react to an attempt by the enemy to stab him. His tomahawk swung in every imaginable direction, sometimes at the man in front of him and sometimes at a man beside him, even at a man behind him. He knew it was a mistake to try for a kill with a swing at the head of his enemy; the tomahawk could get momentarily snagged in the soldiers' cap. So he swung it at the knees, arms, collar bone, face, or whatever he could to wound, if he could not kill.

At one moment, the flash of musket fire lit up Charles' face exposing the red and black war paint around his eyes and on his face. That provided a vision of hell to at least one American trooper, and a cry rose from that trooper, "Indians, God damned Indians!"

It was the yells of Ignace and Charles that broke Ashford from his rage. They were well into the fight and could be seen in the flashes of light from muskets and flares as they swung their tomahawks at the US troops. Then Ashford heard someone again call, "Indians! God damned Indians!"

Ashford looked, with relief, to see the Americans melt into the darkness and run and stumble down the hill.

It was over. Ashford found himself siting on his haunches, sweating, shivering and shaking with fear. Then he felt the hand of Charles on his shoulder and the shaking and fear left him.

Both sides were too exhausted to fight any more. The Americans retreated, but Drummond could not pursue. His men were also unable to press the battle. All Drummond could do was set up for another possible attack and wait until daybreak. That proved to be a long and horrifying wait. Throughout the night one could hear the moans of the wounded and dying men, both American and British, and there was little they could do for fear of another attack.

In the morning a toll was taken:

> British – 778 killed or wounded. Three of Ashford's 'Chosen Men' received bayonet stab wounds that were not serious.

> American - 820 killed, wounded or missing. Among the severely wounded was Winfield Scott, a true American hero and maker of men, the man who trained those brave American troopers in the French way of battle.

It was the last time the United States tried to invade the Canadas, but it was not yet the end of the war.

A New Assignment
Lundy's Lane the Next Day
July 27, 1814

A Lieutenant appeared at a full run with a request from Major General Drummond to report to the General as soon as possible.

"Major Ashford. Thank you for coming in such good time," began Drummond. "I've called you for four reasons. First, I compliment you on the plan presented to General Riall and I. It worked perfectly and I have learned a great deal about your men and how to use them. Second, your action and timing of the rescue of our guns was superb. I am aware that it was a dangerous maneuver because of the possibility suffering fire from our own troops. And those Indians, where on earth did you find so many of them?" He waited for Ashford's reply.

"Sir, as you know I have two Iroquois brothers. They are a very effective part of the 'Chosen Men'. The other "Indians" were my own men. We practiced the Iroquois battle cry many times and it was a good deal of fun, especially when Ignace and Charles laughed at their efforts to learn it. We know it scares the daylights out of the Americans."

"Very well done. That brings me to the second reason for my haste in calling you. Your action and your knowledge of battle is exemplary and for that reason, and in order to have a man of your caliber closer to the command I have placed a request that you be immediately promoted to the rank of Lieutenant Colonel. I decided so very soon after the American retreat as I wish to have you as an advisor in my command."

"Thank you, sir. I am honored."

"I am sure that Governor General Prevost will approve so I have the honor to present you with the stripes and epaulettes of your new rank." Drummond handed the items to Ashford. "I, this morning, sent my request to the Governor General by fast horse."

"That brings me to the third reason for my calling you here so quickly." He looked Ashford in the eye with an 'I wish I didn't have to do this look'.

"I am about to lose you, I hope temporarily. What I am about to say is not to be repeated and you will know why. A few moments ago, I received an urgent message from Major General Robert Ross. It came by way of a fast frigate from London. Because he is in need of skirmishers and cannot bring the 'Chosen Men' from Spain, he has requested some of your men in a venture of great significance. You will be informed upon reporting to him."

"You are to muster forty-eight of your men, plus the two Iroquois, for immediate departure by way of *HMS Pictou* which is at York awaiting your arrival. I am told it will involve a relatively short ocean voyage but am not able to tell you, at this time, where and what it's all about. You are therefore required to muster your group for departure from York two days from now. To that end, I have prepared wagons, horses and all you need to get you there as quickly as possible. You will present this packet of documents to Admiral Cochrane on his flagship somewhere in the northwestern Atlantic. The packet contains a copy of my detailed account of your actions yesterday. It will help him and General Ross to know better how to use your men and I am sure they wish to know more about the Indian and 'Chosen Men' style of fighting you have developed."

Ashford was stunned. He was sure Lord Percival was somehow mixed up in this but wondered how he managed to do it so quickly. It must have been in the planning stage for some time. "Thank you, sir." That was all he was able to say.

"It seems I will lose you, Colonel. But I hope you will be back soon and I can say the packet contains my request that you be returned to my command as soon as possible."

"Sir, I would be honored to serve under your command and I look forward to returning soon."

"That is all, for now. Hopefully we will have more contact in the future." Ashford rose from his chair and departed.

Ashford went immediately to the field and asked Lieutenant Wilson to organize the forty-eight men, plus Ignace and Charles, and have them readied for the trip. He instructed Wilson to wait until he would be able to talk with his Iroquois friends first. In the meantime, Wilson was to muster the men with full kits. Wilson was also directed to have the men clean their uniforms before departure for York as there would not likely be time to do so later.

Ashford then sought out Ignace and Charles and found them, sitting on their haunches and talking.

"Charles, Ignace I have some news and something to ask of you." They looked up, not surprised to see him. They nodded for Ashford to sit with them and offered him some tobacco. Ashford accepted it and began to load his pipe as the talked.

"I have just met with General Drummond ..." Charles interrupted Ashford, "He is good man like the great General Brock. We hope he lives much longer."

"Thank you, Charles. That's why I'm here. General Drummond has received orders that I am to take fifty men on a voyage into the great waters for a battle with the Americans. He knows about you and has heard of your bravery and ways of fighting, not just from me but also from dispatches, messages, sent to him by other generals. He wishes that you join me and forty-eight of my men on this new assignment. All I know is that it will be a great battle, like this last one, and it will be fought against the Americans. It means you will have to leave the Canadas and go further into the American lands. It means you will have to travel on the great ocean. That's all I know, and I ask you to come with me."

Ignace and Charles sat for a few moments, then nodded to each other and rose. Charles was first to speak.

"*Tha-yo-nih*, we will go with you. We will fight with you. We will fight with the 'Chosen Men' because we know it is meant to be." Ashford waited for Ignace to speak.

"*Tha-yo-nih*, we will go with you for the reasons my brother has said and for one more reason. We have seen the big canoes on the great lakes and have been told there are even bigger canoes that the ones we have seen. We would like to see what they are like and how they can move so well without the paddle. We think it will be something we will never forget and we will tell stories about them to our grandchildren."

"Well said, my brothers. I told General Drummond of how you made me your brother and the name you gave me. He found it very interesting and he knows you are great and honorable warriors." They sat and talked for a few more minutes and then Ashford added, "We must prepare because we will leave very soon, less than two days from now."

That night, as he lay awake in his bed, the events at Lundy's Lane kept seeping into Ashford's mind. The dominant part of it all was the bayonet fight and the look on that young American's face when Ashford killed him. The same vision hit Ashford again, only this time as a dream. It would hit him again and again for the next many days. It would come at him in super slow motion, with each detail in vivid colours, especially the reds, blood reds. And each time he had the dream, there was more blood than the last time.

A Not So Friendly Welcome
Bladensburg, New York
July 26, 1814

As instructed, Major Ronald Roy Foster arrived in Bladensburg, New York, on July 26, 1814. He and his men rode into town in a column of fours. Nobody seemed to notice. He reported to headquarters, waited an hour before its commanding officer, William Harrison, finally appeared and gave Foster instructions on where to find the tents and other facilities for his men. Foster did as he was told.

HMS Nelson
Atlantic Ocean near Chesapeake Bay, USA
August 18, 1814

Ignace and Charles were astounded by the large troop ship that carried them from Halifax to Chesapeake Bay. They were overcome by the vastness of the ocean and how the ships could find their way without sight of land. But when they first saw the flotilla of ships consisting of four ships of the line (ships with more than seventy-two guns), twenty frigates and sloops of war and twenty troop carriers, they were completely dumbfounded. The largest ships had three levels of guns and so many sailors on board it was too hard to comprehend.

When the fleet was first sighted and after the two Iroquois settled down, Ashford told them to dress in their war clothing as he wanted them to meet the leader and for the leader to see great Indian warriors. "No war paint," said Ashford. He would dress in the full uniform of a Lt. Colonel, using his short sword rather than a longer conventional one. He didn't have one of those anyway.

When the Jacob's ladder, sometimes just a rope with cross bars, sometimes more substantial and more like a staircase was lowered, Ashford called up to the first officer on board the flagship, "Permission to come aboard, sir. And permission to bring my two Iroquois brothers on board as well?"

"Permission granted. The Admiral is awaiting all of you." The first office could not take his eyes off the two Iroquois. He heard about these Indian fighters and how fierce they were and he was still surprised how fierce they looked, even without war paint.

Ashford saluted as he stepped onto the deck. His two brothers didn't know what to do but knew they could not salute. Instead, when they stepped onto the deck, they stood up in almost a saluting stance and waived an eagle feather in a friendly gesture to all the men present. Ashford and his Iroquois brothers could see open mouths on all the men on board. He knew their entrance would never be forgotten.

"Sir, the Admiral and General Ross will see you in his cabin. He has instructed me to show your friends around the ship, explain things they see, and answer any questions they may have. I have also instructed the crew to treat these warriors with the greatest respect. Admiral Cochrane and General Ross will later wish to meet these gentlemen in the Admiral's cabin, but they must first discuss urgent matters with you. He estimates, for now, that will take about half an hour."

"Thank you. Please show the way." With that, he followed the first officer while another officer came forward to shake hands with Ignace and Charles, learn their names, and ask if they wished some refreshments before taking a tour of the ship.

Both Admiral Cochrane and General Ross rose as Ashford walked into the cabin. It was clean and not too spacious, with large windows at the stern of the great ship and a table large enough to seat about eight people. On one side of the room was a desk, built so it could be folded up into the wall, and a chair tucked under it for writing. On the other side was another table with a small stack of charts and maps laid on it.

"We are pleased to meet you Colonel Ashford," said Cochrane as he shook hands.

"And I am pleased to meet you, sirs,"

'We have much to speak about as we have some special orders we wish to discuss. Please, sit," Cochrane motioned for Ashford to join them at the large table. In front of Cochrane was a folder packed with about half an inch of papers. He opened the folder and pulled out a packet and then looked up at Ashford.

"You are very highly regarded, Colonel. I have reports from General Brock to the war department and from General Drummond and Lord Percival. All of them are very complementary and detailed in their praise."

He looked up at Ashford and saw a smile, the kind of smile that comes with "Ah, I knew it. Sir Percival is involved in this."

Cochrane smiled back and said, "And I'm not surprised you know it." Then he continued, "Yes, Colonel, Lord Percival is, indeed involved in this. It is his network that has brought us all together and to the next battle of this war, a battle in which you will play an important part. As a beginning, I will give you this packet from Sir Percival and ask you read it. He informs me that you will fully understand its meaning and that you are free to talk about all matters concerning your activities during the past years since you met him."

Before Ashford could speak, General Ross stood and asked the Admiral, "May I offer you a sherry?"

"Yes, by all means General, I think it would relax Colonel Ashford."

"All of this is a surprise but I'm not too surprised that Sir Percival is involved. He's an amazing man," Ashford said, and then put his attention to the packet from the Secretary of Colonial Affairs. It was written in Percival's impeccable handwriting;

For Mr. Ashford London,   **June 1, 1814**

    I have the honour to advise that all superior officers with whom you have made contact have indicated a great respect and admiration for you; for the service you have provided to His Majesty and for your initiative and the unique manner of fighting a very different kind of war. As a result, I have instructed that you be promoted to the rank of Lt. Colonel forthwith. Congratulations.

    Now an important message: Our sources indicate that one Major Ronald Foster of the 17th Kentucky Dragoons has been ordered to assemble his men and present himself at Washington, the capital city of the United States. Burn this letter.

                       Sir Percival Worthington
                       Secretary of Colonial Affairs
                       To His Majesty King George III

Ashford knew instantly what the letter meant. It was a veiled suggestion to assassinate Foster, because it was Foster who sent three men to murder Thompson.

When Ashford looked up from the letter his eyes met those of Cochrane and Ross and, before he could say anything, Cochrane spoke, "We are aware of the contents of the packet and its background. No more will be said."

"Thank you, gentlemen. We shall see what happens." Ashford looked into the small fire burning in the potbellied stove, noting it was a hot day for a fire and that Cochrane was prepared. "May I?" Both officers nodded and Ashford rose went to the stove, pulled open the gate and tossed the letter into the fire.

"Colonel, we shall begin by having you describe the methods used by you and the 'Chosen Men'. In particular we ask that you describe the way in which those methods are different from those of the 95th Battalion in Europe. Even more so, we need to know how you incorporated the two Iroquois and the Indian method of fighting into your work. This may be important for our joint task that we will soon put in motion." The Admiral spoke with great respect.

"And I too sir, am eager to learn. It is of great importance to me to know how we can avoid having your men fired upon by our own forces since it appears you and your men are not dressed in the usual red British uniforms," added Ross.

Ashford responded with a long explanation of how they worked in pairs, each member of the pair looking out for the other, and how they communicated. Silence was the key in the forest, he explained. Ambush was a preferred method of attack and setting up the ambush of the greatest importance. He explained how he attempted to make the enemy do as he wanted them to and not as the enemy wanted to do. But the key, he stressed, was that this enemy did not know who or what Ashford's men were or how they worked.

He also pointed out that, in the battle of Lundy's Lane, it was apparent the Americans were trained and used the French method of attack, though he doubted the idea had yet spread throughout the whole of the US army. He then explained in detail how he and General Riall planned the defense at Lundy's Lane and how well General Drummond executed it. He also explained how General Riall planned the battle so the artillery and the Redcoats knew where the 'Chosen Men' were at all times.

At that point, Ashford paused in order to stress his next statement, "I will add that the Americans, until Lundy's Lane, had no real army and it still consists of untrained militia who have never faced 'the line' or grape-shot fire. They break easily. I suspect that is what we will be up against for some time yet because this French method of fighting will not have spread to other commands. We must, however, be prepared to face a well-trained force in the future."

Ashford decided he had to warn the officers of one other tactic he used, "We use the Iroquois battle cry and you may hear it on occasion. It causes fear, especially for the militia. We also use it as a method of signaling each other. As you can imagine, our methods are unusual, but they are very effective."

General Ross spoke again and Ashford suspected the General wanted to demonstrate that it was Ross, not the Admiral, who would plan and take the land battle. Ashford was thankful for that as he believed a naval officer should not meddle in deciding the tactics of ground troops. "Colonel, we will now tell you what is in store for us. We plan to attack Washington itself."

Ross paused to give Ashford a moment to recover. "We do it in retali-ation for the burning of York and we will do only that, burn the capital buildings and walk away. There will be not looting, as there was in York, no setting ablaze of houses or places of business. We mean to show the might of His Majesty's army so this will never happen again. Tomorrow we will gather the officers here," he tapped the table, "to plan our attack. In the meantime, we would rather enjoy hearing about your adventures with this man 'Thompson' and of the attempt to murder him."

Ashford then described, at length, the trip to the west coast. Then he came to the ambush at Murphy Creek. He told them what they found in the pockets and supplies of the three assassins and how it ties with the man named "Foster".

Ashford stressed the somewhat casual approach he had with his men, because they are the 'Chosen Men' and because comradery was a most important element in how they worked. He was also careful to explain how the series 1806 rifle worked and how accurate it is compared with the "Brown Bess" or any other smooth-bore musket. All that took him more than an hour, with intermittent questions from the other officers.

What surprised the two officers was the fact that Ashford so quickly set up the assassins and had them do what *he* wanted. That made their admiration for Ashford even stronger. "This evening we shall have the officers here, in this room, for dinner, I expect you will be asked about your adventures. For now, we would like to meet the two Iroquois and learn more about them. I take it you have great a regard for them."

"I do. In fact, they have made me their brother and given me an Iroquois name. The other officers would best know that these two men are well-civilized and very loyal to me and to the Crown. I will have them dress in non-battle attire as your crew has already seen them in their normal battle clothing. I planned that to show how fearsome they can look and, believe me, in battle they are the most frightening thing any foe could imagine."

"We would enjoy that, and I am sure will learn much. Please inform them that they are invited for 7:00 pm. I will have you billeted, with your Iroquois brothers, in the First Officer's quarters. We have already arranged that with him and he takes it as an honor. Please also inform the two of them that we hope they will not be afraid to talk and explain things to us. We are eager to learn. Perhaps they could also tell us more about your Indian name."

"Thank you, sir. I am sure you will find it all quite interesting. By the way, these two men have been in the company of civilized men for many years. They do not take scalps. They pride themselves in that and in the fact they understand our ways more than one would think. They also have a great sense of humor that stems with being amongst those French-Canadian voyageurs for so many years."

"We shall see you all at 7:00 pm. The first officer will show you in."

When Ignace and Charles met Ashford in the first officer's quarters, they could not stop talking. The guns, the men, the miles and miles of rope, the three decks, and the immense size of it all, were just too incredible to believe. "What is that terrible whistle noise they made when we got on this ship?' asked Charles.

"It is a custom in the navy to blow the whistle called a Boson's Pipe. When an officer comes on board," replied Ashford. One of the rules on a ship is that no one is allowed to whistle because in battle, with the big guns firing, all you can hear is a whistle and the ship's crew will sometimes get their orders by using the whistle."

"What are those flag things they wave around at the other ship?" asked Ignace.

"It's called "Semaphore", answered Ashford. "The flags are used to talk to the other officers on another ship. It is quick and quiet, like the hand signals you have taught the 'Chosen Men'."

There were many more questions, some of which Ashford could not answer and, when he told his brothers they were invited to dine with the officers, they were flattered. Ashford encouraged them to tell any stories they wished and not hold back on telling of their own adventures.

The supper went extremely well. Ashford's stories of the trip to the west coast were received with interest and sometimes disbelief. As to the Indians, the officers couldn't get enough. When Ignace and Charles told the story and reasons for making Ashford their brother, many of them had instantly felt a greater respect for the two Iroquois. When the 'Green Tea' ceremony was told, the whole table erupted in laughter. Those stories were of great value in bringing about a sense of understanding between the officers and Ashford's brothers. And it was a necessary thing because all had to know that these three men would change things on the battlefield like no one else would. It was also necessary as a way to explain a perceived lack of crisp discipline with the 'Chosen Men'.

Admiral Cochrane then rose, "Gentlemen, we shall meet, with more of the officers, at 8:00 am. We have a good deal of planning to do. Good night."

Chesapeake Bay War Council
HMS Nelson
8 am, August 19, 1814

It took some time for all introductions to be made until the group, eight in total and comprising only the majors and higher-ranked army officers who were to take part in the battle, sat for the briefing. Major General Ross rose slowly from his chair, "Gentlemen, in three days we shall take part in an historic event. We shall attack and burn much of Washington, the capital city of the United States of America."

He waited for the mummer to subside, and then continued. "We will do so from the east, through a small village called Bladensburg which is about six miles north east of Washington. Quite frankly, we doubt the Americans have yet thought that out. When the attack begins they'll be in an awful hurry and will make mistakes upon which we should capitalize. Our spies have informed us that there are very few, perhaps 1000 trained troops and 7000 militia, in the area. I know 7000 sounds like a whole lot, but I am informed by Lt. Colonel Ashford that they are poorly trained. Perhaps I could ask the Colonel to tell you what his experience is with such militia. Colonel?"

Ashford obliged, "We have met and fought these militia men and on most occasions and we find they are more of a mob than a true military force. Most of them are just farmers and ordinary people who have almost no training, have never stood the line in battle, and really just want to go back home. In our first encounters, many of them didn't even have a musket. It is our experience that they will fire one or two volleys, and then run like the devil. But amongst them are some expert marksmen and that presents a great danger to our officers. Cannon and grapeshot disperses the militia in minutes. Standing the line, which His Majesty's forces do the best in the world, will quickly send them running like rabbits. They are learning, though, so we should not be too cocky about it. In our latest battle we came across pure "regulars", trained in the French way to attack in columns and then attempt to form a line and those men are tough, indeed."

"Thank you, Colonel. Now, I have a map of the village and surrounding areas of Bladensburg, sketched by one of our spies. I ask that you all look at it for a few moments, think of what we may have instore for us, and then we will discuss it." He handed out eight copies of the map, and then turned to an easel, pulled off the white sheet covering a larger version of the map and then waited for the officers to continue their study.

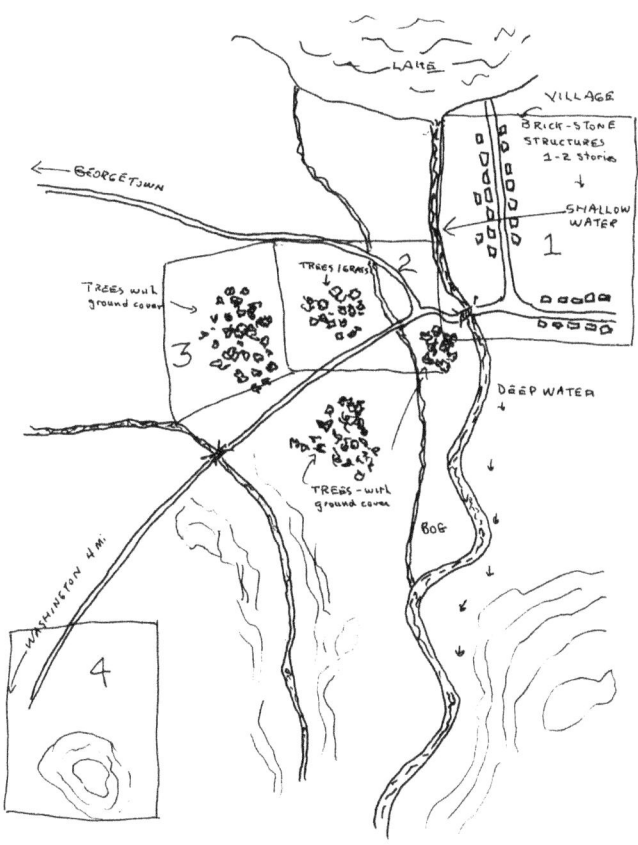

"Here is the road, entering the town from the east at this point. Just beyond this bridge, the road bends to the southwest and runs about six miles to Washington. That is the road we must control to take our objective. I will mark out four areas of importance." He then drew green rectangles and shapes onto the map and numbered them from one to four.

Ashford marked his own map in the same manner.

Area one is the village. You can see buildings sketched here and here. These are brick/stone buildings. One thing we will be concerned about is with sharpshooters or troops in these buildings. They are great cover for the Americans and perfect for causing us a good deal of trouble. Colonel Ashford's men, all sharpshooters, may have to deal with them. By the way, Colonel, please put on your green capot and toque then explain them to us and the way your men work."

Ashford did so, and then General Ross continued. "My plan is to send Colonel Ashford's men and his two Iroquois Indians, in at night. He will reconnoiter the area and set up his men in this position in the trees in area three." He tapped the spot with his finger showing the spot to be in the lower right corner of rectangle number three. "From there he can observe enemy troop movements and give protection while we cross the bridge, here.

"I anticipate the enemy will set fire to this bridge." He pointed to the bridge at the edge of the village, again, and continued. "This bridge is very important. We hope to cross it before they fire it. The second bridge is not so important because it crosses a small steam that we can ford if need be. So, I propose to have the 144th Regiment ford the river, upstream of the first bridge, here. You can see the words 'shallow water' written in. Even if the bridge is not set ablaze, we will still have the 1/44th ford the river at that point in order to flank the left of what may be the enemy positions. It is reasonable to assume the enemy will set up a large greeting party for us when we cross the first bridge, so a flanking move may be needed. Also, the flanking move will assist us in clearing any enemy that may be set up to greet us after the second bridge." He waited as the officers studied the map, and then continued.

"Area four shows a small hill. I am not sure how high it is but we must assume the enemy will set up some guns there. It's not really too useful to them, but we should be aware of the possibility the guns will be placed on the hill. If so, it will be Colonel Ashford's task to inform us and to deal with them."

"General Brooke, you will take that flanking move as quickly as possible. But be aware and make your men aware that Colonel Ashford's men will be located in the trees at Area three. They will harass any attempts by the enemy to move eastward to fire the bridge and may assist you, if needed, in preventing a flanking move to our right. Colonel Ashford, if needed, you will support Colonel Brooke; but if not needed, you will take your men southward, across the road and through this creek, just to the east of the main river and harass anything you see, such as guns set to fire on Colonel Brooke's men. I anticipate guns may be set up somewhere near the road southeast of bridge two, so you may have to engage them. Any questions?"

Ashford was the first to speak. "General Ross, I have a couple of questions. Firstly, I wonder if you could provide me with two good runners I can use to relay messages to you. If the bridge is not fired, I will advise you of that and of any other movement. I have few men to spare for that but, more important, not being dressed in conventional uniforms, my lads may come under our own fire. Perhaps we can get two or three spare red coats I can use for my men if I need them as runners".

"Thank you, Colonel. Yes. I will provide you with two men and the red coats.

"Now, one other thing about which you should be aware. I shall be using Congreve rockets in this engagement and they sometimes go off the intended course. Be prepared to take cover when you hear them. That will most likely be in the first stages of the battle. Also, I anticipate the worst of it will be when we try to cross the first bridge, if not, then sometime after the second bridge will be the worst. So I ask you all to keep that in mind. Questions?"

"If progress is reasonably good and our men are not too tired, we will form up and march, I say again, *march*, into Washington. Colonel Ashford, your men will proceed ahead of us, in whatever manner or forms you think appropriate to harass and prevent any sharpshooters from causing us grief. When we arrive and begin our intended task, to burn all government buildings, your men will remain on the periphery to deal with sharpshooters."

"Yes, sir."

"And, gentlemen, please inform your men that anyone caught looting will be hanged. That is all."

The Bladensburg Races
Bladensburg, Maryland, USA
August 24, 1814

The massing of ships near Chesapeake Bay was an indication to the Americans that something big was about to happen. But they did not think the coming event would involve Washington. It wasn't that they considered it and rejected the idea of such an attack. It was simply something that did not come to mind. But, by late August, they realized the possibility, and then came to realize it was about to happen. They had to scramble together whoever and whatever they could to save the Capital City.

When word came that a large force of British troops was massed and marching towards Washington, panic hit the city. People fled Bladensburg, then Washington itself. Poorly-trained militia, and only a few regular troops, had to do what they could. As a result, mistakes were bound to happen.

At around 4:00 am Ashford's group cautiously advanced into the village of Bladensburg and found it deserted. "Shit", thought Ashford, "They're expecting us."

He ordered his men to check the brick buildings and learned they were clear of any opposition, a glaring mistake by the Americans as the buildings would provide cover against musket and cannon shot as well as great platforms for fire on the Redcoats. That, in turn would allow the Americans to control access to the bridge. "Why not occupy the buildings?" Ashford wondered. "First thing I'd do is burn the damned bridge and make us get wet, dirty, and tired fording the river and then shoot as us at their leisure. Why? Is it some kind of trap? If so, what would they look for? Redcoats, not my men. They'll think my men are Americans and let us pass. Or maybe they're not even here. Maybe they want the fight to go somewhere else!"

Ashford knew he had to find the answer and inform General Ross. He decided to take the risk of running, no, he would march, across the bridge and try to look as American as possible. If it's a trap, the lads could make for the trees as ordered and make a stand there. With hand signals he let the men know they were going to *march*, not walk, across the bridge.

That small ploy must have helped as the 'Chosen Men', including two British 'runners' dressed for now in the cover of green over their redcoats, marched along the road to the other side of the bridge and on to the forest just north east of the second bridge. As they crossed, Ashford gave a signal with his left hand, pointing to the trees just south of the road and, in response Lieutenant Wilson and five men peeled off and ran into the trees. Their job was to prevent anyone from approaching the bridge in an attempt to set it ablaze. There they disappeared into the forest and set up for skirmish action. And a little further down the road the rest of the 'Chosen Men' entered the second group of trees in the south end of Area three.

Once he knew they were ready, Ashford took the time to look, and more importantly, to *listen* to what might be happening. It was telling. There was a great deal of activity about one mile south of the second bridge. He could hear the creak of wheels on wagons and knew instantly that the Americans were setting guns in place in order to fire as the British came over the *first* bridge. Then he heard more wagon noises as well as the distinctive sound of many horses moving northeast from the point where the first wagon noises originated. "They're going to set cannons to bear on the first bridge; but why so many other horses?" He listened more then realized they were sending guns and Dragoons to set another trap, but where? Then realized what the Americans were planning.

They expected us to ford the river upstream of the bridge. They want to secure their left flank for our attack in fording the river. But now they have to prevent an attack by us by way of the bridge. Someone ordered the bridge not to be burned. Now they're trying to set guns to repel our advance over the bridge, but have to also keep their left flank free of any attack. The horses are a desperate attempt to get men and guns close to position on horseback, and then form up on foot. They're moving to set up on the south side between area 2 and 3.

Ashford sat down and took out his little note book to scrawl a message:

1. **Town deserted, bridge not fired**
2. **We are in assigned position – Area 3**
3. **Suspect guns will form up between the trees and our position in area 2-3. Suggest rockets fire there. Will keep my men west of that area while the rockets are fired.**
4. **Suspect enemy is setting up large guns to bear on the road just SE of the 2nd bridge. Hear wagons, men assembling.**
5. **Have set up skirmishers to prevent enemy from burning bridge.**
6. **Will assist Gen T. on his movement if needed.**
7. **Expect major part of battle in Area 4 S-W of 2nd bridge.**

Ashford

He rose and looked for the runner, finding him about three feet away. "Take this to General Ross. Remove your green jacket once you spot some red coats. We don't want our own men to mistake you for American militia. What do you do if you think you will be captured?"

"Eat the message, sir."

"Good man." Get to it.

Ashford then quietly toured his men, "Hold your fire and wait. The only shooting will come from Lieutenant Wilson on the other side of the road. I expect we will have company by early morning. Enemy troops will likely form up between our trees and those over there." He pointed to the trees on the north side of Area two. "Pull back from the edge of our trees, about twenty yards and settle in. I expect enemy troops will want to come into our area to relieve themselves. Just stay quiet and wait. We have to know what they're up to. Take turns sleeping. Eat."

He gave that message to all his men, including Charles and Ignace and asked Charles to stay close to him. That night, a large force accompanied by several twelve-pounder guns, came racing up the road to set up with the guns facing the first bridge. Not only was a good-sized force ready to oppose a crossing, but Ashford and his men were well stuck in a trap. Wilson wisely did not fire on the Americans as he knew doing so was only to give away his position and they were not there to burn the bridge. Ashford, pleased that Wilson held fire, hurriedly scrawled another message to Ross.

"Enemy guns now facing 1ˢᵗbridge north of road, they are located at SW corner of Area 2. Recommend rockets fire there. – Ashford"

He gave the message to his second runner with instructions to take it via the proposed ford north of the bridge and around the village. He was to wear his capot until he sighted British forces because the messenger had to look American at first, then, once close to British lines, like a red coat. "Eat this message if you have to."

Several American troops, militia, arrived at about 9:00 am and took positions where Ashford suspected they would. There were three groups of about fifty men, all on foot except for the apparent leader of each group. Each of the groups had its own banner. Now the trap was even more concerning to Ashford and his men and he could do little about it except hope a barrage of rocket fire would disperse the enemy.

Ashford returned to scouting the enemy and immediately noticed one of those groups had men dressed in the same buckskin jackets as the three men at Murphy's Creek and one of them, on foot, was waving their banner:

17ᵗʰ Kentucky

"Well, I'll be damned!" Then he saw a short man, riding a white horse and dressed in a navy blue jacket with large red lapels, white trousers, and a cocked hat with a huge Egret feather fitted into it and fluttering like a white flag saying "Look at me. I'm so beautiful!"

"Well, I'll be double-damned."

Ashford crept to Charles' position and whispered. "That man in the feathered hat, on the south side of his men is the one who ordered

Thompson killed. His name is Foster, Major Roy Foster. Keep track of him with me. We will both kill him, my way."

Charles looked at Ashford and said, "I will watch him and I will protect *Tha-yo-nih*." and smiled.

At 11:00 am Colonel Ross's men arrived at Bladensburg. The 1/44th, under the command of Colonel Brooke, would arrive at the river fording point within a half hour, as they left for the village about half an hour before Ross in a route around the village. It took half an hour for the rockets to set up and, when done, Ross ordered his Major to fire.

What a spectacular show! The Americans might have thought it was the fourth of July! It was a semi-deadly rain of rockets, all aimed at the positions suggested by Ashford and all packed with deadly packets of musket balls designed to burst near the enemy. The bursting of rockets was incredibly loud and the accompanying flashes of fire were frightening beyond belief. Some rockets went astray and some did not ignite their packets, but they did the job. The unbelievable noise and the rain of musket balls from the sky were horrendously frightening to men who had never experienced it, even to those who did. As soon as the first salvo of rocket fire eased, Ashford could hear a collective groan rise from the desperate militia-men. Then the groan suddenly stopped. Men seemed frozen, unable to walk, or run, or think. They seemed to just stare into space without seeing anything.

Another salvo of rocket fire seemed to wake them. Two groups of militia assembled closest to Ashford's men broke to flee, and as Foster's men were in the way, they had to run southward, to the road and then run like all their worth along the road to the southwest. The men who manned the guns did likewise. There, they received fire from the 'Chosen Men' who quickly moved in position for fire. Many were cut down. The others ran, pulling off their tunics, throwing away their muskets and hats and almost all of them crying in terror.

Foster held, for about three minutes. But he and his men were beginning to break. Ashford and Charles kept watching him as he spurred his horse in a desperate effort to get ahead of his men. He ran down four of them. Then, a shot from one of the 'Chosen Men' struck Foster's horse and it went down, flinging Foster over its head as it hit the ground head-first. It took several moments for Foster to recover, but when he did most of his men were well on their way back the way they came to relative safety. Foster crawled, looking back at his men as if to be sure no one would see him and know he was just a damned coward. When he knew his men would not look back, he rose and ran into the forest in the north of Area two, threw himself of the behind a tree, and waited.

Ashford and Charles followed.

The forest there was unlike the one in which Ashford and his group took cover. The underbrush was scrubbed out and replaced with green, almost manicured, grass and seemed to be an area where people gathered to picnic or enjoy nature. Ashford and Charles stopped to survey the area and then heard what they first thought was a child crying, then realized it was Foster. Above the din of war, they could not tell where the source of the sound was, so they squatted to listen. Musket fire sounded in various places around them, slowing to a relative calm. They listened. After a few moments, they nodded to each other in the direction of the sounds. Ashford then gave a hand signal for Charles to swing around to his right, watch for enemy men, and for the source of the sound. Charles moved silently until he could pinpoint the source of the sound. He stopped and signaled the position to Ashford. At the same moment, Ashford also pinpointed the spot. The whimpering came from just behind a large oak tree directly ahead.

The whimpering stopped.

"Ronald Foster! Stand and surrender! You are to be arrested for murder!" shouted Ashford. He wanted Foster to challenge him. He wanted the man to know who and why he was being pursued. He wanted to kill the man in his own way.

No response, just silence, even from the noise of war.

"Stand, you sniveling coward!"

Then came some movement. It was the grey pant leg on a man struggling to rise.

"Show yourself!"

Foster rose, took a deep breath, and stepped from the tree and turned to the direction of the voice.

"Who are you? Murderer? Whadda ya mean, this is war, not murder." Foster's voice started weak but grew in false confidence as he looked at Ashford.

Ashford walked cautiously toward Foster, watching the man's hands for movement and noticed Foster had no sword or scabbard and no pistol visible on his belt. He did, however, have a knife, a Kentucky Knife hanging from his belt on his right side.

Ashford slowly knelt to place his rifle on the grass, rose and looked Foster in the eye as he walked slowly towards him all the while watching for any shift in the man's weight that might indicate he was about to move for his knife. It was, in fact, an invitation for Foster to pull his knife, not a show of non-hostility as Foster took it to be. Ashford stayed aware of the right hand and waited as the Kentucky man slowly approached, then stopped.

"I surrender. I am your prisoner. Do yuh mind tellin' me what this murder thing is?" asked Foster with a quiver that said he was about to collapse.

"Certainly," answered Ashford; "The murder of Mr. David Thompson." He saw a smile come to Foster's face followed by an instant change in his eyes from fear to hate. He also saw Foster's right hand reach for the knife. Foster's left foot moved foward, signaling a lunge at Ashford.

Ashford knew in an instant that he succeeded in getting the Kentucky man enraged and over-confident, a recipe for death in a knife fight. "This yokel is dumber than a fence post," he thought as he pulled his Navaja knife from his left side, with his right hand, and side-stepped the clumsy lunge.

Foster recovered from the awkward lunge and turned fast to face Ashford and Ashford turned to face him. Both then took fighting stances, feet and body square to the opponent and watching for any sign of an attempt to strike. They moved clockwise being sure never to stand flat-footed and sizing each other up like wolves sizing each other up in preparation for battle. Ashford wanted the first move to come from Foster so he could see how he held the knife, how his feet moved before each feint, how he placed his legs and knees and feet as he did do.

Foster made the first attack, a thrust straight at Ashford's body, then a pull back from a miss as Ashford nimbly moved back to avoid the thrust.

As he watched Foster's movements, Ashford made quick mental notes. He saw that Foster held his knife with the thumb at the side of the handle, and couldn't twist it very well on a sweeping back-hand move. Holding it that way forced him to twist his elbow to get the blade to bear for a cut. That would put him a little off-balance.

Foster then took his squared-off stance again and feinted another thrust downward towards Ashford's lower abdomen but this time Ashford flicked his half-double-edged knife upward as Foster's hand moved forward. It sliced Foster's thumb just behind the first knuckle. Foster jerked back in an instant shock and wild surprise in his eyes.

"That one is for sending LaSalle to steal Thompson's maps," he said.

Ashford thought quickly about what Foster would do next, First blood is always good. Now he's scared. Now he'll have trouble sweeping it at me on the back-hand. He won't try that. He would try to slice at Ashford's body with a forehand sweep. Ashford told himself: stay aware of his feet. He'll move the left foot first, just a bit, then lunge for a sweep with his right foot forward. His left will follow as he sweeps the knife.

They danced some more. Ashford could see that the thumb was now a problem which meant Foster had to do something and fast. Foster's left foot moved, then the right and, rather than stepping back to get out of range of the sweep, Ashford pivoted his right foot behind him, causing Foster to just miss. That put Foster slightly off-balance. So Ashford blocked the back-hand swipe with his own left forearm and stabbed the inside of Foster's left leg, up high and near the crotch.

Stab, then slice on the way out. Ashford thought to himself as the blade came out of Foster's leg followed by the first spurt of blood from Foster's femoral artery. He was taught that each slice outward would cause more damage and afford a better chance to cut an important artery. It could all be done in one basic movement.

"That one is for sending Wyles to kill Thompson."

Foster's reaction to that remark was first of surprise, then of shock and rage. He moved back and Ashford saw him change the grip on his knife. He's desperate, can't use his thumb. He'll come at me over-hand. Less that a second later, Foster did just that but Ashford stepped into him and blocked the charge by grabbing Foster's right wrist and moved to *stab-slice* at the right arm-pit.

"That one is for sending Williams to kill Thompson. Now you will bleed to death even faster."

More rage from Foster as they danced some more. More unsure dancing by Foster. Ashford could see him getting weaker and waited so Foster would lose more blood. He made Foster dance even more as the blood poured down his sleeve and down his leg. Then, in his desperate movement, Foster ran, rather danced, his knife pointed at Ashford's chest as though it were a sword. Ashford simply stepped aside and tripped him so he fell head-first. Foster tried to turn and face Ashford while still on the ground so Ashford drove his right knee into his chest and with his left hand shoved the knife out of Foster's hand.

"By the way, Thompson was not even hurt. He's quite alive. This one is for sending your own brother to kill a good man. I shot him in the left eye as he was trying to kill us." Ashford placed the tip of his knife over Foster's heart in preparation for the final thrust.

But Ashford stopped. It should be Charles who killed him.

"Charles, I give you the honour of dealing with this lump of shit." He rose and let his brother take his place. Charles picked up the large Kentucky knife, knelt beside the dying man, looked directly into his eyes, grasped the man's, hair and violently jerked it up and away from his head and spoke. Foster's eyes met his and froze wide open with fear.

"I tell you why we, the real people of this land, scalp our enemies. We do it so when we kill our enemy his spirit will not run free with the wind and spirits of the land. We do it to be sure his body will rot, so his spirit will not enjoy the beauty of running in the wind, so his spirit will feel itself rot and sink into the ground. And I will kill you with your own evil knife so the evil in it will seep into your body and help it rot."

Foster's eyes opened even wider. He saw the red and black war paint on Charles' face and the horror on his own face froze as if it had been formed in granite.

Charles then placed the tip of the man's knife at his heart and, slowly, so the man would know and feel what was happening, pushed it into his heart. Foster's eyes did not close. He couldn't close them for the sight of war paint forced him to look. His eyes remained opened and frozen in fear like a man looking into the eyes of the devil.

Charles pushed the knife into Foster's chest and then rose to let out the bone-chilling war cry of an Iroquois warrior who had just killed his enemy, and stepped aside.

Ashford bent down next to the body. He felt the jacket for the secret pocket and it .just below the point where the knife penetrated the man's heart. He used his own knife to cut a way into the pocket without disturbing the long Kentucky blade. Inside the pocket Ashford found an oil-cloth packet similar to the ones the three Kentucky assassins had and put it in his own pocket, rubbed the blood off his knife with Fosters' jacket, and rose to face Charles.

"Only you, Ignace, Mr. Thompson and I will know what happened here," said Ashford in a calm and deliberate voice.

"Yes," replied Charles, as he pointed Foster's dead body. "And Charles says *Tha-yo-nih* is a great warrior. But I must tell my brother I lied about why I told this snake I was going to scalp him. I wanted this man to know he was to be scalped, and so his spirit would know that as it rots back into the ground. No, Charles would not scalp him. We have lived too long with the white man."

Charles paused to tell Ashford more, "We are in the place where the Red Bird lives and I have seen him. I have tried to talk to him, but he would not talk to me. Now that I have killed the evil man the Red Bird will talk to me again."

Charles and Ashford carefully took stock of the situation as they left the body of Major Ronald Foster, the 'dandy' from Kentucky. The knife, still buried to the hilt in the dead man's heart would be a flag to all who saw it when Foster's body was found. As he looked at the body, a vision of the kill with the short sword bayonet flashed in Ashford's mind, "This kill is easier because I do hate this man."

As they cautiously made their way out of the forest, they immediately noticed Ignace running towards them and motioning for them 'come quick'. When they met, Ignace quickly informed Ashford that Lieutenant Wilson needs you "up this way", and led Charles and Ashford through the edge of the second group of trees where they lay hidden the past night and stopped.

At that moment, Charles placed his hand on Ashford's shoulder and spoke softly, "Wait, the Red Bird has come to speak to me." He nodded in the direction of a cardinal that was fluttering towards the branch of a tree about four feet off the ground. "The Red Bird will talk to me." The bird landed, looked at Charles, made a sharp "clerk", and then took flight towards the west making more of the same sharp 'clerks' as he flew.

"The Red Bird tells me there is danger," said Charles. "We must be very careful." As they watched the bird, Ashford and Charles noticed Lieutenant Wilson was lying flat on his back with his head uphill on a gentle slope west of the small forest. He was motioning sign language to Ashford to keep down low and come up, fast!

Ashford ran head down, towards Wilson. As he did so he looked to his right, to where the 1/44th was to ford the river and noticed that they had done so and were forming a line to advance up and over a small hill directly in front of them. Although he didn't watch them as they formed, he knew exactly what they would do. It was almost a ritual; a deliberately calm ritual in which they would form the line that was to march, quickly but carefully, up and over the hill. They would walk in short steps, muskets at 'order' positions; cradled against their left shoulder and held in place with the left hand at the butt of the Brown Bess and the right hand holding it steady against the body. It was done with such precision that one would think they were merely practicing and learning as they marched.

But there was reason for that. It calmed them down. It made them think about each step they took, not only in the march but in each individual movement of the muskets as they would prepare to fire. Years of practice and war taught them that they had to perform each step with quick, but careful movements when forming to "stand the line", performing movements in unison and almost without having to think about them. Ashford knew that because he did all those moves before becoming one of the 'Chosen Men'. He "stood the line". He waited for commands, even when he expected a wall of lead to come flying at them at any moment because practice in movements would save their lives.

Ashford reached Wilson and lay down, on his back, to hear what his Lieutenant had so say.

"Just over this hill, behind us, the enemy has set up three guns, twelve-pounders. The guns are set to repeal any attack on the American left flank and will bear directly at Colonel Brooke's advance. The grape shot from guns will cut them to ribbons. We should take a look. Keep low."

Both men slithered on their stomachs and slowly peeked over the hill. Ashford saw the three twelve-pounders were positioned to cut at Brooke's line, and Brooke could not see them. The moment Brooke passed the crest of that hill the guns would open fire.

Ashford also noted a formation of militia, about forty men, standing at the ready behind the guns. He thought for a few a moments, and then looked far to the left of his position, behind the twelve-pounders. Many, very many, militia gathered behind another six twelve-pounders located about half a mile from the first group of guns. That was an even greater problem. Brooke would be cut apart by the first group of guns and then blasted to kingdom come by the second. He motioned to Wilson that they should slink back down the hill to plan a counter-move.

In little more than a whisper Ashford gave instructions to Wilson. "Go back down and return with twenty-four men. Keep low and have them wait until you know you are needed. In the meantime, send your best runner to Colonel Brooke's position, if you have a red coat, make him wear it. He is to advise Brooke of what lies ahead. When his lines are about to crest the hill, your men will fire on the guns below. Make sure they set their sights at two hundred yards and take time for each shot. My guess is that the militia will break and run, leaving the artillery men all alone. Have them re-load out of sight of the enemy, then fire at will as they pull themselves back into position. Keep firing on them until all of them break, then stand up, all of you, to show Brooke the enemy has broken. Your runner will also tell Brooke about the guns to our left. I will take my group, including the Iroquois, to start a similar action on them. I should reach them in time, but Brooke should know he may have to wait until I can form up a good skirmish line. Got that?"

"Yes, sir!"

"Wait. On second thought, you should be the runner. You can explain it all better since you have seen what lies ahead. Have your sergeant get the men up there and tell him what I just told you. Not being able to see you will add to the fear. Once the Americans break, get your men to my position as fast as you can. It's going to be a big one."

Wilson and Ashford then ran, still keeping as low to the ground as they could.

Ashford gathered his men and started the run, behind the cover of hills and in the direction of the second gun group. There were small hills between him and the guns that provided some cover against detection as long as his men stayed low. Wilson did his part without hesitation and was well on his way towards Colonel Brooke's troops, dressed in an ill-fitting red coat, and running like a frightened deer.

About four minutes into Ashford's run, he heard the sound of rifle fire from the hill above the three twelve-pounders. He knew it would take about three more minutes before he was in position. He glanced back to the hill where he and Wilson made their plan and saw the 'Chosen Men' lying on their stomachs, firing, moving to crouch and re-load behind the crest of the hill, then moving back up to fire from prone positions. From that he knew that all the shots would be well-aimed. Wilson was already running up the hill to join them.

"Good men!" Ashford said. "Good men."

Each of Wilson's men fired about four rounds and stopped. That meant the militia broke and was confused, afraid and scattering. "Good men." He looked back again and saw Wilson's men rise to be seen by the enemy and by Colonel Brook, then turn to run in Ashford's direction, motioning to 'keep low' as he did so. In less than three minutes, Ashford's men were ready and sitting just below the crest of a small hill and about two hundred yards from the second group of twelve-pounders.

Ashford looked back at Brook's formation. It was changing as they marched, spitting into two separate 'lines' in order to make it more difficult for the enemy gunners to train the cannons on one large group without having to reposition the guns.

Ashford, Wilson, and the men waited. It would take several minutes for Brooke's troops to get within cannon range of the second group of

American twelve-pounders and even more to get within range of grape-shot. Waiting would also slow the heartbeats of Ashford's own men and make their aim truer.

He peered over the crest, saw the red coated troops act quickly, but deliberately as though it was a practice rather than a real battle. He saw two lines form; one a good distance to the right of the other and spaced so the enemy guns could not be pivoted to fire on more than one line. Splitting the fire meant one group would suffer heavier casualties than the other. It made grapeshot and cannons less effective.

"Good man, Brooke. You know what you're doing," Ashford said to himself.

To call it 'a line' is a bit misleading, for it was really two ranks of men that would meld together to form just one line. The second, or rear rank, was spaced just behind the front row and, when made ready to fire. the rear rank would make half a step into the front line and wait for the order to present and then to fire. The back rank would point their muskets over and between the shoulders of the men in front placing the tips of their muskets about six or eight inches behind those of the front rank. It was a formation that would send a wall of lead to the enemy. There was no 'aiming', just a pointing in the direction of fire as the musket was not accurate enough for aiming.

Ashford motioned his men to line up on top of the hill, in prone position, and make ready to fire.

"Take your aim on the artillery men, lads. Aim true. But make the first shot a full volley. We want them to think there are a hundred of us up here. First shot, first kill. Wait for my order. Select your target and keep your sights on him. Wait for it .... Wait for it ...."

"Fire!"

Twenty-four series 1806 rifles and two Kentucky Long rifles in Ashford's group fired in one big, roaring blast. It caused a great amount of smoke to rise, linger and then float away a few seconds later.

The distance was about 200 yards. Not ideal. But the effect was terrifying to the Americans. The militia stationed behind the guns wavered, looked uncertain, didn't know, at first, where the gunfire came from and were not only terrified, but confused.

About eighteen shots hit artillery men, some in the torso, some in the foot, and some in the hands or arms. But, a moment after Ashford's volley, the cannons spoke. A wall of grapeshot whacked into one of the two British lines advancing towards them and at least ten Redcoats went down.

"Let's hear the battle cry lads! Let them know what's in store. Keep low, shoot from prone positions so they can't see you!"

As was their pre-arranged method, Charles and Ignace rose to be seen by the enemy to give the first Iroquois war cry and many of Ashford's men followed. The result was a collective shock followed by a stunned silence and more confusion.

"Fire as you wish, lads. Fire only at the artillerymen. Keep firing. Lieutenant Wilson, get your boys up there and have them fire a full volley at the militia. If they break, the gunners will break!"

Another wall of grapeshot hit the Redcoats and another fifteen of them went down.

Then a volley of twenty-four rifles created havoc into the militia and, about four seconds later, the militia broke and ran. It was the same scene as earlier in the day. The horror-stricken militia ran in sheer panic. Many of them threw away their long rifles and most tore off their uniforms as they half-ran, half-stumbled away from the scene.

Meanwhile, the Redcoats came on in an effort to gain good distance for a volley of musket fire. When in good range, the lines stopped. Ashford swore he could hear the orders of both officers commanding the lines ...

> "Prepare to fire." Each Redcoat raised his musket to ready it, not yet at the shoulder, pointed more or less at the enemy.
>
> "Present!" Each man raised his musket to the shoulder and pointed it directly at the assembled enemy gunners.
>
> "Fire!" Each man pulled the trigger and the whole world turned to smoke.
>
> "Re-load" It took about twenty seconds for each man in the line to re-load his musket.

Many of the artillerymen went down. Some of them grasping at their body parts, some sobbing and coughing blood, some desperately trying to dig themselves a hole to crawl into and many of them already dead. There was no time for the Americans to spike their guns; no time to give any order to do so, no time to even think of loading another round of grapeshot, no time to even think of a prayer.

There was no need for another Redcoat volley. The Americans could do no more than flee. They did so in pure panic, not in good form. "Lieutenant, please inform Colonel Brooke and General Ross that in my view we should make for Washington as quickly as we can and that I will take my 'Chosen Men' now to provide skirmishing tactics for entry into the town. We will do nothing other than that and will light two large fires near the road to thereby advise him that the enemy has disappeared. Also advise General Ross that your men are at his service. I feel we should have some control over stragglers and such as he enters and hope he will not regard my action as insubordinate."

With that, Ashford gathered his men, and began the run-walk into the capital city of the United States of America.

The 'Burning of Washington'
August 24-25, 1814

It was about 6:00 pm when Ashford reached the outskirts of Washington. On his way, he noted that there were uniforms, not just militia uniforms, but those of regular US army troops scattered here and there along the road. He observed many troops, both dressed and not dressed in uniforms, in a panic to get out of Washington. Some were on horseback and, in their desperation, rode through small groups of troops, knocking them down as they passed. It was almost as though they were in a race to get out at all cost.

Later, historians and the people of Washington would call this battle 'The Bladensburg Races'. It would tarnish the reputation of the American army for many years.

Ashford instructed his men to gather a good deal of firewood, an easy task as there were stacks of it everywhere, and to set the two large fires only on his order. He would wait until it was dark enough to ensure the fires would be seen by the following British troops. In the meantime, he and several 'Chosen Men' walked through the city, on the main and other streets, to confirm the city was deserted. It took only minutes to confirm that.

He would learn, later, that the President of the United States of America fled the city just an hour earlier and that his wife made sure they took the silverware with them. How could anyone ever dream that the British would attack the capital city of the United States of America?

At 7:00 pm Ashford could hear the din of an army marching towards Washington. The noise was not just from the regular noises of clanking gear and boots, but also from the rhythmic pounding of drums. He lit the fires and waited as the troops marched in full order and as though they were on a victory parade in the streets of Washington. It was a perfect show of confidence and bravado. As General Ross and Colonel Brooke passed, he joined them to receive instructions.

"Ah, Colonel Ashford! Pleasant to meet you here! My compliments on your action in aide of Colonel Brooke. He has explained it all to me and I must say that I am very impressed. We shall talk later, but for now I ask that your men accompany us on the periphery for skirmishing. I think you will enjoy the show we plan to make." General Ross was tired, as were his men, for they had marched most of the day before reaching the first bridge. But victory kept them high in spirit.

"And I, too, wish to thank you on your quick thinking and action, Colonel. We shall all toast you at the earliest opportunity," added Colonel Brooke.

"Thank you, sirs. I believe I shall enjoy this moment and remember it all my life."

Ashford and his forty-eight 'Chosen Men' then ran-walked ahead of the column and took positions throughout the city to watch for problems.

The next several hours provided a real spectacle. British Redcoats entered every government building; including the Treasury, the Congress, the Armory and the White House, and set them ablaze. For a few moments it looked like the whole city was afire, but only government offices were burned. There was no looting or destruction of houses or places of commerce. The blaze lasted throughout the night. In the early morning, just before dawn, the drums sounded again. This time it was a signal for the British troops to form their marching columns and depart the city. It took an hour for all the troops to leave, in full order and with a slight swagger in their steps, with drums beating the cadence of the march as they passed General Ross, Colonels Brooke and Thornton, and Lt. Colonel William Ashford in review. As they passed, each column made 'eyes right' in front of their officers.

Ashford, having asked permission to take up the rear of the column, did so and, as they marched out of the city, looked back. It was now a bright, sunny morning, obscured in places by smoke but, in Ashford's eye, a bright day. He stopped a few moments to look back towards Washington. A strange spiral of black smoke rose from one of the government buildings, melded with the white smoke above, and disappeared.

The Flagship
Near Chesapeake Bay, USA
August 31, 1814

It was another meeting of officers in Admiral Cochrane's quarters on *HMS Nelson*, the flotilla flagship. With him were General Ross and Colonels Thornton, Brooke, and Ashford. It was not a planning session but a celebratory one, led by General Ross.

"Gentlemen, I have arranged this meeting for one or two purposes only. One is to celebrate a great victory that may end this war. I therefore offer my first toast concerning that event."

He rose and waited a brief moment while the others did the same.

"A toast to King George and to a great victory, well-planned and well fought."

General Ross stood again. "Now for another, very important toast my friends, to our new Lieutenant Colonel William Ashford for his brilliant and decisive thinking and action in our victory. Without his quick thinking we would have undoubtedly suffered a great many more casualties. To Lieutenant Colonel William Ashford."

All, except Ashford, rose. "To Colonel Ashford! Hurrah, hurrah, hurrah!"

"Speech, Speech!"

Ashford was surprised as it was not often that such notable officers would publically proclaim another, the tendency being to grab notoriety for a victory for themselves. He rose slowly, trying to think of what he should say.

"Admiral, General Ross, Colonel Thornton, Colonel Brooke ...."

He paused, still not knowing what to say.

"I am surprised and dumbfounded by your toast and say I do not deserve it. I merely did my duty. I will say that, without a doubt, the great victory lies with each and all of you. General Ross, your planning and your wisdom in finding and using the map of your 'spy' were the greatest keys to this victory. Without that we would have indeed suffered great casualties. The use of those confounded rockets was brilliant and I say I hate those things."

The assembled officers broke into laughter.

"Colonel Brooke, crossing a river, making sure the men kept their pans and powder dry, forming two lines, and then separating them to minimize effectiveness of the enemy guns, and moving very fast was pure music."

"Music?" someone said in gest.

More laughter.

"Colonel Thornton, your advance on the larger guns, your quick action and decisive moves, which you knew had to be done and would be costly, was a stroke of pure leadership. You knew you would face great peril and you acted in the best possible way throughout your movements. It was a work of art."

"Work of art?" said different a voice.

More laughter.

"It is my great honor to be called here to help in my own way, my honor to serve with each and every one of you, my honor to serve King and Country. Thank you all for that." He sat down, feeling humble but proud.

All present were silent for a few moments and the Admiral then spoke. "Gentlemen, we shall drink some more before we dine."

During the next minutes, well, actually the next several drinks, each recounted moments of the battle, how terrifying it was, how valiantly the men fought, how quickly the enemy broke and fled, how the rockets scared them as much as they did the enemy, how beautiful the march in and out of Washington was and more. At one point, Colonel Brooke would answer the question Ashford had still locked in his mind. "Will I return to the Canadas?"

"Colonel Ashford, there is this 'second thing' I must mention," began General Ross. "I requested of General Drummond that he send your

'Chosen Men' to help us in this battle. I did so because of his glowing reports on how you operate and realized we needed something different to assist us. I promised General Drummond that I would return you and your men when this job was done and I will honor that promise. I would rather break the promise but I shall not."

"I understand, sir."

"I have arranged for all your men, with their supplies, be placed onto *HMS Provider*, a sturdy troop ship. There will also be many of our wounded men on board. They need some extra care. A frigate, *HMS Warren*, will escort the troop ship to Halifax, and then rejoin our flotilla for further action. I have also arranged for the troop ship to pass along side this vessel so we can give all the men on board a proper salute."

"Thank you, sir,"

"Now, gentlemen, we shall dine on roast pork." Ross raised his glass for a silent toast.

York, Upper Canada
September 11, 1814

Ashford, by pure luck, was not present at the debacle of Plattsburgh. It was there, on September 11, 1814, that Governor General Prevost decided he would teach the Americans another lesson before the war ended. But because of his incompetent meddling with the construction and arming of ships that were to take Sacket's Harbour and his sudden retreat against the fort at Plattsburg, the British suffered a humiliating defeat. Prevost was recalled to London where he was tried and convicted of incompetence in a court martial. Although he appealed the finding, he died before the appeal was heard.

Afternoon with a Friend
Montreal, Lower Canada
September 15-16, 1814

Ashford, Ignace, and Charles had to wait two days for a ship that could navigate the St. Lawrence River to arrive. While the men went about visiting pubs and brothels, he and his brothers went in search of David Thompson. It didn't take long as Thompson was very well known. On the afternoon of September 15, they found his house. It was a fairly large two-story grey-stone home with an entry raised from the street by a stairway bordered with wrought-iron rails that invited people to walk up the stairs and knock on the great oak front door.

A man, probably a servant, answered their knock. He saw a tall man in a British uniform and two Indians. He was taken aback, but tried not to show it.

"How may I help you?" he said, cautiously

"Please be kind enough to inform Mr. David Thompson that Ignace and Charles, pointing his hand towards his brothers, and Lieutenant Colonel William Ashford are here to pay respects and provide him with some news."

The servant nodded and turned to find Thompson. A few moments later, David Thompson came to the door, obviously excited and surprised, and gave Ashford, Ignace and Charles each a great bear hug. He was unable to talk and tears were forming under his eyes.

"Please, please come in! What a great surprise. Come, come. Arthur, please get some fine sherry and some tea for my friends! Oh, we have much to talk about. Arthur, please prepare for my guests to stay and dine with me and tell Charlotte my friends are here."

Charlotte, his wife, came down the stairway and Thompson introduced his friend to her, bade them enter the study and sat them down.

"You must tell me everything, of adventures you've had, what you have done, where you have been. But first, I must tell you of my good news. All the work and worry over the establishment of a post at the Columbia River was not a waste. It seems the King decided, possibly in part because of my suggestions, that some other means of establishing our presence was needed," He smiled a broad and mischievous smile, almost letting out a giggle, "The Pacific Fur Company was convinced that the fort built there by that company would be blasted to kingdom-come by the Royal Navy. They sold it all, lock, stock and barrel to the North West Company. We bought it for a pittance."

They sat, Ashford sipping sherry, Thompson and the Indians sipping tea. After recounting much of their story Ashford turned to Charlotte and politely said, "Madam, there is some news I must give to my friend that we must keep between us."

"Oh, certainly. I understand." She rose and left the room.

"Mr. Thompson, we have told you only part of the story of our battle at Bladensburg. There is another part that I am not sure I should tell you but feel you should know."

He reached into his pocket and brought out the oil-cloth packet, which Thompson immediately recognized. "I have not, as yet, opened this packet. I wanted you to see it at the same time as we see it." He handed it to Thompson.

Inside was a neatly folded paper, stained slightly with dry blood that somehow seeped into the packet, and made to look like some kind of official identification. It was a form with blanks filled in:

17th Kentucky Dragoons
Identification

Name – Ronald Vincent Foster

Rank – Major

Date of birth – (blood stain obliterated)

Place of Birth – (obliterated)

Residence – Jeffersontown Kentucky

Thompson's hand shook as he read it. Then he looked up at Ashford and said, "I understand. We need not talk more of this. I understand and I thank you for showing me this and for the message it conveys."

Thompson then rose, walked to the fire-place and placed the packet and paper gently on the glowing embers. A few seconds later, both items burst into flames and burned with an excited white smoke that seemed to hurry up the chimney.

They sat in silence for what seemed to be a long time until Arthur entered the room.

"Dinner is served, gentlemen. Charlotte and the children await you."

It was a fine meal, made more delightful by the reaction of the children to the stories of danger and nature while in the company of their father. It became apparent to Ashford that Thompson had not related much of his adventures to the children and, with each story, Ashford could see admiration of the children for their father grow.

Parting was, again difficult, but not as difficult as York had been many months before.

Arrogance and Incompetence
New Orleans
January, 1815

As a show of strength and power, the British decided to take the great city of New Orleans, Louisiana. They had no spies, no information on the lay of the land, no proper preparation and, above all were filled with an arrogance befitting a great nation that thought it invincible. It was the worst debacle of the War of 1812.

Contrary to songs and myths about the battle, it was not won by brave Kentucky militia and their long rifles. It was lost by the British as they marched, with complete discipline, into volley after volley of grapeshot and were mowed down like the scythe cuts through long grass. The British suffered 2,100 dead, wounded, or taken prisoner. The Americans suffered one casualty.

Perhaps the worst part of the defeat was that the War of 1812 had already ended. The Treaty of Kent was signed in Britain on December 24, 1814. News of the treaty had not yet reached the North American continent.

Orders from the Office of Colonial Affairs
Kingston, Upper Canada
May 10, 1815

"Colonel Ashford, I am directed to present this letter to you. When I read it, I was, at first, worried I would lose you. But as you will see, there was no reason for concern. I will give you some moments to review it."

With that, Drummond left the office. Ashford sat to read the letter.

London, April 5, 1815   **for Col. William Ashford**

This is to advise that you are directed to return to London for further assignment. The war with the United States is over, but there are still some indications that, in the not-too-distant future, another attempt will be made to invade the Canadas. We are of the mind that you have, indeed, come to love those lands and its people so it is the hope of His Majesty that you will consent to remain there in another capacity. You will remain in the military, but in a different manner. If you agree to take on such a task, you are asked to return to London for training and preparation for the new venture. That should take about two months and it will be the writer who will prepare you for the new task.

This letter is being sent to you via General Drummond who will read and retain this letter for his

records. It is our belief that you will be challenged in your new assignment and will find it quite rewarding. As aspects of it are to be kept secret, we cannot at this time tell you the exact nature of same. We also advise that if they wish to continue in the service of His Majesty, your Iroquois brothers will be invited to assist you. You may advise them of that.

> Sir Percival Worthington
> Secretary of Colonial Affairs to
> His Majesty, King George III

Return to London
June 20, 1815

L t. Colonel William Ashford, still of the 5th Battalion, 95th Regiment of Foot, walked smartly towards the two large double doors of Whitehall, the headquarters of His Majesty's Office of Colonial Affairs and paused before opening one of the doors. Three months after his return to Kingston, Ashford was met with another dispatch from Sir Percival Worthington containing instruction to return to London for re-assignment. It was his duty to go.

He pushed open on of the two doors, tucked his cap under his left arm, and walked in. A Corporal immediately approached, "Lieutenant Colonel Ashford, Sir Percival is expecting you. Please follow me."

Ashford walked through the same doorways as he did on his two previous visits. The wall pictures hadn't changed. Ashford sat in the middle chair without waiting to be told to do so and waited while the Corporal knocked and entered Percival's office. The Corporal did not have the time to announce Ashford. Instead, Percival's voice, a friendly and eager voice, offered a greeting to Ashford from inside the office. "Ah, Colonel Ashford is here. Please come in Colonel, we have much to talk about."

Ashford rose and walked into the office expecting to find Percival seated behind the desk, head down and studying something in front of him. But this time, Percival was standing in front of his desk, hand outstretched. Ashford took the hand and shook it. "Good to see you again, Sir Percival. It's been some time."

"Yes, indeed. And much has happened. Please sit."

Percival waited until the Corporal walked out and closed the door behind him, and then looked at Ashford. "As indicated in my most recent dispatch, I have asked for your presence here to request your involvement in another task. You may refuse to take on the job, but I am confident you shall agree to do so. In reading your reports I have concluded that you have grown to like, even love, the Canadas and its people. So I will tell you, now, that your new task will be in the Canadas, will involve military duties and an 'additional' duty. Additional duties require your attendance in London, for about two to three months." Percival paused as if to prepare Ashford for his next statement. Have I correctly assumed for love for the Canadas?"

"Yes, Sir Percival, it is the wild nature and the friendly people that I like. And the air is so fresh, the waters so clean ..." Ashford stopped himself as he knew he could ramble on about the Canadas for hours.

"Good. For a few moments, we shall just talk. I am eager to learn more about your adventures. The dispatches for your superior officers are glowing, so much so that I can truthfully say that I have never come across such admiration and confidence in an officer as shown by Lord Wellington and others."

The two men talked for about an hour. In the process they came closer to each other, more understanding of each other, more trusting of each other. At one point, Ashford let it be known that he was growing tired of killing and war. He was looking for a new challenge that was less demanding in that way.

"I am pleased that you feel that way, Colonel. Because the task ahead will be one of more strategizing, gathering information, and analyzing, then preparing for what may arise. You have demonstrated all the qualities to do those things."

"Thank you, Sir Percival."

"As we have discussed and as you know, we have great distances between us that make it difficult to react to matters in a timely way. We need to devise a method of quick reaction and, to do so, we need to set up a system that gives more latitude to those of His Majesty's Service to take quick action. We have decided that you will become the head of information-gathering and the like in the Canadas and western parts of the land. To use a crude expression, we will have you become a "Spy Master in the Canadas." Percival paused for Ashford's reaction.

Ashford, now quite comfortable with Sir Percival, let out a small laugh, "Although I did not expect this, Sir Percival, I am not surprised. And I am aware that I have no knowledge of this sort of thing, except for the Astoria part. But I would be honoured to do this. I have talked with my Indian brothers and they agree to join me and work with me. They, like me, are tired of war."

Percival's smile was bright and wide, "You will be given the rank of a full Colonel. You will have the task of building a larger force of 'Chosen Men', of personnel that can do the kind of work you presently do *and more*. In essence, you will set up a new kind of military force *and* act as a spy master. By that I mean you will set up an information-gathering network, mostly in Upper and Lower Canada. We still have some concern that the Americans might try to take Canada again." He paused, again to prepare Ashford for the next statement.

"You will also take part in an experiment, one that is not used often enough at the present time. You will set up a method of training young men to become officers in His Majesty's army. We need officers who can think like you, think and engage in tactics like you do. It is my hope that the result will be such that members of His Majesty's armed forces from around the world will come to you and learn from you."

Ashford was stunned. Once again, Sir Percival had surprised him, this time in a very wonderful way. "Sir Percival, I am now indeed surprised and I say I will look forward to this new idea."

"Good. We shall start tomorrow. I have taken the liberty of having some civilian clothing prepared for you, uh, the kind that most visitors to this office usually wear. They are awaiting your arrival at the same tailor shop you visited on our last visits. I will accommodate you within my estate, as much of what we do would be best done in the confines of my properties, for secrecy. I intend to instruct you myself, on everything I have learned in the business of being a Spy Master."

THE END

ACKNOWLEDGEMENTS

To my wonderful wife of fifty-four years I say deep thanks. She helped me, proofread for me, suggested many good ideas and, above all, encouraged me to keep working on this story. I especially thank her for understanding why I had to get up at 4:30 am to work on this story and why I was grumpy at times.

To my sister-in-law, Anne Marie Decore, who also proofread and edited this story for me. Thank you.

To my dear friend Diane Mirth who gave me valuable advice in editing. Thank you.

I have never been a fan of an on-line Encyclopedia. I was wrong. A great deal of information was gathered through Wikipedia and led to even more detailed sources of information.

To the Government of Canada for preserving the stories of the War of 1812.

To Andrea Korsos for the excellent topographical map of Thompson's trip on the Columbia River.

To David Thompson for his daily logs and his Narrative but most of all for his lifetime of heroic efforts in North America.

To Canada, the greatest place on earth.

CPSIA information can be obtained
at www.ICGtesting.com
Printed in the USA
LVHW09s2200191018
594206LV00001B/29/P

9 781525 525087